Mr. GOODTRIPS

by

E. L. Odom

(5.5x8.5 Paperback) ISBN: 979-8-9942135-1-3

First Edition

Printed in the United States of America

Date of Publication: February 22, 2026

Dedication

This book is dedicated to Carlos, who tirelessly tried to get this story made into a film when I lived in LA years ago and I first wrote it as a film. Then he fell ill. But he still lives and so do great ideas like the ones he believed in.

TABLE OF CONTENTS

(((((((((((((((THE BIG INTRO)))))))))))))))))

When I tell people that I wrote a book about someone who makes you high, totally euphoric just by speaking, a huge portion of them say, "That would make a great movie!" Well, when I worked in California years ago, I did indeed write this story as a screenplay, along with my other well received idea called *King Vampire*, a film estimated to cost about $300,000,000 to make. People who liked the idea, went line by line through the script, scouted locations and had numerous investor meetings. Two of the meetings were with groups headed up by billionaires; one from Mexico who said all he cared about was fine cigars, and the other billionaire liked to offer one-thousand dollar tips at restaurants to waiters if they were to delight him with what he considered a perfect apple. If the right eyes are seeing this, you know who I mean. At one point, a famous gangster, who we all know, was found to have a copy of my *King Vampire* script in his briefcase when he was arrested for beating his lady friend in Las Vegas. A member of an investment group interested in financing my vampire epic just happened to be there that night and witnessed the beating. That investor was never seen again. Then yet another deal fell through. Yep, they spent over a million dollars on my idea and I never saw a penny.

So what's the point of the backstory? If Hollywood liked my ideas, I'm pretty sure you will, too! Where *King Vampire*, which is coming next, is more focused on horror action and humor, Mr. Goodtrips is a fascination for the senses. It's weird, funny, sometimes

tragic, chivalrously romantic, enlightened and something to make you frightened. And now it begins ...

1) MEET REG

Am I normal? Well, if normal is being like you, not even close. Because I can do something nobody else in this big, baddie world can do. Got your attention? Can't wait to see what? Maybe you'll figure it out right after I deal with this cop who's chasing me. Hell, I'm just cruising down the Pacific Coast Highway my way—fast! No one else is even around. Too bad, too, cuz I was hoping Mr. Fuzz wanted to play bumper cars with me. Yeah, there's nothing like a little demolition derby early in the morning to wake you up good. He's flashing his lights, should I stop? Or should I wait for this blip in time to turn all horror show on me with more cops in more cop cars, choppers, spike strips, news crews and eventual twisted metal mashup with me as the star? Then those prying questions I don't need to be answering. Better pull over. Watch now, you might just guess what's different about me. Cuz lemme tell ya, there's only one who can do what Mr. Goodtrips can do.

So here I am wasting time on the side of the road, sittin' in my super sporty convertible. Here comes mister serve and protect rolling up behind me. My eyes are burning holes in all before me and my hands are crushing the steering wheel. Do I sound worried? It's called focus. Here he comes, got that hand on that gun. At least one of us better be careful. Swinging open my car door, I hop out of my car all smiles and throw my arms out wide for that big ol' hug he'll be giving me. Man, he's pressed! He's gripping that gun tight now. Our ultra edgy traffic cop instructs me rather loudly and with no lack of irritation to get back into the car. I smile. I look over at my good buddy Otto. He smiles too. He knows what's coming, an anticlimax? "I don't wanna!" is all I said. I didn't have to say one syllable more because it happened; his face went blank, his tensed-up body relaxed and that hand slipped right off that gun. He wouldn't need it, just like that free will I just took from him. I'm in charge, always have been. I take my time ambling up to him. This could be fun. "How are the wife and kiddies? Facey book or ticky-tocky? Got any donuts?" were my so simple inquiries. He doesn't answer. Of course he doesn't. The more I speak the more fuzzy-wuzzy his malleable mind-spring melts. His gourd goes gaga with a flood of endorphins and more mind-numbing chemicals than his brain has ever even experienced before in his life or any other. He is hiiiiiiiiiiiiiiiiiiiiiigh! Yep, you saw it for yourself. Whenever I speak, anyone within earshot of my voice gets high. And not only that, they'll do anything I tell them. I guess the getting high part is a freebie.

I take the gun out of his hand and twirl it around. Then I throw it from hand to hand and twirl it some more, why not? Otto gets out of my red hot-rod and comes up to us. Oh, did I mention Otto? Of course, he's my best bud! He's Mexican-American and has expensive ear implants I got for him. He's the only person currently in the world I know who can talk back to me because my voice doesn't affect him obviously. He's twenty-seven years old, the age Jim Morrison died. I kind of look like Morrison, the hair and leather pants especially. I've already outlived Morrison, or at least outlasted him. He did a lot of living in his short existence. A lotta people live a lotta years and don't do a damn thing worth mentioning. Otto worries about the gun in my hand. "What are you gonna do with that, besides look stupid?" he says. I tell him that I thinnnnnk I'll shoot out some tires. Being more practical, Otto suggests I just tell our police escort to forget about us and go away? It works every time. I ponder a bit and suggest the cop shoot out his own tires. Otto just shakes his head disapprovingly at me. "Hey, the man with the badge shouldn't have stopped my Sunday drive," I remarked. Without hesitation, I rush over and jump onto the cop's cop car and get on the roof. "Catch!" I say loudly to the cop as I toss him his gun. The loudness of my command gets his attention then as he perks up and grabs the gun flying towards him. "I don't think you like your car. Execute it!" I say as the cop just stands there, his mind jousting with obedience and confusion. Then with a big, dumb smile on his face, the obedient employee of the people and me especially stumbles, twists and contorts his body to face his car. Then, still smiling, of course, he waves his gun in the direction of the car and fires it. Otto and I are really enjoying this. The cop shoots through his engine. Otto puts his hands over his ears as the cop fires shot after shot through his car until he finally manages to hit one of the tires with a bullet. This is my fault. People take my directions literally. After all, I did say to execute the car. "Yee-haaaaaaaaaaaa!!! Hit the tires, will you?!" I demand.

I'm dancing now, hootin' and hollerin' and stomping my feet, even a little running in place on the top of this car as the cop unloads the rest of his load into it. I'm having a good ol' time, living my life, doing anything I want—yeah! Otto and I suddenly notice people in cars driving by us slowly. Hey, they're smiling, too. They can't possibly think we're acting like fools. Who, me? "You're being filmed, homie," Otto suddenly informs. I looked over at two smiling surfer chicks hanging out of their side windows with their phones pointed at us as they drove by us ever so slowly. Should I chase them down and get their phones? Can you say escalation? Believe it or not, the world doesn't know about me or what I can do and I wanna keep it that way. I briefly discussed the matter with my bud. The only sound on their phone would be gunshots, except for all that screaming and yelling I did. I wasn't exactly posing, but both our images would be on their phone. Otto didn't care; my Mexican friend said there are so many Mexicans in California now that no one notices them anymore. It might have been a mistake, but I didn't care either. So after I told the cop to forget what happened, we hopped in my car and just took off. So much for roadside fun.

So while I'm driving along the PCH, you're judging me, thinking what a delulu loony I must be. Well, you haven't lived my life; people constantly gather around me if I made the mistake of saying, oh, anything! Yeah, sometimes I like it, many times it amuses me and sometimes I just hate it. They never let me alone. So after a lifetime of watching what I say, I'm gonna start saying and doing anything I want. I decided this morning. Not to worry, though. I'm not gonna tell the prez to hit that red button, turning every town everywhere into Nuke

City. How 'bout marching all the politicians into the sea? Maybe? I could do it, though. I have better things to do, though, like have a gooooood time! And you're gonna have the best time you ever had. No itty-bitta baking—you'll be totally baked! Mr. Goodtrips delivers like no other. Any less would be so cheugy.

As for me, I'm a semi-hulking mass of he-man muscles. I am six-foot tall and muscular because I work out every single day after my three hours sleep. I guess they must sleep less on the planet I'm from. I have no proof of that, but I know I don't seem to fit in on this crazy world. Crazy? Hey, I'm in the right place. I sleep less and I'm a helluva lot stronger than anyone I've ever met, too. Unusual for only being a middle-weight, and, oh yeah, there's the voice thing. And lately I've been having these weird dreams, and I mean really weird!

What to do next? Am I famous? Not yet, although I am so dashing and so fascinating that everyone simply has to stop and take a look at what I'm serving up. Oh, did I mention my age? Nope, I didn't and I remember everything I see, hear or just plain experience. I mention the age part because I was born in the 1920s and now it's the 2020s, yet I look about twenty-one. I guess I'm aging extremely well or not at all since I got to be all growed up. I must take after mumsy or daddio. I never met either of them. For someone who remembers everything, my mind is a bit fuzzy in this one area. I met Otto over a decade ago when I discovered he could actually speak back to me when I spoke to him. I look about a tick of the clock older than when we met. Sometimes I see him staring at me, just taking in every bit of my face as if he were looking for any change at all. I'm just glad he's my friend after so much time alone.

I got off track, what to do next? You haven't seen me talk to more than one willing participant yet. You should see me talk to a group. They all listen. And the way they listen; with enraptured delight as if every single word I say is exactly what they wanted to hear to make everything just right, take their pain away and give their receptive minds the greatest euphoria they could ever possibly experience. And it doesn't matter what I say to them either. I could be speaking another language or reciting Jabberwocky and the minds of the malleable masses would still turn to mush. But how to mold such minds of clay as they stand before me, smiling, submissive zombies staring off into space? "You got that look again. Stop daydreaming before you run us off the road," Otto says as I bury my gas pedal in the floor at a hundred per. Yeah, he thinks I'm weird. I suppose I am ... to everyone but me.

So how does little ol' me make a living in this big ol' world? I make so much money that I can go places and waste time twenty-four hours a day minus sleeping, eating and exercising. And the job I have is the best possible work a person like me could have. I am a telemarketer, probably the most successful telemarketer in the history of telemarketing. I call you up. You listen. You buy. It's that simple, for me anyway. I understand most people hang up on sales calls. Not mine. Mine is a call directly into your mind. I stick to the rich folks, though. I get lists of their numbers and just give 'em a call. You just never know when one of them needs ten tons of horsey manure to dump into their swimming pool? I work from home. The boss wanted me to work out of the office like everyone else in his boiler room, but I told him I wanted to work from home and he said fine immediately. He would have said fine if I told him to jump up and down on a pogo-stick on the flagpole of a tall building.

I suddenly notice my hot-rod going over a-hundred-and-twenty miles per, should I slow down? Or maybe I'll speed up to break a record? There are no cops around. Why not go fast when I have to get to nowhere special? I hear it's just the place the discontent always look for but never find. What am I looking for? How 'bout someone just like me? I can talk with Otto, hang out, but that's it. I need someone who does more than talk. I just get the feeling I will one day. The waiting isn't what bothers me. What bothers me is how I see people treating each other today. In the '60s people would get in your face when they had something to say, to get equal rights or to end a war. Now it seems people get in your face just to get in your face. Use humor to fight your battles and people will laugh even if they don't agree. Yep, I have seen the passage of time. Even though I see no change when I look in the mirror, I know I am here for a reason. Could I be here to change the world or even to destroy it? Either one would be change. I guess I'll just have to find out when I cross that broken bridge that hangs over oblivion.

Sooooooooo here we are; Otto and I, two fine, young lads ambling down the avenue of Melrose, looking for love in all the fashionable places. I don't wear suits—never have—but I do like a nice shirt exploding with color or design, one that grabs your eyes right out of your head. Something with ruffles like Jimbo used to wear is nice, too. Hello, you lovely ladies! I can't help thinking as I pass giggling girls passing me. "Helllllllllo," I say suggestively as I pass a pretty face, her fuzzy thoughts beginning her euphoric cascade of pure bliss as I divert my fashionable self into a trendy clothing store with faithful and hangry Otto right behind me.

Jenny, one hot and stylish enchantress, and owner of the establishment, drops a dress she's currently holding up for a lady customer and rushes over with the most sincere and gigantic smile that a happy face could possibly ever make and covers my lips with her own. Before I can pull away to speak, she raps her arms around me, her lips speaking to me so passionately without ever speaking as they remain against mine. This must be Reg's girl; that knockout face; that smile to end all smiles, the one that says I love you above all others. Well, maybe she does. So does every other pretty face in the crowd, whether I've gotten to know them better or not. What a bachelor's dream, having every willing, able and ready hot chick oozing all over you, if you're in the mood or not. I'm diggin' myself today even better than yesterday. How true.

"Reg," she says with the friendliest of smiles as she backs away and just looks at me. I only met her once before and she remembers my name. Everyone does. "Show me what I like," is all I need say to her. Then this most elegantly gorgeous creature flits about the store like the most beautiful butterfly lighting on such fanciful creations for me to adorn my body with, all lovingly done just for me. She can act no other way, she's high on Reg.

With enough shopping for us to be dripping in drip, Otto and I head out the door. Seeing that pretty smile leaving that pretty face, I wink at Jenny and yell for everyone to buy something. After the usual time lag, shoppers start grabbing at clothes like squirrels on acid digging holes for nuts. Time to go!

Walking along the sidewalk with Otto, I seem a whole lot happier than he is. I don't dig a dour face staring my way either from on high or the sidewalk walkers below. And with all my pontificating, a crowd had gathered behind us and was following us. Like dawn of the dead shoppers, these zombies were all shuffling right behind us, all waiting for their next fix of Reg voice. I shouldn't have talked so loud. The louder and longer I speak the more my voice numbs the mind. But there's a simple fix for that as I turned to face the crowd. "Wait here!!!" I say nice and loud and my work was done. And with that, Otto and I run our asses to my car, hop in it with our shopping booty and make our hasty retreat, because he who shops and runs away lives to shop another day.

Annnnnnnnd here we are just an hour later at the Beverly Center, a mall with many levels. We already had our munch-out at the food court and now we're just wandering about. As if in a daze, I walked right through the milling crowd toward the railing overlooking the bottom floor of the mall. I just stood there and imagined what it would be like if I told everyone to just start taking whatever they want. There's mom, finally getting that smart handbag and shoes combination. Those screaming kids can shut up and finally get all those toys mommy always puts back. There's a tween with a punk hairdo. I guess he doesn't know the eighties are over. I guess that bag mister huff-in-stuff has is full of spray paint. And there's dad with a big knife in his hand and a wild look in his eyes—a little unnerving! Some guy just came crashing out through a store window. Either someone threw him or he just likes jumping through sharp glass windows. Some dude on fire is running through the mall now, and I'm not sure the human torch likes it. There's a guy running through the mall now with a really big ax in his hands. No, my mistake. He's chasing someone with that ax. This fantasy is getting seriously out of control!

Then it happened! I snap back to reality from my fantasy into a horrific reality as the distinct sounds of gunshots are heard in the mall. Not realizing or just not wanting to realize what was unfolding, I looked out over the crowds of people rushing madly around downstairs. A masked gunman was shooting at them, just shooting at them. What I could barely believe was actually happening and had to be faced because gunshots were heard upstairs now, too, and some shots were close! I turn to see where the shots came from and see a man wearing dark shades and a bandanna over the bottom half of his face with a gun in his hand. He was randomly shooting at people.

Otto and I just look at one another. Everyone is now rushing about like the insane asylum doors just broke open. Strangely enough, Otto and I stand still and watch the surreal chaos. Was my bud waiting for me to do something? I wasn't sure if opening my mouth would make things better or worse, so I stood there still. But I wouldn't be still for long, because the gunman sees me. In fact, I now have his full attention. We just look at each other, me and this madman with purpose. Then as if in a Peckinpah film, I watched him raise his hand in slow motion and point his gun in my direction. Strangely still, I wasn't afraid. I was more fascinated. I was more afraid for Otto. What if he's next? I thought a million thoughts at once. I had no more time to reason. I must act. And if each of us is here for a purpose, I was truly about to find mine. No more random collisions in space to make up the man. I would find my voice and its ultimate purpose—so I simply screamed, "STOP!!!!!!!"

I screamed so loud, so long and so strong that everything stopped. As far as the eye can see, no one was moving. And the quiet—it was as if I were standing in a tomb or on the moon. There was no sound. How could there be no sound? Not even the sound of machinery was heard. It's as if every single thing living or not was waiting for my next command. As I glanced over the railing, it was just as quiet downstairs. And Otto, talk about a freak-out! He actually looked scared. He always knew I was different, something not quite right about me, but here it was slammed right up in his face. Up till now it was all fun and games, using my unique ability to talk my way into movies or out of speeding tickets and other silly, stupid things. But what I just did could turn monstrous. I could have these people do anything! Make 'em come raining down over the railings or hop into a buzz saw ... or even kill each other for no other reason than some perverted pleasure. But that's not really me. I might be a lot of things that fall short of the angel's wings but not that. "Put it down," I said so calmly, forcing the masked man to involuntarily lower his gun hand as I walked over to him. I had pulled all the monster's teeth. He was a monster no more, at least for this moment. Otto walked up to the madman and took the gun out of his hand. "Better do something before they all snap out of it," he suggested.

And Otto was right, the people would not remain quiet, remain still forever, and the shooters would start shooting again. I had to make a choice and I had to make it right now! So I walked back over to the railing overlooking the bottom floors of the mall. Then I looked up. Everyone would have to hear me, and everyone would never forget what was about to happen. I was about to speak. That's all. "I know you all like hearing my voice—so listen to me! First, you creeps doing all the shooting, give yourselves up! It's over. Put your weapons in the nearest trash can and wait for the cops to just take you away, to just be gone. To everyone else, go back to doing whatever you were doing or go home. Take your time, take what you want, I don't know?" I instructed.

No one moves. I guess people like me ordering them around. Otto and I, though, have to go! So I speed things along and simply yell, "Now!!" And after a moment of contemplation, the people did start to move, except not like I thought they would. They all proceeded to rush into all the mall's different stores, whilst Otto and I stood around like smiling imbeciles not even realizing that people don't always react the way you think they will. Within less than a minute, people with armloads full of everything they could carry came rushing out of every store, which I'm fairly certain or completely certain they didn't stop to pay for. And they weren't just taking from the stores but from each other, tug of wars breaking out with anyone who had anything that anyone else wanted.

Then Otto and I just looked at one another, something had gone terribly wrong and we were in the wrong place—here! So without hesitation, we rushed toward the nearest escalator, shoving aside frantic, confused shoppers that happened to stumble past us. If they all came to their senses before we escaped, how would they react, wanna thank us for all the free stuff or tear us apart? Even that cop we just blew past us was playing fanum tax day with the mall's goodies with no thought in his head to keep order.

And there they were, two looks maxing super smack snacks! I suddenly stop in front of two beautiful girls, a blonde and a raven haired ravisher. I don't know why I stopped. It's as if I had to, as if one of them made me stop. Otto stops too, a bit bothered. "Think of your dick later. We gotta go!" Otto punctuates. And before I could say anything, the dark-haired one simply said, "Say something," I looked at her devilish smile, all the while feeling as if she was rooting around my brain through those hypnotically beautiful wide eyes. Being a Stooge fan, I simply said, "Something." As I stood cemented in place, I couldn't take my eyes off her. Then she surprised me further by putting her arms around me and kissing me, kissing me like a lover who had loved me more each day for a thousand millenniums. My arms crept up around her as the kiss went on and chaos danced about us. But I didn't care. I was oblivious to it. Now I know the bliss others feel when they hear my voice. Now I knew true joy because somehow I knew I would never be alone again.

Suddenly I could hear Otto yell, "C'mon!" as the kiss ended and I could feel Otto's hand yanking me away. But I stopped. I stopped as my raven-haired enchantress pulled out a business card with her beautiful beyond compare face on it and casually held it out as she smiled, "Take it." I take the card and look at it, the eyes drawing me to it as I hear her say, "Come to me when you're ready." "You can speak to me," I blurted out. "We can do more than speak," she said with a smile so suggestive that my spine was turning into knots. I wanted to stay so bad! But I knew we had to go. Otto and I raced for the exit as I kept glancing back to see that raven-haired enchantress smiling at me, a sly, playful smile that says I gotcha!

2) HAWAIIAN JOE'S PLACE

Have I had an interesting life? If I were to tell you just of the famous people I have met, it would fill a set of encyclopedias, remember those? If I were to tell you how many of those people contributed to mankind in a truly meaningful way, it would fill a handful of pamphlets. When I first moved to Hollywood, someone told me that I would never find more people anywhere that thought so highly of themselves for so little achievement. True or not, I think a good song or a well-crafted film does make the world a better place for that moment in time that it gives you joy, and this is a movie town. As for me, I didn't come here to entertain; although some say what I do is quite entertaining. I am the motivational speaker known as Hawaiian Joe, a name I acquired not from my heritage but from the Hawaiian shirts I wear. I always thought the best way to reach people is with an open hand and a true heart. Those who wear the ten-thousand dollar suits while motivating certainly look professional, but I always felt they're throwing up a wall of superiority. They say it is for you to aspire to be as rich and as influential as they are, but what if that is not all you aspired to be?

All introduced? Good! Then let me tell you of the weirdest experience I have ever had and the most unusual man I have ever met, and there have been a lot! I take you back to the sixties, a time of free love, free expression, the best music ever made and my early journey into manhood. I was with a young Native-American girl. I never knew her name, but I was fascinated by her! I know, if you saw her, you'd be fascinated, too! Beautiful women have an instant fascination. It was more than that, though. There was something about her that went far beyond her looks or her heritage. After barely knowing me, she knew all about me. She could finish my sentences like she was reading my mind. She knew all my dreams, desires and fascinations, and one of them was her. So, she gave herself to me. We became very aware of ourselves physically in the back room of some sixties drug guru's hipster place as people spoke, partied and partook in a variety of chemical substances that only gurus would approve of in the huge outer room.

The outer room went quiet suddenly. It was really odd. It was so odd that my romantic interlude came to a complete stop. Why would I want it to stop? I was having more fun than anything going on out there I thought. Not even the sound of dishes clanking or people moving about was heard, which was insidiously odd. I thought the place was being robbed, everyone was forced to be quiet. My native maiden fair saw the curiosity on my face and told me it was time for me to experience something. She didn't say see or hear—she said experience! That took on a whole new meaning in my life as I was about to find out. Then I heard it, one voice speaking.

My native fair and I emerged in our rags and beads from the backroom to see a young man speaking in front of the crowd that had stopped to listen to this single expression of sound, his voice. And the things he said perplexed me. It wasn't artful philosophy with deep meaning or even beat poetry, which was still popular at the time. He spoke lines from films and gibberish as if it had meaning, intermixed periodically by an annoying laugh or giggle as if he were toying with the crowd and they didn't even know it. And from the looks on their faces, they had not a care in the world, or even a thought of their own. It's as if their minds had been taken over in a casual maneuver, the simple sound of his voice. They were all mesmerized. I couldn't understand it. Why wasn't I affected? Then instantaneously as that thought breached my conscious mind, my native fair told me I'd understand as she removed the necklace of genuine animal teeth I wore around my neck ever since it was given to me by a genuine Cherokee Indian man in the forest when I was just ten years old. More on that later.

Then it happened ... that voice. That beautiful voice! I don't care what he said. I just wanted him to keep talking, no matter what he said. I never wanted it to stop. Because, you see, I was stoned out of my mind. It was the best high I had ever had! If you looked in the dictionary you'd see it under this odd fellow's name and I didn't even know who he was. To everyone standing before him his name was euphoria plus, a magical euphoria you can't get from any other drug. And trust me—this was the sixties—I had tried them all!

I just stood there. I was winking and blinking as if coming out of a deep sleep. My native fair was giggling as she placed the necklace of teeth back around my neck. "Now you know why you were told never to take it off," was all she said as I lost her in the crowd. I was still shaking off the euphoria that overcame me. I don't even know how long it lasted. All I know is that it was dark now and the mystery man with the magic voice had vanished, and so had my native fair. I would only ever see her again during the eclipse, when she gave birth to my daughter.

And as fate would have it, whilst I sit in my comfy office chair in my office in my crammed full house in the Hollywood Hills and fiddle with the necklace of animal teeth around my neck, Luna, my beautiful daughter, my partner in business and my constant source of joy comes into the office. She is holding her phone with something for me to see on it. "Please, not another cute cat video," I tell her. "No, dad. This might be what we've been waiting for," she informs me. She shows me the video of a long-haired young man yelling and acting the fool on the top of a police car as presumably the officer who normally drives it is shooting his service revolver into it. I ask my daughter why I am perusing this crazy person? "Doesn't his voice affect you?" she asks. "Should it?" is the natural reply. "It affected everyone in the house but us," she insists. "I don't understand, how did his voice affect them?" I inquire further. Not paying attention to the video, I suddenly realize who it might be and ask, "Can you highlight his face? I can't tell..." I go numb as she freezes on the young man's face, the same face that scrambled any thought or reason at a certain guru's party in the sixties. "They kinda blanked out, like it affected them. It was difficult for them just to gather their thoughts. And if I play it over and over, they just wanna stay and watch this dumb video," she explained. "It's him! He looks the same, exactly the same!" I can barely believe. "The one with the voice? How does it not affect you?" she inquires. I touch my necklace of animal teeth.

"The one time it was taken off, my mind went away. When he spoke, I had no sense of time. And the euphoria, it's as if heaven on earth had descended on my brain. I never wanted it to stop." I pondered. "How did you know to take it off?" she asked. "I didn't. Your mother did. She wanted me to experience him. I don't trust him. Before she took off the necklace, I heard him speak. His voice had no effect on me as everyone else around me was immaculately stoned. Then she took the necklace off and I was gone. I had no will. I had no need for one. All I wanted was another word from him, any word," I explain. "Wow! The most simple thing in the world, just speaking and you lose your mind. I thought you were a good speaker. He wouldn't have to convince anyone of anything, just speak and they're convinced. If you saw him in the sixties, why doesn't he look older?" she asks. "The same reason you do not. Did you ever wonder why you were born in the sixties, but you still look like you are in your twenties? It must be your mother," I surmise. "Oh, that girl you met once, placed an order with and she made the delivery?" she stings. She notices me fiddling with the teeth on my necklace. "Why are you always fiddling with that? As long as I've known you, you can't keep your hands off it," she ponders. "Touch it," I tell her. "Every time I ever got near that thing you pushed me away. You even yelled at me once for it. Why now?" she simply must know. "Just this once," I tell her. She hesitantly reaches out to touch the teeth necklace about my neck as my hand comes away from it. "I can feel it," she smiles. "It's a good feeling, isn't it?" I ask. "This is why you look middle-aged when you're over eighty—it has to be. It rejuvenates you," she guesses. "May I have it back now?" I say with a smile. She lets go of the necklace now. "Why did you say you don't trust him?" she asks. "The one time I heard him speak, he just—it wasn't so much what he said but the way he said it, like he was one of the gods on Olympus, toying with the mere mortals for his twisted amusement. There is a precedent for this sort of thing, you know. The sirens of mythology, they would sing their song of death on the rocky shores to lure sailors to their deaths by crashing their ships onto the rocks. Imagine if they really lived and had descendants," I muse. "You've been thinking and not looking at the TV. I saw this guy today at the mall. He can do everything you said he can do," Luna confesses.

I just look at my daughter. My mind can hide nothing from her, not merely because she is very perceptive but because she reads minds. That was her gift. Our house was a truly special house indeed; it housed special people with special gifts from all over the world. Mind reading, telekinesis, remote viewing and invisibility are but a few of the gifts possessed by the residents of my house. No, this is no school for mutant X-Men. My home was a refuge for those who felt they didn't belong on this world. They felt they belonged from a truly far off place, the stars. They are the star children. They believe they come from the stars or at least one of their parents does, and for whatever reason they were left here on this world. They all yearn to reach out to their true place among the stars, as do so many of us.

I asked my daughter if she would take a group member and go out to do some mind probing. This is simply walking among crowds of people as you scan their minds to see who's who and what's up. "I was thinking of doing that. What if no one remembers? If this guy can affect your mind, he can also make you forget," she states. "It's worth a try. Someone always knows something," I nudge. "Yeah, but where to go first?" she inquires. "Where would you go? This person appears to have a lot of free time," I surmise. "The mall. This guy has to be a mallrat, but fat chance he's going back there now," she presumes. "Pick a destination. Use that intuition. But remember, I sense a mean streak in this one. He commands an army. All he has to do is command the masses to turn against you and they will. Maybe he already has," I presume. "Or maybe it's just arrested development. This guy lives alone in this world, except for his friend Otto with him. Otto has a hearing problem, probably the only friend with whom he can speak. There could be people everywhere and he still can't get any more satisfaction out of them than a ventriloquist talking to his dummies. He needs us. We could help him focus his gift. He could change the world!" she surmises. "Yes, he could change the world, turn it into a burning cinder of ash," I forecast. "What happened to dad the optimist? This guy is right here in our state. We don't have to travel to another state or even another planet. He's right here! I say we find him. Or, we can just wait for him to show up here," Luna says with a rascally smile. "Why do you say that?" I ask. "Oh, I just have a feeling he might," my daughter continued to smile as if she knew something I did not.

3) HOW HAWAIIAN JOE MET GAWANII

Joe here. Now, let me tell you of that Cherokee man. When I was a child, I went on a camping trip with my parents to The Great Smoky Mountains, and they spread out over several states and cover over a half-a-million acres or over eight-hundred square miles. Why the statistics? Well, one can imagine it is a really big place to get lost in, especially if you don't live there. There are plenty of park rangers and trails there now, but when I was a kid over a half a century ago I couldn't find any of those park rangers nor any of those convenient signs that point my way out of the place.

Mom and dad slept in their old fashioned camper, while I slept outside in my tent under the stars. After all, I was a whole ten years old, why not? I'd learned everything I needed to know in life I thought. I hadn't learned to take advice, like dad telling me I'm not Tarzan and to stay out of the jungle. A jungle is a lot more dense than a forest, except in spots and I was about to find that out. So, after the morning sun and a loud, funny-sounding bird woke me up, I thought I'd do a little exploring. It's funny how you stumble endlessly about like you're still asleep and suddenly realize you're lost. Falling down and then looking about in every direction makes you feel that way, too, especially when every place you look looks the same. I didn't panic, though, not yet. I just picked a direction—the wrong one obviously—and headed back to my campsite.

After walking what seemed like hours, I realized how tired and hungry I was at that moment, with it getting worse every moment. I felt like crying, but I felt too much like a pathetic specimen the way I ended up this way for such a display of grief. Was a search party looking for me or did anyone even care where I was? Then I suddenly had an odd feeling, the kind that says I'm not alone. It had to be a bear. It's stalking me. I'm just the right size for a bear snack. I couldn't move, but I had to. That bear must be right behind me. I couldn't outrun it. I may as well turn around and face my destiny.

I finally got the nerve to turn around. There was no bear, only a very tall man dressed like a genuine Indian. A real live Cherokee Indian man stood ten feet behind this ten year old boy. He must have noticed the look of fascination or relief on my face and he smiled. "Should I call you little lost bear or have you decided to live here?" he inquired. I was so relieved. He was friendly and spoke English; two things I needed right now, along with a way out. I just looked him over. His suede leather outfit must have been made by hand and the necklace of animal teeth around his neck looked just as real.

"My dad's gonna be mad at me," I expressed. "You mean he would rather show anger than find joy in your safe return?" was his wise reply. "I was supposed to wait for him to get up. He's probably looking for me," I told him. "He will see you soon enough. What is it that you seek?" he inquired with care. Even at the age of ten, I heard that as more of a philosophical question than anything else. My father wanted me to follow in his footsteps and do what he did. I didn't know what I wanted to do then. I just knew it wasn't what dad did. He made plenty of money, but he was barely ever home. "I just want my dad to listen to me. Whenever he speaks, it's the final word on everything. I thought we were free in this country to do what we want," I told him. "Gawanii too was restless at your age. He wanted to see beyond his village and he has. There is no place on Mother Earth Gawanii has not seen, in body or spirit. Gawanii hears your name being spoken among honorable men in time to come," he predicted. "Gawanii, is that your name?" I had to know. "It is ... and your name is Joe," he unbelievably replied. I couldn't help but to look surprised at him. How did he know my name? Dad! That's how he knows. Dad hired him to look for me. "Your father did not hire Gawanii," was his immediate response. My mouth dropped open. He either read minds or was the best guesser in the forest. So I asked, "Have you seen my dad? I, uh, kind of haven't." He told me how easy I was to find and that finding my father would be just as easy—for him! I was still lost. I wondered how he found me and at that very moment he told me, "My friends of the forest, they told Gawanii of your arrival." Friends? I wondered. "Oh, you mean the animals. Yeah, I guess they see me before I see them. How, do you talk to them?" I need to know. "The animals, the rivers, the trees, they all speak to us. You just have to know how to listen," was his answer that I still think about to this day.

I was more confused than ever. Then I did something perfectly suitable for a ten year old who knows no better. I asked a dumb question. "How come you don't sound like Tonto?" was that question. He just looked at me. Then he simply shook his head and smiled. "You must not believe everything you see on your television. Tonto is an honorable character played by an honorable man. The way a person speaks is determined by the way a person learns. If you desire to sound ignorant, do not learn anything," he instructed me. So I asked if by chance the animals told him where my dad was. If I'm lost, he might have gotten lost, too, looking for me I thought. Then we must find him, his mind replied to mine.

He just smiled at me and started to walk like he knew right where to go. I gladly followed. For some reason I wasn't worried anymore. I trusted that I would indeed find dad and our campsite and maybe more importantly I trusted the man guiding me. I wouldn't say he was odd, definitely unusual! I just felt I was in the presence of someone very special. And as we walked, he told me about himself.

Gawanii tells, "Even before Gawanii was born, his spirit roamed free. Even when mother carried Gawanii in her belly, he could see beyond her. The rivers and streams, the mountains and trees and all the forest animals who would become his friends made this the true heaven place on Mother Earth for Gawanii. In this time, mother was so young and beautiful. All the young braves and even our chief and our tribe's shaman had eyes for her. She, as all the others in the freshness of Gawanii's life, was Cherokee. Father was something entirely different. His tribe was not from Mother Earth. He was from the faraway place, a place beyond the sky. He and his tribe came to visit Mother Earth. Gawanii never knew why he really came, only that he found mother and Gawanii found life. The entire time father stayed with Gawanii's tribe, the giant ship hovered above the trees. Father looked not like the red man. He was pale of skin, even more so than the white man my people would come to know in the passage of time. Father had such soft eyes for mother as she did for him. Sometimes when Gawanii's spirit left mother's belly, father would smile at Gawanii. He was the only one who could see Gawanii. The gift of my roaming spirit was just one of many gifts passed onto Gawanii by father. Mother's greatest gift to her son was her love and her appreciation of Mother Earth and the people who honored her."

Gawani continues, "Gawanii is born now. Body and spirit, Gawanii comes to life in this strange place, on board the giant ship above the trees. Father wanted a son and he had one in Gawanii. Even as a helpless little one Gawanii could read his thoughts and desires, as he could read Gawanii's. He wanted his son to live with him in the faraway place among the stars. Gawanii wanted only to live with mother and her people, even though father's people were just as much his. Mother looked upon him with such sad eyes. She wanted only her son. She would have father, but he could not stay. From beneath the trees, mother and son watched the giant ship rise high into the sky until it passed beyond the heaven place. Father had searched all the skies in search of one who would bear his child. And with all his great knowledge, he did not consider mother's love for her child or his love for mother. So he left for his home without us. Before he left, he placed a crystal around Gawanii's neck." I looked over at the necklace of animal teeth I had seen before, noticing now the teardrop-shaped crystal in the middle of it all. The crystal would change colors as it gave off a pleasant glow. If everything he had told me so far was a tall tale, it was a good one because I believed him. I just did.

Gawanii continued, "In Gawanii's first few years as a child there was only peace. And though Gawanii lived happily among his people, he had a great sense of loneliness. Because, you see, Gawanii could not communicate with any of his people but grandmother. This was not because Gawanii could not speak or because they could not hear. It was because whenever Gawanii spoke his people would lose themselves. All their reason was lost; they could do nothing but listen. Gawanii loved his people and would never instruct them to do a wrong thing. Gawanii says instruct because his words were more commands into their minds than suggestions, and my people would do whatever Gawanii would say. Gawanii communicated with mother by putting thoughts in her head. Gawanii would listen to her mind for her thoughts or she would simply speak. We understood each other only this way. She would always smile. Others in the tribe thought Gawanii strange, especially our shaman. He always thought Gawanii to be intruding on his power and influence. Gawanii had many friends in the forest: the deer, the bear and the Tsul Kalu." "What's that?" I asked. He tells, "Other tribes call him Sasquatch. Other men call him Bigfoot. There are many beings in the forest. Gawanii was even friends with a Nun'Yunu'Wi, a stone man; a creature that lives between worlds. It has skin as hard as stone, unbothered by man's puny weapons. It carries a wand like a sorcerer and can cloud the mind of any animal, even man. Neither stone man nor any animal ever feared Gawanii. They would always come to Gawanii, even if they did not understand him. Gawanii's people only ever hunted animals for sustenance, not for sport. At the end of their lives, my animal friends would come to Gawanii so he may be sustained. Gawanii honors their gift and their life with the proof of their animal spirit shown in his necklace." I asked him if animals have spirits? He suddenly stopped and closed his eyes. So, I stopped. I just looked up at this fascinating man of the forest. His head began to sway as he looked very serene. He then opened his eyes. "What do you see?" he asked. I was a bit confused about what he meant or what he wanted me to see. So I stopped looking at him and looked about the forest. I couldn't believe what I was seeing. Either he had a twin or someone who looked and dressed exactly like him stood near a tree up in the distance. The double put up his hand and just smiled. The double now lowered his hand and vanished before my eyes. He didn't say a word about what just happened. He just began to walk and talk and I began to follow and listen.

Gawanii tells, "Grandmother, she was the only one of my people who could speak with Gawanii. She was not a witch nor enchanted. Her ears betrayed her. She had such trouble hearing, but she always understood when Gawanii spoke. While most in Gawanii's tribe only thought Gawanii strange, mother and grandmother always thought differently. They were the most special to

Gawanii. Since grandmother could converse with Gawanii, she taught him more than anyone in his tribe could. Gawanii's other great teacher was observation." I told him I had a grandmother and that the other one had died.

He continued, "The cycle of life, so is it with nature. With every harvest comes a celebration and as autumn becomes summer comes the green corn celebration. No corn is eaten or even touched until fasting ends and feasting begins. The men of our tribe dance in brightly colored costumes decorated with many beads and feathers. On this occasion grandmother danced among the others. They did not object because grandmother sometimes acted silly and she looked so happy on this day for some reason. When she was done, she walked up to Gawanii and told him her spirit would soon soar with the eagles. She hugged Gawanii and told him how special he was to her. Then she put a necklace around his neck with beads and polished teeth of the animals that had come to him at the end of their life, a way of honoring them always, she told Gawanii. She then walked into the forest. When hours went by and grandmother did not return, Gawanii went into the forest to look for her. As always, the animals of the forest came to greet Gawanii. This occasion was different. The animals were leading Gawanii to something, so he followed them. Then Gawanii saw grandmother, she sat quietly sleeping against a tree. She was too quiet. Gawanii talked to her and then shook her. He had seen this in the animals that had come to him and went quiet. This was death. Gawanii had never seen death come for one of us, one of my tribe. He did not know what to do or who to tell. Even mother could not make everything right again. Gawanii felt so alone. The one human being on Mother Earth who could understand her grandson was gone. Gawanii walked alone through the forest now and began to weep. Then the sound of a loud wail was heard. It too came from Gawanii. He stopped to listen. No wolf howled and no bird sang. There was no sound to be heard as far as his eyes could see. So Gawanii ran! Running faster and faster, Gawanii thought if he ran fast enough he could breach the sacred barrier and see grandmother again. So Gawanii ran impossibly fast, faster than the mightiest brave in his tribe could. It happened then, Gawanii was flying free. He soared over the trees and beside the eagles. Gawanii hoped he would see grandmother there. Then Gawanii noticed he did not see his hands or his body. He was truly free. Of course he was! He could see beyond his body even before he was born. He had just forgotten how. So he looked down for his body and could not see it anywhere. He suddenly became scared, terrified he would never find himself again! And as his anxiety grew, he was suddenly on the ground and in his body again. His fear was gone. His only fear was not being able to fly again." "Why do you refer to yourself in the third person so much?" I inquired. He just stopped and looked at me. The shrimpy kid had just interrupted his good and poignant story. "It is Gawanii's way," was all he said. He continued to walk and talk and I continued to walk and shutinzee-up.

He tells, "Gawanii wandered through the forest then. In his short life, he had only played games and done childish things. He was forced to see life as not just for games. He was just a confused little brave. And in his confusion he saw his friend the stone man. We just looked at each other. He knew Gawanii was different from the other human beings and Gawanii knew he was different from the other animals. He was more than an animal and less than a man. He was a stranger in this world just like Gawanii. The stone man put Gawanii on his shoulder and we walked through the forest. He sensed Gawanii was lost, in place and in mind. When we arrived close enough to my village, we could hear the sounds of my people so he let Gawanii down. He knew his new friend would be safe now. He walked away now, without acknowledgement or need of thanks. Gawanii just looked at him as he left, probing the tangled web of his odd mind. He turned and looked back. Gawanii smiled and waved at him. His face formed what would pass for a smile. Then he disappeared into his home, the forest."

"Do you know the abominable snowman, too?" I asked. "Did you mean to be funny or inquisitive?" he replied. I thought it was a fair question after a story like that. Suddenly thinking of his double I saw in the forest, I asked if he could do other strange things. He told me, "Just as the spirit can travel beyond the body, the body can travel to meet the spirit. As Gawanii grew to manhood, he discovered more of the abilities passed onto him by father, most of which was being able to finally speak to mother. The power Gawanii's voice possessed to mold the minds of others was truly a part of him now, and when Gawanii could control himself and his abilities he learned to speak with or without taking over the minds and wills of others. Many a leader or tyrant would sell his soul for such power. Gawanii looks upon his abilities as nothing more than gifts to help others, not to control them." I blurted out, "You sound normal to me. What's so different about your voice?" He replied, "Does the face not look different when it wears a mask?"

He stepped away from me and threw his arms out at his sides. Then he said loudly, "Come to Gawanii!" His voice became amplified and echoed throughout the forest and seemingly everywhere. He put down his arms now as every conceivable form of forest animal came creeping or racing through the forest to be my native guide's willing audience. Taking pieces of fruit from a leather pouch on his side, he hand-fed the fruit to docile deer and gave nuts to eager and willing squirrels. The raccoons preferred a sweet treat in the form of a cookie. I realized how hungry I was and thought if I knew he had cookies, I would have asked for some. So he gave me one. And as I chomped down on my cookie, I watched all the animals eating, and getting along and just happy to be around Gawanii. He didn't just have a way with animals—he had a way! In his forest, all men and beasts were friends. I was suddenly glad I got lost because I had truly found something.

He walked on and I followed. We had good friends to keep us company. The animals tagged along for a while, until they got distracted and got along with their lives. I asked him if he always lived here or if he ever left his home.

"Many times has Gawanii seen beyond his land as said before. Joe must listen," he said as I listened more carefully now, him telling me as he grew to manhood his greatest need suddenly was to see what lay beyond the forest home he knew only. And just as he learned to send his spirit out as a scout to see what lay beyond the forest, he could then send his body to join his spirit. Then as he stood before his mother and his people and described what his spirit saw in a far off land, he described little men with strange eyes; they were building a wall that stretched across their entire land. Then he told of a land with strange beasts like he had never seen before and men with a skin color darker than his own. Mother saw the longing in his eyes and the restlessness in his heart. She knew her son's place was no longer only with his people. He told mother his place will always be with his people, he just has a need to see what he has never seen. Then a bird landed on his shoulder. He reached into another bag on his hip and took out some bird seed. He simply held out his hand and the bird hopped onto his arm and fed on the seeds in his hand. Such a simple thing, yet I marveled at it. The bird finished eating and flew away. Then my native guide proceeded through the forest with me in tow. He didn't miss a beat as he got on with his story.

He tells, "So Gawanii left his people. He looked to the sky and let his spirit roam free again, his body appearing in a far off land. Gawanii saw all the animals of Africa. The people there were less curious about his red skin and Cherokee attire than the way the beasts of the plains gravitated to him. Even the fiercest or most gigantic of beasts would not harm Gawanii, only wander up to him in friendship as if all their lives they have been waiting only for him. He is honored again." "Where else did you go? Did you go to the land down under?" I had to know. So he told me, "Gawanii danced with the aborigines of Australia, learned the way of the sword with the Samurai in Japan and celebrated the festival of Samhain with the Celts on the way to countless other experiences he had never experienced before. Then Gawanii caught a glimpse of himself in a nearby stream. In the calmness of the water he could see his face clearly. The passage of time had barely changed him. As those all around Gawanii grew old, he did not. Then he thought of mother and his people. He felt he had betrayed them by leaving them. He had no other place on Mother Earth to see now, only his home. So his spirit took to the wind and found his people in the village where he had left them, except there were many more now. And in the passage of time, Gawanii learned many more things. Earth, air, fire and water, all created by Creator to serve Mother Earth's harmonious nature. So, Gawanii let a gentle wind move through his village, a wind so different it could not even be seen to move the treetops. My people observed this and thought it strange. Then Gawanii saw mother. She moved more slowly now as she walked through the village. She had grown old waiting for her son's return. And even before Gawanii appeared before her, she smiled. She knew her son had come home. Gawanii stayed with his people for the rest of mother's life. Not seeing the world or anything else mattered to him now. Her son's very presence rejuvenated mother. We spent many happy years together. And for all that lay ahead for Gawanii, he would remember this time in his life as the truest heaven place on earth."

"How do you control the forces of nature?" I inquired. Gawanii raised his hand and made small circles with it. Then a gentle breeze came through seemingly only where we were standing. I couldn't figure out if he was causing the wind or just redirecting it. Then I noticed the crystal around his neck glowing and changing color like it was active. Gawanii and I then started to rise up, the gentle wind swirling under our feet was lifting us up like the world's most eco-friendly hover-board. As we rose higher, I looked afraid until Gawanii's look of reassurance calmed me. Then I really started to enjoy the ride as we went higher, swirling and bobbing about without a care in the world, not even what dad would do to me. I had seen something I could not un-see. I was changed forever.

We were now hovering above the trees. Was this all just the wind at our feet or were we actually controlling gravity? Then I saw mom and dad's campsite from up there, a truly surreal moment. They were outside the trailer, arguing I think. Gawanii noticed, too, and proceeded to lower us to the ground. "I think I'm in trouble," was all I could think to say. "Does your father punish destiny? Perhaps destiny demanded you meet Gawanii?" he told me. "Dad punishes me for everything. If he doesn't like it, it's wrong. I don't think I could explain you to him either. That would just make things worse. He'd say I was lying and then I'd really get it," I explain. He told me if he had given me cause for concern, he would explain to father. I just told him it would still be my fault. "Trust Gawanii, father will listen," was all he had to tell me. He just smiled at me like he knew something that I didn't; he could make things right and with the greatest of ease. Of course he could. I felt at ease now as we continued our trek back to my campsite, probably because I now knew where it was or quite possibly because this special man was by my side.

I suddenly blurted out, "Are you glad they made your home into a national park?" "They could have asked Gawanni first. Maybe they did it simply for Gawanii to meet Joe," he smiled at me. That felt good! I'm having the best time being lost in the forest.

He had to tell me just then, "You will leave home one day. Gawanii has left his home many times over the centuries, but he always comes back." "Did you say centuries?" I had to be sure. "Gawanii's father's people live much longer than human beings, a gift passed on to Gawanii by father. Much time passed through Gawanii's gaze and Gawanii remembers all. As centuries pass, Gawanii finds himself to be Mother Earth's true chronicler of time, seeing much of what Man would call progress," he relates. "You mean like the atomic bomb? They made a lot of cool movies about it; Godzilla, and other giant monsters, even one with a giant tarantula!" I tell him over excitedly as any kid would, where in a world of the fifties there was no shortage of big bug and flying saucer movies to explore.

My native guide then moved his hand around and around in a circle as a mirror without substance appeared before us. We observe our floating reflection as he said, "As the thousandth year of Gawanii's life approaches, he looks into this pool of calm and sees his reflection. He sees a man still not yet in his third decade of life. How will he see himself when he looks upon yet another stretch of time as great? Should he yet again venture out into the world as he has done so many times before?"

Gawanii took one of the many necklaces of teeth from around his neck and placed it over my head. And as we stood there and looked at our reflections, his reflection changed very little, while my reflection was that of an older man wearing a Panama hat and a Hawaiian shirt, a vision of the future, my future. And, yes, I am still wearing the necklace. "Wear your necklace always. It will protect you from those like me," he said. "Like you? But you're not one of the bad guys. I know you're not," I had to say. "I meant those who would try to control you, cloud your mind," he said and began reciting a poem.

The Carolinas, where these people did roam
The sacred land of their Cherokee home

To be one with nature is to be one with our earth
Not just for the red man but to all given birth

Mother Earth, I honor you and use what I need
Never will I simply plunder you for greed

Air, I honor you and take of your breath
Never to pollute you with the incense of death

Fire, I honor you, taking warmth from your form
Never pervert you to nuclear storm

Water, I honor you and drink of your life fill
May you never lie poisoned, stagnant and still

A shaman I am now, a bringer of rain
May the skies never cry only tears of their pain

And if man's ways destroys such earthly wonders
The earth will correct with its Seven Thunders

So, Earth, my mother, I honor all that you give
To abandon you now is to truly not live

Pushed out into this world, I can only roam free
Gone is my home with the Cherokee

He stopped as the reflection faded. He waited and looked at me as if for a critique. "That was pretty good, but why did you say I and not say Gawanii as usual?" I inquired. "Because the words spoken were for you, not just Gawanii. The words were for everyone who comes to this sacred place," he needed to tell me.

We reached a place in the forest where I could see my campsite without hovering above the trees. We just stood there. I didn't want to go, probably because I knew what was waiting for me; mom would be worried sick and never stop telling me why and dad would just be a hundred-foot raging monster ready to stomp on me. Maybe I really didn't wanna go because I just didn't wanna go back. Hey, it was the fifties with all my cool music, and flying saucer and big bug movies to go back to. It was pretty fun back there. There was something pretty cool here, though, too. Then he looked at me. I was so sleepy all of a sudden.

I woke up in my tent. I could smell food cooking. I rushed out of the tent! I just wanted to take my medicine and take it quickly. I knew I was about to be punished and I just wanted to get it over with. Mom and dad were smiling. I don't get it. They greeted me and remarked on how long I was sleeping. It was almost noon. It's like they just stepped out of *Invasion of The Body Snatchers*; they're the smiling pod people. Their conversation didn't make sense either. It was a combination of gibberish and double-talk, and the funny thing was I don't think they even knew it. I'm not getting punished, though.

Then it hit me. I just woke up! Was I really in the forest with a thousand year old Cherokee Indian who leaves his body, reads minds and floats on air? Most people would definitely say dream, but it was so real! I didn't know what to do about it or who to tell. I could tell mom and dad right here before me, but why? They're in a good mood already. Why spoil it? So I had breakfast.

As mom and dad came to their senses and we finished eating, they spoke normally again. Dad didn't get mad either. They were both calm and reflective. They were really glad they came here. It was so relaxing for them. I was glad I came, too, whether what happened to me was a dream or not. I felt like I learned something. No, I did learn something! I have to start being more decisive. Life can still be fun.

As I packed up my gear in my tent, I was a bit depressed. We had to go. Sure, we'd be doing other fun stuff, but I had to leave here, this special place that was made even more special just for me it seemed. Do other people who visit this special place have such dreams or was my dream just for me? Did I need to be told something? Yeah, people don't fly; it had to be a dream. Then as I left the tent to start taking it down, I saw the necklace of teeth that Gawanii had given me. I don't know why I hadn't noticed it before, but there it was. And I just stood there shocked to see it, a voice in my head said, "Wear it always."" And except for showering and one party at a guru's house in the sixties, I always have

I walk through a forest. Something seems so familiar about it. No, I don't recognize any individual tree or spot, of course, just that I've been here before. I glance down at the ground and see my foot, such a small foot. Of course I see it like that. I am ten years old again. Then I see someone up in the distance, someone familiar from long ago. My native guide, it has to be him! I have to be sure so I run, running faster and faster as I weave between all the forest trees. I called out to him with no answer. I get closer and suddenly he is up in the distance again. How can this be? I run so fast and yet he only walks. I am closer now. I can't see his face. He walks past a tree and now he is far away again. I run faster! I must know if it is really him. I will reach him this time. I am close again and again he disappears behind a tree, only to pop up somewhere up ahead. My heart is racing. I'm a small boy, not a marathon runner. How much more can I take? I almost reach him and suddenly I must stop, too tired to go on another step. He turns around. It is indeed my native guide. "Why did you stop? If you want to reach Gawanii, you must come to him," Gawanii instructs.

I woke up. I must have fallen asleep at my desk. My heart is racing. Was my native guide sending me a message or is my obsession worsening? I must know once and for all if we really did meet so long ago.

4) SAFE AT HOME

Back at Reg place, Otto and I sit and watch the tube—and look at that! Some bloodthirsty reporter is interviewing shoppers about some odd fellow who just visited the mall. Apparently he saved the day while telling everyone to make off with the mall's contents. Now I was a bit unnerved by having someone try to alter my destiny at the barrel of a gun, but I don't think I said to loot the mall. "When did I tell everyone to turn wacko, nutso crazy and loot the mall? I thought I saved the day," I remarked. "El duderino, you have total recall. You recall saying to take what you want? Cuz I do. You gotta be careful what you say, your one responsibility," Otto jabs. "Are you saying I'm irresponsible or a slacker?" I ask. "I don't think you're lazy. You just need focus," Otto informs wisely. Then it hit me—no one mentioned the shooters at the mall, and the reporter only barely mentioned them. Normally after any shooting incident that's all you'd hear about for days, but it didn't even register. I was the story. I couldn't imagine what was going to happen next, or didn't want to. As Otto kept watching, I tuned out and just turned myself off.

Water ... cool, cool water, I'm floating in it, in an infinity of ocean blue under a sky azure. I have found my place of tranquility. As I sit in my floating lawn chair with my silly straw hat on, I care not how uncool I look, for I am in the middle of nowhere, where prying eyes cannot see me and needful ears cannot follow me. So far from life, I worry not. I need no rescue. I need no brand new friend to bother me. I have found all I need in the very womb of mother earth. I am safe, and free and without obligation to mankind or destiny. Please no one come look for me. As I drift away, leave me be ...

I sip my drink and lay my coconut cup upon the water. I watch it gently drift away. As I hold out my hand, the cup simply drifts back right into my hand. A dolphin bobs its head out of the water like an old friend dropping by to see me. I hum for my old friend, its head turning as if to hear me even better as it makes playful sounds of approval. Yes, even the animals like my voice. If I dare sing for the dolphins, would they dance for me?

As my eyes flutter gently into sleep, my hat blows off unexpectedly, sailing off into the sky farther and farther up as if it could fly of its own volition. I hop up from my chair to watch this floppy straw hat fly farther away until it is out of sight. Then I realize I am standing on wet sand. No water to be found anywhere. It's as if a giant stopper plug was just pulled and all the water got sucked down. Even the cup in my hand is devoid of refreshment now. I toss the cup away, the cup cracking and blackening with heat as I watch it dry up before my eyes. The sand where the cup lies is now drying up, spreading faster, and faster, and faster until nothing can be seen but dry, cracked sand. A big spot of sand under my feet is still wet, though. Why am I untouched? It must be immensely hot, yet I do not feel it. All forms of life exotic and beautiful or even deadly are now gone, perhaps taken with the water or just taken from me. I am alone again, not a peaceful, warm and fuzzy feeling as before but an oppressive one. Nothing but lifeless, barren land for as far as the eye can see in every direction. Strangely, I feel afraid but not for myself.

I am not alone now. Then I stand in the middle of a circle of people; all kinds of people attired all kinds of ways. They seem to be about a hundred feet away in this perfect circle or ring around me. I am exactly in the middle. So I run! I run towards the people. I must ask them why they are here, why I am here. But every time I get close to one of them I am back in the middle of the circle, starting my run over towards a different face every time. But I will reach one—I will! So I run faster, and faster and faster! Every time I get close enough to reach out and touch one of them I am back to the circle's middle—this madness! But I will not stop. So I keep running, even though I feel I don't have the energy to take one more step. I reach one of them, a beautiful woman with a scarf around her neck. As I reach out for her, I collapse, only to find I am on my knees in the middle of the circle again with the scarf in my hand. The sweat rolling off me could refill the lost ocean, and I am so tired that I cannot even stand. I ask again why we are here with no answer, so I scream at them! But still they will not answer me. I wait. Then one of them, a little girl raises her fist and chants my name. Then another chants and one-by-one they all raise their fists and chant Reg! Reg! Reg! Then the chant becomes louder as one ring of chanters is encircled by a second ring of chanters, which becomes three rings, and four and finally the empty sea is replaced by a sea of chanters, all chanting together so loudly that the sound is deafening! I cover my ears, but nothing stops the ring of madness. Why won't it stop!!!

And then suddenly ... all the chanting stopped. I uncovered my ears not only to a lack of sound but to a lack of light. Everyone was looking up, so I got up on my feet now and looked up, too. We all watched a blood red eclipse darkening the dry sand below us. Total darkness is now cast over this desert, though, leaving only an eerily red glow from the sun that is easy on the eyes. A feeling of inner peace comes over me again as I look around at all the reddish haze on all the smiling faces. Why are they happy, or why am I not suddenly?

Off in the distance now, a distortion up in the air can be seen, the kind of distortion you see over the highway on a hot day. Not like a devastating hammer blow but more like a mild breeze the distortion wave of extreme heat gently lands way off in the distance, slowly closing in towards everyone around me. As the wave of heat creeps closer, I notice all these little wisps of ash twirling and floating up into the atmosphere. As the wave gets even closer, I can clearly see to my horror now that those wisps of ash are the people surrounding me. Like souls reaching up for heaven, the bits of rising ash made their way up ever higher as I watched the people around me be incinerated. Why must I endure this? I felt such overwhelming grief, not for myself because I knew for some odd reason I would be spared.

She comes towards me, this incomparably beautiful fair-skinned goddess of a lady dressed in flowing silk-like dress. I feel I know her, but from where? Out of the circle of chanters she steps, walking towards me with her arm outstretched as if to give me something. "Save us, Reg. Save us, my son," she says with a voice so haunting it penetrates deep into my very essence. It's as if she has the same power as me. I feel her voice more than hear it. All I could do is watch with the most pitiful sadness as the wave of heat gets ever closer to closing the circle. As she gets even closer, the longing in her eyes and the futility in her voice is nearly impossible to bear. She wants me to do something I know I cannot do, save her.

Only a step away, she would reach me. I smile. She smiles and reaches out for me. And with a blast of heat, the circle closes. I stand there looking at flames dancing harmlessly over my skin and then away into nothingness. I am completely unharmed. I lift my head up slowly now to see the beautiful goddess, now a statue of blackened ash still reaching out for me. And I would hear her maniacal laughter echoing through the wasteland as if taunting me as a gust of wind takes her swirling up to the sky to join all the other ashen souls. I am alone again.

"See you tomorrow, homie," Otto says as I wake up. No, I don't awaken with a scream, even though you might consider many of my dreams nightmares. You can get used to things, even a hurricane in your head every time you close your eyes. If only I could master my dreams as easily as I use my voice. That would be true power. Then I would feel like I accomplished something. But the gods play their games with you, don't they? Is it simply because they can? Or, are they testing you, seeing if you will be made stronger? I definitely feel the dreams visited upon me are to teach or prepare me for something, but for what? I often feel my dreams are more like harbingers of impending doom. But maybe that is just exactly what they are, twisted portents of a future that I must prevent ... or am I the one who causes such catastrophe? "I just had another dream. Something's gonna happen," I tell my bud. "Yeah, I'm going to go home," was all he said as he headed for the door.

I sat there dazed. What have I done? I did what I had to do, but at what consequence? I speak up quickly before Otto reaches the door. "Why leave now? It's not even dark!" I plead. "This Mexican won't be noticed in a sea of Mexicans. But you, homie, you're like, radioactive. I can't be around you right now," he says. "So you just ditch me? The first sign of trouble and you take off?" I plead more. "You don't listen! Everyone will be looking for you. If they find me with you, I won't be able to get you any help," he says. "What do you mean help? What are you gonna do?" I mystify. "Trust me. I'll check on you in the morning," he says as he heads for the front door. "I made a mistake, didn't I?" I somber. "We all make them. It's just how you deal with them," he says as he leaves and leaves me alone yet again. He leaves and I just sit here. I don't even try to stop him. Why not? Because it's a dumb idea! He's my friend. He'll help, but how? What's he gonna do? So many questions pop into my head with answers in a nanosecond, but I get no relief, no reward for my logic and reason. I hop up and go look out the window. Otto is driving away in his Gran Torino. I got it for him. I'd do anything for my bud. I hope he feels the same. It's not that I don't trust him, I just don't know what he's gonna do. How does anyone make everything right in a situation like this? I look at my watch. I've been standing here for over an hour. Am I waiting for Otto to return or more likely looking for who might drive up?

I watch a movie, but I can't enjoy it. I keep thinking about what's going to happen, and I can't stop hopping up to go glance out the window. I work-out. I look out the window. I eat some protein. I look out the window. Am I truly paranoid or just cautious? It's dark now, a perfect time for them to come for me, but who will come, man or Astroman? Will it be the government, the shadow people or the little green or gray dudes? They're coming to take Reg away la-di-da-ha-ha! To the funny farm with Reg. I'll just tell them to let me go, though. What am I worried about? Then why am I worried? Get some glue, dude, you're cracking up!

I sit looking out the window in a chair I brought from the kitchen. I can look over at the TV and back out the window from here. No one's sneaking up on me. Man, it's getting late. My eyes are playing winkie-blinkie. I can't keep them open. I'm fine. They won't get me. They'll never get me. Was that a yawn ...

How did I get here? I'm at a home I visited as a child. There's that sound, the sound I always dread hearing. That sound means they're coming. It's the faint sound of thumping as if someone were dropping the most gigantic bags of sand on the ground in the distance. I have to know, so I run outside. I see nothing yet, but I know I will soon. The sound is getting louder. Then I see them, the giant machines. I just see a head, and soon a face coming up over the horizon, rising up in the atmosphere as they walk the curvature of the earth until they can be seen in their entirety. Two, three miles high or more they must be. I'm not sure. They stand miles away across a forest, the tallest of trees only brushing their ankles. As I stand there helpless but amazed, they look as if they're coming just for me, and yet I know I will be unharmed. They are still so far away, yet with every step they are so much closer and so much louder. O, the sound, it's almost deafening! The rumbling, the sounds of stepped-on trees snapping; the crushing sounds of buildings crumbling and people's houses being stomped on! Yet I am impressed, these giant machines must have come from a very far off place, another world just to show me this enchanting devastation. Each machine is a different shape; a big headed alien, a lizard, a Samurai, an Indian chief, all forged in alien metal, impervious and unstoppable. These were so massive and impressive that they would make Transformers look like Tonka toys.

They are so close now that I must look up to see their faces move through the clouds. Yes, I feel no terror now, only exhilaration, for they had come this far to show me their awesomeness as they put on their show just for me. A giant foot is lifting up and passing right over me, coming down on the neighbor's house instead. They were never nice to me anyway. I look around to see rubble everywhere, except for my house, unharmed as I knew it would be. I wave to the giant robot machines as they proceed on their way around the earth and I notice how small my hand is. I'm a little kid again. That's right, this happened when I was just little—didn't it?

A knock at the front door pops open my eyes instantly. Yep, dreaming again, unless reality has a whole new meaning now? I stand and look out the window. I'm happy again, or at least relieved. Otto is here.

Otto and I sit and eat a nutritious and delicious breakfast in my grand kitchen. Well, I do anyway. I told him I would fix him some steak and eggy-weggs or porky pig parts, but he preferred to gobble the breakfast cereal I keep in the house for him that's just chocked full of sugar and bright sparkly colors, yum city! So I just had a muffin and protein drink. While quietly consuming mass quantities of gluten and sugar, Otto blurts out, "I think I'm in love." Thinking that more than out of the blue even for my best bud, I ask him to elucidate me further. "Her name's Aphrodite, you know, like out of mythology. She was with Hawaiian Joe's daughter, you know, the one who kissed you last night. I was eating a hot dog on the sidewalk and they just walked up to me. It's weird, like they were reading my mind. They asked me how I knew you," he fills me in. "Somewhat spooky—what did you tell 'em?" I ask. "I just said you might be someone from the hood. I don't think they believed me, though. They kept looking at me. It was freaky. Then they said if I knew anyone who could find you to tell you Hawaiian Joe would be speaking at the Staples Center tomorrow and that he could help you. They gave me another card," he says as he puts a glossy business card on the table. I picked up the card. It had an address on it and a picture of a beautiful girl with the most piercing eyes on the back of it, the mall kisser. I just stared at her picture, and the more I looked at it the more I felt she was staring back at me, like she was right here with me in the room. "Is this Aphrodite?" I ask. "No, that's Joe's daughter. She's not bad either," he adds. "Well, who's the mad kisser here?" I demand. "Luna," he says and instantly I see the sky darken as the sun and moon seem to collide. "She was born during an eclipse," my fuzzy melon spills out. "How are her lips?" he quips. "How are Aphrodite's?" I came back. "I haven't gotten that far yet. I don't think she was interested. They're interested in you. You better lay low. They're trying to find you bad!" he emphasizes. "Interested in me, huh? When I'm finished with 'em, I'll give you leftovers," I smile. "Pay attention! I said lay low, don't go anywhere!" Otto stresses. "Criswell predicts they're waiting for me with a kiddie pool and a bucket of oil," I jest, but not really. "Otto predicts sharp surgical instruments and your dumb ass strapped to a table. What if they work for the government, if they're spies? They're gonna find you before you think. You better start making plans," Otto stresses. "Plans?" I inquire. "To leave! You think you can stay here? Not unless you can put a force field around the place. Can you do that?" Otto asks. "What if the government does find me? What if they lock my bank account? I better get more money out. They can't touch my crypto, though," I assume. "What do you need money for? Just walk in to any hotel and tell them to house you. Walk into any restaurant and tell them to feed you. You've done it before," Otto says. "What do I do with all my stuff? I like my stuff. The feds would just confiscate it, examine it all like it's alien artifacts," I guess. Finishing his cereal, Otto gets up to leave. "I'll be at the speakers convention tomorrow at the Staples Center. If you wanna hang out, that's where I'll be," he says as he heads for the back door. "Tomorrow? How 'bout now? We got all day!" I stress. "You better pack a suitcase and watch out for long black sedans. I saw one last night I just knew was following me. I'm gonna go hang out with the biggest homies I can find till tomorrow," Otto says as he opens the back door of the kitchen. "Why you using the back door? What about your Gran Torino?" I ask. "I got a ride. They're waiting for me. Better take this seriously," Otto stresses. "Why did I have to open my mouth?" I ask. "You mean at the mall? What you did wasn't wrong. Sometimes you just gotta do what you gotta do. Don't do anything stupid before I see you tomorrow," Otto adds as he heads out the back door.

I just sat there. I felt like I had unleashed a Genie out of a bottle—all the Genies! I had to focus like never before. I picked up the card with Luna's face on it. I just kept looking at her image. So much for focus. I'd swear she was looking back at me, though. Wherever she was, I strangely felt she knew I was looking at her. I knew it. I felt it. I would have to find her. Having Joe's address on the card wouldn't make it too difficult.

Trapped in this house because I dare not leave it, the day disappears and night falls. A prisoner of this place will I be no longer. I slip into the night's cloak of darkness, comfortable and safe. It's time to play superhero, my favorite game to pay with the freaks that come out to play. That's the game where Otto and I walk the streets to fight crime in a casual way. I guess I'll do it alone tonight. If I see someone robbing someone, I just tell them to get some self-esteem and get a job. If I see couples arguing, I just tell them to go home and make love, they'll enjoy it more. If I see someone about to shoot someone, I just tell them, "You don't wanna shoot anyone. You don't wanna shoot anyone ever again." Other superheroes have to wear funny outfits, hop around and tire themselves out, and then they make enemies because no one likes to get captured and incarcerated. Me? I just walk on by and lend a kind word, making sinners and saints alike feel alllllllright! There will never be another extra freaky freak like me, another one who can do all the trippy things I do. Yeah, I'm the ultra shaman, baby! I'm Mr. Goodtrips.

So here I am walking Sunset Boulevard. There's a place I like to eat. There's where Tower Records used to be. There's where Belushi and Morrison stayed. I pass a group of regulars. These aren't tourists, I've seen them before. There goes a guy with bloodshot eyes and he looks a bit jumpy, too. He's gotta be on some kind of drugs, some bad drugs! I don't get a very good vibe from that guy. For me, an occasional toke or shot of tequila is good enough to be sociable. If I get wasted, I say stupid things. Then people do stupid things and end up hurt. I don't need to be the cause of that.

I hear a female screaming. It came from behind me, so I turned and ran back down the sidewalk. There's Mr. Bloodshot Eyes; he's pointing a gun at our crowd of regulars on Sunset. I guess I'm the only one here to save the day. He sees me and points his gun right at me. "Hey!" I yell at him, loudly enough to put everyone's mind around us into a haze, except for the man with the wild look in his bloodshot eyes. He's reacting to my voice, but not like I'd expected. He's blinking and wincing and acting like he's in pain—what is this? My voice isn't supposed to do that. "What did you do to me? I'm gonna kill you. I'm gonna kill you! I'm gonna kill you!!!" he shouts. My voice had the others transfixed, but our friend with the bloody desperate eyes and the gun was in a panic. I did have experience using my voice on other people under the influence, mostly stoners. And when the brain is compromised already by one drug, the introduction of another drug either fights the first drug or amplifies it. Stoners usually start to laugh and get too mellow for words. This guy? He must have been on PCP or something else equally insane for the membrane. This guy made me scared! I mean scared like I'd never been before! Although my heart was racing, I had to be calm; at least my voice had to be. So I used a most mellifluous tone on him. "I am calm. I sail on a sea of bliss and tranquility. I feel no more pain. There is no more want in me. I am whole. My need to abuse myself is no more. I am free to live. My body will heal itself, and I will go on with my life and finally find my way," I said to him as if the words were his own thoughts. As I spoke, the tension from his body all but disappeared; his pain did subside and he realized he would truly be free of his bodily cravings. I was realigning his brain for him. He lowered his gun. Then before I could speak, he simply walked away, tossing his weapon into a sewer opening as he disappeared from sight. I told the others simply to forget and enjoy the night. The rest of my moonlit walk was a lot less exciting, which was just fine with me. I just walked on without further incident. No robberies, rapes, murders or meteors crashing into the earth were witnessed by me. I had a decision to make, though.

5) MEETING THE MOTIVATOR

Okay, so I'm here at the speaker's convention. I'm wearing a fedora and sunglasses, just in case no one would mistake me for the mystery mall guy or a bad spy. There are booths set up to talk disenchanted and aimless people out of their money for motivational courses. There's a big stage set up where I suppose the speakers will speak, all, I'm sure, trying to one-up each other and sell the most motivational courses. Sure, they must help some people, but I keep remembering this guy I saw on TV in the eighties who always talked about how he flew here in his helicopter after getting off his yacht. Hey, I'm okay with having nice things, but this guy always sounded like he was rubbing it in.

So after a bit of waiting on my part, Joe walked out on the stage to address the people. From what I know about Hawaiian Joe, he wasn't really from Hawaii. He got his name because he's just a long-gray-haired, friendly guy who wears Hawaiian shirts when he speaks. Joe was young in the hippie days, learning about flower power and other groovy stuff at the feet of Timothy Leary. Hey, maybe he knew ol' Jimbo, too! I'll have to find out.

Joe stands on stage before an eager crowd. I can't tell if they came for the motivation or just to see someone famous. "I was going to ask all of you to smile, but I see I need not ask because I see a lot of smiling faces already. That makes me smile, puts me into a happy state. Like a comedian you all know and love appearing on the stage, everyone is instantly happy, and why not? You know he or she is going to keep making you happy. And you know it is you that really keeps you happy. You can literally walk through a minefield and remain in a positive state. After all, it's only the mine that you step on that you have to worry about," Joe smiles. A few people laugh, I guess they hadn't heard that one before. I hadn't either actually. I usually just avoid minefields when I can. "Simon says don't be manipulated. I don't get it, Marge, do I smile now or not? That's the whole point, it's your choice! So if you have a choice to be happy or anything else, what should you choose to be? What an easy choice. Is a smile a form of manipulation? It can be. If you're happy, just smile. If your car is on the side of the road and you're a pretty girl, a smile's a helluva manipulation to get you to stop, but it works!" he smiles again and the people laugh again. Joe's all right. I can't stop thinking about what that girl on the side of the road looked like. That happened to me once actually. I stopped to help a young lady out with her car. Turns out I couldn't fix it, so she just flagged over another mister helper. I told him to fix the car and deliver it, while I took the girl home. Ain't life grand!

Joe took the microphone off the stand and he's walking around the stage with it as if he's thinking. He's not smiling as much now. "There are a lot of speakers here today. You all have your favorites. It doesn't matter to me. I'm just here to enjoy life. But if I had to pick just one speaker who is more convincing than any of the rest, I'd say it was one that might not even be here today, or is he? I've met a lot of interesting people or personalities in my life. But the one who spoke at the mall recently, that is someone I'd like to meet! If you are here today, I would be honored to meet you. I suspect you didn't really want to reveal yourself the way you did, but we are all very glad you did. You saved a lot of people. Destiny is calling you, my friend. You will have to answer destiny one day. If you care to meet, I would never betray your trust. If you do not believe that, believe this: I know someone just like you," Joe says as he slides the microphone back into the stand and walks backstage. He was all too serious at the end, putting baffled looks on many faces. This wasn't like Joe.

"He's talking about you, mister daydreamer," Otto says as he appears next to me with a beautiful blonde woman by his side. At least my bud would be here to make whatever I had to do next easier. I wasn't so sure about the girl, although she did have a certain appeal. "You must be Aphrodite," I say directly to her, putting her into the usual mind altering dreamy dream state that even I can't release her from. I smile at her and she smiles back, too high to talk back. "Thanks a lot. Now she can't function," Otto remarks. "You know how it works, that's how they react," I come back. "Glad you came. Ready to meet Joe?" Otto asks. "What's the rush?" I ask. "No rush. You can stand around here all night as people react to your voice," Otto states. "Tough! That's what nosey people get," I snapped. "What are you Humphrey Bogart now?" Otto asks. "Is it the hat? I thought my huge cowboy hat would attract too much attention," I mention. "No, it's that mouth!" he complains. I say like Bogie, "Okay, let's go meet Joe. You bring the dame." So we walk away to meet the next part of my destiny.

And like some powerful, mystical force had taken over me, I found myself backstage with Otto and Aphrodite in tow. Joe looked up and so did a couple of his handlers and a security guard, who immediately put his hand on his gun. Not wanting to be filled fulla lead, I simply yelled, "STOP!" The guard went limp as his hand slipped off his gun, while the two handlers' brains went bye-bye. Joe, on the other hand, he just smiled. He knew it was me he was looking for. "It is you, isn't it?" Joe smiles. "Yeah, I'm me. Did I not just pull the sword from the stone? Of course it's me. You mind if I send them away so we can talk?" I ask. "It won't hurt them, will it?" Joe asks. "Not even if I kick 'em in the ass on the way out the door," I add. "Just inquiring, we don't need anyone hurt," Joe states. "They'll feel what I want them to feel," I say, which comes off ominously to Joe. Just stating a fact. Not smiling at me now, Joe says, "How do you suppose I get them to leave?" "That's right, they're here, but they're not here. He's not here, and he's not here and the blonde's not here. All the planets orbiting around me and only I can keep them from crashing into each other. How is it that you can talk back to me, all those drugs in the sixties with Leary?" I ask. "Something like that. Thank you for coming to see me as I requested. I ..." I cut him off saying, "You da man? You think you made me come here? I came out of curiosity. No one makes me do anything. I'm ten times stronger than you. I'm a lot older than you too, old man. No one has ever bested me. You could send an army after me and I could talk them over a cliff!" I boast. True, though. "I have been a speaker for a long time and I know how to use words, how to manipulate if you will. I will not be manipulated by you," Joe says sternly. As the stare down continues, I start to laugh. "I like this old dude," I say. The mood is lightened for all now. "He likes to screw with people," Otto tells. "The product of too much time on your hands, no doubt. Really, may we speak alone somewhere?" Joe asks.

So I speak directly to the others, telling them I wanted to speak to Joe and to forget little ol' me. Then like good little zombies they shuffled away, leaving me, Otto and Joe to rap some. "That's how you got back stage, isn't it? You just told everyone and they let you, amazing!" Joe amazes. "Yeah, I'm like a Shaolin priest, I can walk through walls. Why doesn't my voice affect you like everyone else?" I ask for the second time. "I am not sure. Quite possibly because my brain may have been compromised by certain substances I happened to have experimented with when I was younger," Joe says. "How come when people with no money take drugs it's a crime, but when people with money take them it's an experiment?" Otto inquires. "Don'tcha know, Otto, LSD wasn't illegal back then—off on a technicality!" I add. "You can speak in his presence, too? Why may I ask?" Joe asks Otto. "I have hearing implants. His voice don't do nothin' for me, and I like it that way," he delights. "That's my Otto. He's not stupid, and guess who else isn't? Tell me the real reason my voice doesn't affect you or we're outta here," I demand. "As I mentioned before, I know someone like you. I suppose being around someone with your special gift builds up a tolerance in the listener," Joe explains. "So this person can do the same thing with his or her voice?" I curious. "She has a different gift from yours, one also very special," Joe says with a twinkle in his eye. This person was definitely as special to him as the talent she possessed. It had to be his daughter. If it were, I definitely wanted to meet her. I noticed Joe just looking at me like he was taking in every aspect of my face. Then I realized something. "You've seen me before, haven't you?" I inquire. "A long time ago. You haven't changed. I met a Native-American with her own special gifts once," Joe adds. "Strongheart's Native, but doesn't have my gift," I describe. "Native, yes. Male? No," Joe tells with a smile. "Desert Flower, the prettiest Cherokee I have ever seen. Very illusive. How do you know her?" I needed to know. Joe smiles a sly smile. "Oh, that's how you know her. You must have met her when you were younger," I add. "I always wanted to know her name. But are you sure it was her? I mean, how many more are there like you with your vocal ability?" Joe asks. "You think we're all in a club? How would I know? None as far as I know. Desert Flower pops up to have a kid with someone and she's never seen again. She must be queen of her own tribe by now. Wait a minute! Are you saying you had a kid with her?" I must know. "My daughter," Joe happily smiles. "Why does someone named Hawaiian Joe not wear flowers around his neck? Why the animal teeth? Did she give that to you?" I wanted to know. "She shared herself with me and many a native story. The necklace I received elsewhere," Joe informs. "Do you have a picture of yourself a little younger, or a lot younger?" I ask. "At my house. Why would you need that?" Joe baffles. "If I can see you the way you were, I'll be able to place where I saw you. I remember everything," I explain. "Amazing!

Total recall, too. What other gifts ..." I interrupt, "Not patience. The dance is over. Why did you wanna see me?" I had to know. "There is so much more you can do with your voice. You could empower the world. People listen to you," Joe tells. I guffaw. "You don't get it, do ya? My voice makes people high. That's why they listen. And not only that, they'll do anything I tell them. What if I'm in a bad mood? What if I decide Hitler and Stalin were swell guys and I wanna be just like them, killing millions of people just for funzies? Yeah, I'm not perfect, but that's too much responsibility for me," I explain. "Well, I'm glad to hear that. And I do realize the implications of what you are saying. Myself, I only ever wanted to help the masses in my own small way—but you! You could help this world more than anyone in history. If you controlled or at least focused what you say, you could be the greatest voice for change the world has ever known!" Joe dreams. "You said it, control. I'd just be controlling them, not changing them. The only change taking place in the world would be that they'd never leave me alone. They'd follow me to the ends of this earth I'm stuck on just to get their next hit of Reg. Think about it, Joe, I'm the candy man. I got your fix. Just follow me and it's all free, the best buzz you'll ever have. They'll never want it to stop," I weave. "My god! You're right. But what if there were a way for you to speak without making them feel the way they do? Only you can make them listen!" Joe frantically hopes. "Without the punchline—the high—why would they listen? Sixties strangeness put us together in the sixties, Joe, and they have made us collide again. Adios, speaker man," I say and just walk away.

6) REG MEETS LUNA

I walk down the street with my good bud Otto, the only one who can understand me, or at least the only one who can answer me. I don't count Joe, we don't hang out. "I thought old Joe was smarter than that, kinda disappointed," I feel. "You shoulda stayed. Maybe he could've helped you," Otto hopes. "Yeah, helped me to sell more motivational courses for him," I surmise. "I don't think Joe's like that. I think he really wanted to help you," Otto concludes. "Wishful thinking. Haven't you been around me long enough to know Joe's pie-in-the-sky fantasies will never come true for me? What I can do is my blessing and my curse. I'm the world's true lonely man and you know it," I know. We reach Otto's Gran Torino and I hop in right after he gets in it to his surprise as he looks right at me and asks, "Where's your car?" "Fun fact! It was stolen! When I woke up from a nap earlier, it was gone city. I just told someone to bring me up here. I do it all the time when I go to the late show; that way no one steals my car. Funny how that worked out, huh?" I jest. "You know, homie, if they took your car while you were taking one of your naps you can't wake up from, why couldn't they just take you next time, ever think of that?" he asks. "I am now," I chuckle and ask, "Who are they?" "You think someone just dropped by to use your car? They're trying to send you a message. They know where you are. They can get you anytime they want. Better be somewhere else," he advises. I just sit there, nothing to say. What's to say?

"You wanna get pizza? We can eat it at your place with a movie?" he says, only trying to cheer me up. "I thought I was supposed to leave there. I thought everyone was looking for me," I guess. "I'll drive by. No one there, no problem," he explains. "I should still look for another place, though, right?" I ask. "I would," he wisely says.

So here Otto and I are back at my place. Well, almost. Otto passes the house because someone is sitting in a car across the street from my house. He drives around the corner. A few minutes later I appeared in the neighbors' yard across the street. I sneaked around to get where I needed to be. As I notice the driver looking at my house and not in my direction, I bolt towards the car with Otto's tire iron, smashing in the driver's side window with it as the driver and the dude next to him pull out their pistolas. I quickly end any shootout by yelling, "Hey!!" By that time, Otto had driven up beside the car. Hearing the commotion, the nosey neighbor popped out the front door of the house. "Go back inside, Gladys Kravitz," was all I had to do. Otto steps out of his car. "Take his gun," I say as Otto strips the passenger of his gun and wallet. Meanwhile, I follow suit and take the driver's gun and wallet. Why not? I wanted to know who these guys were. I lean into the car to say, "Why don't you drive this thing off a cliff? Don't ever bother me again!" I yell as I slam the car door shut. The car eventually drives away in an erratic manner, knocking down the garbage cans on the street along the way as if the driver were drunk. Nope, not drunk. It's just what I gave him, a Reg hangover. Otto and I watch laughing it up.

So Otto and I are back in my place. We look through the wallets of the two bad drivers we left out front. "Hmm, FBI? I'm glad I didn't need a lawyer to talk to them. I'm surprised they weren't NSA or CIA," I conclude. "They'll probably be here next. Better get out, homie," Otto advises. We eat pizza as we watch *Faster, Pussycat. Kill! Kill!* Tura Satana's most underrated achievement of her time. She's like a tightly coiled spring ready to snap for most of the film. Her dancing was as exotic and beautiful as she was, too. Even the Big E Elvis himself wanted to marry her. But my mind wanders. What happened to Joe's daughter? Why wasn't she there with dad earlier? I look at her card again, and again she's looking back at me. The cult classic ends and Otto turns on the news. There is a story on the tube about a driver in a big black car who drove off a cliff. The reporter says, "Witnesses say the driver looked like he did it intentionally." Otto pops up. "I'm outta here, homie. I'll be far away when the shit comes down," he almost panics. "So you're just leaving?" I can't believe. "You're hot lava; I can't be around you right now. You want one of these guns?" he asks. I suddenly realize the situation I was in. If I were strapped, everyone looking for me would have an excuse to get rid of me. Because if the powers at be can't control you, they want you dead! "Take what you want, I won't need it," I tell. "What does that mean? You're not gonna do something stupid, are you?" he asks. "Not what you're thinking! You said move. I'm moving. I can't take all this stuff. If you want something, help yourself," I tell him. All he could say back was, "You have any boxes?" I told him there were bags in the kitchen. So as my good friend bagged up my best movies and collectibles setting around, I sat there and wondered what my next move would be. Where I would go? I had moved many times before. It's just that when you've been in a place for so long, you kind of get used to it. I guess I'll get over it—again!

So I find myself at Hawaiian Joe's house in the Hollywood hills. Nice house, lots of security. So how did I get in? After a free ride over here, the receptive guards let me in, of course. I think Joe's over-paying these guys. So I roam about the house, where's Joe? Then I stop in front of an open door where Ravvi Shankar music is playing strangely enough. Well, maybe not so strange in a place like this. Then I see her, a most ravishing and alluring creature dancing—no—undulating to the music, moving like a sensuous serpent ready to entice any mortal to his death if he desires her. Like a siren's song beckoning me at sea, I would gladly crash upon her rocks for the pleasures within. So I moved inside the room and leaned against the wall for a closer look. I don't know if she actually didn't notice me or was just toying with me, but she continued to dance, and I continued to watch. Then she danced over to me and made eye contact with me for the first time. She was indeed Joe's daughter, his daughter Luna. "You came," I heard in my head. Did she read minds? She still dances. "Shaman of sound and vibration, speak. Prove your existence," she states. At least I'm not using up all the oxygen I think. "Thinking of Tura? She was bad-ass!" she says as she still dances, dances as if just for me. All she desires is to dance and my only desire is to watch. A free spirit for sure, or is she still toying with me? She smiles now as if she knows what I'm thinking even before I do. I wonder if she really knew I would come. "Your brain is speaking out loud. Of course I knew. I willed you here. Once you looked upon my face, you were doomed," she toys. "All that power in a simple business card, really?" I doubt. "It's a link. When you looked at it, I could see you, you know. I knew your thoughts, felt what you were feeling. I could pick your mind clean from a distance. You could do the same if you knew how," she entices. "And what do you know?" I must know. She smiles. She knew something, probably all the things I wouldn't want her to know about me. She dances closer and beckons with her hands for me to approach her as she backs away. I am compelled to do so, reaching out as if to embrace her. She smiles and pushes me away. She dances about now, no doubt thinking of other ways to mess with me. Am I to be just another plaything for her, or do I have something she wants? If this is how she goes about getting it, I'm not complaining. I start to speak ...

"Don't talk. Listen. Feeeeeeel the music. Let it penetrate you. Close your eyes," she commands. So I play along, close my eyes. I listen for a bit. "I hear," she interrupts, "No! What do you feel? Listen, yes, but what does your body feel, your essence?" If by essence she means soul, I really haven't really done a lot of soul feeling. I'm not sure what she wants with me, but I'm up for playing along. This is a new experience for me. I open my eyes and just watch her dance some more. She eventually stops dancing and just looks at me with a discerning look of disapproval and says, "You're not even trying." To do what? I was thinking. How come she's not afraid of this uninvited guest in her house? "Of you, should I be? Do I have to kick your ass?" she boasts. "Kick my ass? How does that fit in with all this flower power stuff?" I ask. "Yin and yang, baby! You gotta have both or you're not a whole person. I peace, but I war also, if need be?" she informs. She gets right up in my face. I can't get that look of surprise off my face. She guffaws. Was she laughing at me or just laughing? "Men have such egos. I've never lost a fight, even with a man," she tells. "Neither have I," I confess. "We're physically different from other humans; we have more brain capacity, more muscle, more longevity and resistance to illness. Even our blood type is different," she spills. "Our? You mean there are more freaks like us around here?" I ask. "The people around here are all special. They're not freaks! You must think of yourself that way," she tells. "Nobody can do what I do. I am a freak of nature. I guess you're unfreaky. I think I'll go on down to Mardi Gras, be the Mardi Gras king if I like," I say. "You have too much free time," she informs. "Stiff and inflexible, are we? I bet you have a calendar with writing all over it, just have to stick to that strict schedule, eh? My time is my own. I do what I want when I want," I needed her to know. "Okay, goooooo do it!" She tells me good. Then she walks out of her room and about the house. I follow because, uh, why not? She plops down in a chair in the kitchen. I just stand by the fridge. "Still here? Stillllllll trespassing?" she complains. "I thought you willed me here? To do what, throw me out after dance lessons? Wait a minute. I just realized you can understand me, too, hence the two-way conversation.

How many more around here can do that?" I must know. She just sits there, ghosting me with her stare. I look around. I see no one and I hear no one. "Where are all these special people? Need a lotta sleep, do they? On vacation?" I inquire. "Get me a beer," she says as if I'd do whatever she told me because she's fairly hot, hot as a chemical fire. Anyway, I'm near the fridge, so why not? I've never had a female to talk to me or order me about before. I wasn't sure if I liked it yet, but I opened the fridge. I got her a beer and helped myself to a Yoo-Hoo. We sip and rap. We eye each other. For the first time in my life I was at a disadvantage. My voice didn't affect her and she could read my mind. "I don't know why I'm here," I tell. "Bullshit! You're looking at why you're here," she smirks. She reads minds alright. She catches me starting to smile. She sips her drink, taking it in as she takes in my head. This isn't at all how I envisioned our meeting would take place. "Did you think it would be across a desk, like a job interview?" she asks. "That is really annoying. Get outta my head," I mean. "Get outta my house," she jabs.

"Screw this!" I say as I slammed my Yoo-Hoo down on the table and left the kitchen. Maneuvering my way through the big house, I make it to the front door. I reach for the front door knob and find a hand on it. I stop to look at her as I put my hand down. "Give up that easy, do you? What a wuss! What disappointment," she keeps mewing. "Aren't we the little manipulator, take after dad? You wanna move?" I ask. "Make me," she tempts and makes the mistake of taking her hand off the knob. "This was a mistake," I say as I fake her out and grab the doorknob again. “It sure was. Big brother saw you come in here. They know who you are, you know,” she informs. “You mean the government? They were at my house earlier,” I confess. “What did you do?” she asks. “I told them to leave. What do think I asked them in to bake a cake? They’re gone,” I say. “But not forgotten. They’ll be back, you know,” she tells as I think about their car going over the cliff. She has a funny look on her face. “You told them to drive over a cliff!?” she mews more. “It’s just something you say, I didn’t think they’d do it!” I confess. “You have to watch what you say, someone with your ability. How do you know they were the government?” she asks. ‘Otto and I took their wallets,” and guns I think without saying. “And what did you do with said wallets and guns?” she asks sternly. “Otto has them, along with half the stuff in my house. I can’t stay there–they took my car!” I say with my droopy face looking down. “How did they find me so fast?” drips out of my mouth. “They’re the government, baby. The only time they act dumb is when they’re accountable,” she tells. “At the mall ... why did you kiss me?” I needed to know. She just looks at me a bit and says, “You’re here, aren’t you?” I look a bit depressed. I was hoping it was more than that. I’m not ugly. I’ve got my health, plenty of coin. What am I missing? And again I realize too late that she must be tapping my brain even now. She smiles. “I have a phone call to make. Our house is yours,” she informs as she walks away from me, hopefully not out of my life. I can talk to her.

I’m floating. No, I’m floating in space, I see the stars. Am I breathing? I don’t have any sensation of breathing. But I have to be here, it's so real. It's so quiet, too! It's so quiet it makes me feel like my ears don't work right, like Otto's. "Tell me about it," Otto says. Hey, it's my bud Otto, he's floating up beside me now. "Hey, Otto, you're here, here in space. I thought you left," I surprise. What a loyal friend to come all the way out here in space just to hang out with me. Why not? We've hung out everywhere else. "Hey, let's get something to eat," he drools. "Out here?" I ask as he points to giant billboard that reads: Eat at Joe's, only 3,000,000 light years on your left. There's a picture of Hawaiian Joe on it, and Joe's smiling with a goofy chef's hat on. I didn't know Joe could cook. "Let's go there," Otto requests. "You mind if I ask how?" I query. "You're in tune with the universe, just think about it," he explains. Think about it, really? I just think about getting a ride out here? Why not, what better place? Before long a little space ship painted like a taxi comes up in front of us, the back of the ship opens up and two chairs on poles come out underneath us. The chairs' seat belts swing around us, strap us in, and then the chairs suck us speedily back into the ship as the door slams shut behind us. This back seat section of the space cab was obviously meant to keep possibly dangerous alien mutants and space cab-jackers away from the driver, who sat up front, of course. He spoke to us in his squeaky alien voice. "Where to?" the alien cabby said. "Where's a good place to eat in this part of the galaxy?" Otto needed to know. "You want just food or fun, too?" the alien asked. "Fun is always good," I tell him. "Ooooooooooh, your voice makes me feel so good. Reg you must be. Known all over the galaxy Reg is," the alien swooned.

I saw our driver for the first time as he spun his head completely around owl fashion to get a look at us. He had a small mouth, big eyes and an even bigger head, and a really big cabby's hat on that big head. He was definitely of the alien variety. Otto and I just look at this alien cabby with the big obsidian eyes staring back at us as the space cab narrowly misses a big hunk of space junk. "Hey, keep your big eyes on the road or the universe there, little space dude," I tell him.

He spins his head back around as the space cab weaves its way through a whole debris field full of space junk. Hey, there's an old rocket that has U.S.A. on its side, maybe we have been to the moon. Is that the Enterprise? I have a hunch. And there's a Klingon vessel and even a Romulan war bird! There's the Churchill from *Lifeforce.* I wonder if that naked chick is walking around in it. There's E.T.'s ship. I guess he didn't get home. There's the ship from *Planet of The Apes.* Damn dirty apes indeed! There's the Nostromo and there's Barbarella's ship. I wonder if she's dressing or undressing in there. Oh, wow, the Jupiter 2! They ended up here? Oh, the pain. I suddenly realized something about my magic carpet ride in space. "Driver, how could all these ships be here? They're not even real," I surmise. "Name is not driver. Kropala name is," he tells. "How come these alien dudes all talk like Yoda?" Otto asks. "Tell me about it. What I mean, Kropala, is how are these ships really here when they never really existed? They can't be," I imagine. "Can they not? This universe you create," Kropala informs. "Me create? Universal mind, explain such purpose in this insanely surreal assortment of phantasmagorical images, exploding with shapes and colors onto a canvas of quasi existence!" I muse. "Don't try to explain it, just go with it!" Otto demands. "Go with it? Why not?" I give in.

A giant space diner is just ahead now. Shaped like a big red ball, or possibly a clown nose, this place looked more like a funhouse in space as a set of mechanical eyes opened up and a happy shaped mouth opened up to accept the incoming space cab. On the way into the ship I see a big sign: WE SERVE HUMANS. I hope so, we're hungry! "What do I owe you, Kropala?" I ask. "For you, Reg, no charge!" he says as he pulls a lever and drops us out of the ship. As we fall, a beam of light zaps us, transporting us into two chairs at a small table on the floor inside an empty room in the huge space diner. Then a huge pizza that covers the whole table materializes within a flash of light before us. Table height robotic servers instantly roll up beside us with our favorite liquid refreshments on ice. Man, this place had good service! But where was the fun part? Coming right up!

As we dig into our pizza, a disco ball lowers and the musical selection *Music to Watch Space Girls By*, by the late great Leonard 'Spocko' Nimoy, starts to play. The perfect lounge type tune for a diner in space I thought. And now for our dining pleasure, Luna and Aphrodite are twirling across the dance floor in big cups like at Disneyland. They get out of their colorful cuppies and start to dance for us. Aphrodite shows off her lovely long legs, wearing stockings and a bowler cap reminiscent of Lily Von Shtupp, while Luna wears a cowboy outfit with hot pants ensemble reminiscent of that chick who danced around the helicopter in *Apocalypse Now.* Luna even swung her hips and pointed her guns around like her. Yeah, that's what I was waiting for! Luna's firing off those guns now. No bullets are coming out, just balls of light that explode into sparkles of color. The girls are dancing closer to the table now. Swing it, Luna! They come up to the table now, still dancing. With my limited experience in such matters, I found this to be an excellent dining experience for this part of the galaxy.

"Ready for dessert?" Aphrodite asks. "Why? Are you ladies on the menu?" I drool. "No, you are!" Luna shocks. "Come again?" Otto gulps. "Didn't you see the sign outside?" Aphrodite inquires. "Yeah, we serve humans, what did you think that meant, boys?" Luna taunts. Aphrodite and Luna simultaneously slam bottles of barbecue sauce on the pizza covered table in front of us. "Put it on!" Aphrodite demands as they smile their wicked smiles. "Yeah, you'll taste so much better wearing it," Luna grins.

Otto and I just look at each other in horror. "We're not the diners!" Otto discovers. "We're the main course!" I discover, maybe too late. Then, like out of another dimension, this eight foot tall, monstrous being holding the longest chainsaw you will ever see appears out a flash of light and is already running towards us. It had a giant pig's head like in *Motel Hell*, except this was no guy wearing a pig's head. This little piggy was a real pig! It had piggy hands and that piggy head, with a tall chef's hat on it to add another two feet to his piggy height. It ran towards us on two piggy feet and it wore a long apron with blood stains adorning it. Did this space pig want to get even with us for all that bacon, sausage and barbecue we'd eaten, or was it just that humans were a delicacy in this part of the galaxy? Piggy's getting close! Don't think—run! So Otto and I haul ass! "It's getting closer!" Otto exclaims and frantically moves faster. "Don't worry! This piggy won't go to market!" I hope.

As I continue to run, I notice Otto's not running beside me any longer. I glance over my shoulder and notice piggy is no longer chasing me, only making munching sounds. "Oh, not Otto," I wonder. Then I stopped. I'm standing in the only patch of light in the whole place as I spin around to see only darkness in every direction. Piggy is there, though, for I hear an occasional demented oinking sound echoing around me in the darkness. My heart is beating fast again, I feel it. Calming down now, maybe the danger is over? Stop worrying. Cosmic piggy is right in front of me! I hear a chainsaw ...

I wake up on a couch in Joe's home. Joe and Luna are standing over me. "Why, this is not the least bit creepy," I blurt out as I sit up. "You know you talk in your sleep?" Luna asks. "I didn't even know I was asleep," I confess. "We have made a place for you in our home and in our hearts," Joe smiles. "Wow, that's just swell. An educated eggducator, I am. When I was a kid, I read every book I could find. Can you guess why? Uh, and without reading my mind?" I ask. "Well, if you're as old as you say, I would have to say because there was no television," Joe says as if waiting for me to praise him or give him a prize. "All we expect out of you is for you to be happy here, or at least content," Luna obviously invades my brain again.

"Can I expect her to creep uninvited into my kooky cranium like some unwanted alien parasite anytime she likes while I'm here?" I ask with a smile. "Uh, yeah!" she smiles real wide back at me. "My daughter is our greatest protective force around here. She detects those with ill intentions before they blossom into disastrous realities," Joe explains. "Santa knows if everyone's being naughty or nice, eh? You know the only reason—the only reason—I will stay here under these conditions is because I have someone to talk to. And when I wanna come and go, I'll come and go. I'm not the born to follow type," I say as I wait for and expect the proper response. "There are no chains on you. Most limitations are put on people by themselves. You will receive all the credit or all the blame for your actions, so be careful when you venture out of this place," he says. "Okay, Joe. You have a gym around here?" I ask. "Why, you gonna show us how much of a man you are?" Luna irritates. I look up, not quite rolling my eyes so as to give the cute manipulator any satisfaction. "I have a lot of excess energy," I come up with on the spot. "That's why you were napping?" Luna snaps back. I purse my lips. So it's going to be like this, huh? "My mind just shuts down sometimes. If you don't have a gym, I can just leave and go find one," I say and wait for her return. "We have a fine gym, which you are free to use anytime," Joe says with a smile. They're trying to keep me here pops into my head—uh, oh! She'll be listening. "We just want to keep you safe," Luna smiles, followed by Joe's big ol' smile. "You know, you give me the feeling that staying alone in the woods in the *Evil Dead* cabin would be more fun than this place," I quip. "I know you have been abruptly uprooted from the familiar surroundings of your home. Look upon this as a vacation," Joe calms. "Speaking of home, I need to get a few things out of my house before I say adios to it for good," I explain. "You don't have to do it now, relax," Joe says as I feel I'm being controlled again. "I think it would actually be a good idea to do it now. He might have things over there that big brother shouldn't see. We ought to get them before they get in," Luna suggests. "They might have been there already," Joe surmises. "I don't think so. I think they're still in the surveillance stage," Luna assumes. My eyes dart back and forth between this verbal tennis match. "Then get a few members, get a truck and get it done," Joe commands. I got what I wanted. I'll be getting my stuff. Why am I not happier? I look at Luna with a sly smile. I know what would make me happier. She just turns her head to the side and looks at me with that look of disapproval, like she wouldn't love it!

7) BACK TO MY PLACE

Before I was to head over to my house in the Hollywood hills for the last time, Joe wanted me to meet the other guests of the house. I suppose if any of them could talk to me, I could go along with it. Joe walks me into a large room filled with people all seated and waiting to be dazzled by me, no doubt. I stand between Joe and Luna. I wonder if I will win two out of three falls with this tag-team match.

"Reg, what you are looking at is a group of the most uniquely talented dear souls on this starship mother earth. Telepathy, precognition, telekenesis, psychic and bioenergetic healing, channeling, levitation, invisibility, remote viewing and bilocation are but a few of the abilities of the inhabitants of your audience. They have been called star children, crystal children or even indigo children, which really isn't what they prefer to be called. These star children are special because they believe they come from the stars. They feel they never really belonged on this planet. They can't cope. They don't fit in. Do you ever feel that way, Reg?" Joe asks. "Now is that gibberish or frontier gibberish?" I prod Joe as I scan the audience. No one responding yet. "Isn't Reg funny? He expresses himself through humor. That takes talent! Tell me quickly! Can anyone talk? Is anyone here unaffected by his voice?" Joe asks and waits for a response. "I'm still waiiiiiiittttiiiiiiing," says a male voice that is unseen and comes out of nowhere. Joe and Luna smile as I keep looking about for the mystery voice. Then a young, curly-haired man slowly materializes as he walks up to us and stops. "Reg, meet Roger. Roger has the gift of invisibility." Joe tells. "It's more than that, fellow traveler. I live between two worlds. I'm never really, like, in one place," he tells with a voice that sounds as if he's the world's most mellow fellow. Maybe that's how my voice doesn't make him euphoric; he always feels that way. "How is it you understand me?" I ask anyway as he answers, "I don't know. You tell me." Roger is no help. "On the contrary, Roger is a great help. He can go with us," Luna explains. Wow, my new buddies. I didn't really know what to expect next as I looked out over this unusual looking crowd, like a nerdier version of the X-Men. "Reg, are you still with us?" Joe asks suddenly. "Huh? Oh, I think my mind went to Hawaii. I was staring at your shirt," I inform. "What do you think of our group?" Joe asks. "What a wild bunch," I really don't believe. Then I came clean. "You really wanna know what I think?" I say as I look out over a crowd of geeky, pasty faces all dying for acceptance in this ever maddening world. I wasn't the one to fly them away to safety and happy, happy sunshine land, only make their lives more blissful for the moment in time they hear me babble about nothing in particular.

"I think, if they were a box of chocolates, they'd all be hard caramels. They're a bunch of losers and you know it. Is that why I'm here, to herd around the losers, the in crowd that's not in?" I say to take the smile off everyone's face. "You do have a cruel streak in you. Don't you think they can hear you?" Luna yells. "They're right in front of you and you don't care!" she yells again. "Reg, the souls in this room are the ones I love and trust more than any others in this world. What I saw you do today has never been done before. The way they reacted to you ... it is hard to put into words. You are not a professional speaker, true, but your voice has power, the power to control the mind! We searched for it in the sixties. We searched with meditation, with biofeedback, with drugs, but nothing we ever tried could bridge that gap that separates the mind from finding that ultimate consciousness, awareness, enlightenment, nirvana! You are the ultimate mind bender!!" Joe says too excitedly. "You still don't get it, both of you. They don't care! They don't care what I say. No magical arrangement of words will make them feel any better or worse. They just want the feeling I supply. And, oh, I finally saw a picture of you around here when you were younger. I spoke to you at a party in the sixties. You were with Desert Flower, her mommy. And guess what? I was old even then. I'll be a thousand years old and still be alone, especially if it means having to live around control freaks like you!" I say as I head for the nearest door. I block out the pleas from Joe and his hot daughter. Who cares if she is? Now you know why guys leave beautiful women—all the bullshit!

I leave the house, slamming the front door behind me. Oh, here comes the security goons racing up to me. They don't recognize me. They should! I walked past them when I came in. I yell. I yell so loud that their brains freeze, did I mention I could do that, too? When I talk, you get high. When I'm pissed, I yell and shut off your brain, just like at the mall. It gives me more time to get away before you revert back to boring you again. I go through one of the guard's pockets for car keys. I beep to see which car is about to be mine. Good, it's a big Hummer, great for playing crash 'em and smash 'em on the road, if I feel like it?

Yep, I head right for my place in my new Hummer. I passed a cop. Great, no one reported my new wheels as stolen. I guess all the geeky dweeb mutants back at Frankenstein's castle of freaks still think they can use me. They think I can save the world—that's a laugh! There's my house and here I am. Good, no mystery cars outside anywhere, except–what! There's my car. Maybe I should throw a stick and see if it goes away and comes back again? I walk fast up to the front door. I take out my keys. Let's try the knob first anyway. Uh oh, it's unlocked. Some sumbitch was in my house! Or still is. Should I leave or play action star? This is my house! I am going inside my house! I put my hand on the knob and turn it, suddenly my spidey senses tell me someone is inside. I kick the door open so hard that it knocks that special someone into the wall. I walk in as someone else grabs me from behind. But when you're several times stronger than the average male specimen, you react in a different way. No need for Bruce Lee kicks and Rocky punches. I just pull my arms up easily out of his grasp, grab the dude with one arm and hurl his breaking and entering ass into the nearest wall—yeah! The dudes were definitely stunned, not dead. They started to root around in their side pockets, looking for a badge or a gun probably. I just say, "Why are you in my house?!" I say it rather loudly and it's a better brain freeze than a Slurpee cuz nobody is moving. Then I hear a thud in another room. The joint's not haunted, so I rush about the house, only to find a third dude on the floor. He heard me all right. I drag him into the room with the other two zombied-out dudes, and whadaya know? Luna walks in the door with Roger. "This will happen over and over again, you know," Luna tells. "Wow, you brought the invisible man with you. Who says I need your help?" I ask. "Just checking on you. I knew you'd get into trouble," she quips. "What did you do to them? Roger asks. "I offered them a bouquet of roses and they rejected me, is he kidding?" I say without a smile. "Okay, you did what you had to do. If you stay here, it'll happen again and again until they tag and bag you or just shoot you with a tranquilizer dart. You wanna guess what they'll do to you then?" she asks. "Not really. I just came for a few things," I explain. "Good, get 'em!" she says as if in a hurry. "Then what, back to motivator mansion? I don't regret what I said before. You expect me to do something I can't do. Hey, where's my cape? It's voice man! He'll make you stand there and drool. That's all you'll get out of anyone, do you see that now?" I plead. "I know it's been hard for you not knowing how to focus your voice, but we can show you how. Just please let us try," she also pleads. "What about these three stooges, do I just leave them here?" I ask as I grab a book off the bookshelf and take a stack of hundred-dollar-bills out of a hollowed-out portion of the book. "Just tell them to forget and let's go!" she rushes me. "Did you bring any boxes?" I ask. "Did you?" she snaps back. She knows I didn't bring any. She just has to be logical, too! "As logical as Spock," she smiles. "No mind reading in my house," I add as she smiles and taps her watch. I take more wads of cash out of more books as I say, "Take what you want. I ain't comin' back." She picks up a round yellow smiley face mug and asks, "This an original?" "Yep, from the far out seventies. Pick a body," I say as I take the wallet and gun off one of the dudes on the floor. Roger and Luna do so also reluctantly. Roger looks through the wallet. "This guy's not FBI," he remarks. "I suspect these aren't your typical alphabet agency types," Luna adds "Men in black? Men from Mars? They beamed on down without their cars, just mine," I deduce. "Are we gonna go a little faster now?" she smiles, pretending to be friendly.

I stand in the middle of the room and say to the dudes on the floor, "Dudes on the floor! Listen to me. You will forget your mission, forget I exist. You will leave my house and never come back. Then you will hump each other," Luna rolls her eyes. "Rog, make sure they do," I instruct. "Like, uh, sure, anything, man." he mellows. "You are one smooth dude, Rog. Follow them out the door when they leave, will ya? I wanna talk with her," I say and walk to the back of the house. And, yes, she followed me back. I was busy looking over my exercise equipment when I heard a voice behind me. Yeah, it's her. "We have to bring all this stuff?" she mews more. "I thought you were strong. Get to lifting," I push. She tries to lift a 150 kettlebell. Then quickly grabs a hundred-pound kettlebell and manages to get it over her head with one hand. She smiles like a little girl looking for approval as she holds it over her head. She hands it to me. "Your turn." she says as if testing me. So I drop it and go and hoist up the 330 kettlebell, like you see in the world's strongest men competitions, with only one hand and little difficulty. "Are we both impressed now?" I slyly smile at a face trying its best not to smile back at me. What is she thinking?

She walks about the back of the house and goes into my bedroom. I follow, of course. I don't know if I'm actually going somewhere, but I may be getting somewhere. "I thought you wanted me to hurry up," I curious. "You saw my room, I wanted to see yours," she says coyly. Show me yours and I'll show you mine, eh? I just noticed my heart was beating a little faster. Was it from the weights orrrrrr something else? She suddenly hops on my bed, jumping up and down on it playfully. Invitation or trap? I ain't the mind reader here. I think my heart's beating even faster now, though. "That's called anticipation, or maybe anxiety in your case," she taps my gourd again. I want to go to her, all the while my feet seem glued to the floor. I guess I don't take hints well. Why doesn't she just hop out of that damn bed and rip off my clothes? That would probably do it. And, here she comes, walking towards me–but no! She passes me and stops at my door. Then she simply swings my door closed and turns around to me with a smile I really liked.

Time passes–and whadaya know! We lie side by side mysteriously in my bed. Was I in some alternate universe suddenly where she could stand me? There is a sheet over us. She must be cold. Better answer? Why, that would be indiscrete. "I must have done something right. I noticed you weren't laughing," I say to give her little laugh. She never laughed so easily before. I think she actually digs me now. "I think I better look under the bed for a giant seed pod. It would seem I am with a different person than the one I met earlier," I hint. "Okay, I get it. I'm bitchy sometimes. I have a lot to deal with. Which reminds me, we should be back at the house. Every moment we're not, you're in danger, " she explains. "You mean you have to be somewhere better than this?" I ask looking over at her with my giganticly dumb smile. She guffaws. "Why does every man think that he is the best thing that ever happened to a woman?" I think I was just insulted. Being she was embarrassingly efficient compared to me, or just done with me in every way I can possibly imagine, she suddenly sat on the side of the bed and proclaimed all bossy, "Fun time over! Get your gear and we're outta here." Then she simply got out of my bed and aggressively yanked her jeans and threw on her western shirt as I just watched. Every part of her was beautiful. I had seen such a vision of beauty and I could never un-see it. If I'm the fish here, I'm hooked! "If you're a good boy, there's more where that came from," she tempts with a smile and a wink. Oh, I feel so used. Not really. "C'mon! Get your stuff. I'll get Roger," she says without patience as Roger suddenly materializes in the room. "Like, uh, I'm here," Roger scares as Luna jumps. "How long were you there?" she says and not in a happy way. "Uh, like, it's hard to say," Roger says in his stoner voice. Was he watching us? I just know he was watching us. Too late now! "Everybody grab some shit!!" she barks as I wait for them to leave so I can get out of bed.

With Luna and the invisible perv out of the room finally, I stand looking at my autographed picture of

Steve Reeves on the wall, a picture where he was Hercules. All the great actors, great celebrities who have fallen in the course of my life and I am left standing, unscathed by the ravages of time. Who the hell am I? I hear her voice behind me as I feel her arms wrap around me. "You must have a lot of memories in this house. You don't have to leave behind the memories, just the house," she consoles. "I saw Steve in the sixties, a few years after he was Hercules. I was tempted to go up to him and ask him something. I've seen a lot of celebrities worth talking to, but you know what would happen if I did," I somber. "You'll have someone else to talk with soon," she says as she fiddles with my hair. "Let's see, it's you, and dad and Roger the tokemaster. Does he live in a bag of weed? You know, stoners can talk to me, after they stop giggling," I explain. "Gonna help us with the packing now?" she asks. I take Reeve's picture off the wall. "I got everything I need," I only say.

And after we took all I wanted to take, I stood with her near the front doorway to the house and just looked over the place. Truth be told, it was a far lonelier place for far too long. Solitude can harden you or crush you. Hell, I need a change. We closed the door as we left, like closing a chapter in my life. There ain't no going back.

8) MEET THE MONSTER HUNTER

Percy Pettibone here, a name my father gave me after finding me in the forest as a mere infant. I got a call from a good friend of mine by the title of Hawaiian Joe. I told him I would get back to him as soon as possible, as I am exploring the caves of Peru, exploring them for giants. I am currently entering a quite massive cave entrance with my two English speaking native guides. Strangely enough, we carry no firearms, only cameras, flashlights, unlit torches, a phone ready to film any worthy encounter in my breast pocket and a few items made of copper. They say you need copper to kill a giant. I also wear a special headband to protect me from the giants' brainwaves. You see, it is said those who encountered a giant without such protection would vibrate and explode from the emanations that the giants' massive cranial cavities create. Only one of my guides wears such a protective headband like mine. The other guide seems not to be worried. I, on the other hand, have encountered unusual creatures all over the world, so I am ever vigilant and cautious to find any manner of unusual strangeness. I feel we are not alone, though. I am seldom wrong in such matters.

Without speaking, we venture further into the cave, only flashing our lights on the ground for reasons of safety and the possibility that we actually do find what we are looking for. One of the guides suddenly flashes his light upward as a noisy bat flies right past us. But as the guide's flashlight moves across the cave, it briefly catches what seems to be a face. Out of foolhardiness or merely experience, I flash my powerful beam into the darkness as my guides fearfully and quickly light their torches. After all, fire may be the only thing that protects us, or saves us. And as the torches came to life, our greatest fears came to life with them; three giants standing in the cave less than fifty feet away. Exactly as the ancient tribesmen and the Conquistadors who had ventured here later had described them was true. They were six rods tall or about thirty-feet high. They had massive heads with eyes as big as dinner plates, and long scraggy hair surrounding contorted facial features as if in constant agony. No monster I had ever encountered before frightened me more than what I was encountering in this dark cave in the middle of this nowhere place. But I showed no fear as my guides' fears showed through their trembling and labored breathing. They knew the stories of how these giants came from seemingly nowhere to eat all their ancestors' food, take all their livestock and, yes, have a taste for human flesh. Mythology called them titans. The bible called them the Nephilim. I call them a horrible death if we don't leave this cave in the most expeditious manner.

We slowly back out of the pitch black cave, lighted only by two torches and a flashlight. But our three massive competitors for our tasty flesh were approaching quickly, and legs longer at the knee than a basketball players' entire body ran far faster. Instantly they were right up on us, mere feet away with their menacing stares looking down on us. I could feel a vibration about me; their brainwaves were trying to tear into me, my only protection afforded me by my headband. My guide, who did not feel the need to protect himself in such a way, put his hands to his head as he screamed in agony. My other guide wearing his headband pulled me away as if he knew what fate lay in store for him. Then as a scream so tortured I would never forget it reaches its crescendo, the hapless guide's body exploded. "Grab his torch!" I yell as I load a copper bolt into my special crossbow, the same crossbow I had used to slay many creatures of the night. With a torch in each hand, my overly courageous guide kept the three monstrosities as bay as they reached out for us. Taking careful aim, I fired my bolt through the eye and lodged it in the back of the skull of one of the giants.

"Get out!" I yell to my remaining guide. Not asking why I would want him to abandon me at such a time of need, he looked at me only for a moment and rushed towards the cave entrance with both torches. Meanwhile, I speedily load a bolt into my crossbow as one of the giants takes off after my guide. Thinking only of him, I turn to the giant and fire my copper bolt through the back of the massive cranium of the attacking giant, sending it to the ground as its massive bulk just misses my fortunate guide. Spinning back around, I now had the last and most massive of the three giants frowning down on me with only masticating vengeance in mind. Not knowing if my humongous foe could see in the dark, like me, I tossed away my powerful light to hopefully put me at an advantage. "Come on, catch me! Catch me. Catch me," I laughed as my voice echoed about the cave to taunt the fumbling colossus. "Can't you see me? I'm near the entrance!" I shout as the monstrosity moves into the light of the cave's entrance, only to see nothing. Then, all is quiet. The only sound now heard is the sound of pebbles crunching together as I walk slowly out of the darkness towards my over-sized opponent as it turns to face me. With the crossbow in hand already loaded and waiting, I walk towards big boy as I screw together my collapsible copper spear. "Your move," I calmly said to it, as if I were the hunter here and it was the prey. If the weird look of fear on its face were any indication, he knew the answer already. It suddenly moved toward me incredibly fast. With no time for careful aim, I fired my bolt at my tremendous attacker, the copper death finding its mark in the groin of the wailing behemoth. The harm to my ears was only eclipsed by its painful bellows. Spear in hand, I leaped up twice the height of a basketball hoop, my spear finding its way deep in the wailing, ungodly beast's chest as I plunged it in. I don't know how many hearts the beast had, but the spear soon ended its agony as it collapsed to the cave floor, the cave actually shaking and collapsing as I rushed out the cave entrance.

Standing more than relieved outside of the crumbling tomb of any inhabitants of the collapsing mountainside, departed or otherwise, I waved and called out to my guide, who was watching from down the mountain. No doubt he was relieved to see me in one piece, for he had not lost a new friend, or more simply that now he could be paid for his services. I am more than happy to pay him, including a massive tip.

Back in the comfort of my luxurious hotel room ... okay, it was a modestly sized room with a lack of conditioned air or room service. It did have a slow

moving ceiling fan and no lack of a variety of insect life, most of which would show no hesitation in snuggling up to you the minute your head hit the pillow. I wasn't spending one more minute in this place, though. There is this lake creature I heard about. Maybe I will–no! I did promise Joe. So off to America I will go.

9) PERCY, MEET REG

I lay on the bed in my new room in Joe's house. I keep thinking about what I left behind. Who am I kidding? I keep thinking about Luna. I wonder if she's tapping my brain right now. "Yeah!" I hear Luna say loudly from another part of the house. I can only take so much of this. I get off the bed and look at my surroundings. They gave me a big room, it fits all my personal stuff. The gym stuff I put in the gym. That's where I should put myself, but I feel so weird being here. I don't know what to do with myself.

Luna pops into my room without knocking. "Feeling restless? There's a cure for that, stay busy!" she nags. "You wanna go to the mall?" I inquire as she laughs. "You gotta learn to do other things. Besides, won't they be looking for someone who looks exactly like you at the mall?" she says with anticipation of me catching on. "Oh, yeah. Great, so I'm back to being here again. I mean, the room's not bad. It's big! Did you have to give me someone else's room?" I ask. "Uh, several actually," she informs. "So you're trying to make me feel guilty?" I ask. "We're trying to make you feel comfortable. You're gonna do great things, Reg," she butters up. "I gotta be somewhere else right now," I tell as I start to leave, only to stop as she puts her hand on my chest. "People with bad intention are waiting for you out there. We can protect you," she informs. "From the boogiemen, or the G-men or what? Why can't they just break the door down and come get me here? I'd rather be out there on my own terms, at least

I'd be free," I gripe. "Where you gonna hide, a storm drain?" she smiles. "I think I can do better than that. I can walk into anyplace anywhere and no one will remember I was there," I flaunt. "But do you want to? You wanna do that forever, or until you're caught? Think about it," she gives me something to think about. Looking beaten down, I flop back down on the bed. "I gotta go out sometime. I'm not a fan of gilded cages," I depress. "How 'bout a concert?" she asks. "Yeah! Let's go to a concert!" I cheer up. "Dad is setting it up right now, and you'll even get to speak there. You see, Reg, when you're famous, they won't be able to touch you. You'll be safe. Because after you speak, you'll be the most famous person on earth," she entices. "I hear a 'but' coming, a big Bertha butt. When's the concert? Not today, I'm guessing," I surmise. "In a few days. You just have to lay low a few days. Then you can spread your wings and fly," she assures, but I'm not so sure. "In the meantime, we have a guest coming who you'll want to meet, a monster hunter!" she—really, a monster hunter? "Okay, tell me when Van Helsing gets here," I drift. "If there were a Van Helsing, he would be it," she keeps talking as I nod off.

How did I get here? I'm walking in a forest. It feels good, though; cool but not too cool. I walk among the trees until I reach a clearing. No more canopy of trees, I feel the sun on my face as I close my eyes. I suddenly feel a chilled wind, opening my eyes as the sun is replaced by the moon. Stars fill the sky, though it is lit by only the moonlight that eerily illuminates everything. Over at the treeline, all is dark and glowing red eyes seem to fill the forest, eyes that I just know are looking at me. Then red glowing eyes are everywhere in the forest, in every direction I look. Then the growling starts, growls not like a wolf or even a lion. These growls sounded more unnatural to any earthly beastie, dare I say demonic? But no beast emerged from the forest for me. The frightful sights and sounds seemed to be telling me that as long as I stayed out of the forest I would be safe. Then how would I leave? I could feel my heart beating faster as my anxiety was rising. Then the glow from the moon intensified. I looked up to see the moon growing in size. I soon realized the moon wasn't getting bigger, it was getting closer. As if the moon were a giant eye looking at me, it kept getting closer, seemingly right over top of the forest. I fall back onto the ground as the moon comes even closer, the moon's gravitational field uprooting all the trees around me and sending them up into the dark of space. So why am I not moving? I watch helplessly as the moon comes even closer—it's going to crush me!!!!

Covered in sweat, I spring up in bed. Joe, Luna and a strange man stand there by my bedside. Joe has a stethoscope in his ears as he touches it to my chest. I try to relax and he takes the stethoscope off me and out of his ears. "It's going down now. It must have been some dream, we couldn't wake you up," Joe tells. "My dreams are over when they're over. I have to endure them to the end," I say as the stranger is taken by my voice and almost as quickly shakes it off. "You were right, Joe. His voice is a phenomena," Percy comments. "Uh, am I gonna have a crowd standing over me every time I wake up? I can go to a baseball stadium for that, you know," I complain. "We were just worried about you," Luna jumps in. "I'm sure.

How come my voice has no effect on you, too? You some kinda freak like me?" I say to the stranger. "On the contrary, your voice had a profound effect on this body. I have encountered all manners of strangeness in my travels, but you, my boy, are right near the top!" Percy tells. "You must be Van Helsing." I say as he looks oddly at the reference. "We told him a monster hunter was coming," Luna adds. "Monster hunter, eh? I've never met a monster hunter," I figure. "How do you know you haven't met one? Percy Pettibone at your service," he says as he hands me his card, which has his name on it and the saying: It Takes A Monster To Find A Monster. "Okay, if you want me to trust you, answer my question. Why doesn't my voice effect you either?" I must know. "As I said, it does affect me, though I can turn it off, you know, much like Spock could do. It is simply a form of mind control, much like the way I avoid the hypnotic gaze of a vampire," Percy explains. "Yeah, I try to avoid those, too," I roll my eyes as I get out of the bed. "I'm gonna use the bathroom right now, if that's alright? Oh, and it will just be me, no crowds?" I say and just smile at them, hoping they take the hint that I have had enough for now. I go into the bathroom and slam the door shut loud enough for anyone anywhere to get the point. "Okay, we'll give you your space. Make sure to join us for dinner. The three of us will talk about..." Luna says as I just scream! Am I wrong, or does every single man, woman, child and animal alike like to do their bathroom duties alone?!

Dinner time! I made it! I'm still here, still alive and I haven't even lost my mind yet. I sit at a dinner table with Joe, Luna and Percy, the monster hunter. Yeah, right! He probably hunts giant rats! Everyone seems to be smiling at me. Am I about to be sandbagged or am I on the menu? The maid, wearing protective headphones, pushes a dinner cart into the room and leaves. Why hasn't polite, ever so delicate dinner conversation ensued yet? I keep feeling a giant pterodactyl will come down and swoop up one of us. Which one I could care less. Percy suddenly takes out a silver cigarette case, pops up out of his chair and brings it over before me. "Cigarette?" he asks as he pops open the case to reveal cigarettes on the bottom inside portion and a mirror on the top inside portion. I just look at him and say, "I know." Luna giggles. I then notice him rocking the case back and forth to, saaaay, capture my reflection to his satisfaction. I just look up at him as if to say, are you finished, am I a vampire or not? Luckily, he sits back down. Luna giggles uncontrollably. "I think he knows what you're doing," Luna manages to get out through the giggles. "Let's see, I'm not a vampire, how 'bout a werewolf? Bring zee wolfbane? How 'bout tana leaves? Maybe I'm a mummy," I express. "Iiiii think it's time to serve dinner," Joe wisely says. Luna hops up and goes over to the food cart. "Gimme a hand, Reg?" she asks with a smile. Great, now I work here. I give her a great big insincere smile and go over to her. At least I get first dibs that way. "We have a variety of dietary needs for our guests here at the house," she explains as I look over the feast, trying not to drool cuz I'm just soooooooooo hungry! "Do you eat meat?" she inquires. "I sure do. That steak looks great!" my eyes say before my mouth. Then the smile leaves my face as she carries my steak over to her dad, just like it magically floated away from me over to him so I couldn't have it. She serves Percy his meal. Wow, what's left, crap? She comes back over to the food cart. "Don't look like that. I saved the best for us," she says as she raises the lid on a most excellent and delicious beyond imagination pizza. "Otto said you guys love pizza," she entices. "Otto loves pizza. I like pizza. It's all fat and carbs, not found naturally in nature," I complain. "I'm sure we'll find a way to work it off later," she says with a brief wink and a smile. I realize the implications of that offer and ... "Let's dig right in!" I let out.

So we sit on down and dig on in! I know this monster hunter was here to find out who I am or what I am. Hell, I didn't even know that. "So, Reg, where about do you come from?" Percy gets nosey. "I have no idea. I was found in the forest, you know, like Tarzan," I add. "Remarkable! I too was found as a babe in the woods," he expects me to believe. "Really? Maybe we should start a club," I conclude. Percy takes out his phone, comes over by me and shows me a picture of a baby next to the dead body of what looks like a monstrously deformed human as men in Civil War attire pose next to it. "What the hell is that?" I curious. "That, my boy, is a cryptid," he tells. "When was that picture taken? And why do you keep referring to me as my boy? I'm a lot older than I look," I had to tell him. "It was taken near the beginning of the Civil War, circa eighteen-sixty-one," he says to make me think. "Want to see something even more interesting?" he says as he pulls up the video of what looks like giants in a dark cave. "Oh, that's not real. That's some kind of special effect ... isn't it?" I assume. "I was just in Peru, a land of many giants. They have been spotted all over the world, even here in America," he explains. "You guys see this?" I ask. "Before you popped up," Luna tells. "Do you know how he dispatched them? With a crossbow!" Joe tells. "With copper bolts," Luna adds. "Use silver to kill a werewolf, but use copper to kill a giant," Percy infos. "Good to know—when's the concert?" I ask to change whatever game they're playing with me. "In a mere few days. I am setting it up now. The artist will sing and you will speak," Joe nonchalantly says as if I'll just say whatever and change the world. "That's exactly what will happen, Reg. You just don't want to accept it. You will change the world," she says so decisively. "So why is he here, to see if I'm some kind of monster?" I ask as Percy gets up, comes around to me and sits next to me. He looks right at me and speaks very seriously to me. "Why do you think I put 'it takes a monster to find a monster' on my card?" he asks and waits for a reply. All I could think to say was, "It's catchy?" He just smiles at me and says, "Because I ... am ... a monster!" His face suddenly contorts, his mouth opens wide with huge, sharp teeth and he lets out a strange growl as he lunges forward, causing me to back away and fall to the floor. He changes back to normal as they all have a good laugh at my expense. Percy puts his hand out to me to help me up. "Your food's getting cold," is all I said as I waited for him to go back to his seat. Then I got up and sat down as I tried not to look like a giant wuss. Hey, I don't have monsters in my face every day.

"You see, Reg, that picture you saw was of a mother and her child. I too am a cryptid, the only known civilized one of its kind. Soldiers killed my mother and raised me as their own. Until puberty, I had no idea I was anything more than what I seemed to be, human," he explains. "That's, uh, just swell. But I ask again, what do you want with me?" I asked the freaky monster guy. I thought I was weird. "Joe just wanted me to check you out. You are not like me. You smell normal. You're not any kind of monster. Like Joe's other guests here at the house, you are most likely of alien origin or a hybrid. Your father came down from the heavens, or more likely a spaceship, and had relations with your earthly mother. It's been happening as long as man has walked the earth. It is even said that is how evolutionary jumps in man came about," he over-explains. "Well, that's a lot to take in. I thought I was just here for the pizza. Did you know about him?" I look at Luna. "There's a lot of strange stuff out there, Reg. That's why we wanna prepare you for it," she tells. "By making me famous and a magnet for all the monsters and weirdos? Thanks a lot," I don't appreciate. "The government won't bother you here because we do a little work for them occasionally. So they keep off our backs. The dark ones are our concern," Luna mystifies. "The dark ones, oh no," I say, totally not meaning to bug Luna." "I'm not kidding," she says with wide eyes. "So are they coming here right now? Did they escape from Loompaland?" I say looking serious, but Luna knows I'm not as she barks, "The dark ones are our counterparts, except they are on the dark side. They have black eyes, totally black, just like their souls. They can influence people to do the most evil things. You've seen all the stories lately of people going mad and shooting, or stabbing or killing people at random for seemingly no reason. On several occasions these dark ones were reported being seen by witnesses prior to the events. They might have been there at the mall that day when you stopped the shooting. We envision a world of enlightenment. They envision a world of darkness. Which side are you on?" she asks. "Uh, I'll take Superman over Hulk. I can see how you get government work; you've got mind readers, and fortune tellers and the invisible man around here somewhere, probably while anyone's showering. You wanna add me to your stable here? It's not my thing, man. I'm not quick to trust the government. Ask any Indian. They never met a red man they didn't wanna screw out of his land or break a treaty," I pontificate. "The government, a necessary evil. That's why it is better to have friends in high places that are for us, rather than against us. And as for our Native-American friends, how would you like to meet one with the same vocal gift as yours?" Joe asks. "I know one, Strongheart, remember? I told you before," I stress. "Yes, but can he control his voice, speak with or without influencing others?" Joe asks. "I don't know. I don't think so. We could speak to each other without a problem. He didn't seem to affect anyone else either. He told me certain members of his tribe were immune to people like me," I assume. "Your friend probably did have the power to control, which he probably used only on occasion as a defense mechanism, kind of like a skunk using his scent or a snake using its rattle," Joe explains.

"Why wouldn't he tell me?" I ask, only to look around at tenuous faces unwilling to tell me some hidden truth. "Your friend didn't tell you because he didn't trust you. The power you possess is a great responsibility, the power to turn people on and off, make them do whatever you desire, whether with good intention or not," Joe confessed, making me come to a realization. "Wow, that's it, isn't it? You don't trust me! I'm here to be molded into whatever you want me to be. I'm Reg, pull my string and I'm your dancing puppet," I say as I wave my arms and move like the puppet they want me to be. "Well, this puppet's cutting the strings—I'm outta here!" I rant and commence to hauling my ass out of Controlville! Heading for the door, I see mister monster hunter rise from the table. You bet your ass I stopped! I point my finger at him and say, "You wanna stop me? C'mon! Try to stop me! I'll rip out your teeth with rusty pliers!" I mad! I see Joe motion for him not to try. "Yeah, just try to use force! Is that your way to win friends and influence people, mister motivator?" I leave. Van Helsing can go back and be in a Hammer film, while I do my thing as I've always done—without anyone telling me how to do it!!!!!!!

10) I GO WALKABOUT

I walk the streets of Los Angeles, Sunset to be more specific. There's nothing but freakazoids and tourists here anyway. I should fit right in. I just need to think. I'll never forget a lady running down the boulevard years ago, she said her dog got away from her. I knew even then she'd never see her dog again. The next week I walked that way and I saw a missing dog sign. Which reminds me, animals dig me. I'm not sure if animals get high when they hear me, like the two-legged variety, but they do seem to get more docile. Wait a minute, is that ... I notice a big black car moving slowly down the street behind me. Great! I just looked and I'm pretty sure they saw me look. I can just run away. I run fast, I mean fast like a cheetah! That way if I had to, I could outrun, uh, a cheetah. Okay, I'm babbling. I probably couldn't outrun that car, though. I just have to move a little faster, get to the people standing in front of the Whiskey-A-Go-go. I saw Morrison there. The car speeds up. I speed up—almost there! I keep glancing back—the car door opens! Other cars pull up and stop, too! I didn't figure on that!! "We just want to talk to you, Reg!" one of them yells. Well, I'm here, here with my people. Power to the people, baby! I was about to give it to them. "I am the second coming of Jim Morrison!!!!" I yell louder than I ever had. Yep, it happened. A normally noisy place became as quiet as a cemetery at midnight, even the people driving by were quiet. They had to be after they crashed their cars. They just had to leave their windows down. Then I turned to my followers. All of them were my followers, but only my LA neighbors were my friends and I let them know it. "Friends! Music lovers! This is not peace and love day. This is stick it to the man day! See the man? He's in those big black cars following your leader. Go stick it to the man! He won't stop you!! Go!!!!" I instruct their minds. Coming out of their haze, the normally peace-loving descendants of hippies and freakies all rushed in mass toward the government stooges. Yeah, they'd tell 'em good! They'd give them all a good tongue lashing; they'd defend me. But yet again the unexpected happened. What I hadn't noticed right away was my protectors all pulling out knives and scissors, nail files and sharp pencils, even broken bottles; the government stooges all smiling obliviously with open arms with the crowd moving on them at lightning speed and attacking as if in a mad frenzy, stabbing, poking and slashing every unfortunate government employee until their oozing bodies resembled red jelly. It happened so fast I couldn't believe what I was seeing. I didn't mean for this to happen!! I have to watch what I say! I just wanted them to leave me alone. Why can't they leave me alone!!! What have I done? This wasn't like at the mall. I have to tell them, I have to tell them to stop. Hyperventilating—can't breathe! Can't think straight. Must calm down. Eventually I calmed myself as I screamed, "STOP!!!!!" and it ended. All the madness ended. It was insanely quiet again as I just looked over what insanity had wrought. I finally instruct everyone around me to forget and just go home, something I wish I could do.

I walk along Sunset Boulevard again. It's nighttime now. No one is following me this time. Hey, there are no cars on the street, only people in groups walking about, having a good time. Maybe some event's going on or a movie shoot. They always shut down the streets for that. Yeah, that must be it. A pretty girl dressed like a sixties flower child rushes up to me with a flower in her hand. She has flowers in her hair, too. It seemed appropriate. She holds the flower out for me to take. "Don't you want it?" she says with the most insanely wide smile on her face. "Sure," I say without thinking as I accept her flower. Then she kisses me and says, "Wanna make love?" My first reaction is to think hell yeah! Then I realized she just spoke to me. She spoke as if my voice meant nothing in this strange land where I had just arrived. "What's going on?" I wanted to know. "It's the end of the world!" she said so happily as she spun around. All of her smiling friends come over to me now to join us. "Bring us the end of the world, Reg. Bring us the end of the world!" they all say together like a quire to freak me out. The smile leaves my face as I ask, "Why do you think I can do that?" They don't get high, none of them. They just keep smiling. "Because you're Reg. You can do anything!" the flower girl tells me with that smile that never leaves her face. "End the world! End the world!" They all chant together. "Why do you want me to end the world?" I ask them. "It is your gift to us," flower girl says. "We accept! We accept!" the crowd all says together. "End the world! End the world! End the world!" they still chant and creep me out even more.

Off in the distance, a fireball hits the earth, rising up into what looks like a mushroom cloud. Big and bright the cloud was, just full of energy and power. "I love mushrooms," the flower girl smiled. She then danced around so happily as she and her friends all proclaimed so insanely happily, "It's here. The end of the world is here!" More fireballs hit the earth and more mushroom clouds rise up, crumbling the buildings around us. "Isn't it beautiful? Thank you," she smiles as she leans in to kiss me on the lips. At that very instant, a wave of tremendous heat carried on the wind turns all the buildings and all the people to dust. Is this real or surreal? The flower girl turns to ash in front of me and drifts gently away, yet I am unharmed. I look at my hands, at myself and everything about me is normal. I see heat dance about my skin that must be hotter than the sun, yet I feel nothing. I see only whirling ashes and crumbling edifices to man's achievements all around me. Then suddenly the wind completely stops and all is quiet. I look around me. I turn to look in every direction, beyond any horizon there is quiet, and devastation and nothingness. Then as I just stand there, plants grow and cactus spring up from the ground, all the while I stand in the middle of what used to be Sunset Boulevard. It looks just like another highway through the desert now. Then I hear them, the roar of a thousand machines. I turn around to see a sea of bikers riding around me. They said nothing, just rode past me with intensity and flaming eyes. They ride so close now. Should I fear them? No, they should fear me. I look to the sky to see no stars, only the darkness that has fallen on this place. So I stretch my arms out by my sides and let out a scream as mushroom clouds rise a few feet from my palms, just enough to show the beyond bright intense power I hold in my hands. Then one lone biker drives up to me and spins his bike to the side as he looks in my direction through the dark visor of his helmet. He just keeps looking at me, though I see not his eyes. Then he flips up his visor and laughs. It's me. He looks just like me! And the laughing–why won't he stop laughing? Then his face is suddenly the face of death–he lunges at me ...

My eyes pop open and see Luna standing over me. Somehow I don't mind. "You don't have to go home, Reg, but you can't stay here," she smiles at me. I thought she'd be mad. I stand up from the bushes I was sleeping in right in front of someone's house. "You know we're in The Miracle Mile district? Do you have some sleeping disorder?" she inquires. "What are you getting at, Dr. Frankenputz?" I jest. "Okay, so you didn't quite make it to a motel, or were you hiding from something?" she asks suspiciously. "I don't have to hide. I just don't like people following me. Hey, how did you find me? Did doctor McCoy put a transponder up my ass?" I ask. "Our remote viewer. You can't hide from us. And if you can't hide from us, you can't hide from the government. They have remote viewers too, you know. We better go before they find you, or did they find you once already today?" she asks as if she already knew the answer. I'm not the Grinch, I can't make up a lie as quick and slick. Soooooooooo, here comes the bullshit! "I ... "Don't lie to me. I'll know if you lie to me. See these eyes? They look right through you," she points to her eyes and warns.

"What do you want me to say?" I ask. "I want you to say you didn't have those agents killed! Are you a sociopath? Is that what I'm dealing with here?" she asks. "I just wanted them to leave me alone. I figured peace loving crowd would just warn them off, not what happened. Why did they react like that!! I confess. "Their reaction wasn't very peaceful, was it? What did you say?" she asks. "I think ..." she interrupts, "No! You have total recall like me. You know exactly what you said, what was it?" "I just told the crowd I was the second coming of Jim Morrison and to stick it to the man. It's just an expression—dammit! People have been saying it forever. Look, if you don't believe me, read my mind. Do I feel bad about what happened? Yes! I wish it never happened!" I purge my every bit of grief into her prying eyes. She looks at me for a bit, her face finally saying she believes me. "You gotta watch what you say, Reg. The things you say can result in tragedy by the mere fact that you are saying them. That's the power your voice has, you see that now? You can also heal with that miraculous voice. Please, will you let us show you how before something like this happens again?" she pleads. I suddenly felt such sadness for what I had done and started to feel so very tired. I needed to do something right, but I just couldn't function. She must have sensed how I felt and she was there for me, wrapping her arms around me, giving me a kind of feeling I had never experienced from anyone before but Sunny.

I sit back in the front seat of Luna's sporty little car as she drives through funtastic LA. We must look like two spoiled rich kids. Not me, I'm self-made. All my money came from talking people into buying junk they don't need. "Hey, there's Melrose Avenue! Let's stop and buy a shirt," I request. "I think we need to get you home right now," she bums me out. "I can always get out of the car," I say and the discerning side-eye follows. "Why would you do that?" she asks. "Because you won't stop. It's not hard to figure out. This reminds me of that Sam Elliott movie, *The Legacy*. He and his lady are doing roundy-rounders in jolly old England and they always seem to end up at the same house. In my case it's your house. I said I would help you. I just need some space sometimes, okay?" I ask of her. She finds a parking space on Melrose and pulls in. "Fine! Get your shirt so we can go," she says with such icy coldness. I think my teeth are chattering. "You know, you're the first female I've done this with. I've had to shop with Otto or alone. And if I shop alone, I have to watch what I say or pretend to be mute. Some of us have real problems," I explain. "The only problem I have right now is you. Are you gonna get your shirt so we can go, or what?" she says with those lovely daggers in her eyes. "Great! Let's go get it," I say with a smile. "You go. I stay. It's more than a concept—grasp it!" she snaps. "Okay, but I might go the wrong way when I leave the shop. I might wander miles in the wrong direction, you never know," I say only to get the most bitchy bitch face. "Just saying," I add as I get out of the car and go around to open her car door, but she's already getting out and giving me the evil eye. "And you were so nice an hour ago. Man, you don't have to be knee surgery," I smile. "The shirt, get it," she says with such an economy of words.

I quietly walk down Melrose as she reluctantly follows behind me. I speed up. Then she speeds up. Then I speed up faster, almost to the point of running, forcing her to speed up just to keep up with me. Then I suddenly stop as she rushes past me. "Hey, where ya going?" I ask with a big ol' smile. She turns around with her not too happy face and puts her hands on her hips. This hot dish can be a cold fish. Since I just happen to have stopped in front of Jenny's Fashionable Fashions, I go to the door and stop to say, "Look, I'm just trying to cheer myself up. I just wanna forget. But I can't forget. I can never forget anything," I say with a sadness I just can't hide. "I know. Let's just get your shirt and go. We shouldn't be here," she tells me like she just might have the slightest bit of empathy.

I come into Jenny's shop. Luna quietly motions with her arm as if to say there everything is. Almost immediately there she was, my Jenny, always and I mean always glad to see me! Unlike some people I know. She rushes up to me, wraps her arms around me and kisses me like she hasn't seen me in years, and loves me more than anyone she has ever known. As she releases me, I look over at Luna looking at us with her usual side-eye verging on evil eye. She just didn't understand. "Find me something," I told my Jenny. Then I go over by Luna and say, "She always greets me that way." "Swell, but the swelling's gone down," she bites as I say, "Meow!" and show her my claws. Luna walks towards the back of the shop or possibly just away from me. I walk over by Luna as I look at Jenny dancing about the shop just for me.

"Now that's a beautiful woman, so elegant and full of class. What does my mind say right now?" I tease. "Your brainwaves go through a blender before they reach me. I can't tell right now, hurry up," she prods me. "Can't play brain invader while you're mad, eh? I'll have to remember that," I say as I think I don't know why I love you, but I do. You're not a very nice person, though. "What do you mean I'm not a nice person? Just because I don't like you, don't dig you? I have a great life, I'll have you know. Everyone at the house loves me, they're crazy about me! I was doing just fine before you came along to screw things up!" she purges. "Well, I'm sorry I screwed things up for the mind-reading super-bitch! And I bet everyone at the house doesn't love you. Have you read their minds lately? They're all thinking, boy, if this bitch wasn't the daughter of big daddy, we'd never have to take all this crap from her! It's true, isn't it? Isn't it!" I bother. "Drop dead! Now there's an idea, if you were dead, dad wouldn't need you, so why don't you just kill yourself!!" she yells. "Why don't you just kill yourself!!!" I yell back so loudly and so angrily without thinking. Luna and I just stood there disgusted with each other, unflinching in how right each one of us simply must be. Then I heard a whimpering coming from the front of the store. It was Jenny. She was trembling and shaking with the saddest look of despair on her face a human being could possibly have. Then she dropped the beautiful clothes that she had so lovingly picked for me and stepped out the front door. In an instant it dawned on me what I had said as I yelled, "Jenny, NO!!!!" I rushed to the door and flung it open, only to see my Jenny stepping off the curb and into oncoming traffic as a speeding driver smashed into her delicate body so hard that it practically broke it in two, her body sliding over the car and landing in the street behind it. The screams from the people nearby were nothing compared to the screaming anguish inside my head as I stumbled out the door to see my Jenny lying lifeless in the street. As cars stopped and onlookers gathered, I just stood there as if I were in cement or being crushed. I couldn't move. All I could do was look. Then I noticed other customers from the shop stumbling confused out into the street. They came to die, but there would be no death for them today. All the cars had stopped. What I failed to notice was Jenny and other customers listening to us. My words were like fatal commands sent directly into their brains.

"Reg. Reg! We gotta go," Luna says to me. I see her; she's standing next to me. She starts to pull on my arm. I couldn't leave, but I couldn't stay. I could only feel numb. I wish I could forget. "Did it really happen? Is she really gone? It's not fair, why her?" I say with more sadness than I'd ever known. "I'm sorry," Luna says with tears in her eyes. Why is she crying? She has no heart. But she had a mind and she was reading mine. I broke down. I wept; a loud mournful weeping I couldn't control. It was like when I was a kid and the little dog I played with died. I sneaked out of the orphanage that night just to look at her doghouse. She would never be in it again, and I cried. I cried so loud it was like the wailing of a wounded animal. I could see the lights go on in the orphanage. They all knew it was me and they wouldn't be bothering me. They were probably crying, too. The next day I tore that doghouse to pieces. I couldn't bear to see it anymore.

Luna knew my voice and overly mournful woes would attract a crowd, so she hurried me to her car. We drove quietly for a while until our grief settled down. Out of the blue, she suddenly asked, "Who's Mrs. Grey?" She's reading me again. "When I was a little kid at the orphanage, I used to watch Miss Grey put clothes up on a clothesline outside. She would just smile at me. Even at that age I knew she would be gone one day. I was happy because she treated me so nice, but I was sad at the same time because I knew she would be gone. She died when I was fourteen. That day I went outside and just stared at that clothesline. It became such an empty place. She should have been there." I purge. "Did she run the orphanage?" she asks. "Yep. Every moment in time for me is like it just happened. If it happened twenty years ago or twenty seconds, I can remember every instant of it as if it just happened. Total recall can be great for remembering the happy times. But when they're not, it's like giant stones being piled on top of you. Oh, and by the way, I'm sorry about what I said to you," I purge more. "Ditto. If I hadn't started it, your friend would still be here. Is that why you ran away from the orphanage, Mrs. Grey dying?" she pries. "Well, that was a smooth transition. Actually, I rans zeway cuz some other vile old bag who took over for Mrs. Grey wanted me to have shock treatments because I wouldn't speak, and this was in the early days of shock therapy where if they used too much juice they could barbecue your brain. Noooooooo thanks!" I wanted her to know. "It's hard to believe they ever did that. A lot of our group has had the very same problems. The parents of star children often mistake their children's gifts for bad behavior or even mental illness. They never stop to think that what makes a person different is what also makes them special," she tells. "No one ever told me I was special, except Miss Grey," I confess. "You're starting to depress me. Can't you say something funny?" She asks. "Something funny," I reply. "I should have known better. So you ran away from the orphanage then?" she pries. "If you must know, yeah," I confess. "That would have been during The Depression. Times had to be grim then. How did you survive?" she simply must know. "How do you think? I robbed more people than Bonnie and Clyde and Dillinger with just a kind word. Hey, what if I'm on film?" I worry. "You mean when you were on Sunset? The second you spoke, everyone froze. No one pulled any camera phones out. The only possible film of you would be in a traffic video. As far as that goes, you're just another face in the crowd," she calms. So I relax into my seat and try to forget the madness of the day, but there is no forgetting. My eyes just close and ...

I'm running, running in a field of flowers. I'm smiling, smiling because Luna is running with me. We stop. I picked a flower and put it in her hair. Then I kissed her. She likes it. We embrace and kiss, falling as if in slow motion into all the colorful, fragile flowers. We kiss more as we roll around among the ever changing colors of nature around us. I've never been so happy. Why do I deserve such happiness after ...

Luna stands up and smiles at me. Then she starts to laugh maniacally as my happiness turns to worry. "You don't deserve me," she taunts, backing away from me now as she is seemingly sucked into another dimension. As I lay there, the bright day sky turned to darkness, the area only illuminated by the bright full moon, casting its coldness down on me. I stand up and I am no longer in a place of beauty but one of ugliness. The field of flowers has been replaced by a barren wasteland as if it had burned away by fire or radioactive fallout. "Reg," I hear Jenny say as I spin around to see her several yards behind me. She looks as whole and as lovely as she ever did, as if the accident never happened. "Speak to me," she says with such anticipation on her face. "I'm so sorry," I say mournfully. "Don't be. I can hear you now, really hear you. Your voice gives me power, the power to live!" she explains as she walks towards me. Her beauty survives, yet I feel such uneasiness by her presence. She puts her arms around me like she always did and kisses me, but her kiss was not like before. There was something not quite right about our embrace. There was no feeling. Then she released me, looking at me anxiously for some reason. "Speak. You must speak always—speak!" she demanded. If my voice did give her power, I dare not speak. Her demeanor changed from one of joy to one of a vengeful shrieking demon, constantly demanding I speak to her. But I wouldn't feed the demon, only stand watching her as she started to bleed and started to age, eventually turning into a rotting flesh-covered hag of a corpse. She lunged at me, grabbing me with such strength that I couldn't pry free of her grasp, her rotting face contorting into a smile to taunt me further. "Speak to me!!!" she shrieked in my face as she pointed her boney hand at the ground. Then a freshly dug grave appeared as a headstone with her and my name on it rose from the ground. "No!!!" I screamed, instantly giving her back her beauty and radiance. "Seeeeee! Just speak and I'll always be beautiful for you," she says as she pulls me down into the grave with her, sinking further and further till the dirt starts to cover my face. I reach out, but I can't break free. I can't get out! I can't get out!!!!!!!!!!!!!!

I wake up next to Luna in her car with my arms flailing as if I'm trying to claw myself out of a grave. I calm down and feel a sense of calm. Then I wonder what will happen the next time I close my eyes. "Bad dream?" Luna asks. "Always. Can you read me while I'm dreaming?" I ask as I wipe the sweat of my head. "I'm not the dream master. If Freddy Krueger or some other monster is chasing you, you just have to deal with it. You have to defeat the monster. I can remote influence, though," she says to spark my interest. "Isn't that putting thoughts in someone's head?" I ask. "That's part of what it is," she tells. "So doesn't that mean if you put a thought in my head, I might not know if it's my own thought or yours?" I ask. "That's why it's called influencing," she informs. "Well, that's even better than what I can do. I have to talk to influence people. All you have to do is think about it," I excite. "Reg, I don't feel the need to control people, only to help them. Let today be a life lesson, you felt terrible. By using your voice the right way you'll feel wonderful, have a sense of achievement," she inspires. "Yep, you're the daughter of a motivator all right. Hey, how do you know big brother isn't following us right now?" I worry. "The only people following us are our people. You didn't think dad would let me come out here alone, did you?" She smiles to calm my fears.

We reach the Hollywood Hills and wind our way up towards Joe's huge house. Luna drives up as the gate opens and drives up to Joe waiting out front. She gets out of her sporty car into the loving arms of a father always proud of his daughter. I, meanwhile, get out of the car and just sheepishly lean on it and hope no one notices me. Joe comes up to me and just looks at me. "When I was a child, I did something very foolish. One day when my mother was shopping and my father was at work, I took out his gun. I didn't want to shoot anyone. I just wanted to familiarize myself with it. I pointed around as if firing it. Then I took a magazine full of cartridges out of the gun to make it harmless. I aimed it around some more. Then I did something really stupid. I aimed it at myself. I was about to pull the trigger, and why not? It wasn't loaded anymore. And at the last second I turned the gun to the side and pulled the trigger. Nothing should have happened but a click, but what gave me the shock of a lifetime was when the gun went off. I blew a hole into the wall of my parents bedroom. I was so surprised that I physically couldn't stand for a couple minutes. My legs wouldn't move. When dad got home, I was locked in the bathroom. I thought I was going to get the beating of a lifetime, but my dad knew what could have happened and he was as mad at himself as he was at me," he told me as I pondered the moral of the story. I know he knows

I'm older than him and I don't need a lecture and my face showed it. "I think he gets it, dad," Luna helps out. "You think? Then let me make it very clear! If he leaves the house again before the concert, there will be no concert because most likely he will be dead! My friends in the agency tell me that up till recently you were just a curiosity, Reg. They couldn't confirm or deny your ability. But after what happened on Sunset ... let's just say they don't need people running around who can do what you can, especially when they think you are not on their side. As the bullfighters say, it's moment of truth time. The bull is charging your way. The next decision you make will change destiny, either just for you or everyone," Joe says ... and he's right. I just smiled and shook my head, telling everyone that at least for now I wouldn't do the wrong thing, cuz I really didn't know what to do.

11) WORLD, MEET REG

I leave the house, the house on the farm I used to visit as a child. When I was very young and lived at the orphanage, we were occasionally taken on field trips. I loved the long bus rides. I could stare out the window and see a whole new world, all the places I'd never seen before. And one time we passed this farmhouse. I was immediately drawn to it and I just had to go there. So when the bus stopped at our destination, I slipped away from my group and commenced my long journey back to that house. I don't know how many miles it was, but I just had to get back to that house. So much of the land looked the same, and yet I knew just where to look. After so much walking, you'd think I was tired, but no! I was more charged up than ever. The more I walked, the closer I got I thought, but to what? Then I saw it, my farmhouse. It was down a long dirt road away from what seemed like the entire rest of the world. It was really far from my group and even farther from the orphanage, but I didn't care. I was happy. I knew something special was about to happen.

I walk into the farmhouse. The door is unlocked. Either the occupants are very trusting or maybe they left it open just for me. I wander about the big house. No one is around, yet I know I am here for a reason. I must find someone—that's it! Walking to a back bedroom, I see light coming from under the door. I open the door and see a mother holding a little girl on her lap. The little girl seems sad and then ... she sees me. "He came!" the happy mom says as the little girl's face blossoms. She jumps off her mom's lap and rushes up to me. She just smiled at me, taking me in as I looked at her. I've never experienced anyone so happy for so little. Then she hugged me, laying her little head on my shoulder. I instinctively hugged her back. We had an instant connection. I never felt that much love or pure joy in my life, and I never have again since that moment. She released me and just smiled at me. "Can you speak the special strangeness?" she asked as I looked so inquisitively at her eyes; they were bigger than normal for a regular person I thought. "Your eyes are pretty," I tell her and she immediately tells me back, "So are yours." I knew for sure at that moment she was like me. My voice didn't affect her.

She takes my hand and leads me away as mom follows behind us. I leave the house, the house I visited as a child with her still holding my hand. Then she looks up and waits. And soon they come, the giant ships coming down from the clouds; one giant ship and several smaller ships. What pretty lights they have.

I wake up, from a dream? I'm not a child anymore. A memory from my childhood possibly? I did leave the orphanage many times by myself as a child. Every time I came back I just smiled and whispered into Mrs. Grey's ear. She would just walk away all smiles. Everything would be fine. Then I fully awaken as I notice I'm back in Joe's chair in Joe's office with Luna and Joe standing nearby. "Bad dreams again?" she inquires. I look happy as I think about it. "No, actually it was a good dream, a really good one. Something that happened to me as a kid ... I think," I wonder. "You think? With total recall there is no guesswork, only absolute certainty," Joe explains. "It's just that I have gaps in my memory from when I was a kid. I met this little girl and we ... you wouldn't believe me," I thought. "We are in the strangeness business. As they say, lay it on me, Reg!" Joe says to try and be cool. "I played with this little girl with strangely wide eyes when I was a kid. I ran away from the orphanage just to see her. And I think—but I can't be sure—that we went on board a huge UFO. I say can't be sure because we would always look up at it. Then I don't remember anything else, only that I enjoyed myself. See, now you think I'm nutty for sure," I explain. "On the contrary, your story is quite common in our household. Did you forget where you reside?" Joe asks. "I couldn't breathe," I suddenly blurt out as I think about what happened on Sunset. Joe looks oddly at his daughter who tells him, "He's thinking about the Sunset incident." "Yeah, and you're thinking about it, too. You're thinking I'm some sort of monster. I just wanted them to leave me alone. Why can't they leave me alone? And now you want me to speak in front of the whole planet? I'll probably end the world!" I just know. "Reg, that is why we want you here, to help you say the right things. You must be precise when people take your words literally," he consoles, but I am inconsolable. "It keeps playing over and over in my mind. I guess there's no rest for the wicked," I assume. "I think it's time," Luna says to Joe to mystify me. Luna simply holds out her hand to me and says smiling, "Lemme show you something." "Another one of the wacky neighbors?" I can only imagine. "You'll like this one," she tells me, still smiling. I had the curious feeling she was right this time.

So I took her hand and just held it. Then I hopped up as she let go and led me through the big house to a room I hadn't been in before. "The lady or the tiger?" I queried. "I'll leave you two alone. Come back whenever you're ready," she says to me and just walks off. "Am I gonna love this, hate it ..." I called her. She didn't answer. Something behind the door did, though.

Since I figured standing outside of the mystery door for the rest of my life probably wouldn't work out, I finally opened it. Inside was dark, except for all these tiny lights of stars and planets being projected all over the walls and ceiling from some kind of mini planetarium-like projector in the middle of the room. Then I noticed someone sitting with their back to me in a high-back swiveling chair in the room. "Hi, Reg," a serenely sweet voice spoke to me, a voice I didn't recognize, though I knew somehow who it must be speaking. My anxiety grew until I would be sure. Then the chair turned around. I saw a delicately beautiful young lady with the widest eyes I have ever seen, eyes I knew could only belong to one person, and I smiled. "Sunny?" I could barely get out. I couldn't believe it. After all these years—since we were only children—she is here again in my life. She stands and walks over to me, stopping before me so I can take her all in. "You came," she smiled so bright. "Why didn't you try to find me?" I had to know. "Hard to get around. Why not look for me?" she reasonably asked. "I don't know. I guess I was too busy being unhappy," I just said without thinking. "No more," she told me to bring back the kind of joy I thought I'd never experience again. "Why did I just dream of you?" I wondered. "It's time," she only said. "You mean for me to stop screwing up? That could be just about anytime," I figured. "Reg must not suffer. When you suffer, others may suffer. You speak the special strangeness. You speak it every time you speak. You must always remember that," she reminds. "How did you end up here?" I couldn't imagine. "Why do you not like Joe?" she reads me like Luna or is just way too perceptive. "I like him sometimes, like when he's not trying to put me on a leash," I feel. "I don't understand. You run to life, yet you hide also, hide in your house. Why not live?" she asks something to which I have no answer. "I don't know how to live. I just know how to survive," I tell her without understanding why, like I am compelled to do so. It's like she threw Wonder Woman's magic lasso around me so all I could do was say what I felt. Or it could more simply be that she's the only one I ever trusted enough to tell. I smile at her suddenly and say, "You're tricky. You didn't tell me how you got here, think I'd forget?" "I have been here a long time. Only pain outside," she says as her smile goes away. She probably had it rough like me before finally finding what she truly needed. I sensed she needed this place and was happy here. So I was happy for her. Then she suddenly hugged me, and I know we both felt as happy as the first time we embraced as children so long ago.

The hippie van arrives at my destination and here I finally am—ready to change the world! Joe's pep talks didn't get me here, nor did Luna's seductive looks that were really just false promises of affection as she wrapped me in herself whenever the urge hit her. I couldn't tell what she really felt for me. But I could always count on Sunny to make me feel that kind of special I couldn't get anywhere else. And that's why I am here at this concert to speak to the world. All the calm Sunny washed over me is fading, though, now as I pace around backstage at the big concert taking place just feet away from me out front. I have the proverbial butterflies in my stomach, except I think they're giant thunderbirds. What can I possibly say that will change anyone's mind, let alone the whole world? "Just tell them what dad told you to say," Luna says walking up to me after appropriating my flimsy dodo bird eggshell of a mind again. "You know, you should work for the Klingons as their mind scanner. Is that supposed to be for my benefit? I'm jumpy enough already. I feel like I've taken a whole tub of pre-workout," I say and can't settle down. "I know, it's making me jumpy. Would you relax? You're not going into surgery; all you have to do is open your mouth," she complains. "Easy for you to say, it's not your mouth. What if they hate me? I'll never be able to show my face in public again. I won't even be able to live in a big tree in the forest with elves," I jest kinda. "Look, think of it this way, in an hour it will all be over," she smiles and puts her hand on my chest. "Your heart is racing," she concerns. "Move that hand a little lower and it'll go even faster," I slyly smile. She takes her hand away as Joe walks up. "After their next song, you are on," Joe informs. "Okay, I uh, I'm uh, ready ... I guess," I say distantly, like my mind was detaching from my body. My body could stay here in the safety of this backstage womb, while my voice could go out there to do all the heavy lifting. Too bad it doesn't work that way. "Hey, where's Crypto the cryptid? He's not gonna show up and bite everyone, is he?" I ask. "If you mean Percy, your favorite monster hunter is off on the hunt again—no worries," Joe tells. "You mean he really hunts, like, werewolves and vampires?" I inquire. "There are plenty of psychic vampires in this town. As for the other kind, I cannot say. Now do you remember all the things I told you to say, all the empowering words and phrases that will help to empower everyone on this planet all at once? I know you do because of your perfect memory. Don't let the world down now," Joe emphasizes. "Yeah, sure, no pressure here. Why don't you just tell me the whole world is watching?" I ask as Joe tells, "They are."

A roadie or some stage guy signaled to Joe that the band was about to finish the song they were currently playing. Joe and I moved over near the stage guy with a microphone in his ear. I hear Joe speak and motion me forward. Oh, no! I'm getting that feeling again, the feeling that I'm shutting down. I can hear but understand nothing. I'm wandering onstage. Is that Joe helping me along? Everyone's just looking at me, the band, the crowd—everyone! Who the hell is this guy? Why are we wasting time on him? The crowd all must be thinking. And the crowd! The crowd is endless! Of course, it's an outdoor event. As I approach the microphone, I can only imagine what it felt like to be walking to a gallows. This is it for me, except I'll just drop dead from fright before I get there. No chance, I'm in such freakishly good shape.

It's time. I look out over the crowd; they're all waiting for something special to happen, but what? Didn't anyone tell them it's just me? I feel the tension build in me. I'm going to die right here or my head will just explode like in *Scanners.* Someone help me!!! Then I feel a calmness come over me like an ocean serene had just washed over me. I feel someone's hands on my back. The one and only person on the whole planet who could assure me was here for me again, my Sunny. Sunny simply smiled at me through her dark sunglasses and said, "Speak the special strangeness, Reg."

So I looked over at the crowd again, smiling and confident, and all I did was say, "Hi ... I'm Reg!!!" And it happened, my voice was sent out like a giant sound wave, touching every mind it washed over, in the audience and in the home audience watching on televisions at their homes and everywhere else. Sunny walked away now with her hood over her head. Her job was done. She was my amplifier. When she laid her hands upon me, she not only eased my fears, she amplified all that my voice could do, sending a wave of euphoria around the earth for all listening to actually experience. I looked out over the crowd, totally silent they were. They all smiled or moved their heads about in slow-motion as if to say, my pain no more as I am evolving into this new heavenly creature of bliss. May it never end? Since I dare not take away this feeling from them so soon, I began to sing, caring nothing for all the things Joe had told me to say. I just felt like singing!

I wanted them to experience me, to feel what I was feeling. And as I sang, the crowd slowly joined in, starting slowly like a ripple in a pond that would spread across all the oceans of the earth. We would all be heard! And as we all still sang, the whole world sang with me. I just know they did. This wasn't about me or anyone else in the troubled world in which we live. This was about all of us. If for just this minuscule moment in time, the entirety of the world was united. No one was fighting. No one was in disagreement. No one tried to best anyone else. It's as if we were all allowed back into that garden of perfection that we all lost. We were all one.

Luna, Joe and a lot of Joe's star children filtered out onstage to be a part of history. This was beyond the Age of Aquarius, where peace was but a dream. This was the dawn of a new era for Mankind and they knew it. They had to be a part of it. We would bring peace to the world, not by force, but by just letting the people experience such peace and joy as an actual force that they can feel and experience, rather than just as a concept people yak about endlessly. And on this day when so many felt such peace and exultation, they would never want anything else. Nothing else would ever compare for them again.

I turn around as my eyes search for Luna, seeing her standing by Joe. I go over by them as the crowd continues to sing. "I had kind of a brain freeze; I could only think to sing," I confess as Joe says, "Perfectly all right! It was the emotion I told you, the emotion! Do you hear that? That is for you! Every soul possesses its own special tune. Yours is the most special of all. You just changed the world, Reg. It will never be the same."

I just look at Joe and Luna with a kind of stunned smile that really isn't a smile. Things will never be the same all right. Joe saying that hit me like a ton of bricks, and a few tons more. I'm supposed to be pretty smart, but I didn't know what to expect next. I mean, I know the press will want to talk to me, but I can't even talk to them. At least if I do get press interviews, they are guaranteed to write exactly what I tell them to write. No left or right bias will creep into that ol' mind of theirs when Reg has gotten to it first.

"He's getting that look again. You all right, Reg?" Luna is concerned. I hope she does finally care. "So what's next?" I simply ask. "Absence makes the heart grow fonder; leave the audience wanting more. First, we take you away from here and plan our next event. We will have no problem getting you a place to speak anywhere on starship Mother Earth now," Joe excites. "But I really didn't say anything," I confuse. "... Of substance, no, but now they all know what you can do. Next time they will hear what you say. I think it was better after all that you didn't say anything specific this time," Joe explains ... but was I ready for more of this?

The crowd had stopped singing by now, and the band had resumed playing. But something unexpected had happened, something no one counted on. One of the biggest bands in the world, one loved by millions everywhere was being booed! The crowd now started to chant Reg! Reg! Reg! Over and over they chanted my name. Rather than hearing their favorite music, all they wanted to hear was me.

"Can you help us out here?" a band member comes over to ask. They helped me, so I for sure would help them. I start to walk back to the microphone, but Joe stops me to give me some advice. "Watch what you say," Joe warns. "In that case ..." I say as I scoop up Luna into my arms to her happy surprise. "I'll need someone to watch me," I explain as I walk with her in my arms over to the microphone. "What are you doing?" she asks. "I'm not running away from this, and you're not either," I tell her as I set her down on her feet next to me and take the microphone. The crowd is still chanting my name, so I motion them with my hand to get them to stop. The chanting dies off so I can speak. "Don't you love your women? I wanna love mine. Luna, everyone ... love Luna!" I shout! Then I look over at Luna and say, "Now they'll love you, too." She just looks as if to say what have I gotten myself into. Hey, all this wasn't my idea. After a short silence, the crowd roars in appreciation. "Yeah! That's what I wanna hear. Now listen to Reg. Enjoy the concert. Buy some band memorabilia to remember this special day. Then go home and love that special someone in your life. Don't long for Reg. Long to enjoy life! Then go out and live it!!" I empower!

After a bit of the ol' ultra-quiet, the audience roars!! I sneak a kiss on Luna's lips. She just smiles as her arms flap up and down like she doesn't know what to do next. Then we just grab each other and kiss each other to an extremely appreciative audience. That's when we make our hasty retreat. Joe, Luna, Sunny and I disappear through the backstage and out into a huge armored limo, which takes us away to needed safety. Because, believe it or not, the overly excited audience members just might want a nice souvenir of the event—me!

I pile into a limo with Joe, Luna and Sunny as I wonder why we are leaving in a different vehicle. What was wrong with the psychedelic sixties hippie mobile? I think it was kind of cool. "So do I, but that vehicle isn't bulletproof," Luna informs me as she taps the sap in my wooden head again. "Bulletproof? You didn't tell me they'd wanna kill me after I spoke! Thanks a lot," I sound off. "They don't want to kill you. That is the farthest thing from their minds. They simply want to get close to you. How close would you like them to get?" Joe asks. "I get it!" I said and I did. "The masses all love you now. Get used to it," Joe tells. "Love me? They're all potential stalkers. Where am I supposed to go now?" I ponder. "Where would you like to go?" he taunts. "You mean my place or yours? Where else can I go?" I can't believe. I notice the overly large sunglasses Sunny is wearing and ask her, "You really rock those shades. You wear 'em because of your eyes?" "Very sensitive," she only says as I rub my head suddenly, the thought of one my massive migraines coming on did little to quell my usual anxiety from taking over. "Are you okay, Reg?" Joe show concern. "Swell. So I guess you really know how old I am and everything else about me," I admit. "We know that both you and Sunny were born just before the Depression, which would put your age at about the century mark," Joe tells. "And what could that information possibly do for you? Are you trying to build a race of atomic super dudes to take over the neighborhood?" I jest. "Luna was born in the sixties. You and Sunny were born in the twenties, yet you all look about the same age, very young as if your aging slows down upon adulthood," Joe explains. "How 'bout your monster hunter? He looks forty!" I recognize. "Yes, but he was born during the Civil War and he is of another race or species. You see, Reg, we are building a database of beings of extreme age without the outward signs of that aging. There are aliens whose lifespans are so long that they would in all practicality be called immortal. I met such a man when I was a child. That is why it holds such a fascination for me," Joe really explains.

I suddenly realize how bad my head is hurting. "Hey, let's stop at a drugstore. I got a headache," I inform. "There are plenty of meds at home, we'll be there soon," Joe tries to calm me, not noticing or not caring as I rub my head. "Yeah, my head hurts right now. I want something for it right now!" I hurt! Luna must be reading me because she tells her dad, "He is hurting." I try to open the door, not having any luck because—it's locked! I bend over holding my head. "It's another bad one. Stop the car!" I yell! "We're not near a drugstore yet," Joe says with such caring! I try the door again—it's still locked! Joe and Luna start in on me. I don't pay attention to what they're saying, I just want out! I just want relief!!! "Open the door!!!" I start to punch at the bullet proof glass as I continue to hear their yammering voices. Don't they see I don't like it here? I punch the window so hard now that a crack appears in the bulletproof glass. They look amazed and a little frightened, especially Sunny. I didn't mean to frighten her—I just gotta get outta here!!!

The limo pulls over as I continue to punch at the window, cracking it further and further. One way or another, I was getting out of this luxury deathtrap. The locks suddenly pop up and I shove the door open. I get out of the limo somewhere in Hollywood. I don't really care. I wander down the street with my hand on my head. Luna walks up to me and gets me to stop. I didn't feel like moving fast anyway. "Would you stop and think about what you're doing? You shouldn't be roaming aimlessly around free right now," she nags! "Free? Why can't I be free? Isn't this America? Can't freaks like me be free in America anymore?! Can't I just be free not to be bothered by assholes who just want something from me!!!!!" I yell extra loud to make my head hurt even worse. With my loud outburst, the people passing by on the sidewalk were all starting to follow me. "Reg, this is getting dangerous. Would you look around? Look at your hand, it's bleeding," she says as I look at my hand. I guess pounding on that window didn't do it any good. I'm bleeding pretty badly. I didn't even notice until right now. I didn't even notice when it happened. I didn't feel it. It didn't even start to hurt until just now. So what! I suddenly stopped. "Hey, all you zombies! This is Luna. Love my Luna! Let's all say it together, Luuuu naaaaaa. Say it!!!" I tell my vegged-out followers. And my little clique of zombie followers do say her name, all slow and drawn out like the brain dead followers they were. And they all reached out for my Luna, her fear turning to terror more by the moment as they got close enough to claw at her. "Reg, make 'em stop!" she requests. "Make 'em stop? They all love you. Isn't this what you and daddy always wanted, everyone loving everyone?" I say with my bloody hand holding onto my head as the blood drips down. "Reg, if you love me, stop them!" she pleads. Through my painful haze, I see my Luna so scared and almost in tears now. Barely able to think, I scream, "Get away from her!!!!!!!!!!!! Go home ..." I hit the pavement. I guess I fell. I lie there and watch the drama unfold. As Joe and his driver hurry over to help me, two low-riders drive up. Otto and three tough-looking Mexican dudes get out of their cars and rush up to rescue poor, hurting me. Good ol' Otto, he didn't forget me. His three armed amigos would make sure I got the rescue I needed, by trusted bud Otto.

Otto rushes up to me as I motion for him to lean down. Otto squats down and I tell him, "Take me with you," "Is it your head?" Otto asks as I just nod yes. Meanwhile, Joe recognizes Otto and is grateful for his help. "Otto, your assistance is greatly appreciated. We were about to have a bit of a problem here," Joe tells as Otto stands to face Joe. "You have the problem, the brain dead bunch. We're leaving," Otto explains. "Would you help us get him into the limo first?" Joe asks. "You are not comprehending. We are leaving. Reg goes with us," Otto defiantly defends as he motions two of his friends to carry Reg to his car. Joe doesn't try to stop them when he sees large caliber handguns tucked into the fronts of their belts. "He needs medical attention, Otto," Joe tells. "I know what he needs. You know, I used to respect you," Otto says before going to his car. Otto's middle-aged-plus Uncle Danny stays to meet Joe with a smile. "Hawaiian Joe! I'm Otto's Uncle Danny," he happily says as he throws out his hand for Joe, who shakes it a bit mystified. "Don't let what Otto said bother you. I know you did what you had to do. Now we're gonna do what we gotta do," Danny tells it like it is and is gonna be. "Please take care of him. He can do so much good for this world," Joe pleads. "I know. I'm Mexican, not stupid," he damn well means. "Didn't mean to imply," Joe says as Danny eyes the big driver with the gun bulge in his coat. "Keep the gorilla in his cage and we won't have a problem," Danny says as he heads to the car that Otto and Reg are inside. Luna yells to them, "Tell Reg to call!" Danny stops at his car door to tell her, "He'll call when he wants to call." Danny gets into the low-rider and takes off fast with the other low-rider. It's a culture, man.

12) GIMMIE SHELTER

I'm awake! I'm being dragged down a long hall, my feet barely touching the ground. I glance over at the two massive men manhandling me, each wearing black executioner hoods over their heads. We reach a huge double door that magically opens by itself as we approach it. They drag me up to some kind of judge wearing one of those old powdered wigs like in England. He scowls down at me from up high in his appointed perch. "The prisoner, sir!" The executioners both say in stereo. "How do you plead?" the judge asks. "Plead? Plead what? Why am I here?" I ask. "Ah, you plead ignorance then. You are charged for what you are about to do," he informs. "How do you plead for that?" I ask. "Very well, the jury shall decide. Jurors, what is your verdict?" the judge asks them as my man-handlers turn me to see the jury, all sitting there with dark robes and dark hoods covering their faces. Each one in turn stood, turned their thumbs down and proclaimed me guilty in rapid succession as if they were in a wave at a ballgame. There was something odd about their voices, though. They were familiar, and yet only eleven found me guilty. "Eleven. That was only eleven. It has to be unanimous!" I said frantically. "Foreman, what is your verdict?" the judge asks. The final juror stands and turns downward his boney thumb as his boney hand protrudes from his robe. Then all the jurors pull back their hoods to reveal themselves. Joe, and Luna, and Aphrodite, and Roger, and Sunny and the other star children all smiled maniacally as they said guilty over and over. Meanwhile, poor dead Jenny pulls her hood off and then the hood of the jury foreman, a bloody skeleton that Jenny lovingly kisses on the side of its fleshless face. “Sentence has been reached—guilty! There is your fate,” the judge says as the executioners now turn me around to see a huge guillotine with my name smeared in blood on it. “I thought you couldn’t use those anymore,” I barely managed to gulp out. “We brought it back just for you,” the judge smiles ever so happily down on me. “Don’t I get a last request or a meal? How ‘bout I die of old age and you won’t have to clean that thing?” I jest out of terror. “Oh, a funny man. Let’s see how well you laugh when your head is removed from your body,” the judge says so slowly and deliberately as he grins at me. “Executioners, carry out the sentence!” the judge orders as the executioners drag me towards the guillotine, where a third hooded executioner awaits me. As strong as I am, I cannot break free, only see the light glisten off the giant steel blade as the third executioner pulls the rope down to bring the blade up and lock it in place. I struggle helpless like a child with all my strength as I am laid upon the device, except I am placed face up. With the round hole conveniently large enough to fit snugly around my neck—but no larger—I could not escape, only reach and scratch at the device as I looked up at the shiny blade glistening above as if taunting me. I felt my heart beat so fast that I thought it would explode! But there would be no cheating the hangman as they say, for the third executioner suddenly said, “This is your fate. This is your destiny. You will not cheat yours!” The blade is coming down so fast ...

I lunge forward in the back of the low-rider I am in. Now they're trying to kill me in my dreams. How much more can I take? I notice the older Mexican dude turning to look at me. "I don't believe we've met," I mystify. "I'm Otto's uncle. What are you looking at?" he says gruffly as I see the hearing aid in his ear. "You wear hearing aids too? It must run in the family," I deduce. "I thought you said his voice was special? It didn't do nothin' for me," Danny grouses. "Reg, how's your head?" my good bud the driver Otto asks. "Surprisingly, it doesn't bother me anymore. A nap always helps. So this is Uncle Danny you told me about?" I ask. "Yeah? What did he tell you?" Danny asks with a frown. "That you were mean, nasty, old and Mexican," I reply. "Then he wasn't lying," he says with such refreshing honesty. I just noticed it's dark outside. "It's dark? How long have we been driving around?" I ask. "Hours. You know how you are when you're asleep, no one can wake you up. Where would you like to go?" Otto asks like he'd do anything for an old friend. "Take-out and take it home," I say.

I had a chance now to demonstrate to Danny what my little ol' voice could do for anyone else but him and Otto. So we go to a drive-in window of one of our more popular burger joints and order a ton of food. I let them do the ordering for obvious reasons. Then when the food magically appears at the window, I simply say, "That'll be no charge." Danny looks amazed when everyone just inside the window area freezes. "Man, that is freaky! But when do we get the food?" Danny asks. I lean out the window to say, "You can pass us the eats now," I smile. After the usual time lag, the girl starts handing us the bags of food and—oops! There goes one of the chocolate shakes. I guess one of us doesn't get one.

We drive up to my house in Otto's low-rider as Chotee and Carlos roll up in theirs. We pile out of the cars and look at yet another car strange to the neighborhood parked directly across the street in front of the neighbor's house. While passing the car, I notice two dudes, one holding a camera. So I figure these are not G-men, but rather just pain in the ass paparazzi looking for a story. I tell Otto, "Would y'all go in the house and check for unauthorized occupants?" "Sure, as soon as Chotee and Carlos aren't statues. You gotta watch what you say around them," Otto complains. "Hey, it's my house, am I supposed to wear a pillow over my face? Tell 'em to wear headphones. Back in a sec," I say as I walk towards the car with the pair of paparazzi. Along the way I hear Danny say 'that is so freaky' again.

I walk up to the car and wave at them with my big harmless smile. One of the paparazzi rolls down his window, snaps some pictures of me with a nice camera that will soon be mine and asks, "Hey, you're him, right? You're Reg?" "Yeah!" I say loudly with my smile intact. Yep! They're frozen. I take the camera from him and ask, "Gee, I sure would like to have your wallets." After a bit, they take out their wallets and fumble them my way. I look inside them and sure enough—press! "Forget you were here. Forget about me, and get another job. Nobody likes you guys," I comment.

I go into my house. Otto and his bunch are already chowing down on the fanum-tax yummies as they watch my big TV and sit on my couch. "Don't talk! I left you some in the kitchen," Otto informs me as I go in the kitchen, plop down in a chair in front of the table and look at the bag of greasy goodies before me. I take out what would never pass for the healthy food I usually eat. But I was so hungry I could eat a rhino's ass through a park bench, so I commenced digging in. A house full of friendlies and I'm all alone again.

Halfway through my processed meal, Otto walks in with my phone and puts it on the table as he tells me, "You left your phone here. You got messages." He starts to leave and stops as I ask, "You can't stay?" "The fights are on. We'll talk later," he says, throwing a few punches in the air as he leaves. I look at my phone. I have got so damn many messages! I look at Luna's message. I'm tempted to call her, but ...

I walk into the living room with my amigos all watching the fights. In the house right now there are two people who can talk to me, except they're not talking, just yelling at a TV screen. I may as well be by myself on a mountaintop in Tibet. At least if I were at Luna's place there are people to talk to ... and Luna.

Wakey-wakey, I'm up. I got my usual three hours of sleepy time and no nightmares—yah! Otto's home boys and I went to bed late after a little celebratin' so it's not dark anymore, like when I usually rise. Yeah, that sun is definitely up with a vengeance! No problem, I'll still work out. Where do I have to be today?

I walk into the den to see Carlos and Chotee snoozing on my couch and chair. I guess Otto and his uncle are in the guest bedroom. I casually move the curtains to see if there are any more unwanted guests outside and they are everywhere! A sea of vans with little satellite dishes on their roofs adorn the neighborhood. The media has found me, but why so many of them? I thought they liked to scoop each other. At least they're not knocking on my door. That'll probably come next. I better put more clothes on than just these gym pants. I might have to make a quick getaway.

So I do my workout without the loud music for consideration of sleepers who need more sleep than I do. I'm not going to rush out to meet the trespassers from the theatre bizarre. They can wait for me. All showered and dressed, I go out to see Carlos and Chotee up and looking out the window as Otto and his uncle emerge from the back bedroom. I didn't make any noise, but people talking outside and the sound of loud sound checks by reporters probably did wake up, oh, the whole neighborhood! "Did you see what's going on outside? I'm an old man, I need my sleep," Danny grouses cuz he's good at it. "I saw. It's hard to miss the circus passing through," I reply. "What are you gonna do about it?" Good bud Otto, who can't eat with me, asks. "Yeah, we can't protect you from this. You better make other plans fast," Danny jumps in. "Well, you're not leaving yet, are you?" I sound complainy. "You calling me a coward? We'll go when you're safe. Start figuring out where you wanna be, besides this place," Danny logically deduces.

Reality just hit me in the face pretty hard, and without warning. Either I didn't see it coming or I just didn't wanna. So what do I do next, go crawling over to Luna? She and Joe would just love that. I am not going to be under their thumby thumbs! So I start to use my fabulous computer brain that God or maybe aliens gave me and figure out what I must do. The way I figure it, I have to find a way out of here and I have to get Luna over here without me having to go to her. How to doooooooo? Simple! I will play with the press. These numbnuts must think they'll just stick a microphone in my face and ask me a bunch of innocuous questions. We all know by now that won't happen. One question is all they get. I, luckily, get all the answers, and they'll love and agree with all of them. This will be easier than I thought.

Otto turns on the TV, and look at that! My house is being broadcast on my TV set and probably every TV set on earth, all the entertainment gurus and even political pundits discussing when Reg will emerge from his house and say something, anything to them. I guess they feel entitled. "So, should I go out and meet them before or after breakfast?" I ask. "They're nothing but vultures, they'll pick you clean and move on to the next carcass. We can drive you someplace safe," Danny says. "I thought you wanted me to deal with the problem? Besides, the street's blocked off; you'll never get out of here right now. And even if you could, they'd just follow us. So who wants to go out there and tell them that I'll see them after breakfast? It'll give our home viewing audience a chance to gather 'round the set to see—voice man!" I tell. "Don't look at me, I don't know what to say," Otto gripes. "I can do it. They don't scare this Mexican," Danny volunteers. "Thanks. But, you know, that's not exactly a smiley face you're wearing, it scares people," I add. "You sayin' I'm ugly? Look at this face; it'll be your face one day. It's called getting old!" Danny super grouses. "I don't care about your face! I'm talking about tact! You seem a little too blunt about everything," I explain. "Blunt is honest. You want bullshit, get a politician. Make some breakfast!" he means. And with that, Uncle Danny heads out the front door and closes it behind him. I guess he didn't want nosy reporters looking in either. I like Danny, he's a no nonsense guy. He might be—okay, he is—a little rough around the edges, but that's why I trust him.

So we watch Danny walk in a straight line right down to the street to talk to the reporters, who all looked like they were salivating to get the story of the century. He stopped as microphones were now being thrust in his face a bit too closely for him. "Back off! Show some respect. This ain't your house," Danny informs. "Is Reg coming out to speak to us?" a female reporter asks. "He'll be out after breakfast. You want any?" Danny asks. "Are you inviting us in?" a dude reporter asks. "No! I'm giving you time to go get some," Danny snaps. "Who are you, sir?" a nosy reporter asks. "I'm the one talking to you, any more dumb questions? You're good at it," Danny observes. "Will he be granting any exclusive interviews?" a pushy reporter asks. "Not if he's smart. I'm going in to eat now. Stay off the lawn or I'm coming back out!" Danny scares.

Meanwhile, we watch Danny's interview on the TV with great amusement. Old and cranky can really come off as funny sometimes, like Clint Eastwood in *Gran Torino*. Danny comes back inside now and says, "Tactful enough? Where's my breakfast?"

So I fix everyone's breakfast. We eat it. We like it. Time for someone to go back outside—me! But first! Time to call Luna, gotta make sure she's watching, although I'm pretty sure she is. "Guess who? Are you watching?" I ask. "Everyone's watching? You're not going to be your usual self and say something colorful, are you?" she asks. "Well, it is the perfect opportunity ..." I imply. "Please don't mention any of us at the house here. The world's not ready for us. Will you do that for me?" she pleads. "I'll do anything for you?" I say and I would. "Then come over here. I won't be mad at you," she confesses. "Great! But I have a better idea, you come over here," I order. "You know I can't do that. Dad won't let me without bringing protectors. I think you've blown it with him," she informs. "How 'bout you, have I blown it with you? Bring anyone you want. They'll be welcome. I won't try to run away. I'm sick of running. Can I count on you?" I sincerely ask, and she would know. "I'll think about it," was all she said, hanging up on me first before I could. No time to feel sorry for myself. This only means I have to go outside and be the biggest ass I can possibly be, ensuring she'll have to come over here before I go out there and do it over and over again and mention Joe and his bunch. So, am I devious? What would you do for the one you love? Time to go outside!

So I walk outside all smiles and with my arms outstretched in a welcoming gesture—gotta make 'em love me! I get closer, and closer and closer! Then I let 'em have it! "Hello, planet earth! I'm Reg!!!!!!!!!!!!!!!!!!!!!!!!!!!!!!" I yell! Yep, it happened, every single reporter either plain stopped reporting or dropped their microphone. Can't give interviews that way, can you? So I strut around with my knees bent and my arms flapping, kind of like what Mick Jagger might look like if he were a chicken. That should get Luna's attention. What will this idiot do next? And while strutting around, I sang ...

"Ooooooooooh, I crapped in my bed today
When I went to bed
My eyes were all red
So pinched one off there to staaaaaaay
Oooooooooooh, I crapped in my pants today
When I went to work
My boss was a jerk
So I told him he'd be smellin' me this waaaaaaay!"

I stops my struttin' to tell everyone, "An old Irish folk tune from the sea, as far as you know, dedicated to my 20th century fox. She knows who she is, winky-winky, nudgey-nudgey. So you all think me some kind of fool here? Oh, no answer? I thought this was an interview. Well, without wasting your precious time any further, I would just like to say farewell, buh-bye! And getenzee off my lawn." I then skipped, jumped and twirled my way up to my front door. Then I just went into my house and slameth the door shut.

Back in the house ... "So, what did you think?" I ask all smiley. "That was so cool!" Otto smiles. "Cool? You acted like a fool! Is that how you wanna present yourself to the world?" Danny wins the grousing award! Some people just don't appreciate genius. "Hey, they couldn't respond to me anyway. Why not have a little fun with it? How did those two respond to me being on TV?" I refer to the Carlos and Chotee statues that just stand there because I spoke in front of them yet again. "Your voice didn't paralyze them like it's doing now, but they did say it made 'em feel good. Hey, that may be the answer you need, homie. Just record your voice and people will pay to hear it. You'll be the first trillionaire!" Otto excites. "Holy shit! That's it! I'll be a rock and roll star!" I fantasize.

So hours pass and yet the cameras and reporters still remain; all part of my devious plan to get Luna over here. I can always tell them to go then. On the TV, meanwhile, egghead analysts and those who can actually appreciate such fine entertainment, critique my appearance before the world as if it were a performance, some kind of audition before the world. Maybe it was; I was just trying to enjoy myself. What better way to say I love life than to live it out in front of the whole world? Maybe people will stop taking themselves so seriously now and just do their thing without worrying about what others will think about it. You can never please everyone anyway—blah-blobidy-blah!

Even more hours pass. Ring! Ring! What's this? My phone is ringing. And look who it is—Luna! I think I'll answer it. "Whoever in the world might this be?" I pretend I don't know. "This is your 20th century fox speaking. I must admit, everyone at the house just loved you," she confesses. "But you didn't?" I ask. "I didn't say that, funny boy! Why are all the reporters still out here?" she asks. "Out here? So you've been here all along, eh? Just waiting for me to screw up, huh?" I ask. "Why are they still here? Why haven't you just told them to hit the road already?" she asks. "Because I might have further use of them. You just never know what I might think of to say to them next," I imply. "Uh huh, that's what I figured. You wanna come get me?" she asks. "No no, pretty Polly, you here," I order. "I can't get through the barricade. Last chance, come and get me or sleep alone tonight," she tempts. "I'll be right out!" I say as I hang up, pace around and prepare to go outside again. "Listen up! We're gonna have company. They're friendlies so don't let 'em see your guns," I order. "They'll see them if they're not friendly." Danny rebuts. "Hey, don't shoot my girlfriend. Is that too much to ask?" I ask.

I head out the door and down in front of the camera crews and reporters being corralled in by cops off of my property. Funny, someone else must have asked them to do that, probably Joe. As I get closer, I see Luna and Aphrodite and I yell to the reporters, "Heeeeeey, pendejos!!! And the crowd's frozen. I walk up to and just look at my Luna, who just says, "I don't know what to do with you." "Why'd you bring the dame, sweetheart? She's no good. My voice wrecks her," I say like Bogie, only to be surprised as hell as Aphrodite, says back, "Don'tcha hate that, people talking about you right in front of you?" "You're not doped up like Roger, are you?" I ask as she smiles back. Looks like someone might have some competition here. Luna just moves her head to the side and gives me that look, mind-jacking me again. "You wanna tell them to leave now before that O-so marvelous voice of yours wears off?" she says dripping with sarcasm. "Wow! I am so not appreciated here at the palace," I say as I step up to the crowd and say, "Listen up! Achtung, dummies! Gitt!. You wanna leave. Your job's done. You all feel just great, never better. Those of you watching at home, if you like my voice listen to it there. Don't come here! You don't wanna come here. Uhhhh, now's good!" Luckily the crowd slowly starts to leave, shuffling like zombies as they bump into each other. "I hope you didn't drive here," I say to Luna. "Of course we did, why?" she asks. "Because this place is about to become a demolition derby," I explain. I stand there with Luna's space bud bestie Aphrodite as Luna rushes over to move Joe's vintage hippie van with all the flowers and peace symbols painted on it. "You have an amazing talent, Reg. We can't wait to have you back at the house," Aphrodite tells. "How is that you can speak with me now? Do they have inoculations for me now?" I ask curiously as she smiles and just fondles a necklace of animal teeth around her neck, a necklace I only ever saw on Joe. Meanwhile, we watch all the bumper cars smashing into each other as they exit the area. Luna's exasperation shows as she attempts to maneuver the hippie van through the cul-de-sac of crash happy zombie reporters, only to be bumped, thumped, whammed and slammed by every vehicle that passed her, which didn't go unnoticed if you count the flinches on Aphrodite's pretty face. Entering the driveway now, Luna gets out of the dent mobile and she doesn't look too happy. "Hey, I have a new nickname for you—crashie!" I chuckle. "Dad's gonna be so upset. He's had this van since the sixties," she informs. "Well look at it this way, now you can give it back to the Partridge family," I chuckle more. "Or a junkyard," Aphrodite chuckles. "You too, really?" Luna fumes!

So we three go into the house. Carlos and Chotee start to eye the girls, like, immediately! I can't have that. "Everybody, these are my friends—don't bother the girls," I say with the bug-eyed in mind. "Unless they wanna be bothered," Aphrodite says as she walks her brick-house body right up to Uncle Danny with her smile of fascination showing. "Otto said he had an interesting uncle. He didn't say he was so beautiful, too!" she smiles so sweetly as Danny gets that 'who me' look on his face. "Girl, you need your eyes checked," Danny logically admits. "Oh, I think you're quite handsome, real men are," Aphrodite swoons. I'm guessing Danny's thinking either this girl's loco or he's about to become one lucky son-of-a-bitch! Go for it, Danny! "Where is everyone supposed to sleep tonight?" Danny inquires. "I know where I'll be sleeping," Aphrodite says as she gives him her best seductive look. Works for me. Danny's too cool for drool, so he just busts out with a big smile. "Well, now that that's settled ..." I say as I take two bricks of hundred dollar bills out of the briefcase that has been sitting open on a table all night and all day, and hand them to Otto to give to Carlos and Chotee. "This is for your friends, I won't need them anymore. You and your uncle will get yours when you leave," I tell. Meanwhile, Luna gets this open-mouthed look of surprise on her face at seeing the money just sitting there like that. "You just leave money like that sitting there out in the open like a bowl of Halloween candy for everyone to take?" she asks. "Nobody touched it. I told them not to," I simply say. "But you can see it right there!" she says disbelievingly. "He told them they couldn't see it. They've been walking past it all day. Reg has got some freaky powers, I tell ya. Where will you be sleeping tonight?" Danny smiles as Luna gets an incredulous look on her face. Aphrodite looks all pouty as she says, "I thought you liked me?" "I'm crazy about you. It's just that three doesn't always make a crowd," Danny replies. "We'll be right back. Feel free to get acquainted," Luna tells Danny. "Oh, we will," Aphrodite replies as she disappears into the back of the house with her Latin conquest. "Would you excuse us?" Luna says to Otto with an ominously over-friendly smile as she takes me outside the door.

The nanosecond the door is shut, she slaps me hard across my surprised as hell face. "What was that for?" I mystify. "For yesterday! You ever leave me on the sidewalk that way again and we're finished! If you'd hit me, we'd be finished now. I've had enough of all the lying, and cheating and hurting by men," she informs. "I would never hit you. I've never hit anyone," I reply. "How about fights, that's hitting, isn't it? How about those agents we found in your house? That's hitting. See, now you're lying to me," she tells. "I just tossed them aside. I've never been in a fight. You can read minds, what does my mind tell you?" I ask as she reads me and looks oddly at me. "You've never been in a fight?" she asks. "I've never had to. If someone bothered me, I'd just tell them to go away. Please don't go away?" I say with such sadness. God, what a wuss! I can't help it, she rips me apart. I turn my back so she won't see, but she sees anyway. She tries to turn me around but can't. She puts her arms around me. She's a lot nicer now. I like her better this way. "I'm not going away, Reg. I know you need someone you can talk to. We do more than talk, don't we? Answer me, Reg," she eases. "You don't love me. You think I'm a big baby, just a fool. I know what you think. I don't have to read minds," I purge. She takes my formerly bloody hand and looks at it, but it has completely healed in just a day. "You heal fast. How's your head?" she asks. "Like my hand. Hey, maybe I'm a highlander or a vampire. Keep crypto the vampire killer away from me," I jest. She moves around me to look at me. What is my sly fox of foxes thinking? "I wanna show you something," she says as she takes my hand, enters the house and leads me into my bedroom. "I'm kind of familiar with this room. What did you wanna show me?" She slams the door shut.

Luna and I walk into my den to see Otto sitting in my chair. Uncle Danny sits on the couch with Aphrodite so close she's practically on top of him. Even though Aphrodite's hands were admiring Danny, his eyes were admiring the TV screen, like Otto's. Everyone looks over at us. "Girl, you are loud!" Danny says as Luna's head goes down and she tries to smile with the most embarrassing look on her face. It would seem my girl is not only impressive but passionately expressive in the bed chamber. I try not to smile, why embarrass the poor girl further? "Otto, where are your friends?" I ask. "I sent Carlos and Chotee away like you asked. Most of the press has gone, too. They had some accidents leaving so the cops had to take the reports," Otto informs. "I didn't hear any accidents," Luna states. "Of course not, you're so loud!" Danny says to embarrass Luna to the point that she leaves the room. "Yeah, I miss Carlos and Chotee already. They weren't big talkers, but it was nice to have really dangerous people in my house with tattoos on their face," I remarked. "You know what they say, a kind word and a gun go further than just a kind word," Danny says as he takes out his Colt and twirls it with a smile. "Hey, Luna! He can twirl a gun just like you," I yell to get her attention. "She can? Hey, come back and twirl my gun, Luna!" Danny yells to Luna, who saunters back into the room with attitude. Danny just smiles and winks at Luna, who I'm sure was sick of his playful come-ons and it showed in her face. Luna changes her tune and comes right up to Danny and holds out her hand. "Well, let me handle your gun!" she requested with her outstretched hand. Danny looks a bit surprised. Then he hands her his Colt. "The Colt 45, the sidearm that won the west," she remarks as she twirls it and throws it around her body to the other hand to twirl, impressing the hell out of Danny and Otto. She then shoves the Colt into the front of Danny's pants. "There, now you'll never forget where it is," she impresses. "Careful, I might need those," Danny remarks. "Not a problem. I only shoot what I'm aiming at. I see you wear hearing aids like Otto. It must run in the family," she says as she steps back and puts her hands on her hips. This shapely sheriff was about to lay down the law. "So he can talk with you too, huh, Reg?" she asks. "Yeah, so?" I wonder. "So you want him around to talk to or me? We can do more than just talk, you know," she teases. "He's Otto's uncle, he's cool. I sent the other two away," I tell. "You didn't answer my question, lover, or should I stop calling you that?" she taunts. I didn't like this; she's putting me in a box again. The guys are just looking at me as if to say are you just going to let her speak to you that way, you big wuss? I just look mystified at her. "So go do what you do best, run off and cry some more like a pussy!" she viciously taunts. I just look at her, thinking my thoughts and hoping she would actually would pick up on them this time. Why do you do this to me? Why do you always do this? I'm gonna be a rock 'n' roll star, the biggest there has ever been—and you can't stop me! Then I walked out the door, leaving it open as she yelled, "Reg, wait! I didn't mean it that way." Danny steps up to her and he is not happy. "Is that how you keep a man? There's a word for someone like you—puta!" he defines. "I just wanted to toughen him up. He's never even been in a fight. He needs to know how to protect himself. His whole world is about to change and he's not ready," she sorrows. "Reg has been taking care of himself since before you were born. He doesn't need you," Otto says as he and Danny walk out the door. Luna and Aphrodite just look at each other. They had failed in their one simple task, bring Reg home.

I ran fast and far from my home. No one would catch me. No one would control me. No one would be there for me. I walked out without food, or money or direction. Whatever masterpiece would be sculpted by my life would be sculpted by me. I was alone again, but I wanted something this time and I was bloody well about to get it!

13) ROCK ME-LOVE ME

I never knew my mom and dad, so I don't know what it's like to lose them. I can only imagine. I've heard people say that when you live with your family and one by one you lose them either to them leaving the nest or worse by them leaving the world, the worst part is not always the leaving part. The worst part is when you sit in that empty house and you realize how alone you are. A house once filled with love is now an empty tomb. The only way I can imagine it is when I see the end of *Godfather II* when Michael remembers his family members all full of life and all with him there in the house. Then you see him old and alone. He has his power but no one to share it with. He didn't look very happy to me. As I lay on my bed in my hotel room, I think I know how he must have felt. I must not let the ghosts of my mausoleums drag me down with them. I must prove I am worthy of the power that I have been given, and I must do it alone.

Six months have passed; at least I think it's been six months. Every day blends into the next. I have not seen or spoken to Otto or, Luna or anyone I ever knew from my past. I can't say I haven't thought about them. I'm just a little bit busy now. My life has meaning and purpose, mostly to all the suits, and leeches and hangers-on who just want something from me. But hey, all that other fun stuff was from a former life before I was the biggest, richest, and most sought after singer in music history! I've made billions!! Yeah, that's what I said—billions! Everybody loves Reg—yes, they do! They buy my songs, my albums, my shoes, my cool line of shirts ... Everyone has to look cool like Reg, don'tcha know? They buy my cola, my phones, my Chia Pets with my likeness, my anything that has my face on it or my voice in it. Yeah, I've got it all, all but my Luna. I wonder if she thinks of me when I think of her.

How did I get so far so fast? Simple! I did a little research about where to find a theatrical agent first. Hollywood has the most maddening catch twenty-two of all, you can't get the fame you crave without help, but you also can't get that fame unless you're famous already. You can't really blame every single one of the vapid, voluptuous vamps or any of the well-muscled, macho men filling our movie screens for not noticing you. They're just too busy. You got to go out and get that fame yourself. I should talk, I'm the most famous person on earth now and I have as yet accomplished very little here in Hollywood. I should fit in here perfectly.

And how did I do this? I go into the Capitol building off Sunset, you know, that tall building shaped like a pile of yummy concrete and steel pancakes. I talk my way past the security, walk my way into one of the offices and ask the secretary who was the most influential agent here, the one who could get the job done the fastest? After her brain fog wore off, she told me Zach Zaban, who luckily I was told was here today. If it were anyone else but me, I'm sure he wouldn't have been here.

I didn't want to wait, so I just talked my way past Zach's secretary and walked into the office of Zach, who was on the phone and very irritated that I had come into his office without his divine intervention. That was about to change. No one was going to tell Reg what he had to do ever again. "Put the phone down," I ordered mister big shot. And that's all it took, I had my super-agent. I'm sorry it's not as easy for the rest of you, but hey, I have my own problems, too, as you know by now. This middle aged, beard wearing man put the phone down and just looked at me as if looking for his next instruction. I gave it to him. I put a note on his desk for him to read after I left. The note informed him of who I was and that I would be the next big thing. I never imagined how big! The note also had a list of songs that I would sing. He would take care of the licensing if I had to pay to use them. I also informed him that I would not be singing any songs they whipped up for me. I'm not a product! I made this clear from the start. Things will be done my way or not at all. Needless to say, all of my demands were met.

Back to right this moment six months later, I am in my dressing room as I make ready for my concert. My make-up lady already made me up as Ziggy Stardust. Tonight I'm doing some Bowie. I can relate to him. Some thought he really was the man who fell to earth like in his movie. I'm not sure what I am. I am alone now and that is how I like it! Yeah, sure. I had my security, and my assistants and my various handlers, but I was in control, at least I think I was. I wasn't feeling my best lately and I can't figure out why. I think someone in my orbit was not to be trusted. Some of my people just spoke to me and didn't expect me to talk back. So I didn't, that just slowed up the whole process. "Five minutes, Reg," some assistant barks at me from outside my dressing room door. He's not a problem, but which one is? Who cares? I won't care in five minutes. I'll just have another sippy sip of my Jack Daniels. Funny, I never used to drink. Not to worry, I'm not drunk. I have a high tolerance. I've only had half the bottle. I'll save the other half for after the concert. My door just opened. Didn't I tell them not to bother me? I'll come when I'm ready! I feel a presence in the room suddenly. "I know you're here," I say as I look in the mirror and see a hand holding a business card with Luna's face on it reach around in front of me. I don't even bother to look at who is holding the card. I just take the card and look at it, look at my Luna's face, if she is mine anymore? I lost my other cards with her face on them, or they took them. I put my hand on my head. I don't want anyone seeing me like this. "How has it come to this?" I say with my voice cracking. I have everything, everyone says they love me, yet a simple smile is impossible. Have I really come so far when I've fallen so fast? Then I feel a hand on my shoulder as I hear Roger say, "We're here for you." I needed to hear that. Then something miraculous happened ... I smiled. I knew I would soon be free.

Time to hit the stage! I leave my dressing room. I'm accompanied by various handlers and assistants, all talking at me with me saying nothing back to them. They see that I'm not up to giving the best performance of the century, but they don't care. They just have to keep the cash machine going. I could sing anything sober or not and the people would be pleased, at the concert anyway. The people watching at home wouldn't dig it as much. But as they say, the show must go on. Not for long.

I hit the stage and yelled, "Hey, everybody! I'm here to freak you out! What else would you expect from a freak like me? Only one, baby ... only one. I see a lotta fine looking ladies here tonight. I wonder if there are any I know here. I remember one I was sweet on. But my pretty kitty had such sharp claws. I don't think my wounds have healed yet. Some wounds never do." Am I just purging, spilling out my battered soul to an audience who could care less and cheer at anything I say, or was I hoping just one set of ears was here to hear me?

"Don't worry about the security guards you see. They're just here to keep the naked fugly chicks off the stage." I finally began to sing *Space Oddity*, my favorite song from David 'Ziggy Stardust' Bowie. Born the same day as Elvis he was, and gone way too soon just like Big E. They would like my version of *Space Oddity* even better than Bowie's, which to me was just plain wrong. You can't get better than the original and best. It may sound funny, but I like Bowie's version far better than my own. My voice doesn't affect me. That's why Bowie's version; or any version of any other song that I love sounds better to me sung by those who sang it first. I just sing the songs; the true artists are the songs. They give the songs life. Please don't like my versions better, just enjoy them cuz I'm singing them for you.

I finish singing as the band plays on, and one by one the people start to applaud. Such bright smiles, such love in their eyes all for me. How can I ever leave them? But I must. "Yes, that is my favorite from Bowie. So surrealy real! It makes you wonder if Bowie was actually out in space when he wrote *Space Oddity* rather than just after seeing *2001: A Space Odyssey*. You know what other song is my favorite? The song come and get me!! Yeah, you've been a great audience, just like Tura in *Faster Pussycat*; exotic, erotic and just a bit psychotic! But I gotta go!!!" I yell! That was the signal to those here to get the party started. Come get my ass outta here! My hiatus from something resembling reality is over!!! "You ever seen the part in the *Ten Commandments* where they part the Red Sea? Well, that's what I want you to do for me. Everyone, make a part right down the middle. Do it now!!!" I instruct.

Looking out over the slowly parting sea of audience members, I see my Luna standing there at the end. She really is here for me, and I smiled for only the second time since I've been here. I smiled like I had forgotten what a smile was and wanted nothing else but to run to her. So I ran!!! I leaped off the stage and ran to her like a wild, hungry animal after its prey. She was food for my hollow soul. For a body about to collapse, my need and desire only to reach her kept me going–kept me strong! And I did reach her, stopping just to look at her. "Sorry," she only said and that was all I needed to hear. This was no impostor, no phonies like I had been surrounding myself with. I was free! Then we came closer, embracing and melting into each other like nothing else in the world mattered. I had my Luna and any unpleasant memories from the past were gone as if they had never been. Then we smiled at one another, such insanely wide smiles as we grabbed each other's hands and ran hand-in-hand out into the brilliant shimmering light in front of us like the hopeless romantics, the kooky kids we really were. Then I noticed there was no longer a hand holding mine and I stopped. I could only see the light in front of me. Should I go into it? I turned back to see Luna standing there in the middle of the theatre with me still holding onto her with my head drooping over her shoulder. I'm a burden to her once again, but I just can't move. I have the energy to do not one thing more ... but die.

14) RENEWAL and REBIRTH

Welcome to limbo. It must be. I'm walking in a giant white room, if it's even a room. I can't see any walls, only bright, brilliant white in every direction, kind of like in *THX 1138.* I hear voices. I hear them faintly, but I hear them. Where are they coming from? "Where are you?" I yell. "This way," someone says back. But they just spoke it, not even yelling. How could I hear someone so far away if they didn't yell? It's like no matter how far away they were I'd hear them as if they were right beside me. And something else, that voice sounded familiar. "But where are you?" I yell again. "Stop hollerin'. We're right here," he replied. I know that voice. That's the Big E himself. What's he doing here I thought. "How do I find you?" I say in a normal tone of voice. "Stop looking and you shall find," another voice said. And that voice I knew better than any other. That was Jimbo's voice! Morrison's here? "Help me find you. I have to find you!" I pleaded. "Okay, this way," Jimbo said.

So I start to run, only to stop suddenly. They are right there in front of me, Jim Morrison and Elvis playing cards at a white table. Elvis has his white jumpsuit on and fancy sunglasses and Jim has on a nice ruffled shirt and his leather pants, the way I always remembered them.

"Glad to see you, Reg. I've always wanted to meet you," Jimbo says. "Likewise," I reply. "The King raises the Lizard King three tacos," Big E says as he puts three tacos into the pot, which consists of a growing pile of their favorite foods. "Your three ... and I raise this ..." Jimbo says as he puts a coconut cake and a sugar cube into the pot. "Hold it now, don't be slippin' any of them illegal substances in. I heard about them trippy sugar cubes. Ya gotta raise different," Big E says as Jimbo takes back the sugar cube with a sly smile. Then he shoves a peanut butter and banana sandwich and a cheeseburger into the pot. "Be cool and raise me some of them tomato fritters, and some of that monkey bread, too," Big E insists as Jimbo shoves the bread and fritters Big E's way. Then Big E immediately puts five more tacos and a beer into the pot. Then he lays his cards onto the table—four kings! "Start howlin' like a hound dog, baby—four kings! Five if ya count the Big E," Big E says as he slides his winnings his way, taking a bite out of a taco as I just watch them and wonder if this is another one of my spaced-out dreams, or is it really real? "It's as real as you want it to be. How do you see yourself, Reg?" Jimbo asks. "Normal. No one else does, though. Why couldn't I be like you?" I ask. "Why would you wanna be me when you're Reg?" Jimbo asks. "If you read minds, why didn't you know what cards he had?" I ask. "Don't wanna be cheatin' where we are," Big E says as I look around and say, "Yeah, where are we?" "Where we are," Jimbo tells me. I should've expected that kind of answer from him. "Really, where are we?" I ask. "Where do ya wanna be?" Jimbo asks as Big E says, "It's permanent or temporary." "Yeah, it's for you to decide, Reg," Jimbo tells. So if it's not Heaven and it's not Hell, where am I? "Thinkin' out loud again?" Big E smiles. "Your thoughts are your reality," Jimbo informs. "So that's why you're here. You're only here because I want you here. You're not really here at all," I deduce and feel kind of let down suddenly. I didn't know if they were really here or not. "Lonesome, Reg? Don't be. Big E is really here for ya," Big E says as Jimbo jumps in to say, "Don't your eyes see what you want them to see? We really are here for you." "Then why am I here, here right now at this very moment?" I ask. "We existed. We exist now. We will always exist," Jimbo tells. "And we just wanted ta meetcha," Big E says. "Then I have to go back?" I complain. "Luna needs you, Reg," Jimbo reminds. "The whole world needs Reg—and goodbye!" Big E says as he pulls a white lever that appears out of nowhere and I travel through a tunnel as I hear Jimbo say, "Stamp Reg return to sender." Then I hear Big E say, "That boy was a bit more whiney than I'd hoped."

I'm back in my body. "Awaken me with a kiss, my fair princess," I mumble as I wake up in my bed at Joe's house. Luna sits on the bed beside me and caresses my hair. The long rock 'n' roll nightmare was finally over. There was no place on earth I'd rather be. "I think I'm the happiest guy on earth right now," I say as I put my hand out and my Luna takes it. "You think? You have to think about it?" she asks. "I'm not sure, am I really here? I just got to see Jimbo and Elvis! They looked great and lost all the weight. Apparently you can eat whatever you want where they are. They said my thoughts were my reality there. How long have I been sleeping here?" I ask. "All last night and half of today. I know that's more than your usual three hours, but your body needed the rest. The body always knows," she informs. "Thanks for saving me. You don't know how truly lost I was. Hey, I own a big house now, you know, a really big house. Actually, it's not really a house, it's a palace. It used to be owned by an oil sheikh—it's enormous!" I tantalize.

I hear Joe enter the room as he says, "I wouldn't try to go there right now. I only say that because we know how impulsive you are." "No worries, I feel beaten up, and I've never been beaten up. Is this what it feels like? I don't understand why I feel this way," I comment. "You were drugged, just one of the many ways used to control people," he informs. "How do you know I was drugged?" I ask suspiciously. "We took a sample of your blood," Luna surprises. "Well, thanks, Dracula! You just did that to find out more about me, didn't you?" I ask. "We did it to find out if you were poisoned!" she informs as Joe says, "And luckily you were not poisoned. You did have enough barbiturates in your system to have killed anyone else on this planet, though. Your blood is like no other. You must have been aware of that." "Why would I? I've never been to the doctor," I say to dumbfounded faces. "In your hundred years you've never been to the doctor? How bout the hospital? You must have gone for covid, or for an injury or something," she interrogates. "Well, I went once when I was careless with a tree branch and a crosscut saw—ouch! They fixed me up. I told them to forget and I took all the bloody gauze. I didn't want anyone cloning me," I jest. Then I notice Joe and Luna looking at me like something's wrong. "Is there something you're not telling me? Do I have one foot in the grave and the other one on a banana peal? What? What! Let's have it," I must know. "They think you might have been kidnapped," she tells. "They?" I ask.

"The police!" she says. "Oh, those police. Why would they think that? We ran out holding hands," I recall imperfectly as she looks oddly at me. "Those controlling you are accusing us. You need to get your strength back, but you also need to make a statement to the media saying you were rescued, not kidnapped," Joe explains. "Would you do that for us, Reg?" Luna asks with those beautiful eyes that see right through me. Of course I would. I would do anything for you goes through my mind. She smiles. She knows. "That's not all I'm gonna do for you. I'm gonna give you my palace. You can put all the star children you want in there," I tantalize. "That is a wonderful gesture, but I am quite sure they own the property and all your other assets by now," he says somberly. I laugh it up. "Why do you constantly underestimate me? Every time big money changed hands, I let them do the deal and then I made them forget; bank accounts, crypto, all the code numbers ... they know nothing, like Sergeant Shultz," I say as I tap my head. "It's all up here. Why do you think they want me back? They realize they have nothing without me," I explain. "These people can be very persuasive," Joe cautions. "You mean torture my ass, dont'cha?" I ask. "It's an unfortunate possibility," Joe tells. "I'll give you access to one of my accounts. Beef up security with it or anything else you wanna do with it. I'm gonna marry your daughter, you know," I say to surprise everyone. "Shouldn't you ask me about that?" she asks. You never told me you loved me before. Tell me you don't now and I'll walk away. I'll never be happy again, but I'll walk away. She taps my brain again and tells me, "I'll say it when I'm ready. Please don't fly off again," she pleads. "I put you on a pedestal, you know. Always put a beautiful woman on a pedestal," I jest. "Why, so you can see up her dress?" she smiles. "I wasn't gonna say that ... not now," I smile. "At least he has his sense of humor back. I better go and get the ball rolling on your little problem," Joe says as he starts to go but stops when I say, "Joe. Thanks for getting me outta there. You didn't have to," "Indeed I did," he says before leaving the room. Yeah, that's sincerity alright. I think I like Joe after all. "Hey, let's arm wrestle. I'll show you I'm alright," I say as I put my elbow on the bed near Luna with my hand up. She rolls her eyes and takes my hand. This oughta be a snap. I'll just show her who's really strong and—oh, crap! My arm is going the wrong way. She beat me? I can't believe it! "Believe it!" her mind taps. "I need a protein drink," I deduce. "You need a lotta protein drinks. Stay in the bed!" she says as she gets up to leave. "I really missed you," I say truthfully. She comes back over and whispers in my ear, "I wore out my vibrator waiting for you," she says with a wink and a smile before leaving the room.

I don't know if I'm asleep, nor do I feel awake. You know that feeling when your eyes just pop open in the middle of the night and you don't know if you're still awake or not? That's how I feel right now. I just don't know. There's nothing that I can do about it, but that's okay. I just feel so good. I don't think I've ever felt this good before, felt this way before. I feel rays of brilliant light with ripples of multicolored light emanating from my head. I see them. The light is so bright, yet it hurts not my eyes. My hairs are standing on end, they're reaching out. But how can I see this? Now I know how! I'm standing outside of my body as I look at myself asleep in my bed. I just stand here and look at myself. Why is such a simple thing so fascinating?

I walk to Luna's room. I want her to see this. I walk right through her door. I stand beside her bed. I can't touch her. I can tell her with my mind! Luna, wake up, her mind hears. She opens her eyes. She looks so sleepy. She looks eerily surprised suddenly when she sees me. It's so dark in the room. My body looks like me but transparent. My ethereal body is outlined with energy, like crackling electric sparks. I just smile and motion to her with my hand for her to follow me. Come, I want you to see something, my mind tells hers. She gets out of bed in her long shirt and follows me. I walk right through her door again. She opens it and follows me down the hall to where I am sleeping in my bed. She just looks at my body, the bright rays of light emanating through my head and through my floating hair. I walk back into my body now. Touch me. I want you to feel what I'm feeling, my mind tells her. She gets on her knees in front of me and puts her hands on my legs. Soon the energy flowing through my body flows through hers also. Her head tilts back and her mouth drops open as her long, beautiful hair rises up and spreads out while brilliant light flows up through it. This is beyond bliss, our souls are touching. All feelings and thoughts positive and comforting flow between us. We are one.

I'mmmmm up! I hopped out of bed. No one else is around. Why should they be? It's still dark. I wander the halls alone. I feel like I used to feel when I walked the halls alone in my old house in Hollywood, where Otto and I had so many good times. I'll have to see him soon. He must think I've forgotten him. It suddenly dawns on me why I feel this way. I feel great! That's how I felt when I walked my own halls. I was healthy and strong then and now I am again, but how? Then I remember my dream. Was it just a dream?

Being that I felt so much better than the day before, I decided to work-out in the house gym. Since I was away from any gym for six months, I decided to do my Steve Reeves full body work-out; hit all the muscles from the shoulders down. The more I exercised, the thirstier I got, constantly chugging down protein drinks. It's like my muscles knew what they wanted and I gave it to them. My body must have had the most perfect form of muscle memory one can have because I didn't have to wait months, or weeks or even days; I could see my muscles getting bigger and feel myself getting stronger in real time. I suddenly needed to know where I came from. My people must be like me; they must be superior.

As I pose shirtless in the mirror, I see Luna come in looking astonished at what she sees, a former shell of a man now chiseled perfection. I didn't even hear her come in. "You were at death's door yesterday ... how is this possible?" she says what her mind can't comprehend. "I don't know. I can't figure out why I can do any of the things I do. I just can." I say so confidently. "I was going to suggest you go back to bed, but ... how do you feel today?" she asks. "Never better. I had this incredible dream last night, not like any of the apocalyptic energy sapping dreams I usually have. This dream gave me strength. Maybe it was because you were in it," I say happily to the object of my affections. "I don't think it was a dream, Reg," she informs. "Why are you over there? I know you wanna be over here. Your mind tells me so," I tell to amaze her further. "Then what am I thinking?" she asks, already knowing the answer. "You came for the code numbers for the bank account. I'm sending them to you now. I don't want them written down," I say as I walk right up to her. As I just stare at her, she doesn't look me in the eyes. "I think you're evolving, Reg," she mystifies. "We're evolving," I reply as I kiss her. She likes it. She wants more, but something else is on her mind, the bank numbers. She breaks from me, shaky and breathing hard. "I want to, really I do ... I just have to use the numbers, the numbers to get you that security," she says as she rushes out of the gym. Evolving am I? I hope that's a good thing. With me, you never know ...

15) MAKE ROOM FOR REG

After I simply talked my way past the guards at the gate, Luna drove the hippie van down the long driveway to get to my palace, which kind of looked like a combination of the Taj Mahal and some ancient castle. It was a nice big spread—all mine! Or soon to be mine. After Joe and Joe's attorneys contacted the occupants of my once and future palace, Joe found out to his dismay that Mel, the head of security, had barricaded himself in the safe room in the middle of the huge house. Now most safe rooms in most houses are dinky little claustrophobic spaces to keep you safe in times of emergency. My safe room was as spacious as a small house, with a bathroom, closets for extra food and even a film library. It even had a steel door that you'd need a bazooka to open. Mel could hold up for months without coming out for anything! But being I was even more devious than Mel, I had a rather simple but sinister solution for meddling Mel, which was only to be found in the works of Edgar Allen Poe or a Vincent Price movie. Nuff said! Wait till you see.

Several security guards walk around the house and look suspiciously at the hippie van. After all, it didn't belong there. I talked to them over the loudspeaker on the top of the van and said, "Listen up, contestants! Would all security goons and evil henchmen please walk over to the van you see painted with all the fab, psychedelic colors? Isn't it just like, groovy, man? Get your asses over here—vamonos!" I yell and like in pick your favorite zombie movie, the walking security zombies all came toward the van, two of which came rather suddenly because they came off the roof. First time I knew security was up there. So we hop out of the van as the security zombies come our way. "Everyone! Leave! Don't come back! Outenzee!" I simply say through my bullhorn and problem solved. "You still gotta get rid of the ones on the inside," Luna advises. "No, really? I'll do that as you call your dad. Tell him to send in my special delivery," I say as I rub my hands together and act all sinister.

After Luna gives me that what is he up to look, I go into my palace. One of the internal security dudes says, "You are back, sir." "Yes, I am!!!" I say loudly without my bullhorn as my voice reverberates all over the house and up the spiral staircase to anywhere my voice would reach. "Yeeee-haaaaa! Everybody, listen up! Don't be procrastinatin' or hesitatin', just come on down!" I so ordered. And soon they came, most of my security and the staff, some rolling down the stairs. Meanwhile, Luna comes in and looks with fascination at the mind-numbed mass of employees moving my way. "Kind of reminds you of *Dawn of The Dead*, doesn't it? Except they won't bite you, unless I tell 'em to," I chuckle. "Why did you order a bunch of bricks? What are you up to?" she inquires. "Hey, I have an idea, why don't I just stick my brain in your head? It'll save a lot of time," I remarked about her constant brain invasions. "Didn't have to! I looked inside the truck outside. You're not gonna do with those bricks what I think you're gonna do, are you?" she asks. "Why not? Vincent Price would love it," I tantalize.

So after clearing out the old staff and bringing in a few of our own people, it was time to get down to dealing with Mel locked in the safe room. Joe showed up to show a little gravitas to the situation, and because Mel didn't like me. There was a security camera that overlooked the safe room area so Mel would know if anyone tried to get into it while he was there. My plan was to not get in.

Joe calls Mel inside the safe room. "Congratulations! You found my number. I'm not leaving till I get what I came for," Mel informs as he quickly puts on a pair of headphones. "And what exactly is that, Mel?" Joe asks. "Ask Reg, he knows. You might have more success conversing with him," Mel tells. Joe takes the phone away from his head and covers it so Mel can't hear as he asks me, "What does he want?" "He wants the palace. I can understand him asking for money, but the palace? I don't get it," I wonder. "We might have to get the police involved. There's no way to get that door off. That is a vault door. If you used a torch or explosives, you would do major damage to this structure and he knows it. We ought to make a deal with him," Joe suggests. "Why doesn't Reg just tell him to leave?" Luna suggests. "Because he just put those headphones on. There's something about them that nullifies my voice. It was something they were working on. So, you see, I can't. Besides, he might have explosives in there to blow up the place if we tried to get in, which means there's one and only one way to do this," I inspire Joe to say, "Yes, to get him to come out." "And I have just the way," I say with the biggest Joker-like smile.

So we ignore Mel as bricks are brought in by a workman and a professional bricklayer. Seeing my plan underway, I grab Luna by the hand and rush her up to my giant room upstairs. We go in and she marvels on how big it is. "Spacious! You could practically fit another house just in this room. I didn't say this is the room I wanted, though," she quibbles. "But it's already got all my stuff in it already; some exercise equipment in the corner there, and look at this bed! This bed is so big you could have two girls in it and they'd never meet each other," I tempt. "Uh huh, if you want me in this picture, there isn't going to be another entity added to this relationship, just thought I'd make that clear," she says firmly. "So you're admitting this is a relationship we're having?" I ask with a smirk. "I wouldn't be here if it wasn't," she pleases.

We just smile at each other, the smile that says something good is about to happen. Then without warning, I scoop her up, rush over to my bed and toss her onto it. She goes along happily without protest. She rolls over and just gives me her sexiest look. At this point any look at all would work for me. She slithers around on the giant bed and beckons me hither toward her. I stood and wondered what to do next? Uh, you believed that?

Time passes. Joe bursts into our room! Like dopes we didn't lock it. He walks right up to us. We're luckily under the covers currently and just a bit surprised to see him. "You know why I'm here, don't you?" Joe asks without a smile. "Daddy, can't this wait? This is just a little bit inappropriate, don't you think?" she asks. "You mean my being here or his? You are not going to brick that man up like in Poe's *The Cask of Amontillado,*" Joe figures out. "We won't have to. He'll give in before it's too late. Wouldn't you?" I ask. "I can't get your bricklayer, that huge sumbitch to stop!" Joe complains. "Of course, I told him not to stop, and he has wax in his ears. Hey, relax. We'll be down shortly to deal with the Mel situation, okay?" I ask to cool down daddio. Joe crosses his arms defiantly and won't leave. "We deal with it now!" he means business. "So you think just because we're not dressed we won't get up to face you?" I ask. Joe doesn't move or blink. "Well, you're right. Your dad's no dummy. Look, Joe, Mel is the reason I was deprived for six months of what I'm enjoying now. I was miserable, and from what I hear your daughter wasn't too happy either. I want that bastard to suffer!" I mean really mean. Joe uncrosses his arms but still stands there. "False imprisonment is a serious crime, Reg. You can't just keep him here. This can't end well," Joe informs. "I'm not keeping him here. He's keeping him here. If we call the cops, they'll just have to blow the door off and screw up my palace," I tell as Luna jumps in to suggest, "What if I sent him a mental suggestion? I'll just put in his head that we mean business; we'll leave him in there." "Okay, come do that," Joe agrees. "Now? But I haven't licked chocolate off her entire body yet," I smile to totally irritate Joe and completely mortify my girlfriend, who slides down to cover her face. "I'll be right outside the door. Hurry it up!" Joe says as he walks out of the massive warehouse-like room, exiting the door as he reminds us, "I'll be right outside the door!" Joe's right outside the door now—I'm sure of it! Luna and I just look at each other—ready for more! I reach over for her when a muffled voice says, "I'm right outside the door!" I stop reaching and flop back onto the bed. Gotta remember to lock that door.

Luna and I come downstairs now to join Joe, and possibly invisible Roger. I can never tell. I see the brick wall getting higher, and everyone working on it is wearing protective headphones and wax in their ears just for me. "Glad to see you are on your feet again, both of you. Now get on with it," Joe orders. Luna whispers into the ear of her dad, who then gets on the phone and calls Mel. While polite conversation ensues, Luna sends the mental message to Mel, "You may as well have booked a room with the pharaohs because you'll never leave when that wall is finished." Suddenly, Mel sounds oddly uneasy. Luna takes my hand and leads me out of the room.

"It's done. I hope it worked. Why didn't you send him a message? You mentally sent me the account numbers yesterday," she ponders. "I haven't been able to do it since then," I mystify. "If you did it once, you can do it again. It's like a muscle, you have to work it out to get better at it," she explains. "I'm just glad the crowd isn't here today," I half tell. "The crowd?" she asks. "Yeah, thousands of people show up outside the palace every day," I say, a bit annoyed. "And you want us to stay here?" she complains. "I just tell them to go away every day. They won't leave me alone. I wish I'd never left home sometimes," I complain. "You can't put the genie back in the bottle, Reg. When one door closes another opens, it's called opportunity," she instructs. "Speaking of opportunity, what is it Joe wants from me next, to speak to another big group who really just want another hit of Reg voice? I may as well just sing, like I've been doing," I express. "That's a great idea! You can empower the people in between songs, you know, just sneak it in," she suggests. "So I just tell the people to stop hating each other, and to end global warming and all that fun stuff? You know what I think about that? I think the sun's gonna keep shining and the haters will keep hating. Please don't put all the world's problems on my shoulders. I am no one's messiah," I admit.

We suddenly hear Mel screaming from the other room. We rush in to see him with his hands on top of the small area that the bricks have yet to cover. Mel pleads to let him out as the bricklayer now uses a sledgehammer to knock down the wall that he just put up so professionally. After enough of the wall is broken down, Mel stands sweating and breathing hard before us without the headphones on now. Then he sees me and moves to close the vault door again. "Stop, Mel!" is all I said to end his hasty retreat. We had the workman drag him out. Then Joe overpaid them so they would leave and keep their mouths shut. After security interrogated Mel without me and my voice to interfere, I came back, told him to forget and no lawsuits either. Then we just sent him on his way. Wouldn't it be great if all problems were handled so easily? And now the joint was ours; no more Mel and hopefully no more big problems.

I sit and watch the TV in my room in my new palace. A couple of weeks have gone by and everyone's all settled in to where they want to be. I live on the top floor with Luna, of course. Being restless, I go downstairs to find something to do. I now have a huge place and lots of free time on my hands, which doesn't always end well where I'm concerned and I freely admit. Anyway, as I came down the staircase, there she was coming through the front doors. She never had to touch them because it looked like someone was opening them for her. She just walked in with all the grace and style of the most seasoned runway model, but not too fast. She strolled in slowly as she looked over the place. Then her eyes met mine. She stopped dead in her tracks and just smiled at me with the most alluring smile I had ever seen, possibly even to rival Luna's. I shouldn't be thinking that, but I am. I can't help it. I just stood there with one hand on the staircase. She wasn't coming to me, I had to go to her and she knew I would. I had to at least say something to put people under my spell. All she needed was a look! So I walked over to her, not too fast to give her the impression I was interested, but she knew I was. Long dark hair, the most piercing eyes, a body and face suitable for any Greek sculpture—she had it all! She was no snack. She was the whole meal! And class, she wore a short dress, but not too short like she came for a job interview. She did in a way. She wanted in, and one look at her and she knew that's what I wanted, too! I stand before her. As if I have a brain freeze, I can't think of anything to say or my mouth just won't work. I had babe paralysis big time! I just keep looking into those eyes of hers. Hey, maybe she's a vampire. "I'm Annowre," she smiles as she puts her hand out for me. I take it and immediately get a shiver but in a good way; and I mean in a really good way all the way up and down my spine, and I'm almost certain she knew it. I tried to act cool as if nothing happened, but her twisting smile told me she knew otherwise. She had me in her vise and she loved it! "I'm Reg," I barely replied as she released my hand now and simply said, "I know." Thank God, if she held it any longer I would be embarrassing myself in the most obvious physical way a dude can. "My voice doesn't affect you," I amazed. "It makes love to my ears," she said and she did look satisfied, the way that just rolled off the tongue and those lips of hers. Geez, I better snap out of it! "Why are you here ... exactly?" I wondered. "I belong here," she said so confidently. "I can see that, but I'm not the only one who decides that," I say. I can see that, really? Am I hitting on her already? Is it just me or can no one help themselves around her? "I'm scheduled for an interview. I know I am early. I do try never to come too early," she tells soooooo alluringly. Was that a come on? Of course it was, she's screwing with me. Strangely enough I'm not complaining. "So they're expecting you?" I babbled. She just nods yes, her eyes dancing all over my body. This I liked. Get a hold of yourself. Someone please come for me before I make a total fool of myself. Luna, help me! And I guess my mental request did indeed reach Luna because she walked out of Joe's new office downstairs, looking around and looking puzzled. There was more going on here than I could see on the surface and Luna knew it. She walked straight over to us and just looked at us. "What's going on?" she says puzzled. I don't know what to say. Then Annowre just turns her head and looks right into Luna's eyes. "Do you know her?" Luna asks accusingly. "We just met. She just came in. She can speak with me. She's one of us," I say excitedly, but

Luna is extremely suspicious of her, even cautious as Annowre reaches out to shake Luna's hand. "I'm Annowre," she tells as Luna apprehensively puts her hand out, grasping Annowre's hand for only a mere moment before yanking her hand away. "She's not one of us. She's one of them. Succubus!!!" Luna yells as she backs up and points her finger at her, yelling succubus! Succubus! Over and over until the family members all flooded out of their rooms and approached cautiously. Meanwhile, Joe is walking up behind Luna, most probably wondering what's going on just like I was wondering. "I'm sorry, I don't know what she's doing," I say to Annowre as she just smiles devilishly at me and I see her eyes go totally black for a moment before turning back to normal. That was something I'd never seen before. I don't think I liked it.

Annowre suddenly moved towards Joe. "Don't let it touch him!" Luna yells! But before anyone could grab her, Annowre simply swatted my Luna to the ground on one side of her and easily shoved me away on her other side. Then she laid her hand on Joe's chest, his body shivering before he fell agonizingly to the floor. I didn't believe what I was seeing and I didn't understand it. Luna jumps up and goes immediately to the aid of her father. The other star children gathered round as I saw the huge double doors slamming shut as if by a gust of wind, my eyes not catching who just went through them. I look at the others as if to say you saw it, too? Then we realized Annowre was gone.

Joe lies helpless on the floor unable to move. "Necklace," he manages to say as Luna instantly knows what to do. She has me lift up Joe as she slips off his necklace of animal teeth and lays it in a circle about his chest, making sure it makes good contact with his skin. As we all watch tenuously, the necklace weaves its magic and puts a smile on Joe's face. Now everyone was smiling.

Joe puts the necklace back around his neck and holds out his hand as Luna and my baffled self help him to his feet. "That was close! But why did she try to kill you? Why not Reg?" Luna wonders. "In war, you take out the leaders first, the generals before the enlisted men. And this is a war," Joe explains. "What's all this succubus business? Why'd you call her that, just because she's hot?" I ask. "Put your drool bucket away, she wasn't even human. Do you even know what a succubus is?" she asks. "Sure, I saw the Cassavettes movie. And since you're into mystical crap, maybe she was a sorceress? "Annowre was the name of the sorceress that tempted King Arthur, but he rejected her. Sorceress, wanna bet?" I ask with my book learnin' showing. "Wow! Have any other useless information?" Luna says to totally disrespect me. I just look at her a bit. Then I walk out the front doors.

I'm standing outside by the garden for not thirty seconds when I see Luna rush out the front doors and look for me. She looks relieved when she sees me, probably because I didn't take off again. It did cross my mind. She walks up to me, looks at me and then hugs me. Then she grabs me and kisses me. "Is that don't run off insurance?" I ask with a half smile. "Can't I just let my man know he's my man?" she asks to make me even more suspicious that I'm being used. I look at the bees in the garden. "We ought to get a beekeeper. We can make our own honey," I suggest. "That's a great idea! Let's do that," she says overly happy. "How 'bout we drive monster trucks through the garden? You gonna just agree with everything I say now?" I inquire as I smile at her. "You are so fickled. And I should know, I'm a woman. I'm just trying to make you happy," she admits. "You're just trying to keep me here. You know, when I was in my Hollywood home, all I felt was being trapped there. Now I just wanna get out, go places, see all the things I've never seen. That's all I want," I purge. "Tell me, when you go on a trip, do you plan your trip and pack your suitcase or just head out the door aimlessly?" she says to me, the one who never packs or picks a direction. "Okay, maybe that was the wrong question for you. We can go do things together. We just need to..." I interrupt to say, "I know! Take a bunch of bodyguards and an armored vehicle everywhere so no one who loves me won't get too close to me, to love me to death," I say with dismay. "It's an unfortunate fact of life for you now, but can you think of another way?" she asks, thinking I couldn't possibly have an answer for her. "How 'bout disguises?" I say with a big dumb smile. "Are you serious?" she says to my happy face. "You are serious. There's no talking you out of this, is there?" she asks. "We can go out on a date; get something to eat, see a movie, go to a disco. No one will be able to hear me there," I tantalize. "Do I wear a disguise, too?" she asks. "I think just me wearing one's enough," I say without thinking. "You know, everyone knows I hang out with you. So when they see me, aren't they going to assume that it's you that's with me?" she logically asks. "Okay, we can both wear disguises," I assume. "So, I can just wear, like, a big, dumb hat and sunglasses disguise that looks like I'm wearing a big, dumb hat and sunglasses disguise, which would, of course, fool everyone who's staring at the dummies trying to fool everyone with the dumb disguises, is that about it?" she says sooooo sarcastically. "You're not talking me out of it," I say and walk away.

Nightfall. Luna and my bad self are getting ready to go out for a night of fun and weirdness in Hollyweird. No one could talk me out of it—so we're going! Joe and Aphrodite, wearing headphones, walk out of his office up to me. "Reg, before you have your night of fun, would you do us one small favor? Say something to Aphrodite, would you?" He asks. "What's the point? She won't be answering me," I assume. Aphrodite immediately answers back, "It works!" I look a bit amazed. Then I recognize Mel's special headphones that Aphrodite is wearing. "You finally got 'em to work again, huh?" I remark. "You mean those headphones are blocking his voice?" Luna asks. "Oh, I can hear him, his voice just doesn't make me all loopy," Aphrodite remarks. "Is that what Mel was working on before, the technology to block your voice? Do they mask your voice? I don't think they could find your frequency, if you have one?" Luna wonders. "I don't know how they work. They used a bunch of my money for research and development on them. They said they were for the band so they could play without my voice affecting them while I sang," I explain. "Reg, do you know who made them?" Joe asks. "Lemme think, not Radio Shack. Some electronics wizard made them. They were Frankensteined up, assembled from used parts. I noticed that when the band was wearing them," I tell. "We're going to have to talk to Mel and the one who made them. We can't have these where just anyone could get their hands on them," Joe figures. "So we had Mel right here and now we have to get him back here again?" Luna surmises. "Or, we can just screw it and go have fun before Mel comes back to steal our women and rape our cows," I say to mystified faces. "Just trying to speed things along. Hasn't anyone here seen *Blazing Saddles*?" I say as I head for the front door.

16) RAVE TO THE GRAVE

Luna drives us around in the hippie van in Hollywood. We've both been unusually quiet. Nope, I can't probe her thoughts like she does mine. "Yes, you can. You're just not trying," she informs me. "If I can do what you do, why can't you do what I do?" I ask. "I'll work on it," she blows me off and says, "Lets go to that disco," she inspires. "Ain't no Studio 54 in this town. Why don't we wait till it's dark and find a rave?" I ask. "Aphrodite and I used to rave all the time. You know how we did it?" she asks. "Gee, you two aren't the ugliest buzzards around. Lemme guess, bored Hollywood rich kids fawned all over you, trying to dazzle you with how vapid they were to take you out?" I ask. "That happened, of course, but I just did it the same way I found you at the mall, a simple crowd scan. I'm disappointed you didn't figure that out with that big, bad brain bulging out of your head," she quips. "And are you glad you found me?" I inquire with a smile. "I haven't decided yet," she smiles back. She pulls the hippie van over near a place where all the night creatures meet, all the youthful peccadillo ponies waiting to be ridden in the right direction. She just sat there looking them over, undoubtedly probing the craniums of anyone that looked hip enough or fashionable enough to go to a rave. "Okay! Wanna get something to eat first?" she asks as I curiously inquire, "You found one, a rave?" "Sure. Some of us don't have to shout things from a mountaintop to get attention," she smirks with the intention of saying her power is every bit as important as mine. I never said it wasn't, Professor Xavier. She just smiles at me. Her power was frightening! Especially over me.

After our feast of roast beast, or some equally greasy, gooey, gobble down goodies, we head to the rave. After parking the van, we headed for the super secret entrance. Yeah, I've been to raves before, mostly in the nineties. Most raves are in rented warehouses or big areas that were just taken over. Most organized raves have some big dudes at the door to keep out the icky cheugies, and hopefully really bad dancers. Our rave had a big metal door to breach first. I pounded on the door three times. The metal window in the door slid open and a dude with a pushed-in face was staring back at us. His eyes paid no attention to me, which meant he wasn't gay or just had no taste. His brow raised like John Belushi when he saw Luna, though. He calmly asked, "Password?" "Let me in or I'll huff, and I'll puff and blow your big ass door down," I said with a grin. After my voice started to wear off, pushed-in face opened the door for us. As we walked into the increasing wall of sound, a voice nearby said, "Hey, that's Reg." I just put my finger to my mouth and gave out a long shush. Even my shushes soothe the mind of any man or beast.

We proceed to our night of fun. "I have an odd feeling," Luna warns. "I thought only Aphrodite got those," I assume. "Just watch out. This is the perfect place for you to get in trouble," she double warns. "All one has to watch out for here is the gawky awkwards and roofies," I'm pretty sure. As we proceed into the ever widening crowd of light-stick swinging groovy ghoulies, we both notice that about half the crowd recognize us or me anyway. "I told ya this would happen," Luna expresses as we hear "It's Reg" somewhere in the crowd. And as if they were all curious fireflies lighting about us, all the ravers rave over toward us and then slowly gather around us. The DJ's music still played, yet the only motion seen was all the eyes darting about in our direction. A lone cute girl walked right up to me, quietly smiling at me as if waiting to see which of us would break the silence first. Then she reached over and touched me. Then one-by-one everyone started to touch me. Luna just watched in amazement. It was almost like a religious experience. It reminded me of *Zardoz* when they're all touching Zed. It's as if they were all touch learning, seeing what they could learn from Reg without him speaking. Then it had to happen, one horny raver boy just had to touch Luna, my Luna! She was not into the touching, especially when it was more accurately described as a breast exam. So she cocked that fist back and gave grabby boy a Clint Eastwood right into the camera, or nose—and POW! The bitch boy went down! My girl can hit! Our little action scene didn't go unnoticed as several security thugs rushed over and started getting grabby with me. I just flung two of the burly bison boys into the crowd as I yelled, "Lay off!!!" Yep, all the crowd and all the security guys went still, except for one middle-aged security guy who looked around like, totally surprised, my gosh! "What did you do to them?" he asked as I noticed the hearing aids he was wearing. "I just did what I do. If you're wondering why you're not like them, it's your choice of ear candy. You like money?" I ask as I pull out my carrying around big bucks wad and peel off a few hundred dollar bills and slap them into the hand of the one happy hearing-aided guy as I tell him, "Here. Get 'em to play some disco music, seventies disco. I can't dance to this shit!" "Who are you?" he says, more than a little surprised. "Have you been living in a cave on a desert island? I'm Reg. The seventies disco please?" I ask more than asking. He gives me the thumbs up and goes to find some music that will hopefully let me and Luna boogie with some extra oogie.

I turn to my maiden fair now. "Ready to get down!" I lay down. "If they leave us alone," she jabs. I guffaw and throw up my arms to address the crowd as I announce to all ravers, "Listen up! We are gonna dance and you are gonna dance. No more Reg love tonight, just have a good time!" Suddenly *Disco Inferno* by the Trammps starts to rock the house. "Yes! I hope it's the ten minute version," I add as I start to move and Luna starts to groove. I guess the ravers dug it, too, cuz they were moving with moves I hadn't seen before. It's been a while since the nineties. I love this. I absolutely love this! I'm with my Luna. I'm having a great time. I didn't forget my *Saturday Night Fever* moves. Luna's eyeing me up and down. Yeah, I dig her, too. Yes, I do!

Out of the corner of my eye, I see a young dude walk up to me, open his gloved hand and blow some powder in my direction as he says, "Take a trip, Reg." Luckily Luna is dancing several feet in front of me now and backs up even more as the powder mists all about me and several other ravers near me. I stop and stare off into space, feeling euphoric and totally strange. I'm a statue, yet the ravers around me are dropping to the ground like dive bombing asteroids crashing violently into the earth. Then I see Luna, the look of horror frozen on her face. Was I just poisoned? Why am I not crashing, too? "Reg, we gotta go," she tells me. "Go? Where do we go?" I say in a dreamy haze that seems so totally natural. Then I start to feel sick. I bend over with my hands on my knees. I hear my Luna talking, but I don't think she's talking to me. I straighten up. Oh, the phone, she's on the phone. I stumble away. I think I'm going to die, while I also feel such ecstasy. Yet I have the sensation of falling, falling as if from the greatest height imaginable, and what happens after the fall? You crash. You die. Or was I just fading away? I'm here for a reason—yeah! Me and Superman, we're here for a reason! I can't go this way. I stop, defiant in what destiny wants for me. I'm in control. "I'm in control!" I yell without realizing it. "That's right, Reg, fight it! Expel the poison from your body," Luna instructs me. Why is she keeping a distance from me? "You might have fentanyl on you. I don't have any Narcan. Help is coming," she reassures me. My Luna's reading me even now. It doesn't bother me anymore.

I wonder about the crowd now. No one wants to touch me anymore. They keep moving away from me. Why is he not dead? I hear in their heads. Hey, yeah, that's right! I can hear everyone's thoughts like Luna. I'm not supposed to do that. What's happening to me? I'm evolving again. Does something terrible always have to happen to me to get me to learn anything anymore? I feel like I'm falling again—I am falling!

I suddenly see something I thought I'd never see again, myself. My glowing astral body just went walkabout outside my body again, just like that night my astral body visited Luna in her room. Everybody is looking at me again, a bit more strangely this time. Now I know where that expression shock and awe comes from, they're either in shock or awe. They simply can't believe what they're seeing. I'm getting used to all the weird shit. Can't wait to see what happens next. Let's go see ...

As my compromised flesh just lies there on the cold ground away from an ever widening circle of Reg lovers who wanted no more to do with him, sparkly me lifts off to the sky, flying around the night sky like that glowing car in *Repo Man*. How come my astral body is so visible? I don't know if I'll ever see my body down earth way ever again. I'll just let it heal, whilst this me discovers the universe. I can now. I seem to be able to fly around as fast or as slow as I desire. The final frontier, let's take a trip out into space. I hear it's just the place.

Passing the moon now. I don't see any of those Martians on Mars, just a few giant faces. Yep, Jupiter is a big ass planet. It has rings like Saturn, too. George Harrison would love my next destination. Here comes the sun. Pretty impressive for a big ball of gas. I hover right before it, yet I feel no heat. I am not blinded by its light. This body was made to last! "Awesome, isn't it?" I hear Roger say as I look over to see him hovering nearby. "Checking up on me?" I ask. "One can get lost out here. What seems like minutes can be days. You've already been gone, like, three days. Everyone's worried about you," he informs. "Luna too?" I must know. "Especially her. I can show you all the cool places one night, things you thought never existed," he tantalizes. "How soon can I get back from this far out?" I ask. "Yeah, this is far out, man. Just click your heels and you'll be back from Oz," he says as I decide in an instant where I want to be.

"Boo!" I say as I sit up in my bed surrounded by Luna, Hawaiian Joe and a nurse who's not talking. They jumped a little. I flop back down and just smile at Luna. She smiles back. I thought maybe she'd want to punch me. "I don't want to punch you. A severe ass whooping, maybe? How are you feeling?" she asks sincerely. I breath in a big breath of beautiful air. "I feel great! Nothing like a good solar charge. Those cosmic rays made me even more sparkly, must be good for me. Say, why are all other astral travelers invisible, but I sparkle? Maybe I'm like the vamps in *Twilight*?" I mused. "Yeah! That must be it," she humors me. "Why am I in pajamas?" I curious. "Your body had to be cleaned of all toxins from head to toe, my boy," Joe informs. "Not by you I hope," I really, really hoped. "By a hazmat team. You were sprayed with enough fentanyl to kill a heard of elephants. They still can't figure out why you are still alive," he informed. "Disappointed? Hey, I've been bitten by a cobra and a rattler and survived, hence I'm still here," I tell. "It's nothing to joke about, Reg. Five people died, almost six," Luna informs somberly. "You now see what your night of fun brought you?" Joe asks as if it's my fault again. "Yeah, it's my fault again. Everything's my fault," I complain. "No one is assigning blame. We are just saying how dangerous it is whenever you leave this place unaccompanied," Joe scolds. "So I need a chaperone to go anywhere? I think I'll take another trip into outer space. I'll stay here, while sparkly me goes to Rigel 4, that okay?

And if you call me my boy again, I'm gonna start calling you old fart. Here comes old fart Joe!" I make clear. "Let's not give him a hard time. He's had a hard enough time—how come you didn't ask if any fentanyl got on me?" she asks. "So much for hard times. I was gonna ask! Did it?" I ask. "A little. I'm fine. The first girl that touched you was the one who survived," she informs. "I'm glad ... for both of you," I say as we both smile. "She wants to thank you when you're okay," Luna confuses. "Thank me! For what?" I couldn't imagine. "I think she just wanted to see you again. You know, a lot of those kids whipped out their phones to film you when you were floating around like that. The whole world knows how different you are, maybe too different, if you know what I mean?" she asks. "So they're all gonna break out the torches and pitchforks and storm the castle for me, eh? Kill the Reg monster! He's too, too different. We can't have that!" I assume. "The people still love you, Reg, possibly more than ever. They have held a vigil around this palace since the moment they heard of your illness. They won't leave. I'm afraid only you can get them to go," Joe informs. "No, problem. I used to tell them to adios every day when Mel was here, I remind. "When you are ready, you might want to speak to those outside. I hate to think of what might happen if they suddenly decided to check on you personally," he scares. "Hey, I bet that Fentanyl did get on you. You're immune to it like me. I could probably chug cyanide and eat rat poison, too. The Three Stooges did it all the time," I say as they look at me like I've lost my mind for sure. "You certainly aren't immune to stupid ideas. You do realize the Stooges didn't really eat rat poison. Please tell me you know that," she says anxiously waiting for an answer, so I tell her, "They ate a lot of moth balls, chalk and bars of soap, too! I guess it was quicker than washing with it." I just look at her, waiting for her to catch on that I'm just screwing with her. Then I smile and she smiles—fun time over!

I jumped out of bed. I stand there in my goofy duckies and bunnies pajamas as I ask, "Do these make me look sexy?" "Oh, definitely," Luna piles on the baloney. "Then why aren't you wearing them?" I ask as I head for the bathroom.

Dressed appropriately now in striped shorts and a Spock shirt, I come out of the palace roof entrance to address the crowd. Even I was surprised to see how many people were waiting for me. During Mel's reign, a few thousand of my admirers would encircle the palace every day until I talked them away—but now! People were visible for as far as the eye could see. In the streets, in people's yards, in the fields up in the distance, in the trees—people were everywhere! It reminded me of that episode of *Star Trek* where the people were supposed to occupy every spot on the planet. How many people ventured around this planet just for me? They can't all be from around here, but here they are. "It's the same on the other side," I hear Joe say as he and Luna walk up to me. "It was never this many before. I mean, there were a lot, but not this many!" I say with such disbelief. Should I be humbled or frightened by this display? "Are you overwhelmed yet?" Luna asks. "Oh, I'm light years beyond that. This is for me?" I say as I start to get emotional. Who am I kidding? My vision is blurred by something that mysteriously got in my eyes. No one ever gave a crap about me. I was so alone, hiding from the world with only Otto to talk to. Now this—all this! I feel Luna's hand caressing my back, feeling all my confusion. There's absolutely no one else I would want next to me at this very moment than her, forever and always. "I know," she says with a slight tear in her eyes. "Try to speak now," I hear Joe say.

I step up to the microphone stand, still taking in the endless crowd as I try to compose myself. "Thank you for thinking of me. I don't know how ... I don't know how to return the favor. I wish I could take you all in, make your lives everything you want them to be. I wish I could tell you everything is perfect and wonderful in this world. I guess it is when you listen to me, but that's so temporary. You have to go find your own bliss, each and every one of you every single moment of every single day. That's called life. Life's a struggle, but it's also a gift. It's not given by me. You have to go find that life somewhere else. Please go and be happy with your gift ... just be happy," I tell my quiet crowd. I just happened to glance over at Joe, who had the strangest, most joyful smile as if for the first time he approved of me.

The three of us just stood there silently as the crowd woke up and slowly started to leave. None of them pushed, or shoved or rushed to leave. They just left. They were happy, happy to be where they are and wherever they were going to be, wherever that is.

17) REG TO THE RESCUE

Concert day! It's concert day! Well, for me anyway. I'm doing all the singing. I haven't sung since my big rescue. And unlike before, I've never been more ready. I feel incredible, I feel like singing! I have the world's hottest backup singers, too! I hope they're in a good mood today, especially Luna. I'm crazy about her, but she's like an overactive eel; impossible to grasp and electrifying!

When everyone heard Reg was going to be at Joe's event, it instantly went from an indoor to an outdoor event with a stage set up in a field, and I mean people seemed to be everywhere! You could barely tell there was grass under their feet. These people came to see me! So I would dare not disappoint them, because they were more than just fans. They came for guidance, or just to hear my voice, but they came. I just stand around backstage with Joe and my band, all of whom were wearing Mel's special headphones so they can play while I sing. My personal go-go dancers Luna, Tricia and Aphrodite were there too, all appropriately dressed in hot pants and go-go boots. We were going for a retro look and feel, and the way my girls were dressed you'd have to be dead not to feel the vibe they pulsated out over the crowd.

"I'm just curious, but you're not planning on saying anything to embarrass yourself or better yet me out there, are you? Because if you are, forget it! My dad takes his job seriously, he doesn't need it ruined," Luna gets in my face to say. "Don't worry, I wasn't planning to say anything that might bother you, just whatever flies out of my mouth," I say with a smirk. Two can play this game. "Yeah, that's what worries me. Just sing your song and maybe say a few words to empower the masses. That's what you want to implant in their minds, something positive. Not dumb jokes. That'll just confuse them," she tells as if I'll actually listen. "I thought this whole idea was yours and daddy's? Get into the spirit of the thing yourself. We're here to enjoy ourselves, ain't we? If you don't look happy, people notice. And what's all this business about getting serious? I've made billions of dollars in the last few months. Probably half the people out there have a T-shirt with my face on it. I'm doing okay. Where are the other speakers, as if anyone cares?" I inquire. I guess I talk too loud because Joe looks bothered by my voice paralyzing the man with whom he was speaking. Joe comes over to say, "You have to stop doing that." "Maybe I should put tape over my mouth; just yank it off whenever one of you wants to talk to me?" I say with a grin. Joe the pro ignores my jab and launches, "Do you you want to sing first or wait for the other speakers to speak first? My guess is if you sing first, they might not be able to speak," Joe assumes. "Or no one will care," I assume. "Reg, the others speakers are on the ticket with you. People came to see them, too," Joe says as I point out over the endless crowd and make the point, "How many of those people you think came to see the opening act? I'm the main attraction, daddio, and you know it. Am I wrong?" I ask truly. "He's gotta point, dad," Luna interjects. "Is my own daughter against me now, too!" Joe says overly loud before walking away from us. Luna doesn't look happy now. "Now I gotta smooth things over with him. You could have just pretended to go along with him. Speaking is his job. It's not just what he does, it's what he is. It's important to him," she explains. "He speaky, I freaky. Dadio's gotta learn that I'm not just gonna suddenly say that special something that changes the world," I try to convey to Luna. "I know," she finally admits. "I'm not admitting anything. Your words could change the world or screw everything up. Just watch what you say. Could you just do that for your little Luna," she says with a manipulative smile. "But not little here where it counts," I say as I put her hand on my heart. Before Luna could walk back over to dad, dad walked back over to us. "You sing first," Joe says and walks back away. I guess the speaker was in no mood for speaking.

I walked back by the girls. This day was certainly starting out to be a bit too tenuous for my liking. I didn't know what was going to happen next. I walked over to ogle Luna, Aphrodite and Tricia, another of Joe's hot star children all growed up, in their short shorts and go-go boots, and, of course, the special headphones to mask my voice. "I must say, you girls know how to dress for success; every guy here will stand up and cheer for you, if you know what I mean? Do I get a kiss from my girls?" I lean in with a big grin and wait for one on the chin. Aphrodite gives me a quick and classy kiss on the lips. Then Tricia goes in for the kill, pressing her lips against mine, and then grabbing me to really show me she meant business as she practically sucked the life out of me with her super sucking lips. She let me go and smiled like she just got away with something. She did, but I didn't. Luna just stood there and looked at us with her arms crossed. She's the cute one without the headphones. I wonder why?

Frowning, Luna leads the girls outside, her face instantly turning to a smile as she hits the stage where all could see her. She was happy now or just very professional about it. I stayed backstage as the announcer said nice things about me and eventually announced me. I came onto the stage to monstrous applause, my arms raised as if arriving after some monumental wartime victory had just taken place. I keep my arms raised until the applause fades. I take the microphone and look out over the crowd as if some great profundity would spew forth from my unique voice box, and I simply said, "Skibidi-bibidi-boo! I'm here to sing for you!!!"

After a time lag, the audience erupts again wildly. I just smiled over at the girls, who I have to admit were all happily smiling back. I started my song now. It takes time for the audience to respond and join in with the fun. And you must understand, my audiences are present but never really there. They smile, and nod along and sometimes applaud as if their only desire in life is to hear the very next thing my voice utters, and they never want it to stop. I am their nirvana. I wish I could find my own.

My girls shake it now—and they really know how! Luna's a real dancer with Tricia a close second. Aphrodite looks nice in her outfit for sure, though she's just a bit clunky in the dance department. Hell, who's gonna notice anyway? The old song I chose made looking sexy easy because of the beat and how it described my girl. The song I chose to sing was aimed right at my girl, cuz she made me feel every kind of wonderful and I wanted everyone to know it.

I continue to sing as the girls dance close by, especially my Luna. She knew I must have chosen this song just for her. She's almost right on me. This wasn't dirty dancing, this was her way of saying I forgive you. I don't think she's mad anymore. The song ends. I grab my smiling Luna and pull her next to me and ask, "Did that do anything for you?" "Oh, there was a message in there?" she smirks so well. I smirk back and kiss her on the lips. I look out over the crowd now and spill fourth, "Let's see ... renegades, exterminators, apathetics ... and, oh yeah, brutals and eternals—I see them all! I understand that you fun lads and lassies really dig my voice. They say it makes you mellow. For some reeeeeeeeally mellow. Well, I want you to enjoy it, but what I don't want is for my voice to be all encompassing in your life. Enjoy my voice for sure, but don't let it be a replacement for living. Live your life. Let my voice add to your life, not be your life. Now stick around for some more interesting people. I'll sing another song, too, if you stick around?" I walk backstage with the girls now.

"What do eternals and brutals have to do with reality?" she inquires. "You've seen *Zardoz.* It's the most strange and fun movie you'd ever see that makes no sense, just like my life. How about the song?" I ask. "That was good, too. What do you need a bone every time you do a trick? You have a beautiful voice, Mr. pouty," she says as she grabs my chin briefly to move it around. Aphrodite comes up to complain, "Oh, do I have to dance again?"

"Please no! I mean, no more dancing. My next musical phantasmagoria is a different kind of song. I'm still waiting to see our wrestling speaker speak. I bet you are, too. You just wanna see his giant, he-man muscles, don'tcha?" I ask. "He's got nothing on Percy," Luna informs. "Percy the monster hunter? He's no behemoth of muscled manliness, like some of us," I hint wink. "Percy is a cryptid; he's a dozen times stronger than a normal man. Why do you think you see cryptids crawling under bridges? They're powerful," she informs or maybe warns. Does she think I want to tussle with him? We just smile at each other as we notice a commotion outside, Major Destruction, former championship wrestler extraordinaire and now speaker is on the stage outside. I go to the side of the stage to watch him. No one else backstage seems interested. "Hey, it's him, don'tcha wanna see him?" I ask Luna. "If he hits someone with a chair, let me know," she nonchalantly quips.

Nope, Luna didn't care. Hey, he wasn't Andre The Giant, but the Major was pretty good in his day. Wrestler man speaketh. He talks to the crowd as if they don't listen and obey, they'll be introduced to the pile driver. I guess it's part of his act, but the crowd seems to enjoy it. "Man, he really fires up the people. None of that smiley face stuff like you give them. He's bad-ass!" I admire. "Are you also fascinated by shiny objects?" Joe gripes. I guess Joe's mood hasn't changed from bad!

Watching the Major do his thing, something in the air catches my eye, a drone. It wasn't one of those car-sized spy drones you hear about. It was just this itty-bitty baby drone. It looked harmless enough, but something gave me an ominous feeling about it as I saw it hovering over the crowd, bobbing and darting up and down as if fishing for its catch. Who was controlling it, someone in the crowd as a stunt or was it of a more sinister intention? I point at it as Luna and Aphrodite see it. Our disaster predictor indeed reacted as Aphrodite looked like she was ill suddenly or quietly terrified. Then if it is so dangerous, why do I feel so eager to walk out and confront the flying metal insect menace?

"What are you doing?" I hear Luna say as I walk out onto the stage where The Major is speaking. Everyone notices me there, including Major and the drone that is now buzzing its way over by me. It lowered itself right down in front of me and about a yard over my head, just close enough for me to see that it had a little blinking light on a box attached to mister drone. As if I were speaking right into the mind of the drone's controller, I showed it who was truly in control as I calmly said, "Fly. Fly up in the sky ... very high ... then goodbye." I looked around at Luna and all the scared faces. What a great way to assassinate a world leader, an ex lover, a loose end, a freak who speaks. Then after the seemingly tenuous eternity, the drone started to rise. Then it shot up like it was a rocket launched into space as it exploded so suddenly and with so much force for such a little guy. Such pent up rage extinguished in an instant. Was I controlling machine or the man behind it? I take the microphone to pontificate, "Looks like someone doesn't like Reg. I thought everyone liked Reg. Could it be mister government man who doesn't like Reg? They only murdered millions of Indians. Trail of Tears, heard of it? Well, I've got a message for you!" I yell as I point at the camera filming me. "In the city, in the country, in the streets—everywhere!! The people are on my side! They're all lined up with me, and if you try to take me away from them again, they are going to go to Washington and slaughter you all!! So I better stay in the best of health, government assassins, bumbling bureaucrats. No one likes you anyway—this is our world!" I finish as I just toss the mic to the floor and walk backstage.

Walking towards my star child tribe, I see only shock and surprise on their faces. "Lemme guess, I said something wrong. You don't get it, do ya? Now there won't be any more attempts to snuff out Mr. Goodtrips cuz they know what'll happen, next," I explain as faces take on looks of understanding, understanding of the pure genius of what I just told the crowd, and I didn't even plan it. My thoughts on the subject just popped out of my head like Zeus' bastard children. "Yes, but what if it's not the government trying to kill you? What if it's a madman?" Joe asks. You'd have to be mad not to love Reg," I naturally assume. "Who's Mr. Goodtrips?" Aphrodite asks. "Who I am is what I am," I thinketh. "Okay, mister philosopher, are you going to sing again? You left your audience with some bad ideas in their heads. They need a come down and you're the best one to do it," Joe obviously says to massage and give candy and flowers to my ego. He was right, though.

"Okay, let's sing!" I say as I grab Luna by the hand and rush her out onto the stage with me. "Stools! Two stools for your king and queen," I so order and with extreme haste a stagehand produces them. Two headphone wearing guitar players gather around us to play as I sing and tell, "Would you join me in our bliss? I say that to my Luna and to any of you in the audience who care to listen." Luna plays along and sits on her stool facing me and I sit on my stool facing her. This song was more for her than anyone else. "I want to sing a song now about a man who doesn't really have enough money to go home. So rather than be looked at, oh, I don't know, critically by his family he just goes away. To me this song is a love song, though, because I sing it to my lady," I preface.

So the guitar players start to play and I begin my song. It was an old song; old, melodic and beautiful. No need to rush, I sang it slowly and from the heart. I could sing it no other way to my Luna. And as I sang, the people cared for nothing else. Their raging confusion had been replaced with total contentment as if they knew not nor understood what a negative thought was. And as I sang, my Luna's eyes softened and eventually gave way to wistful tears as if only a gentle rain were falling on her cheeks and she didn't even know it. Yeah, I guess Luna did like it. I had genuinely moved her. That was the whole idea. "*Five-Hundred Miles*, everyone, an old Peter Paul and Mary song. I hope you liked it. Luna, everyone! She's my lobster girl. You can thank her for my being here. You can thank her for everything that I am," I say smiling over at her as she wiped away her tears and actually looked happy. This was as good as it gets. I saved the day and got the girl. Things were looking up! And no more killer drones either.

With the song over, I get off my stool and take Luna's hand as she stands beside me. Gripping our hands, looking out over the vast audience looking at us, we were all synced up, finally realizing there would never be anyone else to be found for each other. Two such extraordinary souls could never live mere ordinary lives. We could be king and queen of this world if we chose to be. Now there's an idea ...

"Every king needs a queen," I say looking into Luna's eyes as I get on one knee, her near gasp of surprise widening her soft eyes as I speak from my heart, "Every Arthur needs his Guinevere, would you be my queen, my only love? I can feel or think of no love greater than the love I have for you. Luna, will you marry me?" Still crying with a bit of trembling, my Luna relents. She nods yes. I stand triumphantly! "All my dragons slain, I have no more conquests or lands to conquer. I have found my one and true love, my Guinevere, my Luna," I say as I sweep my maiden fair up into my embrace and kiss her in front of the audience and probably the whole world. We kissed for so long that our audience actually reacted. I suddenly hear a deep voice in the crowd say, "Can we kiss the bride, too?" Luna and I stop smooching immediately. "We? I think there's a biker gang here. They love to share," I imagine. "Can we go now? I think the whole world's seen us enough," Luna says as if to say—get me outta here!

We make our Hasty retreat backstage as proud dad Joe comes between us with a really big smile for someone who was such a sour puss earlier. "Nicely done, I could not have done better," Joe continued with that wide smile. No more mister bad moody. "Hey, if this doesn't work out, maybe I can get a job with the bomb squad. I seem to be pretty good at defusing bombs," I jest. "I saw Peter, Paul and Mary when I was quite young. *Blowing in The Wind* would have been a more appropriate song to promote peace, but the song you chose worked out quite nicely for our audience," Joe praises. "I wasn't singing it to them," I say as I only have eyes for my Luna. Dad's smile mysteriously disappears as he looks at his daughter and asks, "Are you sure this is what you want, this man ogling you?" "No one makes up my mind for me, dad. You know that. If I said it, I meant it," she expresses. Damn straight! "Oh, where was Otto? You said he'd be in the front row. I didn't see him," I told Joe. "He's living with his uncle now," Joe informs me. "Thennnnnnnnn, let's go see 'im!" I say and mean.

Two limos pull up to Uncle Danny's house in Korea Town. Joe walks up to the house and rings the bell. Soon after, Danny opens the door to see Joe standing there, no one speaking yet as Joe just smiles and Danny realizes who Joe is after a moment of hard looking at him, his normally rough exterior and frown turning into a smile. "Hawaiian Joe—hey! If you're looking for Reg, he's not here," Danny tells. "I know. May I speak with you inside, or would you rather step into my office?" Joe asks. Danny steps outside the door and notices two limos. "Two limos? I didn't know you were that big," Danny jests. "One is for extra security, and one is for a very special friend of Otto's. He apologizes for not coming sooner," Joe hints. "Oh! Tell him to come in," Danny invites. "Actually, Reg had a different idea," Joe interests.

So here we all are back at my palace, sitting at my round table as we wait for lunch to be served. Our star child guests wear the special headphones so we all can converse. "I was curious how this place looked inside. This table looks familiar," Danny mystifies. "It's the actual round table from the movie *Excalibur*. I found out where it was and told the guy I wanted it, and here it is!" I explain. Servants wearing headphones serve lunch all around now. Danny gets fried chicken and taters. "Fried chicken, my favorite! Otto must have told you what I like. Thanks, Otto. You know, my daddy always said chickens do three things well: cluck, fuck and go good in a bucket," Danny jests to audible laughs from me and other diners. I can't seem to stop laughing—uh, oh! There's my Luna—not laughing! She just shook her head as if to say, why do we have to eat with this uncouth idiot? Danny smiled at his successful witticism as he munched away and glanced about the table, noticing only Luna looking disapproving. So, he would screweth with her. He noticed the butter was near her and he needed it for his mash taters. "Would you pass the butter?" Danny just stares at Luna until she realizes he's looking at her. "You want something from me?" she says mystified. "Yeah, the butter for my potatoes ... unless you're saving it for later? I saw *Last Tango In Paris*. I know what you're saving that butter for," he prods as she looks at him smiling at her with his mash tater eating grin and gets the best squirmy look of horror on her face. "Excuse me, what!" she says sooooooooooooo bothered. I'm LMAO! In fact, I could die laughing right here at this table. He was screwing with her and I knew it, and I'm pretty sure he knew I knew it. Some of our other guests got the joke, too. They were laughing with just a tad of restraint. Luna can't lighten up, though. She stands up, grabs the butter caddy, goes around the giant table and slams the butter down before Danny. "Your butter! Thank you, no! I won't need it!" she says with extreme exclamation and goes back to her seat. Danny wasn't finished with her yet, though—oh, noooooooo!

"Thank you. Did I say that loud enough for you? I just wanted to be sure I was loud enough because I know how loud you can be. You should hear this girl. When Otto and I were staying at Reg's old house, you could hear this loud moaning coming from the bedroom she was in. Oh! Oh! Oh! No one could sleep. I told her, 'you are loud girl'! She's loud," Danny says and continues chowing down as if nothing happened. Meanwhile, Luna looks mortified to the point of almost changing colors. And me, it was laughing hyena time again, and I wasn't the only one. The only one not laughing was Joe. Yes, if I were her dad I suppose I wouldn't laugh about something like that, poor Joe. Uh oh, it had to happen; Luna shoved herself away from the table and rushed upstairs. She was looking down so I couldn't tell if she was crying or not, but it wouldn't surprise me. I suddenly felt awful. I rushed upstairs after her. "Sorry, she's loud. Is it wrong to tell the truth?" Danny apologizes.

I come into my room to see Luna just standing there not far away with her back to me. "Stalk much? What do you want, Reg? Can't I have a moment to myself without you constantly on me?" she asks. "How did you know it was me?" I ask. "Because dad can't get up the stairs that fast—of course it's you!" she explains more than a tad pissed. "Hey, honeybee, I'm sorry if he embarrassed you. He's Otto's uncle, he's good people. He's just a little rough around the edges," I smooth over. I move in front of her and take her arms to console her, which was the wrong thing to do right then because she ripped her arms away from me and started to pound on my chest with her fists as she also lays into me verbally, "He's a pig! And you're a pig for laughing!!!" And Oops! She caught me on the lip with one of those downward strikes. She stops thankfully as I step back, the blood streaming down my face. Yeah, I felt that one. "Oh, I'm so sorry. I didn't do it on purpose," she says sincerely. "No, of course not. You were just pounding out dough; you thought I was a pizza. Put some pepperoni on me next time. I'll taste better," I jest the pain away. "You're bleeding," she says as she takes a tissue out of her pocket and licks it, and then wipes the blood off my face, all the while I just look at her with only love in my eyes. She notices. "What are you thinking?" she says as a smile finally comes back to that pretty face. "You tell me," was the perfect comeback for someone of her talents. She just looks at me, my thoughts hers if she wanted them. "You should be mad at me," she reads. I'm not, of course. "And you should be mad at me," I say and she, of course, is! "You bet I am!" she says with with that look she gives when she wants something—me! "Stop smiling at me like that and I'll believe you," I say and lean in to kiss her as she's leaning into kiss me. We are definitely on the same wavelength. I flinch after kissing her because of, oh, my busted lip. "I think we're outta luck. I can't kiss you right now," I say a bit put out. "You won't need your lips," she expresses as she grabs my shirt and rips it open.

After enough time goes by, Luna and I come downstairs. "Did you lose something up there?" Aphrodite smirks. "I was just consoling her, much better now," I just smile. "Yeah, how many times?" Danny asks. Luna lays down the law to smiling Danny now. "Look! I'm not taking any more crap outta you, and neither is he. Tell him, Reg," Luna insists. "She's not taking any more crap outta you," I say and she jumps up and backhands me on my chest. "And you're not either?" she asks or insists, I'm not sure. "Hey, Danny's not a bad guy, he just says what's on his mind," I say knowing I'm gonna get it. "Yeah? You wanna sleep with him instead?" Luna says with that insane look in her eyes that says I better not screw up this answer. Luckily at that moment, to save my dumb ass, a security guard comes in the front door as he puts his special headphones on to speak to me as he says, "We might need you outside, sir. We have a little problem." "Do I have to tell people to leave again?" I assume. "No, sir, actually they won't leave until they talk to you," he tells. "Well, you know how that's gonna work out, what's the point?" I ask. "One of them said he could speak with you. He said he knows you," the guard intrigues me.

Not knowing many people in this big world who can actually converse with me without electronic headgear instantly got the better of me as I found myself on the roof outside of the palace, hearing the roar of a hundred or more Harleys riding round and round the palace. As I just stood there and watched all these bad-ass bikers riding around, Luna, Joe and Danny soon found their way by my side. I was suddenly mesmerized by the sounds of the engines and all those biker movies I saw in the sixties. I always wanted to be a biker. After *Easy Rider*, I talked a biker into letting me ride his hog, something that just can't be done if you don't have my particular talent. Anyway, I hopped on his bike all excited as I hit the gas! The front wheel went up and I went down. So much for riding easy. I went over to the microphone on the roof and said, "Who wants to speak with Reg? Who can? It's a short list." The circling herd suddenly slowed to a complete stop, some of the bikers falling or bumping into each other because I spoke. Then one lone biker answered me. "Hey, Reg! You didn't forget your native brother, did you?" says Strongheart, my Cherokee friend from so long ago.

Wasting no time, I am making my way out of the palace and over towards the front gate. Not wanting to paralyze the guards, who don't wear headphones, I wait for Luna to come up as I signal her to tell them to open the gate. As the elegant palace gates swing open, I take in a sight I hadn't seen in half a century. I mean, I'd seen bikers before to be sure, but these guys dressed like bikers from the past, like straight out of a sixties biker flick. They wore dust covered raggedy jeans with jean jackets or leather jackets, all with ROD on the back of them. They all just sat there on their bikes as we slowly walked up to Strongheart, who sat next to one intense looking biker. Not wanting to speak yet, I sent the message 'who's the leader' into Luna's head. "Reg doesn't wish to disrespect anyone. Does he speak with his friend, or is his friend the leader?" she asks wisely. Strongheart smiles and speaks, "You've been around bikers before. They don't believe he can do what he does. They think it's a trick. Show 'em, Reg," "I thought I just did. These dudes are hard to convince," I say quietly to Luna. Then after a moment contemplating, I say loudly, "I heard there's some bad acid going around. Well, it ain't me!!" Meanwhile, all looks of doubt, curiosity or intensity vanish from their faces as they look like they just scored the best high they've ever had. A few of them even fell over on their cycles. I go over and give Strongheart the arm wrestling handshake. "Why so long? Why now?" I ask him. "I told them I know you. I had to convince them. You could convince them of anything, couldn't you, Reg?" he says to make me wonder about his motives. Why was he here, here now at this exact moment? I noticed Luna staring at him with extreme interest, soaking him in for sure. "This is what I guess you would call my mama. This is Luna. Did you come for the wedding?" I ask. "I came to rescue you from this place," he makes me wonder. "This place? This place has it all! I kinda like this place," I say amused. "Okay, invite us in," he says as Luna immediately responds, "Nope, not gonna happen, sorry." She just looked at Strongheart as if to say Reg is the all powerful one, but she was the light in the forest that showed him the way. He just stared at Luna as if staring her down, with no luck. Then he finally said, "You're Hawaiian Joe's daughter. I know your mother." My Luna suddenly looked so confused. What was she thinking? I couldn't say. That was her specialty. I just know that brain of hers must have been on fire! "Come with us, Reg. Ride with us," he tantalizes. "Is Spock fronting for Kirk? Who's the leader?" I ask him. "What's the difference, man? Step outside this gilded cage prison. Cuz that's what it is. If you can't leave, you're not truly free," he said as if he knew exactly what I felt. I suddenly realized this is just what I needed, a road trip. See America on two wheels, that's what I wanted. "Yeah," I blurted out while staring off into space. Luna just rolled her eyes. She knew when I had my mind set on something there was little chance of changing it. She sent the message 'I don't trust this guy' into my thick head. I just looked at her as if to say I got the message. "We have to rap some. I don't wanna leave without her," I told Strongheart. "Why leave her? A lotta guys here have their old ladies with them," he tells. "Yeah, well, this old lady ain't gonna be passed around like a tray of treats. Just thought I'd make that clear. We need to rap some," I say with a smile. Strongheart was an old friend, but friends change. I just hope this old friend hasn't changed too much. I walk back into the palace as Strongheart yells, "Get us something to eat!" I just give him the thumbs up as I enter the palace and the gates shut behind us.

Back in the palace, I have a rap session with Luna and Joe in his office. Joe sits reading what he sees on a computer screen that he is perusing. "Nice bunch you want to hang with. The ROD on their jackets is for Riders of Doom. They're not your more modern bike club that just wants to ride and hang out. Over half of them are in the one percent club. Do you know what that means, Reg?" he asks. "They're bikers, not nuns. I don't expect them to be perfect," I retort as Joe suddenly stands to face us. "They're outlaw bikers. They run guns, and drugs and who knows what. You think I'm going to let my daughter go with those people?" he asks or complains. "What if I can't talk him out of it? Wouldn't it be better if I were there to watch him?" his daughter asks. "What are you going to watch, them rape and kill him before you? Let him go! Why do you want to sign up for this madness?" the worried father asks. "One of them said they knew my mother. Is there something you don't want me to know, dad?" Luna needs to know as she stares down her stubborn father. Joe just sighs and sits back in his chair, fearing the inevitable may happen. He may lose his daughter, one way or another. "You're not going to lose me, dad. You told me you haven't seen mom since I was born. Wouldn't you like to see her again?" she asks a confused father who can only say, "I don't know." Joe sits forward and tries to reason with us. "What do know about this man who said he knows you? Do you know him? How do you know you can trust him?" Joe asks. "Strongheart is FBI—full-blooded Indian and all percent Cherokee. Your daughter's mother is Cherokee. I don't know what I am. I still don't know where I'm from. I don't look Cherokee. Luna does. We just wanna know about ourselves. That all anyone wants, to know; who they are, where they fit in in this world," I explain the best I can. "I knew this day would come," was all dad could say.

With a few things packed, we left the palace to ride with Strongheart and his gang, who were busy chowing down on the cornucopia of good eats and treats the staff gave them. We walked right up in front of

Strongheart as he sat eating in front of his chopper. "What do think you're going to a fashion show?" Strongheart asks, almost laughing as he sees me in my trippy-drippy leather jacket and sunglasses. Luna asked the questions so I didn't make happy eating bikers choke on my words. "So, why do you do all the talking when Voltaire there is the leader of your band of merry men?" Luna asks as she motions at Voltaire, the leader who has that look of intensity that says anyone who screws with him is dead, and not in the best way. Voltaire just eyed Luna before speaking. He didn't have to act tough or cold. Those who actually are tough never have to run their mouths, only those insecure types to prove they're anything but. He spoke plainly without rushing, with a choice of words to demonstrate he didn't have to say what snowflake ears needed to hear to be all safe and cozy. "Patton loved his men. My men have followed me into hell ... and will continue to do so. If you are looking for some joyride playtime to pass the time, you won't find it here," he says ominously, which also intrigued me. I don't dance on the razor's edge, I skateboard on it! Luna wasn't having it, though. "Yeah, I don't dig wusses either. Wanna arm wrestle?" she asks as Voltaire smiles and many of the brother bikers laugh. "I can think of something better we can do," Voltaire says to get under her skin—and mine! I immediately walk over to Strongheart, grab his shirt and drag him speedily away a good distance before letting him go. He jumps to his feet not looking too happy about it. Being we are hopefully far enough away for his biker buds not to be affected by my voice, I speak up quickly before my angry friend hits me. "If you think I'm disrespecting you, you just did that to Luna and me. We're even. Now, why are you really here?" I must know. He calms down as we both glance over to see that some of the bikers have sprung to their feet as if ready to all pounce on me. "That wasn't smart. What if they come over here? They like to do things as a group, you know, like beat your ass!" he states. "Then I'll just tell em to stop," I say. "They don't think that far ahead. Look, Reg, I thought you'd like me coming here. You can go back into your big, pretty box or come with us. What do you really want?" he asks, still hiding something from me I'm sure. "Do they know about you, what you can do?" I ask. "I don't have your vocal ability. I'm just their token Indian," he says. "They must have noticed how strong you are, how you don't age. How long have you been with them?" I inquire. "Not that long. Listen, Reg, we have an opportunity for you," he informs. "What did you get board? You did the biker thing, go looking for America and not find it anywhere? I don't need money. I have enough green to shovel into a furnace all day. You need some? I'll give you some," I tell him. "I didn't come looking for a handout. You don't get it! This is an opportunity for you! You can unite all the biker gangs. If they were all united, it would be like a chain across this land the government could never break, but they have to be united. When Voltaire saw what you told them when they tried to blow you up with that drone, he was impressed. You didn't back down. You didn't flinch an inch," he buttered up. "This Voltaire seems like someone who likes to be leader. Why would he let me just step in and do it?" I must know or won't go. "You're the tip of the spear, the ten foot flaming sword that can cut through all the bullshit! Your voice, it's the only thing that will unite bikers that would rather kill each other than ride together. Because you can make them listen. You're the only one who can do it. It's gotta be you, Reg," he says truly. "First Joe wants me to empower people with happy talk. Now you want me to unite them with it. You are aware that whoever hears me just gets high when I speak. They don't give a shit what I say. I can't wrap it up with a bow and make what's in the box what you want it to be. That's just the way it is," I say hoping he understands. "You think just because your voice doesn't affect me, I can't see what it does to everyone else? If you think you are unique, you are not. There is another who can manipulate the minds of others with only words, but he chooses not to do so," he says to intrigue me further. "So he never speaks?" I ask. "You don't understand. He can speak with or without affecting anyone. He can control it. It is you who cannot. Come with us and you shall meet him," he says and knows now I must follow. To meet someone like that, I would follow anyone anywhere. But I say anyway, "I always have to leave this place with bookoo security or everyone follows me. I hate it!" "Did you notice we got more than a few guys here? No one's gonna bother you or they get bothered. And the more that ride with us, the stronger we are. Who's gonna mess with an army of bikers coming their way? Opportunity just rolled a big hole in this place for you to ride out of. It's up to you, Reg," he entices. I didn't have to think twice. I knew what I was going to do.

18) RIDERS of DOOM

So I decided to saddle up, rev up and head out on the highway. Actually, I ended up riding along with Luna in the hippie van since not one biker wanted to lend me their bike. I guess I had impressed no one with my bike riding skills as of yet. Someone Strongheart could trust rode his bike because he rode in the van with us. I didn't know if it was because he just wanted to see me up close and personal after all these years or to simply keep an eagle eye on me, hear every word I would possibly have with Luna. What he didn't know is that Luna and I could hold whole conversations without saying a word aloud, and we made sure we kept that to ourselves. He was my friend all right, but you never know? I drove. If Luna drives, she gets distracted, making it harder to probe each and every mind around her.

As I drove down the highway, the two-wheeled rolling entourage rode behind us and ahead of us, protecting us in their traveling cocoon of chrome and leather. Luna's eyes darted from biker to biker, soaking in the exploits of each biker without them ever knowing their secret thoughts were secret no more. On occasion I would glance over at her to see her face contort, no doubt by the disturbing images flooding her mind. Strongheart sits between us, just staring quietly ahead as if his only objective were arriving at his destination. Nothing else mattered. I hope our friendship still did, so I asked, "Getting any closer?" "We won't run outta gas," was all he could muster. "Wow, you're a blabbermouth. Tell me, do they trust you, knowing you're immune to my voice?" I ask. "Why is she immune?" he asks about Luna, who looks his way now. "Maybe it's a gift passed on to me by my mother. You said you knew her," Luna says and waits. "Desert Flower. I know her. Of our kind, she is one of the oldest," he says and stops, still saying just what would grab our interest but nothing more. As Luna just looks at him, 'he's blocking' me pops into my head. My old friend obviously had other talents to be revealed. "You'd make a great magician, Strongheart. You leave everyone wanting more. Tell me this, are we all related, you know, our kind?" I must know. "You are not Cherokee, but you are still my friend," he tells and stops again! "Good to know. What else can you tell us?" I ask. "You'll know soon enough. We are not all related. Like out of mythology, the gods came down and mated with mortal women. In our case, the star people visited themselves upon our women. Who is to know if they are not one in the same?" he poses. "Wouldn't that make us demigods?" I ask. "Maybe you. Only you and one other can do what you do," he hints at knowing another such as I. "You're doing it again. Who is this person? I didn't come along to pick strawberries, I wanna know. I need to know," I say and hope for more as I look at him more than the road. He points at the road as I look back just barely missing a fellow biker. "His name is Gawanii," he finally blurts out as Luna excitedly says, "That's the name of the man my dad said he saw in the forest as a kid. We are talking about the same man?" "We are," is all he would say. "Is he where we are going?" she asks. "Your mother is. Gawanii lives in the Great Smoky Mountains. Exactly where, no one knows," he informs. "Gee, my Native friend, that's kind of a big place. How will we even find him if we were to go there?" I ask. "If he wants you to find him, you will," he mystifies. "There's a spooky answer. And, oh yeah, this is California; thousands of miles away from his super secret home, piney home," I inform. "As we traverse this great land—that used to be ours—we will unite our fellow bikers city by city and town by town. By the time we reach our destination, we will all be united. That is what you can do," he says to fill my head with a thousand racing thoughts. Then our rolling entourage turned into a huge roadside bar.

Trapped between the rolling herd, I reluctantly follow the van into the parking lot. "Did they get thirsty?" I ask Strongheart. "This is your first test," he smiled at me ominously. "Test? You're not enhancing my cool, dude," I say with my semi-worried look. "Our kind are all super soldiers, Reg. If you are as tough as I know you can be, you should be just fine," my old friend worries me even further. "Wait a minute, are you gonna do what I think you're gonna do?" my Luna anxiously interjects. "No, he is. I want you to go in there and pick a fight with one of them," Strongheart explains. "Just one? Hey, no problem," I say happily as our van doors open and Voltaire stands by me and says, "The time is now." I look over at Strongheart, who says, "No talking or you fail the test, clear?" I just nod my head and get out of the van as another biker immediately puts a big piece of duct tape over my mouth. Looking concerned, my Luna comes to my defense and says, "We don't need this, Reg. Let's just go home." I just motion with my hand and follow the other bikers as they lead me up to the bar. Just one guy, eh? If I only have to make not so nice with one biker, why do I get that feeling I'm going to the gallows again? Every step closer I get to the bar makes me feel like I'm climbing the world's highest roller coaster. The big drop was coming—me into this bar! We stop at the door as Voltaire says, "I like your voice. Don't get hit in the throat." Just standing there, I was introduced to busty Cassandra, an old lady of one of the bikers I'm sure. "I'm Cassandra. I'll be tagging along to make sure you don't get naughty. No talking. Anything else goes," she says with a great big smile that does nothing to reassure me.

So I enter the huge bar with my date for the next few minutes and just stand there as we look over the crowd drinking, playing pool and being mildly rowdy. Hey, why spoil their mood and make them mad? I can't get over that stupid smile that won't leave her face. Then Cassandra suddenly whistles loudly to get everyone's attention. With the bikers from a biker club other than the one I am currently riding with all looking at us now, Cassandra loudly says, "I found this stray dog in the parking lot. He says he hates bikers. He said you're all pussies!" I just look over at her with my eyebrows raised up into the top of my head. Cassandra just smiles at me like she just got the house, the car and bow wow in the divorce. Then it happened, the biggest biker I have ever seen walked up to me. I knew I was still stronger than him. I just wished he would wait for me to tell him that. So I got a better idea, I held my arms up with my palms raised and figured I would show him. He took the hint and interlocked his Andre The Giant-sized hands and fingers between mine and I waited as he pressed down, pressing and pressing as I stood there without moving or wavering an inch. Every muscle in my body was tensing to keep this elephant's foot from crushing me. We just looked deeper and deeper into each other's eyes as he tried to trash compact my much smaller frame without me budging. Me being in better shape than the greatest Olympian and him being overly bulbous and not in the best of condition was ever so quickly taking its toll on his ravaged body. Then the fat bastard cheated and kneed me in the midsection. I went down on my knees and tried my best to breathe through my nose, the tape over my mouth not making it any easier. But being I recuperate at warp speed, I snap my neck up to look up at the huffing puffing pile breathing even harder than me. I smile. I leap towards the behemoth like a big cat attacking its prey, my fingers sinking into the sweaty, gooey glob of fat and tossing him like a huge bowling ball across the floor as he slides towards the bar and crashes into it. I hear 'holy shit' as I look about the place. They all looked a bit taken aback or even scared. They knew what they just saw wasn't normal, just wasn't right, but they all wanted a piece of my ass!

And here they come! With fists, with bottles, with pool cues, with bar stools, they came at me, all trying their best to best me. But I was never so focused, so ready to rumble. I had never really been in a fight. I had seen all the Bruce Lee and Chuck Norris movies, though, and I had taken notes! And even more than that, I was mad!!! The Hulk had nothing on me! I could see every punch and every swinging object coming at me as if they were in slow motion, and these were bad dudes, real fighters. No wusses here. I was just once more bringing out the superior me as I tore through them like a blowtorch through butter, hitting some of them so hard that they never left the floor. And when they hit me, I barely felt it. I just kept on going, going until there was no one left to challenge me or no one left who wanted the futility in trying me. Then I glanced over at Cassandra just standing there. She wasn't smiling anymore. I don't know if she respected me or was just plain afraid. Then I saw Voltaire, Strongheart, Luna and a bunch of other ROD bikers standing just inside the doorway with pretty much the same looks on their faces. They knew there was no one on this earth like Reg. You better believe it! I walked up to them and ripped the tape off my face. "How was that?" I said as I saw Strongheart smiling ear-to-ear. No one else was. I took Luna by the hand and walked out of the bar.

Walking outside the bar with Luna, I blurt out, "Am I officially a bad ass now or what?" I reach the van, open the door and just sit on the edge. "Are you hurt?" she says, looking concerned. "You know, every time I do something different, I realize how different I am," I say as I collapse into the van.

I instantly realize I'm walking through the desert as my eyes pop open and I raise my head. Was I sleepwalking? I should feel more hot, but I don't. I see the blur of the heat rising up from the desert sand in the distance. Isn't Luna keeping an eye on me? Why didn't any of those bikers try to stop me, let me just wander out here? I must have told them not to. Yeah, that's it. I see something familiar up in the distance. As I keep walking, I notice that it's a headstone. I've seen graveyards in the desert, but why here? This is the middle of nowheresville. I walk up to the headstone now; it's the grave of Jim Morrison, 1943 – 1971. But he belongs in Paris. I know, I've been there. "I knew you'd end up here eventually," Jim says as I turn to see him standing there. Yeah, Jimbo is right here for me now. "I think I screwed up big time, didn't I?" I ask him. "No more than I did. I've left all regrets," Jim says calmly. "But you ever regret, you know, leaving this world behind the way you did?" I ask him, not really knowing what to say. "Does it matter? Reg, there are no more regrets now. Life's just one stop on a train, you gotta get off sometime," he says Morrison style. "I think you got off before your stop, though. I just wanted to say I've enjoyed your music, your poetry, what you left behind so much. Nobody will ever forget you, Jimbo," I tell him. "Just Jim. My friends real and true call me Jim. Call me Jim, Reg," he says sincerely. Call me Jim, wow! Now this is cool—the definition of cool! "I don't think I'd like being a ghost, it's so lonely ... Jim," I say. "We're not ghosts, not even close. And it's never lonely where I am, Reg. If you want to come with me, you'll get to meet Ray," he interests. "Why, am I done here? I thought I was just getting started. Everyone wants something from me, everyone needs something. I've never seen so many needy people. Why are you really here? I was hit in the head with a bar stool, wasn't I? I have a concussion, right?" I must know. "The world does need you, Reg. Luna, too. Hey, I liked the way you sang to her, it reminds me of when I sang to Pam," he smiles to bring me a smile. "That is high praise. And let me tell you, you did six great albums, not just three like so many say," I say. "Is that what they say?" he just stares at me for something stupid I just said. "I never tried to please everyone. I won't see you again, not on this side," he informs. "But I will see you again?" I ask. "What do you think? Plenty of time in the infinite. You have a lot to do yet, Reg. Never forget you're not like the others. You'll find your ancestors in the constellations," he says to make me wonder. Then he simply fades into the heat of the desert and out of my life. I look over at the grave again. What grave? It's gone too.

My eyes pop open. I am in the back of the van with Luna, who perks up and looks at me. "How do you feel?" she asks with concern. How do I feel? I make two fists and make my knuckles crack just like Bruce Lee did just before he took out a whole Karate school. I felt strong! "A nice nap always makes me feel better. We still at that bar?" I ask. "No! We are faaaar away. Some of those guys didn't make it. Now they're looking for us," she says with a worried look. "The cops?" I ask. "The biker gang from the bar!" she tells. "Better than the cops. They never stop looking. No, wait, that's the mafia. Do they even know I was the one at the bar?" I inquire. "You mean the famous Reg? You know, I didn't stop to ask them," she says with attitude. "Are you mad at me?" I ask. "You know I had to pee in a bucket in here? Some of those bikers have some really unclean thoughts in their heads. I don't wanna be alone around them," she says. "Hey, if they get near you, I'll just tell them to go away," I say. "Not if you're unconscious! You don't know the madness running through all your new biker friends' heads. They can't decide whether to worship you or dispose of your body," she informs. "I pick option C," I say with a chuckle. She's not laughing. I sit up. "I'm hungry," my mouth and body say. "Good! Let's go home and have a pizza. I'll drive," she really means. "You mentioned going home twice now. I thought you wanted to see your mother," I thought. "Not if it means we get killed! Or worse," she warns. "Where's Strongheart? Go get him," I order. "I'm not leaving this van without you. Reg, your romanticized notion of these bikers is not mine. They don't just ride around and get a little rowdy like in a sixties biker film. They do insane things. I heard one of them saying he was gonna go kill this guy for misspelling his tattoo," she stares at me with an intense look. "I have things to do. I can do things no one else can do. I want you by my side when I do these things," I say as I just stare at her. "I don't want you to die by my side," she says with sad eyes. "You wanted me to toughen up. I have," I say as I kick the back of the van open and get out.

I stand there and look at a bright full moon illuminating the desert across the highway. On our side of the highway was me, Luna, a ton of bikers and a run down looking shack of a house. Not exactly all the comforts of home, but I felt good again. I look back over at my girl defiantly unmoving. I put my hand out to her and simply said, "Come with me." Hesitantly she gets out of the van and just gives me her famous bitch face, not taking my hand. She instead crosses her arms as I put my hand down. "I feel really good. It's peaceful out here, makes me wanna roast marshmallows. Look, we live a long time. We have time for this. This, being here now is what I need to do, and I need you with me. When I first saw Sunny, she was so happy. She knew I was the one, the one who could speak the special strangeness. When I first saw you, I knew you were the one, the only one. I need you to help me navigate genius from madness in that strangeness. I think you know that. Now will you come with me?" I say as I once again as I hold out my hand to her. She takes it this time. 'A softened heart is not a weak heart' I think as she smiles at me.

Luna and I walk together among the groups of partying bikers. Campfires, good eats and good times abound. They seemed happy, except the ones that stopped smiling when they caught a glimpse of me. I guess they didn't know what to think about me. I don't blame them. I don't know what to think about me either. Maybe if I live long enough I'll live on a planet where people don't judge you out of their fear. Maybe this one.

I suddenly stop walking, throw out my arms and yell, "Strongheart!!!!!!" The party atmosphere stopped, but no one minded because I spoke. They feelin' good now! Strongheart made his way out of the darkness up to me and Luna. "Why'd you ruin the party?" he could only say. "Ruin it? I started it! Isn't that why I'm here, to unite all you guys?" I ask. "These dudes are already united. We've wasted a whole day while you slept. Why do you sleep so much?" he asks. "I only sleep three hours—unless! Unless my friend tries to get me killed. Then I have to heal myself. See me now? I'm stronger than before. See how strong I am?" I say as I get right up in his face, take his hands and hold them in front of me as if we were both a wall pushing on each other. Not knowing how to react, Strongheart barely pushes back at first. Then he pushes harder as I push harder. "Why am I really here, old friend?" I ask as I push, his own great strength really pushing back now. "I told you, to unite us. What are you on something? Why is he doing this?" he says as he strains and looks at Luna, who is busy trying to probe his mind. Perhaps she will have more luck with this little distraction we cooked up. "I think I'm here for something else. Any thoughts on that, old friend?" I say as I drive him down to his knees. "Maybe there was something else," he admits. "Maybe? Indecision is a killer. See that car up ahead? It's about to hit you. What do you do? You move!!!!" I say as I push my friend to the ground before I break him. He is still my friend, I hope. "What the hell's a matter with you?" he complains. I look to Luna, who tells us, "He wants you to unite the bikers, except for one club. That one he wants dead, he or someone here does." "She's a mind reader," he says as he gets up on his feet. "Did you know I was one before? You were blocking me," Luna explains. "I wasn't blocking. If the mind is emptied, there is nothing to take from it. Hey, you know if they come to their senses, they are all going to jump on you. Don't you know how bikers roll? Mess with one, mess with us all," he explains. "Yeah, I heard. Then maybe I should keep talking, or just tell them not to jump. I know how tough your buds are. So are a yard full of prisoners, or terrorists or superheroes. It doesn't matter. The more the merrier. I love crowds! More to do what I tell 'em, whatever I tell 'em. But then you know that. That's why I'm here, righty right? I'd rather it because we're friends, not just to be used," I gripe. "Uniting our fellow bikers is a noble thing. Are you still going to help us?" My friend asks with a worried look. "He'll help you, that's what he wants. Murdering people? No! Clear?" Luna lays down the law. "You're a tough squaw. I'm sure you're part Cherokee," he says smiling at my girl. "Who's the one who wants someone dead, your leader? You wouldn't go to all this trouble for anyone else. Reg will just open his big yap and make him forget. Problem solved," she assumes. "I don't know. Voltaire's a Captain Kirk type, very dynamic. He might forget and one day he comes across one of the biker's who killed his brother and then ... I don't know what he would do, besides ruin everything," Strongheart explains his dilemma. "I have an idea, why don't we cross that bridge when we come to it? Now, when do we see this woman who may or may not be my mother?" Luna asks with her hands on her hips.

"Let's show 'em who's boss," I say as I look to the night sky, my eyes roll back into my head and my sparkling astral body leaves my body, floating about over all the campsite as the bikers look on in their special I've seen it all but this bizarre bullshit! I land in front of Voltaire, and say, "You are the leader, but who do you follow?" Then with an explosion of light friendly to the eyes, my brilliant astral body streaks up to the sky and directly into outer space, passing all those puny planets and heading right for the main power source, the sun. I stand there briefly soaking in its power. I couldn't feel the heat or radiation, though I knew it was making me stronger. Back on earth, I threw out my arms and gave out my primal scream of power, and in an instant my astral body dropped like a light bomb right back into me. I opened my eyes to see Luna and Strongheart by my sides and every other biker gathered round me in a big circle as if waiting for my triumphant return from battle. I walked over and just looked at one of their chromed Harley masterpieces on wheels and I felt strong. I felt strong!!! Then I threw my hands on it in a couple good spots and hoisted it over my head. Then I just held it there. I just saw it and knew I could do it. I could do the impossible. Then I told everyone, "I will come with you and you will follow me, and we will go wherever destiny takes us. We shall rule the world!!!" Then I gently deposit the bike back onto the ground and walk over to Luna and Strongheart as the other bikers enjoy the high I have given them and hopefully understand the true meaning in what I have told them. They both look like they don't know what I'll do next.

"My love and my friend, don't fear me. Guide me ... because I don't know what's gonna happen next," I tell them as I put my arms around them and walk away. "Sorry I was so rough with you, Strongheart, that I doubted you. It won't happen again," I tell him. "Your abilities have awakened. Now I know you must meet Gawanii. He can teach you what no one else can," he informs. "Wow! Sounds like Yoda," I say cuz he kinda does. I turn to look at Luna and ask, "Why do you put up with me?" "You tell me. Maybe you'll pay off one day," she says with a smile. We walked off into a night as beautiful as any day. All color may be stolen by the night, but there will always be the stars to guide ship Reg.

19) DESERT FLOWERS HAVE THORNS

Driving the hippie van, I followed our herd of bikers down a long dirt road to a huge farmhouse. It immediately reminded me of the farmhouse I had visited as a child with Sunny. It's funny how some things remind you of other things. I looked over at Luna, the look of anticipation filling her face. I hope she likes what she finds.

Whether it was the sound of all those roaring engines or perfect timing I couldn't say, but Desert Flower walked out onto the huge porch in front of the house, followed by over a dozen young people, all males. Other than looking young, they all had other things in common. They looked unkempt with raggedy clothes, and grime and ground in dirt on their skin as if washing up were a punishment. They certainly didn't look like a superior crowd to me. So many assessments of them ran through my head in an instant. People who didn't care for themselves in the most basic manner certainly wouldn't care for others. This looked like the clan from *The Hills Have Eyes*, all except for their mama and one other; he was well-dressed in his leathers and turquoise jewelry, and he wore a ring of animal teeth around his neck like Joe. He just stood there with his long raven black hair and sleek muscular physique. He had to be mama's favorite, and he looked Cherokee, unlike the rest who all looked like white trash without the brains to hide it. How could they be from her? They were obviously controlled by her, or mister well-dressed. I got the sickest, most sinking feeling standing there. Meanwhile, Luna had that look of anticipation on her face, while the look in her eyes showed she didn't know what to think. "Is that her?" Luna asks. "Desert Flower? That's her," I say with no excitement whatsoever. "You two never ..." she almost says as I tell, "No! I don't think she likes me. I hope you're as good at reading people as you are minds cuz she's kinda tricky. She'll be really nice to you when she wants something. Then when she's got it, she'll have no other use for you, like a conditional friend who just uses you," I explain. "Why are you telling me this? Don't you think I can read her? Don't you think I can do my job? My job is protecting the family," she says as if I disrespected her abilities somehow. "I'm just trying to prepare you for disappointment. I don't want you to be hurt," I needed her to know, because she was only looking at her mom and not the rest.

We pile out of the van as our biker buds get off their bikes and mill about. I got the impression that they wanted us to have our space and do our thing. Luna walked slowly and hesitantly towards the porch as I followed her, all the while my spidey senses telling me this was all things ominous. Why couldn't my girl pick upon that? Then as Luna got close enough, Desert Flower opened her arms, smiled a welcoming smile and asked, "Do you belong to me?" Luna came to her and embraced her, holding onto the mamma she never knew like someone would suddenly snatch her away. I just looked at Desert Flower, taking in her forty plus years look, which was years older than the last time I saw her. She was aging badly for one of us. I didn't think all this would affect

Luna so much. My Luna was a strong-willed, no nonsense girl, but I dare not speak up and take this moment from her. I think it's quite possible she came along with me only for this moment. The embrace finally ended and they looked at each other. "Hi, Reg," Desert Flower says to me with no discernible feeling. I just smile back with the same lack of interest. Nope, she does not like me.

"What's your gift? Everyone here has a special gift, what's yours?" she asked Luna, who looked as if she didn't think she should divulge any great secrets just yet. So, I jumped in to say, "Is this information for the CIA or Santa Claus? Wanna know if she's naughty or nice?" "Well, if it ain't the richest man in the world. Wadaya doin' around all us poor folks? Shouldn't you be off somewhere drinking Cognac and lighting cigars with hundred dollar bills?" she needles me. "Don't drinkey or smokey, and I see you haven't changed, never let up on the ball-busting," I remark. "Not where you're concerned. Why you with him? Couldn't you find a nice native boy?" she asks Luna, who looks trapped as I say, "Still playing control freak? It never worked with me," I jab. "Well, boy, you spent all your time trying to get into my pants," she return jabs. "More like I would never let you into mine," I return jab. "You think she'll believe that?" she refers to Luna. "Oh, she's very perceptive," I say and look at Luna, who after suffering through our verbal tennis match, suddenly looks more curiously at Desert Flower and asks, "Where exactly did you meet my father?" "Well, now that's no way to talk to your mamma," Desert Flower says with a smile that I can tell my Luna just doesn't buy. "I really wanna know. I need to know," Luna says sincerely to her new mom, who decides there is more to be told here, but not in front of me. "Come on inside. I'll tell you anything you need to know, including a few stories about your dad," she says with a smile I would never trust as I start to move toward the steps. "Just her," Desert Flower insists as her clan step up to prevent me from going in the house. I just look with concern at my girl, who tells me confidently, "It's okay, Reg." I felt so helpless as I stood there and just watched them file into the house. I noticed one of the dirtier clan members also had a string of teeth around his neck, except they looked like human teeth. As I stood there outside the house, I saw Luna stand there inside the house. So simple a thing it was to just look at her and feel such pleasure, all the while thinking it was the biggest mistake we would ever make; her going inside and me thinking I really had to be here. Then I noticed the well-dressed Cherokee, walking slowly from the end of the porch towards the door as his eyes never left me. He casually stepped inside the door and just stood there with his look of intensity, a look I'm sure he used to dominate others. Was it my imagination, or was I experiencing waves of bad energy being beamed my way? It sure felt like it. The more I stood there, the weaker I felt. But I give as good as I get and I stood my ground and gave him no satisfaction, only the blankness he gave me. Then he suddenly smiled. Then, still smiling, he flung the door closed. At that moment I knew I had made the biggest mistake of my life.

I suddenly yelled, "I'll come back in a few hours if you're not back!" I didn't want to smother my girl, make her think I have to be involved with every aspect of her life. After all, we all need our space. I know I do. Then why do I feel like I'll never see her again? Snap out of it! Go have some eats with Strongheart and the boys. So I walked back over to them.

Strongheart and I and my new bad-ass biker buds did indeed go out to eat. I paid, which made them all happy. Strongheart and I caught up on what we had missed in life and done in life, more importantly. I tried not to think about Luna. She had a lot of catching up to do, too! Strongheart told me we would gather more bikers to follow us as we made our way to Sturgis, where we could all meet up and gather an unlimited number of followers, for what I'm still not sure. Then night fell and I realized I had not heard from Luna, so I called her from my fancy phone. No answer. "Luna's not answering. Something's wrong," I told Strongheart. "You worry too easily," he said. Maybe I thought. No, dammit! Something's wrong. "I have to know. I have to go check," I told him. "You have to go check? I thought I was your friend. We have to go check," he assured me. "Thanks. Now when you say we, do you mean all of us or the royal we, just you and me?" I asked. "They will go if you ask them," he informs. "I hate to ask them, but there are only two of us. Desert Flower had a dozen of her clan waiting for us," I say as my friend interjects, "More than that. You see what she wants you to see." "Well, if you thought she was that conniving, why'd you let me come down here and do this?" I ask a bit bothered. "Worry does not change the future. If you want us to check, we will go check. That is what brother bikers do for each other," he says to reassure me as he puts his hand on my shoulder and walks away to talk to the rest of his fellow bikers. I just sat there and thought ... I didn't know what to think, as usual.

So Strongheart and I rode in the hippie van as I headed back to where I hoped my girl would be, safe and happy for her trouble staying where she thought she would learn more about herself, or at least what came before her. My biker entourage followed behind as I led the way this time. This time I was the quiet one, driving with total focus on what I needed to do, get back with my girl. I somehow thought I had betrayed her by leaving her behind, but that's what she wanted. I kept thinking she would find out things about me that would make her not need me anymore. Hell, I didn't used to be a gangster or anything like that. I wasn't anything before her.

We arrive back at Desert Flower's place. It was totally dark. My heart was sinking already. There was something wrong and I would make it right immediately! The second the van stopped, I jumped out of it, rushed up to the house and kicked the door open. I went slowly into the darkened house. There was no one to be seen. No one to be heard. It was lifeless. Strongheart suddenly came in and snapped on the lights. That made it even worse. Then I could see how lifeless this miserable place was. Then I saw it, Luna's phone setting on the middle of a big table in the middle of the room. I walked over to the table and picked it up. "Is that her phone?" Strongheart asked. "Yeah. One thing, only one thing and it's her phone. If that's not a message, I don't know what is," I say and don't know what to do. "We'll find her. And the more bikers we have to look, the more eyes we will have to look," he reassures me. "Look—that's it! Joe has a remote viewer at his place," I say as I put my phone on speaker phone and call Joe. Joe answers, "Reg, something is wrong with Luna." "I know, she's gone!" I inform Joe. "So that's it. She has been trying to contact me," Joe tells as I jump in to ask, "What did she say? Why didn't she call me?" "No, no! With her mind. Luna is trying to send me mental messages, but she obviously doesn't know where she is," Joe explains. "You've got remote viewers. Get 'em to work on it," I order. "She is working on it, but she has had limited success. It would seem Desert Flower can block her. There's something I have to tell you, Reg," Joe says to put an immediate lump in my throat. "Now you're really worrying me. Well, tell me," I must know. "Before Luna was born, Desert Flower tried to kill the child. She went crazy at the hospital when she was born. She wanted only sons. You did notice she has only male children, didn't you?" Joe asks. "You're not saying Luna's ..." I can't bring myself to say. "She is fine, for now. We must move quickly if she is to remain that way. I have sent for outside assistance," Joe tells. "You mean like, elite commandos or something?" I ask. "That is precisely what I mean." Joe clarifies. "We got plenty of ex-military guys. We don't need others in the way of what we gotta do," Strongheart interjects. "Who was that?" Joe asks. Strongheart interjects, "Joe, this is Reg's friend Strongheart. We met many years ago. Listen, if you send a team in here to find your daughter, it will only cause conflict between our guys and your guys. My guys will not take orders from anyone, except Reg." he tells Joe.

"You're probably right. My only other option is to find someone who can see my daughter without ever seeing her," Joe says exasperated. "We both know such a man. You are his friend, ask him," he tells Joe truly. "But I haven't seen him for so long. I wouldn't know where to look," Joe somberly says. "You know where," he advised Joe. "Perhaps. You know, I always wanted to know Desert Flower's name. The hospital staff barely saved my daughter from her. She fled before anyone knew her name. Luna needs you now, Reg. Please don't fail her," he says somberly and hangs up before his voice cracks.

I see Strongheart looking at an unusual lampshade on a nearby lamp. "Come on, man, we gotta go!" I stress as he says, "You better see this." I go over and look at the tightly stretched leather-looking lampshade over the lamp. "Human skin," he tells me. Like in a haze, I drift about the house, looking in other rooms and seeing bloodstains on floors and bits of bones everywhere. Then I went down into the cellar. It was a big area, and part of it was a huge walk-in freezer. Like it beckoned me, I had to look inside it. So I did. What I saw would have shocked Norman Bates. It looked like mummified bodies sitting around the walls as if they were sentinels frozen in time. They couldn't be real. Then there were the hooks. Some looked like pigs on hooks ready for barbecue. But the others, they looked kinda human. It has to be my imagination. This can't be real.

Then I put my hands on the sides of my head to keep it from exploding. My Luna was with them—with them!!! Or is she right here? "I know what you're thinking. She is not here," I hear Strongheart say as he comes in and stands with me. "How could I have let this happen!" I practically fly apart into pieces. "We'll find them. We'll never stop till we find them," he reassures me. I just stared forward for I don't know how long, my eyes about to burn holes in the wall. "This is messed up, man," I hear Voltaire say as I see him and a few more bikers looking around now. I'm glad they were here. They'd know what we're dealing with and would help. Our only quest now would be to find Luna–AND VENGEANCE!!!!!!!!!!!!!!!!!!!!!!!!!!!!

So here I ride in the hippie van, on the way to Sturgis. I ride alone, only my thoughts to torture me, and a growing army of bikers to follow me. Was rounding up more bikers instead of looking for my Luna my way of giving up on her? Hell no!! My kind have been living amongst you for centuries. We know how to hide. If I am to find what I am looking for, I will need all the eyes I can find for the looking. And if I don't eat, don't sleep, don't have a minute's pleasure and only pain, that's fine. In my task more sacred and noble than finding the Grail, I shall not stop! I will not give up nor give in. And if there is much pain, and suffering and blood! I will make sure it is from my enemy, which is Desert Flower's clan or anyone who gets in my way. This is no time for mercy as I have no well to draw it from. Come ride with me ...

20) SEEKING

I'm riding a Harley now. I traded in the hippie van. It's got too many happy symbols on it. I'm not into happy right now. I'm pretty much an atomic bomb with a short fuse riding through Hades without permission. I'll find my girl or end up like Billy in *Knightriders.* So Strongheart and I discussed the matter, because speaks with anyone else I'm riding with is rather limited. Where would Desert Flower go? She wouldn't leave the states, she considers America her land, as a lot of our native friends do. So would she be just miles away or move cross country? She's not a city girl. She would have to have a place that Luna couldn't escape from so easily, unless she's chained somehow. I hate thinking about that. We're thinking possibly a huge farm or place with lots of space. The clan would have to go out for provisions on occasion, unless they're preppers. Man, it just gets more complicated. We haven't informed the law to help us find them; that would just take the ability and the supreme pleasure away from what I am going to do to them when I find them.

Joe calls sometimes, he thinks maybe Desert Flower's got dark forces helping them. I'm not sure what that means. Is that like the devil or just one of his demon buds? Anyway, I am on my way to Sturgis, and at every stop I sound off and add more bikers to Rolling Thunder, more eyes to find my Luna.

Strongheart signals me to turn into yet another giant roadside bar. So Rolling Thunder, now hundreds strong, parks outside the bar, and everywhere else they feel like parking. With Strongheart by my side, I go into the bar and straight back to the stage where a band is singing. As I go up the stairs to get onstage, a big dude gets in my way. "Move," I calmly told him and I was on stage. I guess the band didn't hear me cuz they kept playing, until they recognized me. The stunned lead singer gave me the mic as I simply held out my hand. Strongheart smiled next to me; he knew what was coming. So I stood silently before my receptive audience in my custom leather vest open to my beautifully ripped bare chest, my sunglasses, and all my studded leather fashion badassery and calmly said, "You are today's Knights Templars, the knights of the highway, rolling through life your own way; taking what you want and not saying pretty please because why the fuck should you? Because, you see, a ride is not something you do on just weekends or special occasions, riding is a way of life! And when you ride with Rolling Thunder, you have found your ultimate purpose, to ride with Reg. Well, search no more, you have found him. I am Reg. I am the shaman. I am Mr. Goodtrips. Join me."

Before a couple hours go by, I'm at another bar, on the stage and ready to rock and roll as I entice, "I know what you've all been waiting for. You've been waiting for it all your life. Well, here it is, the ultimate high, with no cost to body or mind. The ultimate experience with no consequences. Wanna really be free? Join with me."

A few hours later and—you guessed it! I'm on stage at another bar as I proclaim, "Do a lotta drugs? They mess with your head, empty your wallet? Well, have a free hit of Reg. He'll soothe your savage mind and you'll never want it to stop. I'm Mr. Goodtrips! And I roll with the thunder!! Join me!"

And that's how it is for me now, town after town and bar after bar of me thinking of more cute and profound ways of stealing souls to join my ever increasing army of bikers for our cause. I'm getting hard—very hard! When I think of my girl, I harden fast and hard! No weak thoughts, only total focus on my goal of building my army and constantly moving. Joe called me the other day. He told me if I wasn't so filthy, stinking rich, I wouldn't be able to pick up the check for my rolling army. They eat a lot. They drink a lot. They party a lot. Nothing's too good for my men. Did I mention we are thousands strong now? When we roll through a town, it's our town. Local fuzz stays out of our way. People are quitting their jobs and becoming bikers just to join Rolling Thunder, or just to cozy up near me. We don't need the sissy soft. We want the hard and fast and born to last. We cull out the weaklings by making them pay their own way. Then soon they're gone.

I'm running through a clearing in the forest. But why am I running? A cabin, a cabin in the distance. I see it. I must reach it, but why? Luna is there, she must be. And if Luna is there, they must be there, they who I must destroy! I hold out my arm and a sword appears in my hand. It feels good, like it belongs there. And I run even faster, seemingly folding space as I leap forward ever closer to the cabin ahead that never leaves my sight.

And I see them, they who would keep my Luna and my vengeance from me; Desert Flowers' pitiful offspring chopping wood and waiting for oblivion. I would give it to them. So I raise my Conan-like sword and scream my presence known as the two diseases made flesh turn to me with their puny woodsman axes in hand and look upon me with their exquisite horror. And I swung my sword, only to see dust dancing about the air as I had vanquished only lifeless statues. I wanted blood!!! "What trickery is this, witch? Show yourself!!" I yelled, hoping to summon the hag from her cabin lair.

And the witch did appear. The cabin door opened, only to have total darkness displayed within. Then Desert Flower floated out of the cabin within a circle of red mist that dissipated as she hovered just outside the cabin door, all the while cackling like the true witchy woman she was. Where's Luna? Where is your family, your sons? I want you to witness what I shall do to them. Then it will be known what awaits you," I said with eyes that could pierce any armor. I would have my vengeance.

"Then have them," it cackles as all her bad boys emerged from out of the darkness of the cabin, each appearing with a different weapon, as if such fumbling hands could ever use them. They surround me now, standing in a perfect circle around me in the distance. I pick up the cheap wooden-handled ax left on the ground and just look at it as it transforms into a shiny broadaxe right out of the Middle Ages. Such a lovely huge blade it has, perfectly suited for the bloody hacking it must now do. I didn't have to wait for long, though, as they all came at me, swinging their swords and sickles, their axes and maces my way. But I was the only true warrior, and I swung my sword and chopped my ax faster than any human could as clan member after clan member simply exploded into dust, each a different color that rose up and just hung in the air. I was tired, breathing hard. Then the witch proclaimed smiling, "You will become tired of swinging such heavy weapons. Then they will have you." "What are they? Why don't they die? Why won't they bleed? I want blood–your blood! And I will have it!!" Then all the different colors floated down and formed into clan members once again, all ready to hack, and chop and beat me to death as I just waited for it to happen again and again for all time. Must I be like Sisyphus and roll this rock uphill for eternity?

Then she appeared, that incomparably beautiful fair-skinned woman from my dreams, floating down and hovering above the battle to take place. Without speaking, she opened her hand to reveal a tiny ball of twinkling light. Then she simply tossed it into the mud within my circle, winked at me and floated away.

And the clan members moved to attack, only to stop as the mud began to rise up and take the shape of a giant, featureless being. No one knew how to react. What was it? Or who did it come for? Then as the clan members began to move my direction, the ten-foot mud man simply opened its eyes and mouth as brilliantly bright light streamed out of him and he rotated his head to focus the light on all the attacking clan members as they exploded into dust once more. This time the dust fell to the earth instead of rising. They would rise no more.

"She invoked a sun golem! Such powerful friends you have, but you have not your Luna," the witch barked as she pulled Luna out of the darkness of the cabin and held onto her so she couldn't come to me. "Luna!" I yelled. "Reg. Reg, don't leave me!" she yelled back with such anguish in her eyes. "Never! Break free. Break free of the witch. You're strong, you can do it!" I empower her. At that moment, Luna did break free, pulling away from the old hag and rushing out of the cabin. She was so happy, both of us smiling as she ran towards me. And suddenly as she was almost right before me, she was yanked back by some unseen force back into the darkness of the cabin as the evil witch cackled on the doorstep. "You'll never have her–never! And you'll never see her again," the witch mocked me with her disgusting laugh as she too was sucked back into the darkness of the cabin and continued her mocking laugh. "Luna!" I could only scream, lunging forward as the cabin door slammed shut. Then the cabin ripped itself off its foundation and rocketed up into the sky as I watched helplessly.

My eyes pop open. I suddenly feel as if I will never find her. I haven't smiled for so long. I won't until I find her. No word about her is getting to me. I stare straight ahead riding my bike all day. When I close my eyes for sleep, it's like I just blinked and I'm up and ready to go. I look at my phone to make sure I got my three hours. I see all my men sleeping in whatever desert or field we stopped at for rest and I realize it's still dark. I have hours to kill without waking them up. I can't travel with big weights, so I use really strong bands so I can workout when I rise as I have for so long. It keeps my mind off the bad thoughts in my head. I think I'm cracking up sometimes. Is this the life I really wanted? No Luna breeds no sanity. News better break soon about a clan member sighting or I might end up driving my rolling army of followers off a cliff. I've thought about it, you know. Don't tell them. It would be so easy. But then I realized my Luna would never be free and I would never desert her. I will find her. I guess you'd say I need hope. Hope is bullshit! You wanna know what hope is? It's an empty glass in the desert. You fill it. There's your hope. Then hope walked up to me.

Out of the dark he came, a middle-aged man; an average looking man of average size and Japanese descent I would soon learn. "Come with me," was all he said. The serious look in his eye said he meant business. But how would I converse with him? It turns out I could. He didn't have any special quality in his voice, though he was immune to mine. He was a fellow traveler. He was like me. As we walked and talked under the bright full moon illuminating the desert, I learned he was much older than me. I learned that at one time he was a Samurai. He told me that he had studied lost mystic arts in Tibet. And for some reason he wanted to teach poor, pitiful me something. According to him, I had potential, the potential to destroy the world while trying to save it. Because of my unique abilities, he knew he would be able to teach me what I needed to know in much less time, as our time together would be very limited.

Then, as we were far enough away in the desert for no one to see us, he abruptly sat on the desert sand, crossed his legs and put his hands together as he made a kind of chanting or grunting sound. I didn't interrupt him. I was patient, for I knew he must be doing this for a reason. Then I saw him, a Samurai wearing armor walking towards me from out of the desert. The Samurai stopped right next to some large cactus and just looked at me. I could only see his eyes through his helmet, eyes I recognized as from the man sitting on the ground beside me. The Samurai suddenly gave out a yell, drew his sword and sliced a cactus cleanly through. Then as the freshly pruned cacti fell over, the Samurai simply vanished. My new friend stood up now and asked, "What did you just learn?" "To be freaked-out? Yeah, I learned that!" I said as he looked a bit disappointed. "Think! What else did you learn?" he said and expected an answer. So I thought about it with my defective computer brain and said, "That was from your mind, wasn't it?" He smiled and said, "Yes, from my id!" "Yeah, I saw an episode of *Kung Fu* from the seventies where the monk conjured up images like that," I said to impress him, but I was unsuccessful as he just rolled his eyes and said, "Crude example! You must learn more. You are an infant!" "Hey, I'm no kid, you know," I barked to get under his skin even more as he just said, "Infant! Do you wish to learn?" "What you just showed me, yes! If it will help me find my Luna," I said with my melancholy showing. His demeanor softened or he just took pity on me as he tried to instruct me in this ancient art of conjuring from the mind. Before the darkness was to be obliterated by the light of day, I asked him if he wanted to work out together, as was my habit every morning before the others rose. He just smiled and said, "We will one day." Then he just walked back into the darkness and sea of sleeping bikers never to be seen again.

As I workout away from the men by a cactus in the desert, Strongheart walks up to me. Like me, he doesn't need as much sleep. "Why do you workout? We are going to live a long time whether we exercise or not," he brags. "I like it, keeps me strong," I tell him between huffs and puffs. "Andre The Giant never worked out and he was stronger than anyone. He used to brag about not working out," he tells me. "I am not a giant. And besides, Andre only lived to forty-six," I told him. "Well, I'll show you my workout later. It involves pumping twelve ounce cans of brewski between my arm and lip," he describes as he demonstrates the fine art of pumping brew. I stop between sets to find out why he's bothering me! "Is there something you need to tell me that can't wait till I'm done?!" I say a bit bothered. "Yeah! There's been a sighting. It would seem Desert Flower needs money. Some of her boys robbed a few stores," he tells me. "Close?" I asked. "A couple towns back. You know what that means? They have to be in that area," he fills me in. "Maybe. You know what they say, never steal in your own back yard," I imagine. "I don't think she's that smart. We're not all are that smart. And for her to do the things she is doing, she must have the soul sickness," he tells. "She doesn't have a soul! She doesn't use her head or her abilities," I say as I think I haven't been using all my talents to find Luna. "What are you thinking?" he asks a distant-looking me. "I'm thinking this might be our only chance. It's been almost three weeks. I just get the feeling if I don't go for it right now, I may never see her again." I stress. "Okay. But I suggest we do it alone. Big crowds tend to get noticed," he advises. So we commenced to sneaking around to get our bikes without anyone going wakey-wakey until we managed to leave. A few did wake up, though. I just told them to go back to sleep. I drew the line on singing them lullabies.

So here Strongheart and I are, driving the dark and lonely blacktop of night. I'd call it a peaceful ride if not for all the mangled thoughts I was thinking. I didn't know what I'd find. Not finding is not an option. Speed was the only option, and we rode like we just sprang outta Hell as we burned a flaming path behind us. I wasn't going back without her. The more I rode, the more I felt like I was actually getting somewhere, where she would be waiting for me. Don't ask me how I knew—I just did!

We rode past farmhouse after farmhouse, field after field. Then I heard my name being called. Was it a message from my girl or merely my mind wandering? But my name kept repeating in my head, and now it sounded like Luna's voice was saying it. It has to be Luna! She's sending me a message. I know she is! Her voice calling my name is louder than ever now. Then suddenly it stopped. I looked over at this big farm behind a field of crops and I pulled the bike over in front of it. Strongheart pulled up behind me. "She's here," I blurt out. I just hoped she wasn't calling out from some lonely, forgotten grave on this massive land. There were several buildings on the property. It didn't look like a farm. After looking through a small pair of binoculars, Strongheart said, "I see Halloween decorations. I think they're getting this place ready for the holiday, like some haunted hayride deal. She can't be there." "She's here," I say, staring straight ahead without really seeing. This was the time. This was the night. This was revenge night; all scores would be settled and all wrongs would be righted ... and there would be suffering.

"Did you see him?" I suddenly blurted out. "See who?" he asked. "The guy I was talking with earlier in the desert, the Japanese guy?" I ask again. "I didn't notice," he said as if I made it up. "Well, I'm not a loony, I was talking with the guy. He said he was a Samurai. He was like us. You don't know him?" I asked. "I don't. Only you do," he says like I'm nutso for sure. "Hey, I saw him, okay?" I stress. "Okay, you saw him. Why are you telling me now?" he asked. "He came to teach me something. I think it was for this very moment." I explained. "What?" he seriously says back. "To make images from my mind, bring them forth, give them power," I say. "You mean an avatar or tulku like in *Forbidden Planet*, make a monster from your subconscious?" he asks as I just get the most twisted idea and purge forth, "A monster, yeeeaaaaaah. That's just what's needed here, something monstrous."

I get off my bike. I just stand there not really sure how to proceed, the story of my life. Strongheart gets off his cycle and takes two cloth wrapped objects off the back of his bike, and as he unwraps them he tells me, "Not to disrespect your abilities, but your voice won't work on Desert Flower's family members. These will. Ever seen *Prime Cut* with Lee Marvin? These are M10's, an older but reliable weapon. See how the magazines are taped together? After you empty one, you just pop it out and slap in the other side. It's quicker that way. Hell, why give your enemy a chance to kill you? It's us or them,

Reg. You do realize that, don't you?" "More than you know. They're going to die, all of them, and I won't need a weapon" I say staring straight ahead. "Reg, I know you're psyching yourself up, but fists won't work against heavy artillery. They robbed a bank or whatever. They have weapons. You can't go in there defenseless," he explains. "Would you like to see what the desert man showed me? That's what's going in there," I say as I look up at the power lines overhead. Then I sat on the ground and crossed my legs. An image started to form in my mind, one more ghastly and horrible than any of my twisted nightmares; it was of a shapeless form, a mass that took the shape of the wretched and deformed faces and limbs that would pop in and out of it. And as this form of mental madness rose up in the air above me, I made sure it would have the power it needed to reek the monstrous mayhem it was intended for as it rose up into the power lines, drawing power from them as the electricity arced and crackled with the power sent within the undulating mass as if madness itself had been created and was trying to escape into the world. I could see what the form saw, watching it fill with power and the look of amazement on my friend's face as he just looked up at it from down below.

Then the form drifted its way in the air over the field of crops, wilting and burning them as if to say nothing will be allowed to live where I roam. Sitting on the ground, I saw what the form saw. I saw Strongheart crouch down and move through the fields with his M10. Let him do it his way. Let him feel useful. So I would let the monsters in the house meet a real monster.

Eerily quiet the form crept up towards the buildings behind the giant field. If one were to witness this medusa in all its glory, one just might go mad. And as the form reached its destination, I saw no inhabitants anywhere. There was no one outside. Could I have been wrong? I was in tune with great power, I must not just use my eyes, though. I would have to listen, listen with my mind! Luna, where are you? "I am near, down here," she faintly said in my head. Of course! She was under the ground! I sent my form through the buildings, nothing but Halloween props and spooky jump scares waiting to scare no one. No one was there. Then the form ventured under the structures—but nothing! Luna, where are you? I can't find you. I must find you! Then the form moved through the last structure and there they were, Desert Flower's clan, eating, and drinking and having fun! But no Luna! But they would have fun no more. My Lovecraftian menace reached out for them, grabbing them with its claws and tentacles, and swallowing them whole, and I could sense what they were feeling. Hell had come for them, to take them where they belonged. My form made quick work of them all, but where was my Luna or Desert Flower? Then my form suddenly passed through the floor—and there she was, my Luna! She was just lying in a bed as Desert Flower sat across the room and read to her from a book. Needless to say, that vile hag dropped her book and looked on at my form in eye-popping horror.

As I sat there, I realized my little experiment was out of control. I had conjured up something I could no longer control. Then my eyes sprang open as I sprang to my feet and I ran! I ran across the field like I was running for my life. I ran as if I were an exploding bomb of anxiety and only running faster could stop it. I had to get there before now. And soon I was there, smashing through the front door and down into the basement. There was Desert Flower and there was the form. I think it knew it was part of me so it didn't attack. Then I walked over to Luna just lying on the bed. She looked so weak. I tried to smile, but I didn't know if I should. I didn't truly know that she was okay. I was so torn between happiness and vengeance. Then there was the form, just hovering there as it waited, but for what? I sat on the bed next to Luna and took her hand. She managed a smile just for me, and instantly my need for vengeance was just gone, replaced with eyes that could not see clearly through the mist filling them. The long nightmare was over, I had my Luna back.

I wiped my eyes and asked her, "Can you speak?" She faintly said, "You have to send it away." I started to rise up from the bed, but I sat back down as she pulled on my hand. I came closer as she whispered something in my ear. She smiled and I smiled as I stood up to confront the form, while Desert Flower still cowered in her chair. I ignored her as I told the form, "You cannot perish. You are part of me, but you cannot stay. Oh, and take one more with you." The form now turned on Desert Flower, moving towards her as the hag could only sit and witness her coming deserved end. Then my mind form opened up for her to see the horrors within it, something I could not see from where I was standing. But she could. And from the look on her face and the scream she let out, it was probably a horror left unseen for curious eyes. The form now simply sucked her in, but not in an O so delicate way. In an instant, it compacted her down into atomized particles like a spaceship getting too close to a black hole and sucked them in. Nothing would escape it. Too bad it didn't take longer. It reminded me of the things they would say in the old mad scientist movies. There truly are some things man was not meant to meddle with, and I had unleashed a power I best send as far away as possible. So in my mind I imagined the form rising up into space where it could do no more harm. Then bursting with power, the form did indeed rise up through the house and up into the air. In my mind I could see Strongheart outside just looking up at my form rising up into the darkness. Then he rushed towards the house.

Strongheart rushes into the basement with his M10 to see me laying on the bed next to Luna, who has a firm grasp on me. "I didn't see anyone. They must have cleared out before we got here," he surmises. "Forget about them. Call an ambulance. The bastards didn't feed her. They didn't want it said that they killed one of their own. They'd just let her die," I say feeling weaker. He takes out his phone as he tells me, "She's taking your energy, a way for her to survive. Just don't let her take it all." "She can have it all ..." I say as I fade to black.

I guess I fell asleep. I'm awake now. It's still dark. Uh oh, I've been sleep walking again. I don't know how I got here, but I wandered into a graveyard. Why can't I wander into a fridge and raid it like everyone else? It is peaceful, though. So quiet. Well lit, too! Look at that full moon. I walk among the tombstones. They're very old. This graveyard's been here a while. What? Someone just walked past a large tombstone up in the distance. There she is, a woman wearing a long grey dress with long, raven black hair. I didn't know they wore dresses like that anymore. She's turning toward me. She sees me. She's coming this way. And the way she turns as if in slow motion with her dress and her hair blown around by a gentle breeze, yet there is no breeze. It's Luna! She should be in bed. She's not well. She's ... she's so beautiful. Maybe it's just my eyes or the way she looks in the moonlight, but she looks pale. And her eyes, they shimmer as if made of liquid silver. She stops before me. "Reg," her voice reverberates in my head. She approaches me, puts her hand on my face. It's so cold! As if the words from her mouth came out ever so slowly she smiles, "You love your Luna, don't you?" "Yeeeeeeeeeeees," I can only say. "I need you," her wispy voice says as she smiles, showing her glistening white fangs. How curiously reel they look. I don't care, it's my Luna. She caresses my face, looks deep into my mind with her beautifully shimmering eyes. I wish this would never end. I'm mesmerized by her. I want her. "I know you do. I want you too," she says as she kisses my neck. She looks up at me, her fangs growing out even more as her silvery eyes are filling up with a bloody red. I knew what was coming and I didn't stop it. I feel a sharp sting on my neck. I don't protest, don't say a thing. She needs me. I feel tired suddenly. "I think you're taking too much," I say as I turn my head to look. She turns her head, her beautiful face snarling at me as blood—my blood—gushes down her chin. "Don't look at me!" she says more with her piercing red eyes than her hungry mouth as she once again sinks her fangs into me. I try to push her off me—but I can't! She's too strong and I'm too weak. I feel my blood, my very life force being drained out of me. My mouth drops open of its own volition as I feel my weakening body being emptied and collapsing in on itself. I try to scream—but I cannot! I feel my eyes being sucked into my head. I can't see. I can't see!!!

I spring up in a hospital bed, my Luna in the bed next to me with Joe sitting in a chair by her side and two security guards that I recognize from my palace sitting nearby. It's rather comical the way they are all staring at me now. "You just disabled the nurse. We might need her," Joe says with a smile as I look over at the frozen nurse dropping the clipboard that she was writing on. "How'd I do that? I've been asleep, haven't I?" I ask mystified. "Until you woke up raving. Tell us, can you see?" he asks. "I don't see Strongheart. Where is he?" I ask. "Try looking out the window," Joe tells me as I hop out of bed with all my energy returned and then some. Then I go look out the window to see a sea of motorcycles and my Rolling Thunder army in the parking lot down below. "Wow! And I don't see 'im," I say as Joe says, "No doubt. The hospital requested, when you're available, to kindly ask them to leave. They do tend to frighten people away." I rush over now next to Luna, who lays there with intravenous drips attached to her. I look at her with such concern as she just looks at me. "How long have we been here?" I ask. "Only a day and a half, not long enough to rectify the damage they did to her," Joe comments. "Well, they won't do it again," I casually remark as I can't take my eyes off my girl. "How do you know that? No one knows where they are," Joe suspiciously says as I look directly at him and say, "Would you rather find them or have her?" Luna barely manages to speak to defend me by saying, "Dad, don't give him a hard time. I wouldn't be here if not for Reg." "That's exactly right. You wouldn't be here if not for Reg!" Joe accuses. "Yeah, it's my fault again. Hey, did you hear I shot Kennedy and Lincoln, too?" I jab. "Would you please tell your rolling entourage to leave," Joe requests. "Sure. Where are my clothes?" I ask as I just look at Joe. "Have you never been in a hospital? They're in the closet," he tells me as I go retrieve them from the closet and tell him, "I want everyone out of the room. I want to talk to my girl ... alone." "You can't talk in front of the statues here who won't remember, or is it me? I feel as if there's some unspoken truth here," Joe insinuates. "About what?" I ask innocently. "About her mother. People just don't disappear!" Joe further insinuates. I come over to Luna again and just look at her as I ask, "You didn't tell him?" She just smiles and gives me that innocent look. I guess I get to do all the heavy lifting on this one. "Come on, I'm waiting. Someone tell me what?" Joe demands.

"Ever heard of the id?" I ask him. "Oh! What did you do now?" he asks or rather—bitches! "So I'm guessing you have. Well, I kinda, you know, conjured up a little monster, mothers little helper to save the day. Those guys had guns and Strongheart wanted to storm in there with his machine gun. I just thought my way was better," I say. "So you conjured up a monster? I'm guessing you didn't put the genie back in the bottle, did you?" he asks.

"I sent it out into space, take that!" I jestfully jab. "I wouldn't mess with that kind of power again. Where on earth did you learn to do that?" he gets inquisitive. "Mess with? I can juggle all the hot coals, baby! If you must know, some ancient Samurai showed up that night to teach me just that skill. He demonstrated it, conjured up his own Samurai bad self. Don't tell me you're not happy with the results," I say as I look at him and wait for his reply on that one, yeah! "Nothing in this world could make me any happier than seeing my Luna again," he says with meaning and I jump to say, "And nothing could make me happier than to see my Luna." A little dueling Lunas there. "You are leaving out one thing, though. Where are Desert Flower and her clan?" he asks me so slowly and deliberately as I tell, "Have some of the security guys go to the house where we met the clan originally and take pictures." "Why?" he speedily spits out. "Because it's a house of horrors. I'm talking *Texas Chainsaw, Deranged, Psycho*, take your pick. Ever heard of the Sawney Bean Clan? Your one night stand must have been traveling around for centuries, thinking every poor stiff she encounters is potential take-out," I tell him. "My God!" he can only say. "Still care about what happened to them?" I say and then think of something. I go through my mind when the form was vacuuming up clan members and I can't see the well-dressed Cherokee. "He wasn't there," I blurt out. "Who wasn't there?" Joe asks. "The one that dressed so nice. He also wore a necklace of animal teeth around his neck, just like you do. Right now, get more security for this place. He might come for her," I surmise. "I have two outside the door, but you may be right in this case," he says and instantly gets on his phone. I stop pacing about and go over to Luna again. "You can't leave, can you?" I ask Luna, who just gives me an 'are you serious' look. "You're not out of the woods, are you?" I ask her. "I'll be okay," she smiles at me. "Can I get you something before I collect up my rowdy riders outside?" I ask her. "In-N-Out Burger," she says as dad jumps in to say, "No solid food yet!" I lean over Luna to say, "Please don't go away. I would have to go away, too," I barely get out and kiss her. Then I turn so Joe can't see sloppy me and head for the door. "Reg!" she simply says to stop me before I open it and tells me, "I love you." 'That's the first time you ever told me' I mentally send to her. 'I'll have to say it more often', she said in my head. Like Captain Kirk, I can't have burly bikers seeing me like this, anything less than perfect. So I composed myself at warp speed and I just left.

21) HELL ON WHEELS

Since camping out in the hospital with a few thousand bikers was not an option, I took to the road with them again to round up more bikers to make Rolling Thunder the biggest, baddest and freest army on earth. Sit in your cubicles. Sell your stocks. Grind out another meaningless, forgettable chunk of time and life, while we roll past you and show you what real freedom is. How much trouble could I get into? Okay, I'll try not to destroy the world.

I'm the leader, no doubt about it! Strongheart rolls by my side. They say there are so many of us now that when Rolling Thunder moves, you can see us from space. I dig that. C'mon, aliens! Try to invade! We're waiting for you. Turns out, I've been going about feeding my men the wrong way. Why should I pay for it all? How 'bout merchandising? We coordinate our travel now so that at every stop local vendors have every kind of good eats and Reg or biker stuff to sell, and fans waiting there to buy it. Some come for the bikers or just the circus, freak-show atmosphere. There are usually plenty of fights, which means there are plenty of cops. It's funny how fuzz never want us around, till I tell them they do. Most of all, the crowds always come for me. I can't change that. I'm learning more and more when to talk and when to keep my mouth shut. Still, there is an empty spot, my queen to ride by my side. She'll be with me soon enough. Can't ride into Valhalla in the end without her.

I had a good day. I got to see my fans, make more money for me and my men, round up more members for Rolling Thunder and nobody even got into a fight. We pull off the road into some desert somewhere, I'm not exactly sure. The men break off into their groups, build their campfires and get ready for a night of partying till they get tired or just pass out. I'm with Strongheart, of course. As we sit and enjoy eating mass quantities, something in the sky catches our eye. A helicopter lands safely just outside of the perimeter where it wouldn't el crasho and whopper chopper up my guys. Then I see what looks like a familiar face get out of it, a female. After walking closer and talking to some of the bikers, she walks in the direction they were all pointing, my direction. It didn't take long for me to recognize her. Hell, who else would it be? I got up and started to run to her. Then she saw me and started running to me. Weaving between bikers, and cycles, and cactus, we ran like there was nothing more pure in the world than the need for the one to see the other. There was screaming, and cheering and smiles like the whole world just got happy! Then my arm went out and my hand reached out, and her hand reached out! Then we were there in each other's arms. My Luna was back!

Then I kissed her, or she kissed me. We're on the same wavelength for sure. Time seems to stand still when we kiss. After leaving smooch city, I just looked at her, just for the pure pleasure of it. "Are you sure you're better? I don't want you doing this just to make me happy," I tell her truly. "You're forgetting, our kind heals faster ... and Sunny came to the hospital. She makes everyone feel better," she explains. We walk and talk our way through the crowd back over to my camp area. "Reg, what's at the end of this rainbow?" she asks as I answer, "Whadaya mean?" "I mean, when does this train stop? When do you get off? Where are you going with allllllll these bikers?" She prods me. "Going to Sturgis! You know that," I say. "Yeah, then what?" Yeah, then what? I'll have to ask Strongheart. "Yeah, why don't we do that?" she taps my brain. "You haven't lost your ability to crowd my cranium I see," and say. "You know, you could be a great leader if you weren't so easily led," she says as we reach my spot among the masses.

Luna looks around and sees Strongheart, our two motorcycles and camping stuff. It's what she didn't see that bothered her. "Where's the van?" she asks. "It's, uh, somewhere," is all I could come up with. I hope she doesn't find out I sold it. Crap! She does now. "You sold it! That van was in our family since the sixties. What did you sell it for? You don't need the money," she complains with her hands on her hips. "I traded it in for two wheels. Can't be a biker without a bike," I tell. "Yeah? Well, track it down after you finish playing biker and get it back," she expresses. "Lots of good memories in the back of that van, eh?" Strongheart smiles, but she doesn't. She turns her interrogating skills on him next. "You know, I was always a bit fuzzy on why you're doing this. What happens after Sturgis?" she inquires. "Reg does not just play biker, he is a biker now. No one has done what he has done, unite all bikers," he tells. "For what? For what!" she persists. "You and I are of Native blood. Our ancestors lived free on this land and we will again," he says to mystify her and me. "You're not saying you want to take back the land, are you? Is this another stolen land argument? The word is conquer! The Romans did it; the Mongols, the Ottoman empire ... "I interrupt all excited with, "Oow! Oow! Vlad the Impaler invented shish-kabob." For some reason she looks at me like I'm the loony of the month and finally says, "More of your useless information? And for your information, it's thought that the Turks invented shish-kabob." "Yeah, because after they saw what Vlad 'Draccy baby' the Impaler did–impale a bunch of really unfortunate invader dudes on big sticks–they got the idea for meat on a stick, mm mm!" "Been hit in the head again?" she asks after looking at me like I just took a big step into wacko territory, and without missing a beat she turns to Strongheart to say, "You know, a lot of people live in their little boxes on this land. I don't think they're ready to just give it up," she tells. "Not theirs. The set aside land that the government steals and says belongs to all of us, when really it belongs to no one. That land can be ours once again, and it would take from no one," he explains. "Does that include the national parks? Doesn't your Gawanii live in one of them? What does he think of this?" she asks. "You will know when you meet him at the end of our journey," he tells her. "That's good to know. I'd hate to just rush into things, like going to war with the most powerful army in the world; an army with enough tanks, and planes and bombs to wipe out everyone here in minutes. That did occur to you, didn't it? I'd hate to see Reg guided or misguided into ending his life so pointlessly. I kinda like this guy," she says wisely. "The greatest wars are won without firing a shot. I kinda like this guy, too," he agrees. "Gee, I'm glad someone around here does. You are aware that big brother can't wait to get rid of me. I mean, I appreciate all the free protection, but Rolling Thunder is also a really big target and hard to miss. Let's not give anyone a reason to screw up our rolling good time just yet, okay?" I say as I wait for a reply to all this news that's news to me. "We have lived free a long time, and in time we will live on land that is ours. You will always be welcome to live there with me," he believes.

Out of the corner of my eye I see a knife moving through the air, twirling its way towards us. Like I was the Flash, I could see the knife slow down as my hand reached out and grabbed it just before it would have hit Luna. We three all looked surprised naturally. Then we looked over in the direction the knife was thrown. And there he was, the well-dressed Cherokee. I was merely surprised, but there was only a look of hate in Luna's eyes. Then the well-dressed Cherokee took off running through the crowd as Luna snatched the knife from my hand and took out after him. He was fast—really fast! But Luna! She seemed demon possessed. Even though he was stronger and faster, she drew upon her hate to get ever closer to him with every step. He occasionally glanced back, which only slowed him up as she got even closer to her prey. Because that's what he was now, and no one on earth better get between predator and her prey. I hate to think what he did to make her act this way, but I'm on team Luna, baby! With the bikers finally catching on to what's going down, one of the bikers trips the well-dressed Cherokee, his body crashing and tumbling across the hard desert sand. Not quite back on his feet, he feels the hot blade of his big Bowie knife in his back. Luna put it there. He stands reaching around for it, painfully unable to reach it. Strongheart and I have both reached Luna now as we and all the fellow bikers just wait for the man with the knife in his back to make his next move.

"I want him!" she speaks with her eyes on fire. She would have her revenge for whatever unspeakable evil she experienced with him and I dare not stop her. Not being able to reach the knife or to be killed so easily, the well-dressed Cherokee started to laugh at us. If Luna tried to get closer to him, he would simply reach his arm out quickly and scare her to back off. "He's not getting away," I say unnecessarily. "No shit!" she did not elaborate further. Then Strongheart bravely moved closer to her and whispered something into her ear. After hearing him, she actually smiled and simply said, "Yeeeaaaah!" My friend had finally said something she would agree with, and sooooo happily!

So here we are, all of us. This is apparently what Strongheart whispered into the ear of my girl. Normally she would be against doing something like this I'm pretty sure, but something changed in her. Like me, this whole journey, this ordeal of finding her must have been a cake walk next to whatever she experienced. I don't know whether to ask her about it or forever remain silent. If she ever tells me, it will be only when she's ready. And if she never does, that's fine too. I have her back, that's what really matters.

The well-dressed Cherokee is on the ground with long chains secured to his arms and legs, and the chains are secured to four motorcycles pointing in four different directions. Luna stands over him with the bloody Bowie knife that was in his back not long ago. She just stares at him, possibly taunting him by sending messages into his head. She would give him no quarter, no relief, no mercy. Strongheart steps up to tell him, "You dishonor your people. What do you wish to speak before your trip to Hell?" "When you are through, I will come back and finish what I started. I will come for you all!!!!!!!!" the rotting soul on the ground said. "When he says what I want him to say, that's the signal. Do it then," Luna says. "I will speak no more!" It said. Luna smiled now and simply said, "Oh, yeah?" Then she quickly brought the huge blade up over her head with both hands and plunged every inch of that blade down deep into his happy sack ... happy no more as he SCREAMED!!!!!!!!!!! It was music to her ears as she backed away and all four motorcycles took off to the north, south, east and west. In *Braveheart* days, they'd do it another way. Our method required a bit more horsepower.

Then we all witnessed what was left of our madness shaking violently on the ground as if to get up and seek vengeance against us all, like in some old horror film. "Why won't it die?" I can't believe. "We do not die easy," Strongheart said. "Then how do we kill it?" I simply asked. "What else do you do with trash? You burn it!!!" Luna yelled a primal yell that had to get out and just walked away, wiping her face, her eyes with her back to me as she worked her way through the crowd into the desert. She came among us to such great joy, only to leave to such sorrow. “I know you want to go to her. You must not. Some things must be done alone,” my friend advises me. He’s right. I can only watch Luna get farther and farther away. ‘Please come back to me ... when you’re ready’ was the mental message I sent to her. I hope she gets it.

It’s dark now. Campfires dotted the desert, especially one in particular. Even from where I was camped so far away, I could see Luna’s form standing vigil over the burning funeral pyre, waiting as if its inhabitant weren’t truly dead? She would stand there unmoving until the fire died out to be sure, and I could only watch her from where I sat with Strongheart. And when that fire finally did die out and Luna left it, I felt as if a little bit of us died too.

Lying in my sleeping bag, I cannot sleep. I have all the stars in the sky to keep me company, a truly overwhelming sight. The thought that I could travel up to them right now was truly tempting. Then Luna walked up to me. “I’m cold,” she said as she rubbed her shoulders. I threw open the double-wide sleeping bag as my invitation. “I just wanna sleep,” she informed me. Not being an exhibitionist, especially in front of a sea of bikers, that’s all I wanted too. She picked up on that as she got in the bag with me and looked up at the sky like me. “That’s what I like about the desert, it’s so dark you can see every star in the sky,” she remarks. “I thought you were gonna ask why the sleeping bag is so big. It’s big enough for two, you know. I could have been sleeping with all the other biker mamas,” I smile. “I’d know. Why did you get one this big? Every rattlesnake in the desert can crawl in here," she poses. "Is that why you slithered in?" I smile. Suddenly, a loud ouch is heard across the desert. "Must be a scorpion. They're everywhere!" she assumes. "I talk to them, make 'em roll up into a ball. They're like everyone else here; they don't love me, just my voice." I know truly. "You know it's funny, all this riding around and you're not getting anywhere. How long are you gonna do this?" she asks. "Uh, a lot of that riding around was looking for you," I remind her. "Well, this is what you got. I'm not happy, Reg. It's like I forgot how to be," she says so somberly. "What can I do to make my girl happy?" I ask sincerely. "Let's just leave. Let's just ride into the sunset. Let's just go anywhere," she tells me. "Now?" I ask. "If not now, look around one day soon and I just won't be here," she warns. I think about that and finally ask, "Does that mean you'd be happy somewhere else?" "Don't be a philosopher. I have to be worried about what happened today, too!" she hints. "You mean the Cherokee who took the four-way ride? They're not gonna blame you. I won't let 'em. In fact ..." I say as I spring up out of the blanket to my feet and shout out, "World, hear me!!!" And when I did, it happened again, that familiar quiet was all around as if everyone and everything had my complete attention. This time was different, though. When I spoke, there was an eerie echo to my voice, echoing again and again as if it were a wave of sound reaching out far beyond just the desert. It was the strangest sensation hearing my voice echo like that. Then through the ultra-quiet, I told my men, "There was no drama in the desert today, no Cherokee being stretched like taffy, just good times. You'll never forget such good times, and that's all you'll remember. Go back to sleep." Then I simply sat back down by my girl. "Thanks," is all she said or had to say. I laid back down and listened to the sounds of the desert. There were none. I just laid there. It was a while before the sound of a howling animal was heard. Life came back to a quiet world. Then I noticed Luna sleeping now.

My eyes pop open to the sound of sobbing. Luna has her back to me as she sobs quietly, not always quiet. I don't know whether to grab her and hold her tight or give her space. I feel like when Superman lost Lois, he had the power to turn back the world to save her, but should he? I've never felt so helpless. Acting on impulse, I told her, "If you don't sleep, you'll feel awful tomorrow." She hears and is quieter now. "You know, you're the strongest one I know. You showed me how to be strong. Whatever chains are binding you, I know you can break them. We're not like the others, we are the strong," is all I said. She went quiet. After a while, I closed my eyes again.

My eyes pop open. It's still dark. I feel great! Luna still sleeps peacefully beside me. I feel better than great now. I wonder if I got enough sleep. The stars are different. I'm fine. I try to slip out of the sleeping bag without waking her. As I slide out of the top, she suddenly pops up and looks at me in terror. "Just getting up," I stop and say as she calms down instantly. "Let's just go now," she and her eyes say, more than asking. "Just leave everyone? They'd be lost without me," I explain. "Who do you wanna be with, them or me?" she says with her eyes drilling through me. "I never wanna be without you again. After not finding you for so long, I just wanted to drive them all over a cliff. I couldn't take any more. But I couldn't leave you in whatever hell you were in. You're the only one who kept me going," I say to my only love in this life. Her tone softens as she asks, "Then will you leave with me? Because I'm going. I just am." I know she means what she says, so I tell her, "Tell you what, let's enjoy the day, all of us. Whatever this day awaits us, good, weird or whatever, we leave together at the end of it. We ride off into that forever sunset, just you and me." I say happily smiling as she breaks into a smile. I mean what I say, too!

Leaving Luna to sleep more, I take my bands into the desert to workout. While doing so, my old friend Strongheart walks up to me. "Interrupting my workouts is getting to be a habit," I remark. "You remember when you said 'world hear me' last night?" he asks. "Sure, I remember everything. Oh, and it's still night, what's your point?" I ask. "I checked my phone after you said it. At that time, there was this strange quiet all around the world. People are reporting it from everywhere. Scientists are saying it's some kind of phenomena. It was you, Reg," he informs. I keep working out. Then I realize the meaning of what I just heard, except I didn't understand. "What's it supposed to mean?" I ask dumbfounded. "Can't you figure it out? Somehow you amplified your voice," he says. "Just like Sunny," I say reflexively. "Well, now you can do it, too. Again, you discover another ability, my friend," he says to make me think. "But I only did it that one time. I do a lot of weird things once that I can't do again," I assume. "You are wrong. You said you remember everything. If that is so, you can remember the exact moment you used your ability to recreate that ability," he tells. "I haven't yet. Why haven't you tried?" I ask. "I do not have total recall. Each of us has different abilities, different gifts. You have so many and many yet to discover," he says to make me think. "Well, ain't my life just the comedy/tragedy see-saw, wanna get on?" I halfway mean. "I am on this ride with you. I will not abandon you," he says as I immediately think of Luna. If she's leaving, what do I do?

The day begins and Rolling Thunder hits the road. As many of the herd wanted breakfast, we stopped in a little town along our journey. Either the town was too small or the herd was too big, cuz I came to the instant realization that my rolling army was getting to be unmanageable. All the little places to eat simply couldn't supply enough food for thousands of hungry, irritable men. Because they were more than that. They were the warriors of the road. They deserved better. They rolled with Reg—they were Rolling Thunder! Luna and I just looked about the town, this surreal sight of bikers brawling, and howling, and smashing and trashing the town simply because they could. Small town cops couldn't stop them and reason certainly couldn't. My men had my back, so I had to have theirs. They did as they so desired and all I could do was lean back on my bike and watch the spectacle with my girl. "Has it been like this the whole time?" she asks. "I didn't notice. I kinda had other things on my mind," I say smiling at my girl. "I'm glad you realize it's time to quit," she remarks. "Yeah, but how?" I pondered out loud. If I told them all to go home, would they really listen to me? You can't just storm the castle with a few angry peasants and torches and burn it down anymore, especially when the monster within has grown so big.

Rolling Thunder rolls again, onto another town, another event, another giant brawl without end, rhyme or reason. Our shiny chrome was losing its luster. People were beginning to fear my army rolling through their towns rather than look forward to it. Or maybe they have all along and I didn't notice it. I had keeping my girl on my mind. I have her now and must move on with only her, but how?

Luna holds on tight behind me as I roll on down the highway with Strongheart beside me and Rolling Thunder behind me for as far as the eye can see. My specialty is my voice, not super hearing or eyesight. But even I could see what lay ahead as we approached another small town—trouble! In the ever closing distance I saw a barricade across the road with a tank right in the middle of it. The sideways angled tank suddenly turned and pointed its massive gun turret right in our direction. I slowed down and stopped less than fifty yards from the barricade. A tank pointed at you tends to get your attention. The whole rolling herd came to a stop behind me now. The ones in the back didn't even know why yet.

"Turn back!" a voice blared out over a loudspeaker in our direction. I was stumped. How do I turn back a herd of this size, and should I? "Any ideas?" I yelled over to Strongheart. Moving his head about like he didn't quite know what to say, he just said, "You can go talk to them." "You are not going to talk to them. Time to quit now!" my girl wisely said. I just sat there and sat there, my growing frustration turning to anger the more I sat there. I don't like being put in a box.

I finally got off the bike and walked up a bit defiantly, just close enough to be heard by them. "Nothing stops Rolling Thunder!" I defiantly yelled. Either I wasn't listened to or just not heard inside that tons of armored steel tank, because the tank's gun turret raised up suddenly and just stopped. My heart skipped a beat or two about then. Then the tank suddenly fired, its devastation wreaking down on a spot in my rolling army a ways back behind me. Everyone turned around to see flying men and machines a few hundred yards back. They would not see home again. I turned back to the tank, stepped up even closer and yelled, "Stop! Don't do this!" I didn't know what else to say. Then the tank adjusted its turret and fired again, raining its exploding projectile of doom down even closer than before, and more of my men were dead. I was confused. I didn't know what to do—and I was mad! Madder than before, madder every second I stood there without acting. But what do I do? Then the tank fired again, and again its fury rained down even closer than before. I had let down my men. I had let them die! I was even more confused.

Then I looked up. We all looked up. The monstrous form that I had created to rescue my girl was there, coming down from the sky, more massive and powerful than the last time it appeared. And it opened up in front of the barricade, sucking in the tank, the barricade and everyone and everything near it as if sucking up tiny crumbs at a picnic into the most powerful vacuum while it compacted down everything that entered it into atomized particles. Was it demonstrating its rage or just feeding itself? Yes, I was mad, but I was also amazed by what I witnessed. Such immense power created merely by thought, by my mind. I thought I sent it out into space, yet here it was again to protect me.

Then the form rose up and turned its fury on the town, sucking up the long empty strip mall and all the buildings that lay in its path as easily and violently as it had done already. How would I control it? I must control it! I cannot let it destroy the houses, the inhabitants of the town, too! I must send it away as before. I concentrate. It is part of me and all of me wants it to go away. Into space my mind tells it. Into space you must go and you must stay. And soon the form rose up high into the sky. As I looked out over where the town was, Luna walked up to me. "Tell them to go home. It's over, Reg," she informs and I know it's true. "Then I failed," I utter staring off into space. "You didn't fail. You didn't have a chance to fail," she consoles me. "I didn't get them where they wanted to go. I don't call that success," I know truly. "Some of these men need medical attention I'm sure. Let's get it for them and go," she prods me. Strongheart suddenly walks up to us and says, "We need to remember our dead." "You mean bury them?" I assume. "That is not our way," he says as Luna figures it out saying, "He means burn them. More funeral pyres coming up!" she states. "There are plenty of trees and tumbleweeds for a fire. An honorable life deserves an honorable death. Why did you want your tormentor to be given such an honorable end?

He did not deserve it," he needed to know. "I just wanted to see him burn!! I just wanted to know he's dead! How many more dead do you want? And what are they going to say about that form? They'll assume Reg had something to do with it. They'll be afraid of him. It's impossible to know how they'll react," she figures. "They will do what he tells them to do," my friend says staring at my girl. Then he walks back to the men. "He's trying to control you," she tells as I snap back, "And you're not! This is a noble cause, uniting these men for a purpose. I can't abandon them now! Could you please just be on my side for once!!" She looks at me, the love of my life giving me a stare of icy coldness. She had her melon filled with her needs and I had mine. "The day's almost over," she reminds me with my promise in mind I'm sure. Then she walks away from me. All these people are so near and not one of them wants anything to do with me. How could I screw things up so quickly, so royally? I guess I'm just good at it. Then I got inspiration.

I walked back over to Luna and called out to my friend before he mixed in with the crowd, my voice paralyzing them and giving him little choice than to come back over to me. "I thought you weren't going to talk around them," he complains. "Look, there's something I have to do, something I have to see. We'll be back later. I can't help out here anyway," I tell him while knowing full well he would never see me again. Luna must have been crowding my cranium again because she smiled and gave no protest as she hopped on the back of my bike. I got on the bike with her ready to ride forward through the empty town as Strongheart spoke overly loudly, "Reg! Remember your men." I looked over at him, his eyes staring right through me like he knew what I was about to do.

We rode, me and my lady. I left my men behind. I left them for all time. I left them for my girl. Was I wrong? It was either them or her. Why am I so bad at all the hard choices? I have my girl. I should feel great. Then why don't I? I feel shitty a thousand different ways. Then her arms moving about me almost make me feel better. Then I proceed to where I said I wanted to go, down the Extraterrestrial Highway. Luna must have seen the sign. Area 51, here we come!

Annnnnnnnnnnd we're here! At the gate anyway. I hop off the bike as she just sits there. "Don't go in there! You'll get arrested," she barks. "Haven't yet. Don't you wanna see the aliens? I wanna see some big-headed aliens; big heads and big eyes. They say they got 'em here," I say. "Yeah, maybe they'll march them all out here so you can take inventory," she teases. "They would if I told them to. Hey, you think they know who I am?" I ask. She suddenly gets a worried look on her face and motions to me with her hand for me to come over to her. I do, of course. She whispers to me, "Don't say your name. You shouldn't have come here. You know what they would do to you if the had you?" Her words worry me but for a moment. Then I realize mister government man tried his heavy hand on me long before I'd discovered all my powers and abilities that transform man into superman. "Screw 'em! They can't do anything to me. I'll send my form after them," I threaten. "You better keep that monster in the closet. That thing you conjured up could end up destroying the world," she explains. "No, really? How could it do that? I didn't give it that much power," I wonder. "I know, so where did it get it? That thing's off getting stronger by itself. You should be worried about that, not your biker buds," she tells me. "Why do you say I was thinking about them?" I ask. "That's all you thought about coming here. You think you're not being loyal by not helping them? How 'bout your extended family back at the palace? How 'bout my dad? How 'bout your fans? How 'bout me?! You got me now, you wanna keep me?" she asks much louder than a whisper by this point. "Hey, I'm here. I made my choice. I made it the moment I saw you. How 'bout you?" I needed to know. "The minute I saw you? It takes me longer to lose my mind," she says with a smirk. I look up on the hill to see a vehicle obviously watching us, so I throw my arms out and yell to them, "Hey, camo dudes, I'm Reg!!! Do something about it! Hey, aliens, come down and get me!" I laugh as I look up. "I think it's time to go before they really do decide to come and get you," she warns as I ask, "The camo dudes or the saucy saucer men? They're coming to take me away, ha ha!" "If only. Would you come on? I can't drive this thing, you know," she tells me, now she tells me.

Suddenly that familiar sound is heard, the roaring of a thousand plus engines. We look back to see Rolling Thunder driving our way. How would they know we're here? "A tracking device, it's probably on the bike somewhere. Or, it may be that your friend has abilities he's not telling you about, like the ability to get you to do anything he wants you to do. If only I could do that," she says with a not too happy look. "You don't wanna be here, do you? Or is it just me?" I ask her as she just gives me her cold stare. "It won't be much longer," I tell her as she says with her eyes more than her mouth, "You got that right."

And soon they came, all my men on all their machines, crowding the road and driving on the desert sand surrounding it, too! They take up a lot of space and need their space, crowding out everyone who would intrude upon it. Strongheart drove up to me as other bikers crashed the gates and rode right into Area 51. "Hey, amigo, I knew you'd be here," Strongheart smiles. "Uh huh, how?" I ask suspiciously. "This is the only place around here I just knew you would have to see. It's not hard to figure out. I mean, I don't have to be a mind reader," he keeps smiling. "You know, it's fifteen more miles to whatever military base they got here. I don't think they'll be met with flowers and candy if they keep going," I warn my friend. "Relax, they just wanna ride around, show the man they can. Some of the men quit on us. We'll have to round up more to make up for it," he informs. "Scared off?" I ask. "Whatever reason. Some were destined to quit. Some had cheap bikes that blew up. The desert will do that. We need soldiers, not the weak," he says. "Soldiers are for war. So when's the war start?" Luna asks seriously. "The inquisitive squaw. When we have enough men for Washington to take us seriously, Washington will listen," he informs. "The misguided red man, you're on a suicide mission. No one takes madmen seriously. They just take them out!" she hopefully gets her point across. In this surreal moment of madness, I watch my best girl and my best friend ready to come to blows, all the while an ocean of bikers flood in and out of Area 51. I guess they all wanna to say they were here. I'm not sure what the ones doing wheelies and roundy-rounders inside the place are trying to say.

"Hey, you're my girl and you're my friend. I don't wanna lose either of you. Why are we doing this?" I ask about them and about my life coming to this. "Yeah, why are we doing this? You, take us to see this Gawanii now or we ride," she lays it down to Strongheart. "Is that not for Reg to decide?" my friend asks. "It sure is. Decide now, Reg. Decide or I'm outta here, I'm gone. I can't do this anymore. Look at these idiots. This is madness. Someone is probably on the way here right now to stop this. Well, I am not waiting. Decide, Reg," she says, staring impatiently at me for an answer. "Decide!!!" she can't wait. Again I'm in a box. But can I blame her? "I know you've been through so much, but I've come so far. How can I stop now?" I say staring directly at her. "Oh, look! I can ride one of these," she says as she revs up my bike and looks ready to roll. "I just hope one day you do find what you're looking for," she says without a smile as she spins the bike around and drives away from us, all of us searching for that Eldorado that I fear we will never find.

22) A FRIEND of THE FOREST

Luna here. I knew this day would come, the time when dad would have to venture back into the forest to see that special man who influenced him so long ago. This time I would be going with him. Maybe that would end the madness. We'll be bringing along guests, my bestie Aphrodite and Roger for some reason. After getting off the private jet that Reg so generously gave to us, we rented a camper and drove to the same spot dad said he camped at as a child so many years ago. Why a camper? Memories. His mom and dad may be long gone, but so many fond memories remain.

After parking our camper near all the other campers, we all commenced the long hike into the forest. There would be more signs there now to guide us to keep little lost bears from losing their way as dad would say. While dad had the necklace of animal teeth that he wore since childhood to rejuvenate him, his body was no longer as young and strong as it used to be. He stopped to rest on the giant stump of an old tree. I sat next to him. "When I was a child, it was so easy. I just got lost and he appeared," he tells us. "Why don't you call out for him? Didn't you say all you have to do is ask and he'll appear?" I ask as Roger interjects, "Yeah, like, a genie." Intoxicated by what, I have no idea. "Good, good idea, Roger," I say and suddenly realize what a wonderful idea it truly was as dad hopped to his feet, energized and ready! He asked of the very forest, "O sacred place, O rocks, and trees, and animals of the forest, tell your friend Gawanii of my need for him." Nothing happened. Then suddenly the forest went quiet. I instinctively knew the forest was preparing us for a meeting. A gentle breeze that did not sway the treetops, only lifted up leaves and forest debris as they swirled and danced about as if putting on a show for us told me something truly special was about to happen.

Then as all three of us just happened to be looking in the same direction, a seven-foot man slowly appeared before us, body and soul walking out of the forest up to us. The open-mouthed look on the face of Aphrodite was priceless. Even I was amazed as I slowly stood up, all the while remembering the legendary tales dad told us of the Native man of the forest and once and for all proving the old man telling them wasn't crazy after all.

"Is Little Lost Bear lost again?" Gawanii smiled, and dad smiled like he was just given the best gift he was ever given. From the look on dad's face, this was indeed the man he had met as a child, and he had not changed, according to dad's thoughts. "I knew my journey wouldn't be in vain. I wouldn't come if it were not important," dad tells him. "Gawanii knows. Tell Gawanii of your friend Aphrodite and this one," he says to the surprise of Aphrodite. "Like, uh, I'm Roger," Roger manages to tell him. "Mmm, too many puffs on the peace pipe this one," Gawanii deduces. "Yes, well, he has other talents. Aphrodite is our Nostradamus. She can sense disaster. What do you sense, my dear?" Joe asks. "Only good things," she says with the sweetest smile. I just stood there and took him in, but not his mind. That mind of his was an impenetrable barrier I couldn't even begin to get passed. He must have known that because now he is walking right up to me. "Be not troubled, Luna," was all he said as he reached out his large but soothing hands and placed them around my face and head. I showed no apprehension as he did. I felt a euphoria like I had never known. It must be what others feel when they hear Reg speak. But it was more than that, O so much more! I felt all the tension, and the grief and the horrors in my life just vanish, just wiped away as if they were never experienced at all. Then why am I crying now? They are only tears of joy, the best kind. No one else knew why I was experiencing this, only that it was a good thing.

Gawanii released me and turned to the others. He talked with them as I just listened. Why had he chosen me first to help? He didn't even know me. My leaky brain must have purged my problems right into him. While I was trying to read him, he was reading me; a million racing thoughts and troubles I just couldn't deal with, all healed with a simple touch. After all these years, all dad's fanciful takes on just one meeting with this man and I knew in an instant they were true. I was more than impressed, I was enlightened. His touch not only healed me, it gave me the wisdom to move on. And in an instant I realized I shouldn't have left Reg. I realized I really did love him.

I walked right up to them. I walked right up while they were talking and rudely interrupted them to say, "Thank you." They all simply stopped as Gawanii turned to me. He wasn't bothered. He must have known the change in me and just smiled. "I have to go to him. I have to find him. I should have never left him," I say somberly. "She's referring to the one called Reg. Have you heard of him way out here?" dad asks. "Gawanii has been known to leave the forest. Gawanii knows," and tells. "Then you know what he can do with his voice. The only other one who could do that is you. How is it that you can control it and he cannot?" dad asks. "He will discover his many gifts as he lives his life. He has the time to discover them," Gawanni tells. "Yes, but this world moves at a much faster pace than in the centuries past that you have lived. In just the years since I have seen you last, we went from rockets that could destroy our world in hours to annihilation in mere minutes. We have to find him, show him how to use his gifts for the betterment of mankind. I know you wish to remain anonymous, but Reg is anything but that. I don't think there is anyone on this planet that does not know who he is, what he can do. All they want to do is listen to him. If only we could teach him what to say. Then tragedy could be avoided," dad confessed. "What dad means is Reg has said things on occasion that people took the wrong way and bad things happened," I tell one who knows all too well as he says, "Yes. Caging a beast does not tame a beast. It will not go against its nature." "What?" suddenly wafts out of Roger's fuzzy brain. Feeling all the time in the world wouldn't help explaining to Roger, I moved on and asked Gawanii, "Could you help Reg like you helped me?" "Gawanii can teach him what he needs to know, but only if he is worthy. Such power in evil hands of just one with our abilities could destroy Mother Earth," Gawanii speaks truly. "Yes, why try to push the masses over the cliff when you can just talk them over it? No, I don't think Reg is an evil man, just a bit misguided," dad deduces. "Yeah, right now he's being guided by a Cherokee named Strongheart. You know him?" I ask. "A good warrior and a good human being. If he is there for Reg, he is there for a noble purpose," he tells. "He's there to unite all the bikers to take back all the Government land for his people, including this place. Did you wanna move out of here?" I ask. "Even my people can be foolish. He forgets, he was born here. He can survive here. Modern man cannot. People are spoiled. They would not survive here without all their modern conveniences; their gadgets and video games. What a waste of time. Gawanii will have to speak with him," he tells. "Then you don't want people to visit here?" Aphrodite asks. "To visit, yes. This is a sacred place; a place not to be destroyed with bulldozers and shopping malls. This is a place where all Gawanii's friends of the forest can live," he says as he simply puts out his hand and the most beautiful and friendly bird lands on the hand of his outstretched arm reaching up to the rays of the sun as if right on cue, as if an old friend just stopped by to say hello. We all just looked up at the bird as it sang its song for us, unafraid of us or just unafraid of the man with the magic. Then the bird took to flight as he lowered his arm. Kind of impressive for a simple thing.

Then I noticed something more than a bit strange. I could see everyone's aura. I had only heard of this till now. We had someone at the palace who could do this, and now I could. Gawanii's aura was the biggest and brightest of all of us, extending far out from his body. But all the light became too bright. I had to cover my eyes. "Sensory overload," my mouth spilled out. "What's wrong?" dad asked. I opened my eyes and the light was still there. "The light's too bright!" I complained and once again Gawanii came to the rescue, holding his hands feet from my head and closing them in until he touched my head as he said, "Then we must put the light back in." And suddenly there was no more light. I looked around strangely at everyone looking strangely at me. I started to laugh. "I'm okay. I just saw everyone's aura. Not to cast blame, but is that because you touched me before?" I said looking at Gawanii. "A gift. You must learn to use it, use it as all your other gifts," he tells. "Other gifts? She reads minds. If she has any other gifts, she hasn't told me," bestie Aphrodite complains. "I'm not holding back. I didn't know I could do it. It's funny, I always tell that to Reg, that he has so many gifts yet to master," I say as Gawanii simply says to me, "As do you. Would it surprise you if Gawanii told you that you can do all the things your friend does, that Gawanii can do?" Like a bolt of lightning striking me I knew in an instant it must be true, but I asked out loud for everyone's convenience, "You mean I have his vocal gift, too?" "You do if at least one of your parents is one of the star people, and if they came from the same place. The heaven place is truly a big place," Gawanii tantalizes. "Yeah, but that would mean I probably don't have it because fat chance of all the places in the universe that the same set of horny star people would keep coming here!" I proclaim. "I sense in time you will," Gawanii says calmly with a smile to calm me, only confusing me more. Then I realize who my mother was and my bad feelings start to flood back in. "Do not go there. She was not worthy of you," Gawanii taps my brain to assure me. I don't know if I like it. Now I know how Reg feels about my constant brain drains on him. "Her mother was Desert Flower. The manner in how she lived life is not in question here, only the manner in her death. Reg created something truly frightening," dad explains. "Yeah, dad didn't see it, but I did!" I say looking at Gawanii and hoping he would take the hint and look into my mind once more so I wouldn't have to describe the hideous form Reg created to deal with problems he just didn't want to face. Because let's face it, that's what it really was. At times we'd all love to conjure up a monster that would solve all our problems and fight all our battles for us. Reg really can. Then it dawned on me, maybe I can, too! "You do not want to conjure fierce beasts. There is never a leash strong enough to hold them, nor a cage secure enough to protect you from them," Gawanii tells me. "Not a problem. Creepy critter conjuring is not on my list of things to do. I just thought I'd tell you so you can be on the lookout for Reg's form. Reg keeps saying he sent it away. But every time it comes back, it's stronger," I tell him. "You must all be tired. If you wish to leave now, Gawanii will understand. If you wish to stay, Gawanii will show you something you have never seen before," he said to spark our fire of fascination so bright that we would have to see ... whatever. Then he just smiled, and with that simple gesture, he took all my fears away again. No wonder dad liked him so much and could never stop talking about him.

We walked and talked our way through the forest. The rare chance to learn the wisdom of someone who lived countless centuries was beyond fascinating. Then we came to a pit covered by a huge tarp. "What do you see?" is all Gawanii said. We all looked at the tarp draped over what looked like the outline of a body, but it couldn't be a body, unless that body were thirty-feet tall. Before anyone could speak, Gawanii raised his arms and a gentle wind lifted up the tarp and carried it away. What was left was the most unbelievable thing I had ever seen, the skeleton of what could only be called a giant. "Is that real?" Aphrodite asked with wide eyes. "The Bible called them the Nephilim. Mythology called them titans. They are no myth. Believe what your eyes tell you. Behold a giant," Gawanii shows us, but for what reason? "We have a friend who showed us images on his phone of such creatures. I can only imagine now that they are real," dad refers to Percy the monster hunter. "In the seas, in the skies, in the forests, true monsters do exist. Why do you think so many people go missing every year in the forests of Mother Earth? Monsters get hungry," Gawanii says to frighten or just to enlighten. "You mean there are monsters here in the forest right now, now in this day and age?" Aphrodite asks. "You are safe with Gawanii," he says to reassure us. "Yes, but why are you telling us these things? Why are you showing us?" I ask him. "Do you not wish to know?" is all he said to make us think. "Find your friend. Bring him to this sacred place. Stay with him if you like. But he, at least, must stay for a time. He must live here. He must survive here, here among the animals, and the beauty ... and the monsters. Only then will he be worthy of an audience with Gawanii," he says as he walks away from us and simply vanishes.

We made our way out of the forest. We were definitely not on any clearly marked path any longer. We had to guess our way out. Every time we hesitated which way to go, a gentle breeze would make itself known, stirring any debris on the forest ground in only one direction. No doubt a tall Cherokee had something to do with it. But my mind was on Reg again. What mischief he could make without realizing it. I had to go find him.

23) SNAKES

Reg here, here in the desert again with thousands of bikers—again! It was fun at first, but I'm getting damn sick of camping out in a desert; hot as hell during the day and cold as a tomb at night, or still so hot you can't sleep. Nope, no moderation here. Strongheart fixes us eats as I just sit here staring straight ahead. No relief from the heat and no end in sight, and no Luna. My eyes keep playing winkie-blinkie. I guess I'm just tired.

Strongheart suddenly shakes me to wake me up. "You've got to tell them to stop!" he frantically tells me. I feel dopey like I'm still asleep. I look around in my haze to see all my biker army fighting, fighting each other. "Why are they fighting?" my hazy brain manages to get my mouth to say. "Because you told them to!" he stresses. It's not stressing me, though. "Did I tell 'em that?" hazy brain me says. "Yes! You told them to kill each other. Now they are. Make them stop! You must tell them to stop!!!" he yells, leaning right down in front of my face. I guess I should feel more excited, feel more urgency to the situation, but I don't. Let 'em do their thing, man, and I'll do mine, just sit here and watch. A couple big ass bikers just grabbed Strongheart and are carrying him away. That's cool, too, I guess? Doesn't bother me. Nothing's bothering me. I'm too mellow, just like Roger.

Hey, look at that dude. Some dude wearing a long, black tattered gown and a hood is walking among the crowd. No one is attacking him. I guess they don't see him or don't care. He's turning now—whoa! He's got no skin. He's got boney bone hands and a bare bones skull under that hood. He has a long scythe in one hand and a crystal orb in his other hand. Every time one of my biker buds gets knocked to the ground and stops moving, a little light comes out of their body and travels into Boney's orb. Hey, he's making his way over to me. "You look familiar," I say to Boney in my happy haze. "I am here for the reaping," it says in a waaaaay too spooky voice, but that's cool! Adds to the atmosphere. I giggled up at him, "Hey, I don't fear any reaper. I'm never gonna die." "I am here because of you. I wanted to thank you personally. You throw so many hapless souls into my grasp, and today is such a good day to diiiiiiiiiiiiiiiiiie," that creepy voice of his creeps out. "Dude, I love the voice. You must get a lot of work at Halloween," I tell him with a smile. "I love your voice too, Reg. It's the voice of death!" he says echoing into my brain. I suddenly don't feel so calm anymore. I blink and day has become night. I see my breath and feel the sting of the cold. I hear only silence and see only bodies on the ground. No life stirring anywhere, not even a desert mouse. No sign of our reaper either. Of course not! His job is done here and all too well.

That's a full moon all right. Brightens up the desert real good. And as I just stare at that moon, I notice it kinda looks more and more red, the only color I see in the dark of night. The moon is blood red now and dripping blood from the sky. I wouldn't call it a rain, just red drops dripping from the sky onto all my dead biker buds. It must be blood. Blood gives life and it is giving life to all my men. They keep rising up from the ground.

Are they dead or undead? What's the difference? They're all on their feet now, all rotting perversions of their former selves. None of the blood has fallen on me, though. I am not marked. Yet it's kinda odd, all their heads are turning and looking at me all at once. I don't think I like that. They're all shuffling my way now. I definitely don't like that! Yeah, fun time's over for sure. I stand up now and glance all around, and they are all around me, stepping and stumbling their way in only one direction—mine! This zombie movie had an all biker cast. Too bad Romero's not around any more to make it. I look for a place to run, but there is none.

Feeling that they are not all approaching me for huggywugs and kisses, I start to run! I weave in and out of their reaching grasps. After all, they weren't that fast because zombies move like, well, zombies! I fortunately was fast. I avoided their grabby arms at every turn. How long could I keep this up, though, running this way and that in this monstrous maze of dead bikers? With every turn I could only see pasty gray arms and deformed faces following my every move. And my heart, it was beating too incredibly fast even for this super fit body. Then I suddenly stopped because there he was, Voltaire standing right before me. "Still love the voice, Reg. Too bad it doesn't do it for me anymore," he tells. "Why not?" I mumble out. "Cuz I'm fuckin' dead!!" it yells at me as the rotting flesh in leather lunges at me.

My eyes pop open. It's nightfall. All the men are in their groups, doing their thing and all is fine. Not a zombie in sight. As for my twisted dreams, I only have Morpheus to blame. Strongheart notices I'm up as he stirs a pot of something that smells sooooooooo good! I stumble to my feet and go over to look and maybe drool some. "Like it already, huh? Wait till you taste it, if I let you have any? I had to cut the meat, chop the peppers, even get the firewood. You are impossible to wake up. Good thing you have so many guardian angels, and Hell's Angels and every other biker club you can imagine looking over you. We'll be in Sturgis soon," he tells. All I was concerned with was how soon was that heavenly delight in a pot ready. "I'm gonna sneak off and use the desert. I'll critique the cuisine when I get back," I tell the cook.

I work my way through the crowd without speaking to find a nice cactus to stand behind. I unzip and do my business as I think I hear the distinct rattle of a snake. I finish my number one task and zip up as I hear even more rattling sounds. Then out of the darkness they came, what looked like hundreds of snakes; rattlers and sidewinders all. They were all around me. They did keep their distance, though, like they came to me only to leave me a message, not to intimidate or even frighten. I thought again I must still be asleep, but this seemed so real, like it could really happen. Then I did what I do best, I spoke to them and asked, "I didn't even speak. Why did you come?" I foolishly stood there and waited for a reply that could never come and suddenly all was quiet, not a rattle to be heard. Then the rattling resumed, but only one at a time. One snake would rattle a bit. Then another would rattle until seven of them had rattled. Then the seven snakes rattled in the exact same order again, only this time I caught on. There was a pattern, a code. They were using Morse code to spell out the name Gawanii. "Gawanii," I then said only. That's all I had to say. The message was delivered and all my reptilian messengers simply slithered away into the darkness. I walked my way back through the desert and through all the men, and not once did I see a snake.

I walked up to Strongheart and said, "You're not gonna believe what just happened." Then I told him. He had no trouble believing me. He said Gawanii knows of me and will meet with me soon. For a century old, I still feel like the young Jedi knight and not the ancient master. I dreaded such a meeting like dreading a dentist. I know I wasn't ready. When would I be ready? What could I possibly say or do to impress someone like that? "Eat! Stop daydreaming," he tells me as I sit to eat with my friend. He dished it out in a bowl and I took it more than happily. I taste it and it's gooooood! He can tell I like it without asking, but I really had to ask, "What, uh, kind of meat is it? I mean, I see an occasional rabbit around here." "Not rabbit," he, of course, only said and there hopped away all my hopes of something I could stomach. "It does kinda taste like chicken, but I'm guessing it isn't," I comment. "You guess correctly, it isn't," he tells me to confuse my stomach even more. "Does this mystery meat fly, swim or moo?" I ask. "You forgot slither," he smiles between bites. I had to ask.

I changed the subject. "Where did you go to school?" I ask him. "There were no schools when I was that young," he tells me. "That old, huh? I don't know why I thought of it ... but when I was a kid, I had this really big history teacher with a skullet at the orphanage, and this guy just did not like me. He couldn't get me to talk ever, and I couldn't for obvious reasons. Anyway, one day he just announced to the class that he'd be right back and not to talk while he was gone. So he got up and left the room. After a whole minute, half the class turned into a blabbermouth. That is, everyone but me. I just sat there. I don't know what made me do it, but I turned my head and looked out the room's windows—and there he was! I remember making the stupidest funny face shocked look, like Curly, or Mel Brooks or something and he just stared right at me. And everyone saw the quiet kid make the goofy face and looked out the window to see the teacher snarling at everyone. Then he came back into the class and punished everyone who spoke; everyone but me. And he was mad about it, like he left the class only to catch me talking and I didn't. He told me to wait after class. And with everyone gone, this big ass teacher stood over me with a nice thick ruler and told me I was gonna talk for him. So I did. The beginning of my larceny to survive began. I told him to take out his wallet and give me all his money, which he did. Then I told him to shove the ruler up his ass and flap his arms like a chicken as he ran around the orphanage. The cops had to come take him away. We never saw him again," I laughed and so did my friend. It was a good time.

Then the tone changed. "Soon it will be cool enough for sleep and I will sleep. What will you do?" he asks to my surprise. "Why'd you ask me that?" I had to know. "You slept already and I know you are restless," he explains. "I don't know, ride into town, watch a movie. Take a nap before everyone gets up. Is that okay, daddio?"

I ask. "Would you like a couple of our insomniacs to ride with you? I know you get lost sometimes," he insinuates at me possibly cutting out again. "I used to go to the late show all the time when I lived in Hollywood. I'll be fine," I reply. "That was before you were famous. Everyone knows you now," he says to bother me even more. "You know, I'm getting that boxed-in feeling again, like when I was at the palace. I'll do what I want when I want. Thanks for the grub!" I say as I throw down my bowl and walk over to my bike. Get on it! Rev it!! And ride it the hell off!!! It's time for me time.

24) OUT of PLACE

I left my friend and my men to look for a nearby town—to look for some action! The desert is boring! Pretty but boring. Will I go back with them? Maybe. Even I can't be sure. I found a big bar in a small town. Why would I find myself at a bar? I don't drink, unless you count the few months I sang drunk and drugged out of my mind by Mel. Much better now, if you call this better?

I find myself walking into this bar with enough rednecks to cause even me trouble, if I keep my mouth shut. I see people sitting in a nice dark booth in the back, one where I'd prefer to be sitting. So I amble up simply telling the group of three dudes and three dudettes, "I like this table. Snap out of it and move your asses!" Okay, I was in a bad mood. I'd soon have a nice, cozy darkened area to sit where no one would bother me. So when the soused six stumbled away from the table without really grasping why they were, I sat on down facing the crowd and the band on stage. I had a table of empty and half empty booze bottles staring me in the face, but not for long. I just put the back of my arm on that table and swiped it clean—bottles flying everywhere! For someone who wanted not to be seen, that sure wasn't the way to do it cuzzzzzz they're all looking at me now. "I'm not here!!!" I said kind of loudly. Nobody's bothering me now. Nobody's doing anything. Yet another surreal moment in time as everyone is frozen in time. Yep, Reg's not here. But how's anybody gonna serve me? As I sat there, I just listened to the quiet. In this party place full of unruly rowdies, I just looked at all the happy, empty smiles and I thought of something Luna said about focusing on a moment in time where I did something that I have yet to do twice, like when Luna and I were exchanging thoughts in our heads without speaking. So I tried it. I stared at a waitress and put into her head that I'd like a tall, cold, frosty root beer. I just stared at her. Did she get the message? She soon disappeared behind the bar—and yep! Here she comes with a big mug right towards me. She puts it right on the table in front of me as I toss her a twenty. She looks confused as if she didn't know why she was even there. Then she swipes up the cash and leaves as sound and life return to the bar.

I sit and sip and, yeah, it was root beer. She got it right. I was relaxed, but I was alone again. In a bar packed with people, I was completely alone. They couldn't see me or converse with me, like I was some ghostly walk-in that didn't belong. I don't like this feeling. Why did Luna leave me? I suddenly think to take out my wallet and take out Luna's business card, the one with her face staring back at me that originally drew me to her. I just stared at it, staring and hoping somehow she would answer me. Then I heard 'I see you' in my head in her voice. Was it really Luna or was it wishful thinking? Was I cracking up? "Where am I?" I quietly said aloud. 'In a bar' her voice said. "What am I drinking?" I ask. 'Taste it' the voice said. I tasted it. 'Root beer' the voice answered. "You're batting a thousand. Why did you leave me? I'm lost. Ship Reg is sailing rocky waters and ready to crash," I mumble out. 'If you want to see me, leave the group. I know you're not content' her voice nags. "I've never been content. I'm out of place any place. When I was with you, I was happy. Romeo needs his Juliette. Randy needs his Julie, and I need you," I say. 'Randy needs Julie'? She doesn't get it. "*Valley Girl*, nineteen-eighty-three," I inform as I get up and rush from the bar before I see a tear in my root beer. Once again, I'm without direction. Where should I go, forward or back? I'm oblivious to oblivion, what does it look like?

I hop on my bike and hit the road through the desert back to my men. At least I'd get some respect there. I ride faster, and faster and faster! I just want to get somewhere, anywhere—fast! I just needed to escape where I was and be far away from nowhere. What? Is that—I swerve! But I can't miss the coyote crossing the road. I'm going down!!!

25) FORM of CONFUSION

Pain!!! Pain like I'd never felt before, crushing me as I lay on the side of a dark road and look up at the night sky. I can't move. Am I paralyzed or just a wuss, not willing to get up, to try? Does it end for me like this? The sky sure is pretty, all those stars and only one of me. Maybe I'll just close my eyes and it'll all be over. So I do. Now it's total darkness, it's lights out. Just let the pain go away, even if it means I go away.

Then I realized ... there really is only one of me in all this vastness. Does that mean I actually do matter? I hate to admit it, but I need help. But in all this vastness, who really is out there who can help me? Luna's too far away. I'm not falling off a building, so Superman won't swoop down and save me. My biker buds are all sleeping—nowhere near here! The form! With my eyes still closed, I summon my form. Will it hear me? Will it obey me? Does it still exist? I sent it away. After enduring enough agony, I finally opened my eyes. Right in my line of vision I see something out in space. A UFO? A quire of angels coming for me? Probably not. It's my blessing and my curse. It's the form. It must be moving at the speed of light to reach me from space this fast. It's even bigger than the last time now—it's close! Coming down from the sky it is. It hovers in the desert just above me now. I know of its ability to destroy with a touch, but can it heal? I guess I have little choice than to find out. Staring right up at it, I see the stars disappear as my form gets ever closer.

I'm inside the form now. What a strange sensation. I keep thinking why I have to bear such pain still when all I do is give pleasure. How 'bout a little ecstasy dammit! And the form obeys. It's as if the form were a form of bliss here just to float my cares and pains away. And I feel like I am floating. I am floating! I'm up here in the sky with my head sticking out of the top of big fluffy. You'd think I'd be terrified way up here, but I'm not. I'm too mellow. The rest of my body rises up and I ride the form across the desert like it's a magic carpet. What a view. As I glide silently across the open land, I hold my palms down as lightning from my form fills my hands. Then I turn my palms up to the sky as the power in my hands arcs lightning up into the sky and instantly a gentle rain comes down to bless the desert. It feels good, just what I need. I am one with the form, with the desert. I am free, free of need. I am one with ... everything.

The rain is long gone now as my fluffy ride floats me into camp and over my oblivious sleeping men camped out under the canopy of night. No one sees me. No one shows fear. Then I float over where Strongheart is lying. His eyes pop open just as the form hovers in the sky way over top of his line of sight. He thinks nothing of it because my trickster form seems like just another cloud in the sky, until he sees me being lowered gently down from the sky as the form remains on high. I land right in front of him now. "Am I bleeding?" I ask. He looks me over and tells me, "I don't see any. Your jacket's ripped. Discovering new abilities?" he asks with a more than normal look of fascination in his eyes, and maybe some fear. "I'll need a new bike," is all I say. "Did you have an accident? I noticed you didn't walk back here," he states the obvious. "Coyote. I just lay there. I couldn't do anything else, just hurt. Then I thought of the form. It didn't wreak havoc this time. It healed me, just healed me," I content. He looks up at the form still there. "It hasn't left," he reminds. I look up and wish it away. It obeys to the sky. "You should have got it to disperse," he tells. "I thought energy couldn't be created or destroyed. Besides, might need it again," I surmise and silently go to lay down, no more madness or weirdness to deal with this day. If I hadn't summoned it, I'd still be rotting on the side of the road with insects chewing on me and buzzards pecking at me. Now see, this is why I can't sleep, gotta stop thinking about stupid shit!

Still dark, my eyes pop open looking directly into the eyes of a man dressed in all black standing before me with a big knife. My sudden stare and extreme calm must have spooked him because he just stands there as if he can't decide to use the knife. The more he looks into my eyes, the more I know he sees something I don't see. I feel completely unafraid, yet he reeks of fear. Shouldn't it be the other way? I stand up casually to face him as he fails to attack. "Go ahead," I calmly say as Strongheart hears and pops to his feet in defense. "I'm alright. He wants to complete his mission, but he can't. Go ahead, mister murder man, use it," I tell him calmly as I just stare right through his soul. And the more I just stand there and look at him, the more he shakes and quivers, like with all his training nothing has prepared him for the horrors he is seeing. But I'm not doing anything, I think? The decision has been made, he runs off. Dropping the knife, my aimless assassin runs out into the dark desert night not to be seen again—ever! I pick up the knife. "Someone will find his bones littering the desert a century from now. Here, have a souvenir," I say as I hand Strongheart the knife. "Good knife. It's military issue. That makes me wonder how many more like him are out there. But why didn't he kill you?" he asks. "I was wondering the same thing," I smile. Should I smile? "I can't sleep anymore. I'll make us some breakfast. Try not to attract any more flies or madmen before then," Strongheart informs.

As breakfast is readied, the sun begins to rise over the desert. What a pretty sight. I can't do that. Then as I just watch the sunrise, I realize part of me is trying to figure out how to get to that sun, take all its power. I have power now. But you know what they say about power; it's never enough. But why am I thinking this? Could that form have left a form of itself in me? I mustn't let the new tenant in this body take over.

I sit. I eat. I enjoy. It's the simple pleasures in life that really count. At that very moment all I wanted to do was to see Luna. But I had responsibilities to my friend and my men. It wouldn't be too much longer. Still, I took out a picture of Luna to look at it and look at it some more. Strongheart notices and, "Not thinking of cutting out, are you?" "You know, they oughta write a song for you: *By The Time I Get To Sturgis*. Don't worry, I'm here for the weirdness, the story of my life," I just know. "There's talk that Voltaire wants to take over. A few words from you and that's over," he informs. And I think about it. "Let him," I reply as my friend instantaneously replies, "What! He's more unstable than ... some of us I know." "Thanks a lot. How 'bout if he's in charge for now? Just remember, if anything goes wrong, he takes the blame, not Mr. Goodtrips," I remind. "Do you want things to go wrong?" he asks. "Don't you think I've had enough drama in my life? I just have a feeling something is gonna go wrong," I say prophetically.

Then the phone rings, Strongheart's phone. He looks at it. "It's your lady," he surprises me. "Luna? Why is she calling you?" I mystify. "I don't know. You want me to answer it or what?" he asks. "Yeah, but I'm not here," I tell as he answers her call on speaker phone. "Hey, wild squaw, am I your new phone pal? Why call me?" he asks her. "Because Reg won't answer his phone. Look, you have to find him. Something terrible is happening," she informs as I check the cracked phone in my back pocket, which I show to Strongheart and then toss away. Then I motion for him to hand me his phone, which he does. "Hey, wild child, what's going on?" I need to know. "Reg, they think you're dead! People are going nuts. You have to show up somewhere and tell them you're okay," she tells us. "What! Why are they doin' that?" I can't believe. "You remember telling the world to attack if they killed you, you know, at the drone concert? Well, they are! They descended on Washington and are attacking all the politicians, anyone in a suit. You have to stop it!" she tells. "Politician bashing, is that a bad thing now?" I and Strongheart laugh. "Your fans are getting hurt too, people who love you. Are you gonna help them, Reg?" she asks seriously and I think about it seriously and reply, "Of course I will." "Why didn't you answer your phone?

Are you still mad at me?" she asks. "It got broke in the accident," I scare her. "Accident?" she stops. "Hit a coyote last night. I think I died last night. The form came for me. It didn't destroy a single town, just float me away and heal all my wounds. Need a new bike, though," I inform. "Forget a bike. A chopper's coming for you. Stay put!" she orders. "Okay, ma. Oh, and you know what I'm gonna do when it gets here? Get to the chopper!" I and Strongheart both say simultaneously like Arnold. We laugh it up, cuz it funny. "Ha ha, funny boy. Reg?" Luna asks with a serious tone to her voice. "Yeah?" I ask in anticipation. "I should have never left you. I love you. Please wait for me," she requests. "You have a funny way of showing it," I only said as I ended the call and gave my friend back his phone.

After I hand Strongheart his phone, he tells me, "You don't have to go anywhere to stop it, you know. Remember that night when you told the world to hear you? Just tune in to that moment. I know you can do it." And in an instant, I get the epiphany, "Tune—that's it! What if I were to tune in, you know, like a tuning fork, to the exact same frequency as someone like me? I could take on their abilities and they would have mine. You think that's possible?" "Like a Vulcan mind meld? That might work. Might. You better get on what's going on now," he says truly. I give him two thumbs up and walk alone out into the desert. I had something of the utmost importance to do and I knew only I could do it.

The sun rose more with every step as I ventured out into the desert. Then I just stopped. I formulated my thoughts. What could I possibly say to stop all the fighting on this savage earth? Silly me, it's me! They'll stop. Then I simply outstretched my arms as I drew in the sun's power and proclaimed to the world, "World, hear me!! Reg lives! Stop your fighting! Stop your killing! Rest. Calm your minds. Live your lives. I will see you soon." And once again I heard that eerie echo of my voice reaching far beyond the spot on earth where I was standing. I also felt the sun on my face and felt the calm everyone everywhere was feeling. I felt I had done a good thing, perhaps the best thing I had ever done. Does it make up for all the bloodshed and screwups? What's done is done. Maybe Joe's right. Just keep filling that half empty glass to keep the emptiness away. If only it were true. At least it's true for now.

I lower my arms and continue across the desert, not back towards my men. Would I soon be lost in the inferno of heat to come and have my bones found in the desert one day also? Nope. I remember everything, every moment in time and every step I take. I know exactly where I am. I know how far we were from the road when we entered the desert last night and I know where a road cutting through this dusty hell is ahead of me. Just a few miles more. Strongheart will never expect it. I'll see him in Sturgis. I've saved the world. Now it's time for more me time.

As the day begins for Rolling Thunder and they prepare to roll, Luna lands in a chopper not too far from the men. As she exits the chopper and heads towards the men, Strongheart quickly races in her direction. They meet up far away enough to be heard over the chopper's spinning blades and still be away from the men. "Where is he?" Strongheart angrily shouts. "What do you mean, where is he? You think I'd stop off in the middle of the desert just to see you?!" she yells back. Strongheart just looks at her, studying her. He suddenly believes her. "Then where is he?" he asks. "Trying to pretend he's not here? Trying to get rid of me?" she asks back. "Look, I know we don't like each other and we certainly don't trust each other, but you can look. He's not here," he calmly tells her. She just looks out over the sea of men and looks more than a bit discouraged. "He doesn't have a phone, does he? That means he can't be tracked. That means we don't find him unless he wants to be found," she says somberly. "You're welcome to stay with us till he comes back, hopefully before we get to Sturgis," he obsesses. "Yeah, that's not gonna happen, not without Reg around," she knows damn well. "I wouldn't let anything happen to Reg's woman," he fails to reassure. "I have a better idea; I'll look in the air while you look down here. There is one thing he needs to know if you find him, though. It's stopped. The madness stopped, and I mean everywhere! All over the planet, any fighting, any attacks, they've all stopped," she ponders. "I know," he only said with a smile. "What are you not telling me?" she asks with mistrust. "Remember the night you were here and Reg told the world to hear him? Well, it did," he says and waits for it to sink in. "You mean he can amplify, like Sunny?" she assumes. "Reg has so many gifts now. He needs to see Gawanni, to know how to use them," he tells truly. "I finally met him. Dad and I went to see him. I was gonna tell the bonehead before he hung up on me," she complains. "He will come back when he is more content with you than without," he expresses. "Would you do something for me? Would you call me if he comes back?" she asks. "Reg is like having a tiger by the tail. I could always use the extra help," he smiles at her. She smiled back. They might not ever be the best of friends, but at least they had an understanding of one another. Luna turned and went back to the chopper. And as the chopper flew away, Strongheart could only wonder what would become of his great plans without his friend Reg.

26) LOOKING FOR MY ELDORADO

After walking through the desert till my feet hurt and my tongue swelled, I made it to a road cutting through the desert. I was actually tired. To walk any great distance through a desert when it's truly hot is a real test of strength, or madness. Why do I do this to myself? I put out my thumb as I see a car approaching. The sumbitch passed me! The next one can't. I need out! I practice what I will say when they come, but I can barely get out the words. My throat is so dry. My focus suddenly turns on the car driving my way. My mind sends out waves of stop for me to its occupants. The car approaches, going slower. Its occupants give me the once over. They drive on. I must look too sweaty, too disheveled. What did they expect, a tuxedo? It's the desert! I collapse on my knees, my palms dropping into the sand as every last drop of fluid pours out of me. Is this my fate, to be cooked to death? Last night it was a coyote, what will it be tomorrow ... if there is a tomorrow? I suddenly feel strong arms pulling me to my feet. I'm being carried towards a big rig. I can't hold my eyes open ...

Crap!!! I'm in the desert again, the middle of the desert with no roads in sight. It's funny, though. I don't feel very hot. Not sweating much. What kind of desert is this? I see a large group up in the distance. I wish to be closer to them and suddenly I am, like I just folded space in an instant. I wish to be closer again, and again I am closer, jumping through time and space like a giant desert jackrabbit time jumper. I have arrived, but at what? Hey, it's all my biker buds, and Luna—and even Joe! He's wearing a Hawaiian shirt and holding up a brewski as he winks at me and takes a cool sip. "No more lying! No more false promises! No more being betrayed by those who work for us!!" Voltaire proclaims on a big stage as my biker bud audience erupts with agreement. Then I noticed why. A whole line of men in suits, who are all shackled together in heavy chains as if on some well-dressed chain gang, come shuffling onto the stage. They even had metal collars around their necks. They were all congressmen or senators, how odd. One of them was unchained and placed before Voltaire as he foretold, "Would you like to say anything before we pass sentence on your lyin' ass, senator?" "I don't understand, I didn't do anything," the senator declares. "Exactly right! You did nothing! Nothing for us. Nothing but lying, and stealing and lining your pockets with our money! How do you plead?" Voltaire asks. "Is this what you call justice?" the senator asks. Voltaire looks him over smiling and asks, "Is there a spine in there somewhere? No, senator, this is what we call justice!" Suddenly a big silk is yanked off a giant wheel like you'd find on a game show on the stage, except this wheel didn't have dollar amounts on it for the winning. This wheel displayed what kind of punishment you would receive. The senator looks up in horror at some of the punishments to choose from, including pictures of knives, big hammers, a noose, a gun and a prison cell with an open door and a get out of jail free card on it. "So, senator, would you like to spin the wheel or grovel for your life?" Voltaire says with the most sinister of grins. "Do I have a choice?" the senator quivers. "Everyone has a choice and everyone gets a chance. Show him what he has to choose from, Smasher," Voltaire says as a huge wrestler in a Santo mask displays a huge, shiny chromed meat hammer that is flat on one side and with deep metal teeth on the other side right before the pompous politician's bulging eyes, which I'm just sure is for some maniacal meat tenderizing. "Clubber, show him what else he has to choose from," Voltaire says as another huge wrestler in a Blue Demon mask displays a big chromed club with spiky knobs jutting out of it. Then Clubber smashes a watermelon on a table with the club as watermelon showers the audience. "Cassandra, show him what else he has to choose from," Voltaire says as Cassandra, who tried to get me killed in a bar full of unfriendly bikers Cassandra, struts up on stage with a long dagger and taunts the goodly senator with it, smiling and jabbing it in his direction as she says, "They've been stickin' it to us forever, haven't they? It's about time we stick it to them!" She touches the dagger to his crotch with her own devilish smile just before exiting the stage. "I'll explain how our little game is played for our viewing audience. You get a chance to grovel for your freedom! All you have to do is get on your knees before the audience here and ask for their forgiveness. If they are magnanimous in their sympathies for you, you go free! But, if they are not so forgiving, well, you get a little justice—French style!" Voltaire explains as big silk is yanked off a guillotine dripping blood from its blade rising up from the stage. The senator looks up at it and clutches his chest, turning into a skeleton in a suit as he falls onto the stage. "Scared another one to death! Let's try someone else," Voltaire says as a man in shorts and a pith helmet is dragged up onto the stage. Cassandra grabs the helmet off his head and wears it. Voltaire and the man are seated at a table covered by a big silk covering something moving. "The man you see before you is not a politician. Let's just call him the bug man, because this man thinks we should all be eating bugs," he says as the audience boos their sentiments. "Tell us, bug man, why should all us poor, unwashed slobs be eating bugs, while Grey Poupon chugging assholes like you gobble good red meat and caviar whipped up by your chef and served by your butler?" Voltaire asks with a stare that would terrify anyone, let alone one of minuscule courage. "Well, what I was actually suggesting was ..." Voltaire interrupts to say, "Add them to our salads? In that case ..." One of the bikers rips the silk off the table to reveal bowls filled with a variety of creepy crawly buggies in all sizes and shapes with bottles of condiments nearby for some reason. Meanwhile, another big biker in leathers and a big chef's hat puts a big bib with a roach symbol on it onto the bug man as he angles him in his chair right in front of one of the brimming bowls of bugs! The audience reacts and they're just eating this up, not the bugs. I think Voltaire had the bug man in mind for that. "I think you're just gonna love what we have prepared for you. Mmmmm, all your favorites!" Voltaire smiles as he handles the condiments one at a time and taunts or possibly tantalizes our buggy guest, depending on how much he really enjoys chowing down on such creepy crunchy goodness. "We have all your favorite salad dressings. We have barbecue sauce. Who doesn't like barbecued bugs? We have chocolate syrup if you like to drizzle your bugs. We even have some Nutella if you like to dip your bugs. That oughta make 'em easier to get down that delicate palate," Voltaire delights. The bug man looks over the table filled with crawling protein and contemplates what he must do as he picks up a big bug and just looks at it. "Go ahead, buggy, chug-a-lug a bug," Voltaire says to make the audience roar for more. Looking like he's about to take a big bug bite, the bug man suddenly lowers the bug from his mouth and says, "I don't think it's safe to eat this variety." And the audience boos its disapproval. "Then let us help you," Voltaire says as three bikers in chef's hats bring over a huge funnel and plunger and stick the funnel into bug man's mouth as one biker holds him still, one biker scoops bugs into the funnel and one biker crameth it all down with the plunger. As more and more buggies are crammed down the funnel, bug man's throat expands way out in size like a bullfrog to accommodate the movable feast creeping, slithering and hopping down his throat—yuck! Bug man's body expanded suddenly—then kabuggyboom! No more bug man, just Flying bugs filling the air. I looked to the sky at the moon eclipsing the sun. Then I looked down and everyone was gone, only tumbleweeds dancing across the desert. No man, beast or bug to be seen.

I wake up next to a big truck driver driving into a truck stop cafe. "Feeling any better, son?" he asks me. "I thought I'd be more thirsty?" I blurt out. "You drank your fill when you got in. Then it was lights out," he tells me. "I don't remember drinking anything. I usually remember everything," I say mystified. "Dehydration will do that for ya. You coulda died out there," he makes me realize as I also realize that he's answering me back, but I see no hearing aids. "You have some kind of hearing implants?" I ask him. "I do! But how did you guess that?" he asks all surprised. "I'm Reg," is all I say as he just looks at me before saying, "I'm Buddy. You some kind of a rock star or somethin'?" "Used to be. You really never heard of Reg?" I ask with my ego a bit bruised. I thought people on other planets had heard about me by now. "Maybe, I do a lotta drivin', sorry," is all he says. "Well, Buddy, how would you like to be a millionaire?" I smile at him. "Are you serious?" he asks halfway believing me. "I assume you pulled in here for eats and provisions. Here, get me a burner phone with lunch," I tell him as I reach into my pocket, and yank out a wad of hundred-dollar bills and hold it out for him. He just looks at it. "You don't hafta do that," he says with an odd look to him. "Buddy, I got more than I know what to do with. Just take it," I tell him. Hesitantly, he finally takes it. "What did you wanna eat?" he asks. "Anything without mayo," I tell him. "Hey, I'm the same," he smiles as he exits the cab.

Buddy and I had way too much to eat in his big rig as he rolled down the road. He told me about his kid, and his ex and how his life didn't turn out the way he liked. I told him I was a century old, could leave my body, ride a mind form across the desert and other interesting stuff that's slightly hard to believe if you're not me. He kept giving me looks like I was either plain crazy or just insane. He believed the money part, though. And most of all I told him about Luna, how she drives me crazy when I'm around her and even more when I'm not.

Anyway, we rolled into California. I'm practically home. So many miles from where I was and too many miles to just turn around and go back. We stopped where I could get off near the boardwalk in Santa Monica. As I started to get out of the cab, he stopped me by saying, "Was all that stuff you told me really true?" I just looked at him. I can tell he wanted to believe me or at least believe in me, so I told him, "I don't know if I really chose the life I got. I just know it's one like no other. Goodbye, Buddy." He looked reassured with a big bit of I don't know what to say mixed in. Hell, what do you really say at the end of the road?

I got out of the cab and walked till I made it to a vendor on the boardwalk who was selling tourist stuff. I bought a hat and sunglasses and immediately put them on cuz people tend to stare, and I just know some of them are sure it's me. Then I wandered around the boardwalk as I took out my burner phone to call Luna. She answers, just saying hello several times as I just listen. I didn't want her to know where I was. I just wanted to hear her voice. Then she said, "I know that's you, Reg. Why don't you talk to me?" I was tempted to; I really was. Then I saw a surfboard shop staring me in the face. Yeah, that's what I want. I wanna surf! So I toss my phone away and go right in the shop and tell the owner to show me how to surf. He eventually did ... and sold me a surfboard.

So I go straight as a laser down to the water with my new board. I've never surfed before, but I've seen *Big Wednesday, Point Break* and *Endless Summer*, if that helps at all. Oh, did I mention I bought some cool shorts and a shirt? I took off the shirt before hitting the water. I paddle on out. So far so good. Then I hop-pop onto my feet to ride a wave, only each foot hits each edge of the board as I hop, slip and crash onto the board. I hope no one saw that. The beach is only full of no one saw it. So I shake off my board bash and get to my feet again. Any more screw-ups like that and someone's gonna tell me to go back to the valley. Luckily a big wave is coming. I think it's lucky? Look at that giant curling beast. That wave had my name on it! And the closer it got to me, the more I didn't know what to do. Did I panic? Not exactly. I just stood there. I guess it was that time of the day for me to almost get killed again. I hope three isn't the charm because here it comes! I thought it would be gentle. After all, it's only water, but it hit me like the biggest heavyweight boxer coming in for the knockout. I was down! I didn't know where I was. I was floating in bubbles and all the ocean's foam and fury, and I was beginning to nod off. Now wasn't the time for that! I knew I had to stay awake or sleep forever. But I didn't know where I was. Left or right, up or down, I was nowhere and everywhere all at once, being tossed around like so much seaweed. It was vertigo-a-go-go! Then as I almost hit the ocean floor, I saw a nest of crabs right before my face, all reaching out for me with their snappy claws. For some reason, that gave me the strength to swim straight up to the surface, and I did. I survived again! With barely enough energy to move, I see the shore. It's sooooo far away. But I know I can make it because I'm strong! I feel weak. I feel dizzy, but I am strong! I keep telling myself that. I have to make it to shore. Hell, I'm stronger than anyone—I hafta make it! I will make it!! I'm so close now! I see people coming for me. I'm gonna make it! I'm there!!! I'm tired. I lay on the wet sand unable to move. Now's a good time for a nap, yet I can't sleep. Through the glare of the sun, I see a familiar shape with a gentle halo of sunlight around it, but I can't see its face. Though I don't know who it is, I feel who it is, feeling it in my bones and every part of me. She always does that to me. I reach out my hand as the shape slowly comes down from the light and I see my angel's face, my Luna. All I wanted was to kiss her, to forget any memory of anything keeping me from her. And she did kiss me, kissed me as though she loved me from the dawn of time and always would. And all my silly reasons for avoiding this moment were gone. She's on her knees smiling over me now. "How did you find me?" I ask so surprised. "Synchronicity," she then laughs at me and says, "Uh, a lot of people spotted you here, spotted you since you got here. See, there's a new app called Reg Tracker. You can't escape it," she shows me pictures of me on her phone. "Wow, big brother's everywhere," I just know. "It is where you're concerned. Why don't we get outta here before they wake up," she says as I notice all the people just standing around the beach as they look at me with their gaping mouths and drooping eyes.

So, all energized, I hopped to my feet, grabbed her hand and hand-in-hand we ran down the beach, two giddy, happy lovers being kissed by the sun. I had to get to nowhere special and I was just thrilled that she was along for the ride. When it seemed like we'd run out of beach, she slowed down, her way of getting me to stop. She was breathing harder than I was, of course, as we stood there. "You keep going and they'll never catch up," she pants. "They?" I inquire. "Our security team. You don't think I came alone, do you?" she says to turn my smile upside down. "Now don't be like that. You know you need them. Look around. Half the people on the beach recognize you. You want the security guys around you or them?" she asks as I see all the inquisitive looks I'm getting from the crowded beach. "Maybe they just want me to rub suntan lotion on them," I jest. "Maybe if you get me outta here, I'll let you rub some on me ... anywhere you want," she raises and lowers her brows. Yeah, I was smiling, too, for some reason. So I did the only thing I could think to do, scoop her up and run with her through the crowded beach full of sun worshipers, sandcastle makers, escaped beach umbrellas and gawky gadflies of all shapes and sizes. I didn't know where I was going, but I'd find out when I got there. I pretty much plan all my trips that way.

And even I eventually got tired. I put Luna on her feet as we were between the beach and the parking lot now. To avoid unnecessary interaction with anyone, I just looked away as passersby passed by. "You know, you're the worst person on earth to hide in plain sight, get my meaning?" she hints at leaving. "Well, I hear wherever Reg is is where it's at, you dig?" I ask. "Okay, mister super cool, what's the plan?" she asks as I see a familiar face walking our way from what feels like a hazy dream state. Then I realize she's the cute girl from the rave where I was poisoned. She came to thank me. The closer she gets to me, the more widely she smiles. Luna isn't smiling for some reason. The girl holds her arms out to hug me, all the while I glance over at Luna watching her like a hawk. Smiling up to the very moment she approached me, the cute girl hugged me, wrapping her arms around me with all the softness of a warm silk blanket. Then she whispers into my ear, "This is for my girlfriend ...." I didn't notice till the last second her arm on the opposite side of where Luna was standing was slipping down and stabbing me in the side with a knife that she must have secreted away just for this moment. "Reg!! Luna yelled as the dagger dug into me too late to react. Obviously feeling the sting, I jumped back as the girl raised the knife with the most diabolical look of pure madness on her face someone could possibly have as her sonic scream confirmed her madness. Then as I just watched, too stunned to stop the knife dripping with my own blood coming my way, several shots are heard as they strike the not as cute as I thought knife wielding maniac, sending her blood-spattered body into the sand in a dead heap. Just one more horrific thing I would never forget.

My security guys were the real heroes; they saved the day. There was talking going on between them and Luna as I just stood there, not even holding my side. Then my ears heard Luna say, "Do you wanna lie down?" I ignored everyone. I was too busy trying to heal myself, making the bleeding stop. It's yogi Reg! I hate the damn hospital! But I see an ambulance ride in my future and I don't think it's taking me to Disneyland. Still hazy, I hear one of the security guys calling for that ambulance that will never come because I yell, "No!!! No ambulance! No hospital!" This bothered Luna cuz I just hypnoed the security dudes. "Great! They're useless. How do we get outta here now? You need to go to the hospital," she gripes. "I know what I need," I say as I look up to the sky and soon my form is coming down to wrap us in the fluffy healing place I needed to be right now. Luna looked more than a bit apprehensive. She had only seen the form as a destroyer. I, though, had tamed the beast, taken its claws away and made it my benevolent servant. The form rose up to the sky and floated us away to safety, safe from all those prying eyes and hungry ears waiting for my next word on anything, meaningful or not. "How do you like it? It's like the Wonkavator, it can go anywhere," I smile as she grabs onto me, apparently thinking she might drop like a stone down to earth at any moment. "You're alright," I reassure. "I can't feel my feet standing on anything," she notices. "While we're here, where would you like to go?" I ask. "How 'bout the ground?" she complains. With our heads poking out of the top of the form and her arms glued to me, we floated over the Hollywood hills and far away, where I wanted to be. We touched down in a deserted cornfield and I told my form, "Till I need you again. Now off to the sky," I commanded and my cloud drifted away as Luna just watched it cautiously, less trusting in it than in awe of its power. "That thing creeps me out. It had this weird tingle," she informs. "Pure energy, baby! All courtesy of this," I say as I tap my head. Then she looked at my side, only to see blood on my clothes. She smoothed her hand over where a wound should be, finding none. My fingers interlocked with hers as I just looked into her eyes. She caught on and smiled, "That's why we're in the middle of nowhere," she said as she started to undress. And we made love, made love like never before. We were synchronized ocean waves gently washing over one another with only one thought in mind; may this never end.

Our bodies lay unclad together amongst all the stalks without a care in the world. If I were ever more content than this, I couldn't begin to remember when. "You think there are any snakes around here?" she asks. "Copperheads like corn, or just cornfields. Why don't we just eat all the corn and they won't bother us?" I jest. "I met Gawanii," she casually mentions, no doubt to spark my interest. "Big dude?" I ask. "About seven foot," she only says trying to get me more interested for some reason. "Like 'em tall, eh? I could be seven feet if I got one of them taffy pulling machines and stretched myself, you know," I say as if she'll believe anything I say at this point. She ignores my attempts at humor and simply states, "He wants to test you." I think about that. "I'm guessing not with plenty of No. 2 pencils. What kind of test?" I wanna know. "You against the forest," she said to puzzle me. "You mean, like, against any besties I might find there? You forget, animals dig me. No problema," I brag. "Not exactly. He mentioned something about monsters. It would seem all those people who disappear in the forests of the world every year is because—well, monsters," she says so casually or to just plain screw with me. "You know, I thought I did all the joking around. What's with the monsters bit?" I asked a bit bothered as she snapped back, "Just telling you what he said." "Well, what does he want me to do about it?" I need to hear. I only like my monsters in the movies. She explains, "I think what he wants is you to spend some time in the forest, and quite possibly you might come across some things you've never experienced before." "Monsters?" I still can't believe I'm asking. "You don't have to go alone." she tells. "I thought I did," I assume. "I can go with you, but only if I want to," she stops and makes me think about it, making me shake and quake like Fat Albert on Halloween night. "Well, are you?" I ask to make her giggle. "So you want me to get eaten?" she asks, definitely screwing with me now. After she stops giggling again, she tells me, "I don't think anyone's gonna get eaten. Gawanii likes me. I don't think he'd want that for me." "So, we're doing this together, huh?" I ask. "That's right—huh!" She mocks me. "Why does he like you?" I had to ask. "He has good taste—I don't know. How are we gonna get home? And don't say your mind form!" she means really means. "Okay, we'll go to the forest. But if I see any of those creepy, icky space squids, you're on your own," I joke.

We got dressed ... eventually. Then we made our way out of the cornfield to a main road. Being this was a rural area, traffic was slow. So we walked and waited for a ride. Why didn't she just call for assistance? A whirlybird ride could be just minutes away if she so desired. Did she need alone time, too? Or was it the most obvious answer, was she here just for me? Did she really love me? She suddenly stopped me. "I do love you, Reg," she said and I believed her. "Then marry me," I say looking right at her. "We have plenty of time, remember?" she reminds. "Oh, yeah? Convince me," I told her and without hesitation she grabbed me and kissed me, my arms finding their way around her. I think I'm convinced. And suddenly a pickup truck with school-aged teens drove past us. Both of us immediately waved our arms about trying to flag them down. Luckily the giggling girls of the slow-moving vehicle recognized us as they started yelling, "It's Reg! It's Reg! Stop the truck!" And it did stop to pick up a pair of loony lovers lost in nowhereville. I had found my Eldorado, my city of gold in her eyes. I knew my greatest adventures yet to come would only be with my Luna.

27) REG MEETS GAWANII

So here I am on my private jet with Luna, a minimal security detail and hopefully a pilot. Before we left for our forest experience, we said our goodbyes to all, especially to Aphrodite, who couldn't shake her feelings of dread in what awaited us. I kept asking her, "Is it the plane? You mean the plane? Trouble with the plane? What about the plane?" I babbled the plane, the plane more than a neurotic Tattoo. So she finally relented and told us what we needed to watch out for lay only in the forest. Wow! She should have a psycho bedtime story hour for children. Try ever getting to sleep now, kiddies! She did hug me and Luna, though, which was nice. She told me if anything ever happened to Luna that she'd be there for me—which was nicer!

Our plane landed. Then we were driven to the super secret spot to get off near the forest entrance. We were on our own then. We both had canteens on our belts. I also wore my backpack and had my girl by my side. "Well, we're here. So where is he?" I ask dumbly. "Gee, I don't think he's with the forest welcome wagon. We might have to search a bit," she says and leads the way. I follow, of course. "If this guy's so all powerful, why isn't he here? I thought he wanted to have a meeting. Why doesn't he know we're here already?" I annoy her for some reason. "You know, Reg, your questioning is like a cheese grater on my brain sometimes. Would you just relax and try to enjoy the whole damn experience?!" she was annoyed for sure. "Sorry," I mumble out. "Don't sulk now. Enjoy the beauty. Look at all this beauty," she says as I look around. "You mean like, the trees? And more trees, annnd more trees?" I can't help but notice. "There's plenty more than that—you'll see," she reassures me.

After what seems like waaaay too long, we come to a large tree stump and she sits down on it. "Tired?" I ask. "No," she just smiles. Then I catch on. "Oh, is this the magic spot?" I curiously inquired. "It was for me and dad?" she informs. I commenced dancing around like I'd seen American Indians do in movies, while woo wooing as I'd seen them do, along with some ha-ya-has and other native calls I had seen as Luna just looked at me like I was the loony of the forest for some reason. "Hey, big red, can'tcha come out and play? Let's have a pow-wow, big dude!" I say and continue to chant and dance my cool moves. Suddenly, I see Luna's eyes transfixed on something, something behind me. Then I got that weirdo feeling that something really was behind me.

I suddenly spun around and there he was about thirty-feet away. At least I think it was him. I had never actually met him, but the seven foot part and actually being a Cherokee kinda convinced me. He wore his native garb, too—kinda cool. What he was wearing that I didn't like was that look of discernment looking down on me. Luna hopped up off the stump and came to my side as the big man slowly walked up to us. All was quiet as we waited for him to speak. Then he said, "You will be called He Who Dances Badly." "Well, there are no discos here in the forest for practice," I say as he just looks at my embarrassed dumb ass. Luna has to hold back her need to laugh as she introduces me by saying, "You have to forgive him. He's not always like that. Sometimes he uses his brain. Gawanii, this is Reg." He held out his hand for me to shake, which reminded me of Richard Kiel's hand in *The Longest Yard.* So I put my tiny baby hand into his really big hand and he gave it a little squeeze just hard enough to get my attention and say he was the king in his forest. "You have much to teach and even more to learn. I am Gawanii," he made it known. "Yeah, uh, I'm the other guy, you know, the one with the funny voice. I'm sure it doesn't affect you," I was certain as he began to say, "You have a gift. You should always endeavor to use it properly." "Dad and I have been trying to teach him that for a while. Maybe you can help," my Luna says with only my best interests at heart I'm sure. "Gawanii must know first, is this your man, the man you trust; the man you live for, the man you would die for and the man you love more than any other man?" he asks. "I'm afraid he is," she says, trying not to laugh or cry. "And you, do you feel the same for her?" he asks me. "Since the moment I saw her," I say sincerely with a glance her way. "Then you will live together or die together," he says to just a little bit scare the crap outta me. "What do you want us to do exactly?" I needed really needed to know. He simply extended his arm to a forest that we had yet to explore. I had an encyclopedia of dumb questions left to ask. I just assumed they wouldn't work. I've been outclassed. "Well, I guess this is it," I remark as I head off into the forest with my best and only girl. The wind suddenly kicks up and my backpack is yanked off my back and flies away landing at Gawanii's feet. I turn around naturally and yell, "Hey. We're gonna need that." He just smiled for the first time and said, "Gawanii appreciates your gift." Since going back for it seemed liked the worst idea I'd have all day, I just yelled to him, "Hey, where's the food around here?" He simply said with a smile and a wink, "You are." The big guy was either taunting me or had the most wicked sense of humor in the forest. Luna did get a kick out of the comical look of terror on my face, though. "Stop worrying, he's just messin' with you. You do it!" she points out. "Yeah, but he's so smooth. He should give lessons," I admit. "Maybe that was the first lesson," she makes me think. "What are we gonna do about food? I need my protein," I complain. "It's called intermittent fasting, try it," she says and keeps walking. "You just say that because you can go without eating longer than me. I guess that's from from what happened to you with Desert Flower," I fill in, which makes her immediately stop to tell me, "Reg, I don't remember what happened there, and I don't think I want to." "Don't remember? We remember everything," I say somewhat confused. "He took it away. Whatever it was, he took it away. Can we just keep it that way?" she asks and continues walking. I respected her wishes and dropped the topic as we walked onward. In my case, it was better to quit while I'm ahead, a motto I should have adopted long ago.

Our trek through the forest seemed endless as Luna stopped to rest on a tree log. I sat next to her. "The things I do for you," she says a bit tired. "Oh, yeah? Try walking hours through the desert. Which reminds me, I'm thirsty. Going without food is one thing, but without water ..." I ponder. "You've got your canteen," she reminds. "Yeah, and when that's gone?" I complain some more. "Want some cheese with that whine? Then we find a stream! It's not that hot out here. The temperature will drop tonight, though," she thinks. "Shared bodily warmth, babe," I smile at her. "Yeah? If I let you," she smiles. "I am so sure, your valley bestie would say. The second it gets cold you're gonna be grabbin' my ass," I brag. "This ain't no cornfield," she tells. "Who's the one who ripped their clothes off first in that cornfield, huh? Huh?" I smile over at her to get her to smile. After sitting for a little while, she finally says, "We better make a plan. You know how big this place is? There are places no man has ever set foot on in this forest," she ponders. "Okay, that's it! Call the bellboy to get our bags," I say to get a reaction out of her. "It's not funny, Reg. These are the elements. We could die out here. We better use our heads or we just might not make it," she says seriously as I take her hand and say, "Hey, I will live with you and I will die with you, too." "Let's choose life. It's so simple!" she says as she hops up excitedly and continues, "I feel like a fool! Just leave your body and search for a stream." So I stand up and close my eyes. After standing there a bit, I hear her blab, "Concentrate." So I try to concentrate, but the magic ain't happening. "Are you concentrating?" she blabs again as I mention, "How can I? This annoying bird keeps crowing in my ear!" Then I open my eyes suddenly—cuz she smacked me! "Sorry, mosquito. Look, just remember that moment you did it before and just let it happen," she says as I close my eyes and do just as she advised. And in an instant, sparkly me was rising up out of my body and up above the treetops. I floated over the trees until I found that body of water, filled with fish and just beckoning us to come to it. The astral me came back to me instantly and I opened my eyes to say, "Want some seafood?" "You found it!" she said so smiley. "Yep! Thisa way," I say as I walk onward and she follows. "How far is it?" she asks. "It's, uh, this way," I mumble out. "I see that, how far?" she nagged. "A few miles give or take," I say to make her sigh. So we headed right in the direction of that stream. But we needed to make haste, though, for light was soon to be a precious commodity.

I knew we were getting closer to the stream that I saw, but by now it was near dusk with darkness waiting for us with all its surprises. "Hey, I just realized I haven't seen any animals," I notice. "You can walk a forest for days without seeing any wildlife. Then suddenly there's a bear to rip your head off. Yep, this is bear country," she says so nonchalantly as for some reason I start to look around for big hairy objects.

"Hey, listen!" I say as we hear the familiar sound of flowing water. We picked up our pace and exit the woods near a riverbank. We both chug-a-lug our water cuz now we could get more. "Ah, the simple things in life. You have a fishing rod on your bat utility belt there, Batgirl?" I ask. "Do you see one? Use your knife like Tarzan," she tells me and notices my dumb expression. "Don't you have a knife?" she asks. "Sure ... in Gawanii's new backpack," I say with my droopy face. "Always keep your knife on your belt where you can get at it quick," she schools me. "Thanks, Daniel Boone. What were you, one of those boy scout cub scout types as a kid?" I figured. "Sure was. I can make it out here if I have to," she tells me as she takes out her folding Buck knife, opens it and hands it to me. “What’s this for?” I ask if I didn’t know somehow she wanted me to catch a fish with it. “See the knife? See the water? Get in there and catch us some fish, and don’t drop the knife! We need it to clean the fish,” she instructs. “It’s cold in there,” I complain rightly. “You know what else is cold? The grave! Get in there or we don’t eat–or live! You want your protein? There it is. Get fishing!” she orders. So I move towards the water and she yells, “Hey!” So I stop naturally. “Take off your clothes or you won’t have anything dry to put on,” she instructs. I take off my shirt and shoes only without dropping the knife and hand them to her as I say, “Ain’t takin’ off the pants. I got nuttin under them. I don’t wanna excite any passing mermaids.” “Mermaids are in the ocean. Get fishing,” bossy says. “Wouldn’t it be quicker just to go find whatever we’re supposed to find and just go back?” I ask. “Reg, it’s not just about finding something; it’s about survival. We eat, we search, we sleep and start it all over until we accomplish what we came here for. Now get some fish,” she has me understand.

So here I am standing in this moving water as I try to find a fish without the rushing water knocking me down. I keep seeing these old wildlife videos running through my head where the bears waited for the salmon to hop out of the water into their hot little claws. No bears, no salmon and no luck! Hey, there’s a big fish! I hurry over and hop on top of it, holding onto it like a slippery football. Better not fumble, or drop the knife. With the fish and the knife held firmly against my chest, my super fit body managed to get to my feet. Then I walked my way to the shore as the damn fish tail flopped around enough to run a motorboat, but I got it there. Up on shore, Luna waved me in more, probably so I don't drop fishy back in the water. I drop the fiendish flopper on shore and say, "It was either him or me." She rolls her eyes and grabs the knife from me. "You wanna prize? Start a fire and I'll give you one." she says as she starts picking up small twigs for a campfire. I help out by putting my clothes back on. We find rocks to encircle the wood. Then it's time to make the fire. She takes out her trusty lighter, flicks it again and again annnnnnnnnnd nothing happens. "Shit! It's almost dark," she complains this time. "I have a way that might work," I say as she snaps, "Go for it!" So I simply slap my hands together, put them over the wood and just move them around. And soon there was smoke. Then suddenly the twigs burst into flames. "Chi-gong, what do you think of that?" I smile. "Wow, you didn't completely waste your life," she remarks. "Wow, yourself. You make any insult sound like a compliment. How do we cook the fish without a pan?" I ask. "You have never been in the wilderness? We put it on sticks to cook it, just like marshmallows," she clues me. She started to clean the big fish because she probably sensed I didn't want to do it—and she's right!

We sat eating the fish she prepared. "Nice grub, Wishbone. I can't believe people used to live this way, having to hunt down their meals every time they wanna eat," I imagine. "So you realize it's going to be that way for us for the next few days," she alarms me. "Few days!" I complain. "At least! Your friend Strongheart thinks this land should be lived on by his people. A noble gesture, only his people—my people—are civilized now. We like all the comforts of home like everyone else. Most wouldn't make it here," she says truly. "If you knew it was gonna be this hard, why did you come with me?" I ask. "The world needs you, Reg," is all she said. "Just the world?" I smile at her. She eventually smiles back and tells me, "Eat your fish."

The big fish feed was over and all we had was the dark, a fire to keep us warm and a flowing stream nearby to lull us to sleep. This was new for me. It wasn't bad at all. "You look tired," I tell Luna. "Good guess. I was only walking alllllll day," she says with her eyes getting all winky-blinky. "Where do we sleep?" I ask. "On the cold, hard ground. We could sleep against a tree, but that would be too far from the fire," she explains. "You mean to keep us warm?" I inquire. "Yeah, that and any kind of four-legged critter passing by that wants to take a bite out of us," she makes sense. "The two-legged kind are the worst," I remark. "That's for sure," she says and has to catch herself from falling asleep. Then she takes out a small folded up space blanket made of shiny silver, unfolds it and wraps it around herself. "Is there room for two in there?" I ask. "Barely," she hints at wanting to be left alone. I get up and walk away. "Hey!" she yells to stop me and says, "Don't go off exploring and get lost. I know you—restless Reg!" she says cuz it's true. "You can see this fire from way off!" I tell. "Good! Bring back more wood," she advises as she huddles by the fire. I head out into the dark forest to explore. If there was something out there that wanted me, my Luna would be safe by the fire.

As I walked, my mind kept careful track of how many steps I took and in what direction. Unless I fell into one of those spinny carnival rides, it should work. I glanced back occasionally at that fire. Like the light at the end of a tunnel, I needed to see it. The more I moved into the forest, the more the trees got in the way of that fire, though, and I realized I could see the fire no more. The moon was really bright, but the forest was really dark. Keeping my step count was even more important than ever now. Then I saw them, two yellow eyes shining at me from out in the darkness. Then pair after pair of shiny yellow eyes suddenly appeared as if they all stepped out from behind a tree for a peek. Because the eyes were not low to the ground, like by a wolf or coyote, the eyes were human height or taller. I won't say I was scared, but my heart was beating a tad faster by now. "I'm Reg, friend of Gawanii," I suddenly thought to say. And like that was a signal, something started moving in my direction. I say something because I heard it more than I saw it; the sound of loud footsteps walking right in my direction, and every step sounded as if a big log was being bounced off the ground, vibrating the earth to make its presence known. It must have had its eyes closed or was looking down because those eyes only became visible as it got closer, yellow eyes that were as high as a basketball hoop. A brightly glowing green orb suddenly floated towards me and just hovered there as it illuminated the area for what was to come. And here it came. I looked up at this hairy beast from the light of the orb and I could clearly see what must have been ten-feet high—and it wore pants! I couldn't move. I just stood there looking up at this creature unnatural to nature that could only be one thing—a werewolf. It just looked at me. Then it started to shrink down until it was a man just over six-feet tall, a man wearing only pants.

"You're not afraid, are you?" he said smiling at me, hopefully not hungry. I tried to say something, but—okay, I was afraid! How many giant monsters do you meet in the forest at night? Then I finally managed to ask, "Are you what I think you are?" "And what would that be?" he asked. "Uh, a vampire?" I said to really annoy him. "Oh, come on! Did you not notice all the hair? You get all your knowledge from the movies? Vampires are blood suckers, the scum of the earth! We are the noble wolf, protectors of man. We only hunt vampires, not humans," he made clear. "Good to know. Hey, I was gonna say werewolf because wolves have yellow eyes. What kind of creature has red eyes?" I needed to know. "You're that inquisitive in a situation like this?" he asked, a bit surprised. "I only ask as I see a pair over there," I say and point, making my hairy new friend do a double-take as he looks over at the red eyes peeping at us from a different part of the forest. He turns and yells, "Hey! Go home. Go back to your own dimension," he turns back to me and continues, "Just a Bigfoot. They'll leave you alone if you do the same. Could be one of those peeper monsters. They hang around loggers; hide behind a tree, grab a logger and it's snack time! Peepers, they're just the pervs of the forest. Don't worry about 'em." A tad unnerved, I ask, "Was I supposed to meet you? Gawanii had me to believe I'm here to meet someone or experience something," I ponder. "I am here to meet you. And what's with this Gawanii crap? This is our forest. You've been chosen, you know," he says to make me think. "Chosen?" for what I can't imagine at this point. "Yes, chosen. A certain someone wants you as an apprentice. There hasn't been a being like you on earth for thousands of years. Even I can't do what you do," he says to make me feel special, I guess? I look at all the pairs of glowing yellow eyes in the darkness behind him and ask, "You said 'we' before. Are they all like you? Are they all werewolves?" "Yeah, my family are allllllllll werewolves, wanna meet 'em?" he asks me. "I'll take your word for it," I nuff said. "The famous Reg? But they wanna meet you, and maybe eat you," he says with the most sinister smile before yelling, "Big Bob! Little Bob! Grab the barbecue sauce! Come get a leg and a wing," Then a big and a small werewolf come charging toward me from out of the woodsy darkness. I don't know if I was being screwed with or I was on the menu, so I screamed, "Wait!!!" Suddenly the big and little hairy beasties stop right in front of me and revert back to their human forms while looking like they just smoked a bowl of me. Yeah, my voice even affects werewolves—lucky me! "Well, look at that, you make us high, too ... except for me. Relax, I said we don't eat humans. You're lucky you're not a vampire," he says with a wink and grin as he disappears into the forest with his wolfy family.

Me? I figured it was time to haul ass back to camp. I made it back into camp, looking around to see only Luna sleeping peacefully by the fire. Not wanting to disturb her, I went to sit by a tree for a little slumber against the lumber. All smiles, I suddenly realized that I hadn't rounded up more wood. So I got up, got more wood, put some on the fire and went back to the tree. Now I can relax. Was I worried about being away from the fire? Not really. I just seemed to know instinctively now that whatever was out there in the forest, was there to protect me. Each of us had a different purpose. Maybe they knew that. And I closed my eyes.

Look at all those stars, passing them pretty fast. Wait a minute, they're on a screen. I look around. I'm on a ship, a spaceship. It's pretty big in here; everyone's just floating around. I see a familiar face, Aphrodite. She floats extra fast over to me and just hovers beside my chair. Hey, yeah! I'm the captain of this ship. "Orders, Captain Goodtrips?" she asks. "Orders?" I ask as if I just woke up. "You been trippin' again, Captain?" she asks with her super sly smile. Then a multi-colored bong with smoke wafting out of it floats past us. "Uh, maybe. How'd you know to come over?" I ask. "Oh, captain, you know you wanted me," she smiles with a wink. "While you're here, where we going?" I can't wait to find out. "Our heading takes us to the one and only planet worth tripping on in this ever so trippy part of the galaxy. Welcome to planet Psychedelica," she whispers in my ear as we approach a planet with an atmosphere swirling with every color imaginable. As we enter the planet's atmosphere, a super sexy female voice fills our ship with, "Welcome to Planet Psychedelica. Would you like a rest dome, a mellow dome or a pleasure dome?" Meanwhile, Luna floats over on the other side of me and hovers about. "Oh, hey, you. Any suggestions?" I inquire as I look as my two hot ladies eyeing me up and down. "What would you like, captain?" Luna says as she and Aphrodite both look at me like I'm an ice cream cone ready for a good licking. "Gee, its so hard to decide. Uh, what are we deciding, exactly?" I hope I get a prize for the right answer. "Don't you love it when he acts sooooo innocent? There's no wrong answer, captain. Pick one or pick us both," Aphrodite hints at something I don't think Luna is up for. "Its okay just this one time, Reg. Anything goes on this planet," Luna says to make me happy as the voice from the planet says, "Pleasure it is." Hey, my shirt's being ripped off! I feel hands on me, at least two sets. It's my girls and their lips have found me, too! It's good to be the captain. Is it just me or is it getting hotter on this ship? Wait! The ship's entering the planet's atmosphere on a trajectory that's too steep. Nooooooooooooooooo! Equipment malfunction—premature ejection!

I woke up—dammit! At least it wasn't a sucky dream. I see Luna still sleeping, the campfire still flickering and the darkness still remaining. I felt great! Normally I'd work out, but, alas, no workout equipment. I thought I'd use the forest, so I walked in a direction different from where I saw the yellow-eyed beasties earlier. As I was doing my business behind a tree, I saw a ball of light through the forest. It was too big for a firefly and it didn't flash like one, just dip and rise with its constant eerie glow. I finished up and walked towards it. It wasn't scared off. In fact, it came closer. I put out my hand and it came to it, bobbing about as it lightly touched my hand. It felt like some sort of energy. This wasn't ball lightning. This was life! So I asked, "Are you alive?" "Used to be," it softly said. Then as if they trusted me, balls of light from all around came to join in, bobbing about happily as if joining a fun party. Then I glanced over at the campfire and noticed Luna looking straight at me with that I can't believe what I'm seeing look on her face. So I motioned for her to come join the party. She stood up and slowly walked our way as the motion of the glowing orbs started to change as if they were apprehensive. I told them, "That's just Luna. You'll like her, too." So they stayed and Luna came, marveling at the sight of them with the most joyous smile. "See, they like you," I assure her. "They?" she asks. "The spirits of the forest. Spirits, are there other surprises for us here, good surprises?" I ask them. In unison, I hear the word 'surprises' giggled about by most. Then one lone voice warned, "Not all surprises good." Then with so much light from the orbs illuminating the area, we could clearly see what looked like a five-foot tall gnome step out from behind a tree to meet us. His head was huge and his body stout, and he wore a huge red coned hat on that big head as he said in his goofy gnome voice, "Welcome, Reg," "You know of me?" I amazed. "Everyone knows Reg," he smiled. "This is weird," I say to make the orbs giggle. "Of all beings, you should know what is strange to others is normal to you," he tells. "That's for sure. Do you live here?" I say to more giggling. "Why, how naive of me to think that gnomes and fairies don't live in the forest, too. Are there fairies?" I thought I'd give it a shot. And at that moment, a glowing little entity that looked like a butterfly zipped around from out of the forest right in front of Luna and then over to me to amazed looks by both of us. It looked like a tiny woman with wings. "Why are you revealing yourselves to us?" Luna asked. "Gawanii asked us to help you if you needed help. Do you?" the gnome dude asked. "Only with my sanity. I can't believe this is happening!" I say to more giggles. "You were not born to live a mere man's life. Reg and Luna are special. You must realize all your gifts so you may use them, both of you. You must go through the tuning," gnome says. "Tuning? You mean like a merging of minds, like Spock?" she asks. "Exactly! Then you can share skills, be true equals. Then you can be king and queen of this world or any other," gnome said to our surprise. "You mean an actual king or just a leader?" I needed to be clarified. "Reg can be anything he wants. You are a descendant of the sirens," he says as he points right at me. "The sirens from mythology, those sirens?" Luna questioned. "Indeed!" gnome dude stresses. "But didn't they make sailors crash their ships? They don't sound like the fun crowd to me," I deduce. "Myth and legend have been twisted over time. Some of the sirens were bad and some not. Your mother still lives. She may yet still be here, here on this world," gnome says to make me think. "How 'bout my father, who was he?" I needed to know. "Your father also comes from the stars. He will return one day for you," gnome says to surprise me. Would I have a choice when he comes? "If there were really sirens, were there also really ... gods?" Luna hesitated to ask. "Yes, but they are not really gods. They also came from the stars, possessing a form of energy so powerful, the Greeks mistook them for gods. Any mortal would," gnome explains. "Why did they leave?" I ask. "They were benevolent, but they were also cruel, thinking themselves as actual gods. Merlin finally drove them away," gnome tells. "You mean the magician? How does a magician send away a whole race of powerful space beings?" Luna had trouble understanding. "When the universe was formed, much energy was released. Some of that energy formed into vessels with enough power to create a whole other universe, a creation wand. Merlin possesses one. Some say more than one," gnome says to fascinate us. "If that's true, he could destroy the universe with that kind of power," Luna remarks. "Merlin is good. You have a true friend when you have a friend in Merlin," gnome says. "Yeah, that makes me feel better. Where would I find mom?" I wanted to know. "When her kind were here, they came down from their ships and lived on Olympus and other mountains where the mortals could not reach them. The sirens lived on islands in the Tyrrhenian Sea off the south-west coast of Italy, some say. But you will not find her there. You will only find her if she wants finding," gnome says to disappoint me. "Where will we find what Gawanii said we needed to find in this forest?" Luna asks. "You search for answers. Have you not already found them?" gnome smiles. "You mind if I ask what they call you," Luna asks. "Gnome," Gnome says. "I know what you are, I mean your name," Luna clarifies. "Name Gnome. I am the first," Gnome also clarifies as he turns to leave. "Hey, before you go, you got any of those cookies from your tree?" I ask as Luna rolls her eyes and Gnome and all the orbs giggle. "Silly! Reg silly. Elves are the cookie makers. They live on the other side of the forest," Gnome replies as he and all his friends disappear into the forest now, leaving Luna and my baffled self to just stand there and wonder if what just happened really happened.

"I'm just wondering if we should tell dad what happened," she says out loud. "Yeah, well, you tell him. He doesn't listen to anything I say anyway. Back to camp?" I ask. "I'm going to use the little girls' forest first,"she says and goes to do that, while I head back to camp. I put a few more sticks on the fire as Luna came back. "Going back to bed?" I ask. "How do you sleep after that? I can't stop thinking about it," she says with a yawn. "I don't need any more sleep," I smile. "Swell. Wake me if a unicorn trots by," she says as she lays back down by the fire with her silvery blanky. All of a sudden, the unearthly howl of some unknown beast is heard from out in the forest. Luna immediately pops up and remarks, "That was a Bigfoot. I know what they sound like—I'm outta here!" "Could be a werewolf," I comment. She just gives me one of her looks and commences putting out the fire. What a night!

28) THE INTERVIEW

We made it out of the forest! Yippy! Then we flew back home, after we had a big meal of anything other than fish. So we're at home now? At the palace? Oh, no! Joe set up an interview for us with the press. It seems we need to clarify what happened recently with the politicians being attacked. Joe said this way we could avoid getting a subpoena by congress. I can't wait.

Luna and I sit on a stage in a bulletproof glass box overlooking the press seated below. Since I can't say anything without a mind screw to anyone asking anything, I mentally relay my answers to Luna and she repeats my answers to the press and to the world, because they'll be watching for sure, wouldn't you?

The first male reporter asks, "This question's for you, Luna. How is it that you can talk to Reg when no one else can?" "I'm not the only one. Certain people with hearing impairments can speak with him because what comes into their ears is perceived differently, giving them the ability to have a conversation with him," she explains. "Interesting. But how can you speak to him?" the first reporter asks. "I'mmmm not sure. I just can. Someone else?" Luna asks. The second male reporter asks, "This question's for Reg. Reg, as far as we know, no one can do what you do, no one on earth. Are you from earth?" I mentally send my answer to Luna and she relays, "As far as I know, I was born on earth." "Wait a minute, what's going on? I asked Reg," the second reporter squabbles. "I'm his mental link. He sends me the answers," Luna says to surprised looks as the reporter sits down. The third and female reporter quickly stands up happily and adoringly asks, "Reg, when's your next album coming out?" I send my answer to Luna and she relays, "I hadn't really thought about it. Maybe we can do a duet together." The happy female reporter sits down as the fourth reporter pops up and asks, "Why do you think so many just came to Washington and started attacking our congressmen and senators? Some say you had something to do with it." I didn't like where this was going. I kept going, though, and sent my answer to Luna, who relayed," "I do nothing but help the world, make people happy. Why would you say that?" The fourth reporter persists and asks, "But you told the people, and I quote, 'The people are on my side. They're all lined up with me, and if you try to take me away from them again, they are going to go to Washington and slaughter you all'. Do you remember saying that?" Without waiting for me, Luna jumped down the guys throat with, "That was last year at a concert, a concert where someone tried to kill him! What would you say, please come try it again! They try to kill Reg all the time. He does so much for the world. What the hell do you do! Next question and not from you!" Luna just stares him down until he sits down. The fifth reporter stands and delivers a snarky little question with, "Reg, I know you've helped a lot of people, but a lot of people have been hurt by your actions, directly or indirectly. Care to comment on that?" 'Do pussies like you ever go to the gym?' I mentally relay to Luna, who just looks at me and says, "I'm not going to say that." "Come on, what's with the act? We know you're answering the questions," mister snarky butts in to say as he looks directly at Luna, who then drills his mind good and says, "You know what my specialty is? I read minds, that's why I relay the questions, and I really see a dark, tangled forest in your mind. Did you ever tell anyone how you murdered your neighbor?" The audience gasps. "You're out of your mind? You expect anyone here to believe any of this?" snarky replies. "You buried her in the back yard," Luna says, staring right through him. "Hey, you can come dig up my yard anytime. There's nothing there," he says not too confidently. "You kept trying to kiss her, but she kept pushing you away. You shouldn't have strangled her. She's buried by your childhood home ... by the fence. Wanna do some digging there?" she says with her eyes never leaving him, his breath getting heavier, almost hyperventilating with a look of recognition and pure terror. Then he suddenly bolts from the room. I wonder when the cowardly sheriff comes to slap the bracelets on him?

I've had enough. So I step out of the bulletproof box and give my best Tarzan call, and I mean, like, reeeeeeeeeal loud! I motion to Luna and she leaves the box. As we move to leave, an older male reporter surprises us by saying, "This is the quietest I've ever seen them." "Hearing aids?" I ask. "For a while now. Reg, you mind I ask you a simple question?" he asks. "Go for it," I instruct. "I'm not going to ask you who you really are or why you're here. I'm sure living in your own skin is a challenging one. I simply want to know, are you happy here, here in our world?" he asks to make me think. But it's such an easy answer. "This makes me happy. When you've found your true happy one, you've found your true Shangri-La," I say as I look over at Luna. "And now for our home viewing audience, we're gonna go boogie-oogie-oogie our way outta here—wanna watch?" I smile as I grab giggling Luna's hand and run her out of the building.

We rush outside and stop. There are people everywhere! So I scream!!! And all was spooky quiet. "I didn't come back for this," I say looking so blue I just didn't know what to do. "Don't run off again, Reg, please?" she asks in a way I can't refuse her. "I told Strongheart I'd meet him at Sturgis," I say and mean. "How 'bout your future wife, does she get a say in this?" she asked in a way that forced me to come up with something quick to satisfy her and keep my word to my friend. I needed that light bulb over the head moment annnnnnnnnnnnnnnnnnnd—I got it! "How 'bout we make Sturgis an event? We do the tuning there, in front of the whole world? You'll be my true equal in their eyes. They'll respect and listen to you just like me," I say to make her really think about it. "What if Gnome's idea doesn't work? We'll disappoint the whole world," she imagines. "Are you afraid it will work? If it's our destiny, why don't we just meet it, get it over with?" I ask as she gets an idea. "I know! We'll have a concert and kind of work it in somehow? We'll get this huge tuning fork and have it on the stage," she says to freak me out. "You been reading my mind again?" I wondered. "Not lately, why do you ask?" she asks as I tell her how Strongheart and I already talked about tuning before Gnome ever mentioned it. I even talked about a tuning fork. "It's synchronicity, it has to be. I don't know how to go against destiny. Let's just do it!" she concludes. Then with the crowd still quiet, more stunned than being zapped by the Enterprise with full phasers, we simply walked away. Because like it or not, when I'm around, the only opinion in the room is mine.

29) BUMPY RIDE

I just can't shake this feeling of dread as I sit alone at the round table in my palace. The other members of the circle slowly filter in and sit down with their special headphones on to converse with me as I just ignore them with my dour wandering thoughts. "Reg? Reg! Luna says to finally get my attention. "Are you with us?" she says with concern as I search for an answer and finally blurt out, "Something's gonna happen ... something terrible." "Where?" Luna asks with concern. "Not here. Sturgis," I mumble out. "Are you sure? Even dad likes your Sturgis idea. Are you trying to talk yourself out of it? Do you not want me to have your power?" she accuses. "That's not it! If you have my power, you'll understand me better. You may become a target like me, though." I assume.

"Aphrodite, do you foresee any catastrophe for us?" Joe asks. "Not at the moment, but I will meditate on it," she reassures. "Sunny, does Reg speak truly?" Joe asks. And Sunny, my lifelong big-eyed, beautiful friend looks about so curiously and says, "Yes. I see something in the clouds. I hear her call your name." "Who?" I must know. "The one you seek," she says only to make me wonder further as I pry, "Sunny, I love you, but you gotta stop with the cryptic answers. Who? Who? *Horton Hears A Who*, can you just tell us?" "Mother, your mother," she tells. "Mumsy? Wow, I finally get to meet her. If she's in the clouds, is she in like, a plane or a spacecraft?" I assume. "Just clouds," she can only say and I can only think to say, "You know with answers like that, everyone at the palace here is gonna think you're as nutty as me."

"I see what I see," she sweetly smiled to make us all think something for sure would happen. I thought my musings of madness were just bad dreams visited upon my non-sleeping brain. My concerns were given flesh by Sunny, even though I had no clue as to what or how to prepare. We would just have to be ready for anything. Now we go to Sturgis.

With more bikers than you've ever seen and more than normal for the usual Sturgis event, cuz of Rolling Thunder joining in, we all came. Joe, and Luna and the whole palace gang, including me, traveled via my jet. Luna would have no part in traveling all the way there via two wheels, no matter how customized and cool I made it look for her. I had a surprise for her when we landed, though. Luna and her dad sat across from me. Joe was reeling off facts and figures as if I actually cared, which showed in my over the top facial expressions. Luna started to giggle when she caught on to my antics. Joe caught on last. He should look up more. "Am I boring you?" Joe said with his eagle-eyed stare and frown on display. "Oh, no! You're just fascinating, as Spock would say. Tell us more, Joe," I meant not at all. "I will have you know, mister richer than everyone, if you keep spending your money like you do, you may actually run out of it one day. Did you ever think of that?" he asks. "No, really? How 'bout I just ask everyone to gimme their money? Then I'd have all the money," I say to him with my eyebrows raised with such excitement!" Please tell me you're joking. It's always so hard to tell with you, I think even you don't know sometimes," he deduces accurately.

"Well, I don't know, Joe, do you? Why don't you ask her? Ain't she the mind reader of the family?" I ask. "Don't let him push your buttons, dad. Besides, everything is fine while he's here, where we can keep an eye on him," Luna knows. So I close one eye and look at them with one eye, while winking constantly with my other eye. I was gonna enjoy this ride. Then something outside the window caught my eye.

Storm clouds were suddenly filling the sky where we were flying. "I thought this was gonna be a clear day," I say. "That was the forecast," Joe says as he now looks out the window, his alarm showing as he watches the clouds gather and even spring to life out of nothingness just to show all on board what true fear was. Then thunder cracked! And lightning's awesome power was seen all about the plane as the power winked. Was the plane hit? Everyone showed their alarm as the pilot had obvious trouble steadying the plane. Then he came over the PA system to announce, "Sorry, folks, a little turbulence, but we'll carry on." I looked out at the gathering clouds, the unnatural way they were moving as if they were intelligent, as if they were planning an attack. And what a perfect place for one, the sky. Who would think anything more of it than just the weather? Then thunder cracked again! And the lightning made its presents known like the untamed beast it was as the light went off in the plane. The emergency lights popped on to see only faces of terror on my plane, Luna's most of all, clutching the hand of the person closest to her, her father. I dare not let her down. I cannot let whatever force is present take control, take my love away. So I drowned out the sounds of the panicked screams and I concentrated. And soon it came, my form. It could destroy, it could affect a rescue, it could heal, and now it would defend.

As the clouds made ready their next attack, I watched my form come down from above and make itself known to the mere clouds as if to say to them it was the god over all clouds, the Zeus over all clouds. And as their thunder and lightning was released, my massive form spread itself out capturing the storm electric of all the sky's clouds; its limitless vortex of power easily swallowing all the clouds and all their explosive energy. Such puny displays of power they were next to my form. My crew would have no more excursions with fear, even though they knew not why. I think only Luna knew what I did. Do her eyes not see? Through the window she too saw the clouds vanquished in the oddest battle ever to take place in the sky, quickly won by the one form she took a ride on. Was I shaping, sculpting such power only by thought, or was it learning? Such power need not always be destructive, but could it be trusted? Luna knew not what to say or to communicate to me, only to show blessed relief as my form drifted off again up into space.

And as quickly as the clouds came to fill the sky and make war, their battle was over and they were gone. "You alright, Joe?" I ask as he rubs his necklace of teeth, one just like Gawanii wore. Now I know for sure Joe's secret. That's why my voice has no effect on him. I get up to address the crew of very nervous star children. I just felt I should. "Everything's fine. Just forget the bumpy ride. You can't wait to see Sturgis," I reassure as Roger butts in with, "Like, bad trip, man." "I thought I said to forget?" I kinda ask him. "Forget what?" he mellows out. "Are we talkin' about the same thing? Never mind. I can't make you forget, can I?" I ask of my Sunny. Always the wise one, she just smiles sweetly at them. "You care for them. What did you do?" she asks. "Don't need rainy days or Sundays raining on our parade. So I got rid of the clouds, that's all," I say to keep her smiling. "What you are going to do will change everything," she says to worry me. "I hope you mean that in a good way," is all I could think to say. "I always thought it would be you," she says out of the blue as she starts to cry. "What do you mean?" I ask sincerely. "You know what I mean," my first love says. My god, did she mean she always wanted me? I went back over to sit down across from Luna and Joe. "Did you ..." "I heard," Luna says before I can finish. "Now I feel weird," I say. I feel. "She's always loved you, Reg. We all do," she assures me. If Sunny loves me, maybe we could work her in one one night, a little threesome action I thought. Then Luna gives me that look suddenly. She has definitely not stopped with the Klingon mind sifter on my naughty noodle. "Hey, thinkin' it ain't doin' it, you know," I complain. "Sure!" she says before slamming her fine self back in her chair. Again, I should have quit while I was ahead.

30) TO STURGIS AND BEYOND

We landed at an airfield not terribly far from our destination. My private jet was really big! It was more of a party jet. It had minimum seats and maximum extras, nothing too good for my precious cargo. And waiting in the cargo hold were two custom motorcycles, my surprise for when we landed. After disembarking, I hurried Luna around to the back of the plane. She acted like she wanted to just go with the others and her dad. It seemed like everything I wanted was a waste of time, immature or just plain unnecessary in her eyes. That's what I thought, so that's what she must have picked up on, or just saw me looking putout. So she stayed and I got happy again as I unveiled the two custom rides with paintings of our likenesses on each of them. I could see that she digged them, but I asked anyway, "What do you think?" "I think you like to spend money. They're beautiful. It seems a shame to ride them, though," she says to worry me. "These are to ride to Sturgis, just you and me," I inform. "We have to prepare for the concert, Reg. We'll have to do the sightseeing later," she says all businesslike. "Don't you know by now I live my life by happenstance, a dash of whimsy? Let our people set up the concert, that's their job. Our job is to ride in there like the king and queen of the world. You know that, don't you? You just don't want to admit it," I say with such wide eyes and hope that she'll understand. "Reg, I don't know what's going to happen. I still don't know how it will happen," she confesses. "I don't either. I just know I want to find out with you. All the great and terrible things happen when we're together. This is the one that will define us forever, I just know it," I felt it in my bones. She just looked at me like she knew it must be true, too. Together we would find our ultimate destiny before the whole world.

So as we were ready to saddle up the mule and get on each of our cycles, Luna surprised me by saying, "You mind if I just ride with you? I had trouble riding one of these before. I'm more used to a dirt bike." "So you don't like big things between your legs?" I smirk as she just gives me her deadpan look. Okay, I thought it was funny. So I get on my bike as she just stands there. "Have you ever ridden these roads up here on a motorcycle?" she asks. "Now you know I haven't, why?" I asked back. "Because there are a lot of switchbacks, those suddenly ziggy-zaggy roads that dip and rise and get people killed, get my meaning?" she asks. "As in be careful? I think I get it," I thought. "You know what I think? I think we oughta ride dirt bikes. They're smaller and easier to maneuver on dangerous roads," she clues me. "Too bad we don't have any, climb on," I smile.

And before I could rev my engine, two dudes wearing headphones rolled out two dirt bikes that I somehow knew we'd be riding. "Think I didn't know about your bikes? They're nice, not practical. Dirt bikes will get the job done, too. You climb on board," she says like I'll just follow her orders. "They're just wussy little bikes. I like my bike," I told her good. "They're not that small. Steve McQueen rode dirt bikes. He raced them, remember? Now stop complaining if you want me to go," she says like I'll just do it her way. Standing there with her hands on her shapely hips, I'm pretty sure I'm doing it her way–again!

This is fun. This is freedom, riding Iron Mountain Road and Needles Highway—and the beauty! With no two hills the same and huge rocks that jutted way up from the earth, these Oglala Sioux Black Hills were every bit as sacred as Cherokee Gawanii's forest. And my girl hasn't stopped me or complained once. I guess she likes it, too. We suddenly have to come to a complete stop as buffalo cross the road up ahead at life's own speed.

"Are you still mad at me that I wanted to do this?" I ask Luna next to me. "Not at all. This was actually a good idea. I never told you this, but dad took me here when I was a kid. I rode in a sidecar next to him," she surprises. "Joe was a biker?" I can hardly believe. "Dad's tried a lot of things. He just wants to live life. I guess I can't fault you for wanting to do the same," she finally admits. No, I don't read minds like her. I just sensed a kind of calm in her that I rarely see. The beauty, the vastness, the feeling you get traversing this sacred land does more to heal my restless soul than the most opulent of palaces, including my own. And I suddenly realized I might never see my palace again. It could be stuffed with gold and jewels and not compare to this. No wonder Gawanii loves his forest and Tarzan loves his jungle. They are so much a part of them. They belong there. Where do I belong? I now notice Luna's questioning eyes, she senses yet more restlessness in me. All I know is that after years in my dungeon of a house in the Hollywood hills, I can no longer be still. This eagle's wings can only fly. She must understand this if she is to fly with me.

Then something makes me look over at the buffalo; one of them moving its head about and stomping its feet as if it were mad at us. It suddenly breaks from all the rest and charges towards Luna. I speedily hop off my bike as it falls over and I step out in between Luna still on her bike and the ton of mad beast charging our way. I simply held out my arms and made the most pleasurable sounds I could think to make, kind of like the cooing of a happy child who knew not what fear was. The hairy beast slowed and eventually trotted up to me, its rage instantly replaced with total contentment. It had found a friend. Nothing more needed to be said. I just smiled and pointed to his herd. Then the happy beast turned and trotted slowly back to be with its kind. I picked up my dirt bike as out of the blue Luna said, "Sorry." Curiously, I asked her, "What for?" "Because I could have got us killed. I was just trying to communicate with one of them," she says, laboring to breathe. "You alright?" I ask as I kick my kickstand to hold up the bike and go over to her. "My heart's still racing. I've done it plenty of times before. When I was a kid, I used to sit at my window and get the neighborhood pets to come to me, or birds to fly into my window. Sometimes they're the only friends you have," she purges. "Sounds like dad wasn't around a lot," I assume. "He was building his business. Get on your bike, I'm okay," she snaps at me. "After our buffalo friends finish crossing the road," I inform. "Friends? Friends don't let friends get trampled!" she complains to cover her fear. "Animals dig me. You were never in any danger. It's good to have the Reg around, huh?" I ask, smiling at her. "Okay, they've crossed the road. We can go now," she lets me know. "Okay, where do you think Strongheart and my loyal subjects will be, Deadwood or Crazy Horse?" I ask. "Your friend is crazier than Crazy Horse. You do know the tribes in this area were screwed over when gold was found on their land. You think he's gonna let that lie? He probably wants you to do something about that, too," she informs. "You still didn't guess where he is," I say like I might have gotten one over on her for once—but no! She whips out her phone as she says, "Your rolling army of the assorted delulu and dangerous is slowly filling up all the free camping areas so no one else can." "Hey, they're not all lunatics. Some are kinda swell," I mumble out. "Some? I have spent time around them, you know. I know what they're thinking," she complains. "Tell me, are you the one who shows up at all the kiddie parties to let the air out of their balloons?" I ask her, getting only a discerning look. Then she just takes off on her dirt bike. I follow, of course, cuuuuuzzzz I wanna be abused some more.

I arrived with my sanity intact in Deadwood. I thought Strongheart would be in Crazy Horse. But since I like movie stuff, I figured that he would figure I'd go to Deadwood—and there he is! Luna came, too, probably to keep an eye on me. "I don't have enough eyes to keep on you. Let's get this over with," she prods. Gee, this is only my life! Why get things over with? Anyway, we rolled slowly over by Strongheart as he had munchie-wunchies with a nut-covered ice cream cone. "You came, wow! I see the squaw's not thrilled about it," he says looking at

Luna, who forgot to take her smile to work today. I look around at all the familiar faces and some I know not. "Are these all ours?" I ask. "Man, I lost track. You never know what'll show up at Sturgis," he adds. "Do you expect for all this to last beyond today or is this it?" Luna asks Strongheart, who looks more than a bit broken. "We got here on momentum only. It can't end this way," he says with his melancholy showing. "You know if you expect Reg to talk to everyone and make everything alright, it'll only be temporary. I should have listened to him when he kept telling us he can't change the world, only make people stoned. I really should have listened," she says to bring us down even more. "Hey, *Don't Bring Me Down* is a song, not a way of life. Maybe I was wrong. Maybe I can speak the special strangeness that will change everything. Maybe that's why I'm here. Where do we get some of that ice cream?" I drool. Before he can answer, we three hear a rather loud argument far enough away not to be influenced by me chattering away. Then all of a sudden it's wham time! This guy just knocks another guy out with one Danzig take-down punch. Luna gets off her bike and yells over at the guy, "Can't you lay off for just one day? This is our night!" I guess the guy didn't like that because here he comes fast walking over to get in my girl's face and complains, "Mamas should be seen and shut their yaps!" I stare straight forward with my mouth shut as I just look at Strongheart enjoying his cone and trying not to laugh. Should I help, or would Luna take it as butting in? "Get outta my face," she calmly tells bigmouth, who hasn't recognized me yet. He must not belong. "Where is your man, hiding under some bed ... or is this the wuss of the hour?" he says, probably smiling, as he shoves me in the back. We're almost to a Billy Jack moment. How much more of this can I take? I'm not smiling now. "I wouldn't bother him. It'll just get worse," she says, sticking up for her man. So which road do I take here; just tell him to go away or knock what little brains he has out of his head with one super Reg punch? "I have an idea, why don't we just do it, and do it, and do it in the road until your girlfriend there grows some balls?" bigmouth just has to say to her. "Or you could grow some," she says as she jumps and ball crushes the guy with a super Luna ball busting jump kick. I wish I'd seen it, although I did enjoy Strongheart's seal of approval smile. I turn my head now to see the guy holding his nards and gasping to speak as Luna says, "What was that? You want more?" And before you can see Clint Eastwood punch into the camera, Luna was rearing back for a little knockout action of her own and—yowsa! That fist has knocked that dumb sumbitch out! I get off my bike now and just look at my girl. "God, you turn me on," was all I could think to say. She just smiled at me, cuz sheeeeeeeeee knows it!

31) TO TUNE or NOT TO TUNE

The big day was here. And before it would end, I can only think my life will take another tumble into the theatre bizarre. Joe requested a stage to be set up right in front of the Black Hills where they slope upwards right behind the town of Deadwood. The city council said No! So I had to show up and say a word or two. Guess what they said then?

With the stage being built where we wanted, a panoramic view awaited the whole world. I had sung at many a concert, all with their share of surprises or near disasters, yet all was proceeding normally. Joe was happy. He could use me yet again for more motivational crapola! The star children seemed happy. Their nerdy selves got to mix with all the bikers, kinda like throwing your kids in the cage at the zoo with the gorillas and polar bears. No danger there. Luna seemed happy, or at least she wasn't flashing me the bitchy bitch-face. And my fellow bikers were happy. I bought 'em a brewery.

As concert time neared, I walked up to Luna and just looked at her. I wanted her to break first. "Okay, I'm not mad at you! I don't know why I ever am, it's a waste of time," she tells. "Nice! Have you seen Sunny and the rest of our gang with the rowdies? Why don't you just rub 'em down with raw meat and throw 'em in a tiger cage?" I jest to make her laugh as she says, "I know, we're watching them. They never get out." "You should let 'em get out more, you know, like me!" I hint! "Sure, leave whenever you want. There's only an international incident or two whenever you go walkabout. I know you're a free spirit, Reg. Just understand that everything you say or do could affect everyone, not just satiate your mood of the moment," she says sincerely. "Are you ready for this?" I query. "I still don't know what I'm ready for," she confesses. "It's having my ability that scares you, isn't it? It's that you'll be like me, and you don't want that, do you?" I ask seriously. "Your voice is what makes you special to the world, Reg. I know for you saying the right things must be like dancing a high-wire over a minefield sometimes, but I don't know if I'd be any better at it," she confesses. So I tell her like Bogie, "So the kid comes clean. It's not so easy being the Reg, is it, sweetheart?" And I just looked at her. I wasn't mad at her either.

It was late in the day now. There was a slight wind blowing around for some reason. As far as omens go, I can't tell if it was good or the other guy. The crowd down below consisted of about ninety-nine percent bikers and a few tourist families that were hopelessly trapped amongst them. Luckily my biker buds were too drunk to notice. Yeah, even they liked my voice. So when I start singing, my enormous adoring crowd down below will be drunk and stoned. Noooooo problem! As I stand around near the freshly assembled bottom steps leading up the side of the mountainous hills, Luna and bestie Aphrodite, wearing headphones, walk up to me. "Hey, it's the hot twins. Are y'all gonna dance for our guests? They might not rush the stage," I jest as Luna gets that get serious look about her. "Joe just wanted you to know we go like, totally live in five. Are you ready?" Aphrodite asks with her so sweet smile. "For you, anytime-o-rama!"

I say to yet another look of anything but approval from my girl. "You see, you see that face? You've known her longer than me. How long has she had that look? She always has that look like there's something permanently stuck in her craw," I jest. "I've known her long enough to know she loves you, she really does," she says about my girl. "Really? It's hard to tell sometimes. I still say we do something about her craw. How 'bout a crawectomy? Then she can be my lobster girl again. She'll have claws instead of craws," I say to puzzled looks from the valley girl. I guess *Annie Hall* was before her time. "Hey, funny boy, when does this tuning business start?" the serious girlfriend asks. "Business, huh? Everything's business with her. No funny business? How 'bout some monkey business?" I say like Groucho and then say, "Hey, if she ever gets tired of me are you interested?" I ask Aphrodite, who just gets that "hell yeah' smile about her, at least that's how I interpret it.

Suddenly Luna grabs me and kisses me, wrapping her arms around me as I naturally do the same to her. Just as suddenly, she breaks free and backs away to say, "Got your attention?" "Since the moment ..." she interrupts to keep saying, "Good! After you sing, the big tuning fork will be wheeled onto the stage. Then it's tuning time I guess. Now what are you going to say?" "Is there supposed to be a script? I don't know. I'll play it by ear. My whole life's been that way. You expect me to change now?" I ask cuz I just don't know—babble-de-babble. As Luna starts to speak, her bestie butts in to say, "May I? I think Reg is right. What is the right thing to say at a time like that? Just say it from your hearts, both of you."

So my girl and myself just looked at each other. Whoever thought we'd ever get such simple wisdom from the tripindicular valley girl? I'm stoked!

My band started playing as Joe walked out onto the stage and up to the microphone to pretty good applause from those in the crowd who still could applaud. "To all those here and all those at home and around the world, welcome to Sturgis!" he said to some real applause this time! "I say the world needs someone like Reg. The world could use a little healing. Tonight you won't have to think about all your problems, or all the wars going on or anything else! Tonight the healing begins and only one being on starship mother earth can give that to you! Tonight the world unites! I bring you planet Reg!!!" Joe excited the crowd and said more nice things about me than I think I ever heard him say.

That was obviously my cue, so I sauntered out onto the stage up to Joe. He hands me the mic and walks off smiling. "Hi, I'm Reg. I said without yelling. I'd yelled out my name enough. They all knew me now, and with just those three simple words they were already under my spell. "Let the euphoria begin!!" I yelled that time. I gave it to 'em good and they loved it! Then that wind, that eerily odd wind out of nowhere was back. Then thunder was heard in the suddenly forming clouds above. My only thought was I hoped it wasn't going to rain, but I felt that wasn't it. It wasn't my form, was it? It hadn't even crossed my mind. Then I heard a female voice singing, filling the atmosphere with her serene song. "Reeeeeeeg," it said as I looked up to the sky to see a beautiful face in the clouds. And in an instant my brain accessed where I'd seen that face before. It was in my dreams. "Look about you. What do you see?" the serene face in the clouds said seemingly only to me. I didn't get it at first. What was I supposed to see? The crowd was still under my spell, or was her voice the one taking control? I looked over at Luna. She could only stare blankly up into the clouds. I fought to rush over to her through the strange wind resisting only me. "Luna!" I yelled at her, but to no response. Even she was not immune to it. Even Aphrodite and all the band members wearing my voice blocking headphones couldn't help but stare up at the face in the clouds. That face, that voice, it could only belong to one entity, my mother. I moved back onto the stage and yelled up to it, "You are my mother, aren't you?" The face could only smile, but I knew. "Come to me, Reg. Come to me," her melodious voice said even to affect me, me who is immune to such strangeness. Her voice didn't give me euphoria, though, only a sense of peace and calm as if I'd do anything to follow it, like a sailor at sea. She must be a siren. "Where will I find you?" I simply spoke to her. "Come to where I am," she simply said as if I would just know. And while everyone was under her spell, I left the stage. I didn't want to leave my fans, my friends and most of all Luna. I just had to find her and know why I came to exist.

32) FOLLOWING THE SIREN'S SONG

I tossed away my phone, got on my dirt bike and headed straight for the little airport where we landed. The pilot was instructed by Joe to wait for our whole group. I instructed him otherwise. Since the pilot needed overseas charts for where we were going, I had to wait while he went to get some. I made him forget why. This was a trip I had to go on alone. It was dark now and I was trapped here. So I laid back and relaxed and said out loud, "Show me where to find you, my mother. Send me a beautiful dream." My eyelids fell.

My eyes pop open. I am standing near the edge of a rocky cliff overlooking another rocky cliff just opposite me with about a couple football field's distance between the two cliffs. Suddenly men come charging across the divide below. Even from the great distance above them I could see that they were huge men all. They were giants. They started to climb the cliff below me, seemingly straight for me. With men of normal size, anyone would easily have time to move away, to escape. But these giant men, they gripped the cliff rock so easily with their great strength and propelled themselves up toward me faster than I could believe. I feel I should try to escape them, yet I can only stand transfixed by the incredible sight and just watch them come. Then the clouds above began to swirl and thunder lit up the sky as what must be Zeus himself proclaiming, "Go back. Go back!" And as the giants still made their way up towards me, the clouds gathered into a huge ring that glowed with the power they were certain to unleash. Then a thunderous and bright electric madness struck the side of the mountain below me, sending huge bits of rock raining down on what I now realized were the titans. Even the huge menacing behemoths were no match for the giant boulders crushing them or Zeus' thunderbolts thrown down with such precision to explode them.

I throw my arms out and scream, "Mother!!! Where are you?" "Reg," I hear a sweet voice say as I lower my arms and spin around to see an incomparably beautiful woman floating towards me in a huge flowing dress whipping about as if time stood still. I just watched as she came closer and closer. I smiled. I was so happy. I was finally going to meet her, whether this was just a dream or a vision of some truth soon to be made known to me. She was so close to me now and she smiled. She was happy, too. She came closer. She held out her arms as if to hug me. So I held out mine. She floated right up before me and smiled so brightly that rays of light emanated from her. She was now close enough to touch me, to embrace me. Then she pushed me—pushed me over the cliff!! I'm falling. I can't believe it! Why would mother ...

My eyes pop open as the plane flies over the ocean. We were on our way. But did I still want to meet mumsy after a prophetic dream like that? More than ever! She wouldn't do that to her own son, not to me! Not to Reg! Everyone loves Reg. She has to love me. I would find her. If I had to search this whole planet I would find her. I have the resources and I have the time. O, so much time. I can use my time wisely or otherwise. I just know I have all the time I need to find her, and now was that time.

We landed at an Italian airport. I told the pilot only one thing, to get me an interpreter. I would take it from there. Then he was to fly home and forget all about little ol' me, forget everything. I would have no unexpected company come to call on me. I needed no protection. I needed no phone. I needed only to find what I was looking for and some occasional protein. Must stay strong. Must be focused. Must never quit. Must find a ship. What kind of ship? A pirate ship! Scalawags and toothless hags beware. Reg is coming for ya. Ye best be doin' what I tells ya or ye be walkin' the plank, matey! Better wait for the interpreter to tell 'em all that.

As I exit the plane, my new interpreter walks up to me. "You need interpreter? I am Anzio. How much you pay me?" he barked in his Italian accent. I reached into my pocket and gave him the usual folded pile of hundreds I carry with me to his wide-eyed surprise. "Can you understand me?" is the one question I needed to ask, only to get a response more than anything he would say. "I speak English. I interpreter," he spat out quickly and indignantly to my surprise. "Just checking," I say as I look to the sides of his middle-aged head for hearing aids. I saw them as he snapped back, "What you looking at? I not fagala!" "Don't worry! I don't like you in that way. I have a girlfriend—I'm Reg! The Reg, heard of him?" I ask as I wish my pilot was still here—so I could strangle him! "Oh, you one with funny voice. Anzio not laughing," he prods. "You want this job? Or would you rather get back to your herd of sheep, if you know what I mean?" I imply. "You say I fuck sheep? You fuck sheep, sheep fucker!" he says loudly as my eyes roll up in my head to match my raising blood pressure. "I don't see you givin' the money back. You want the job or not?" I ask about to really lose it. "Sure, I do job, not blow-job," he annoys. "Fine! We'll keep it strictly business. Now where can I charter a sailing ship to sail around the Tyrrhenian Sea?" I wanted to know. "Why not get tourist ship? Why go to all trouble?" he asked. "You wouldn't believe me if I told you," I said as he eyed me ever so suspiciously. "Okay, if you must know, I want to find my mother. I'm the descendant of one of the sirens. They live around here, right?" I ask as he looks like he doesn't know what to say, suddenly blurting out, "You crazy!" Exasperated, I see a group of passengers walking across the tarmac and tell Anzio, "Okay, watch this. Hey!! Say hello to Anzio, world's dumbest interpreter." And you guessed it, everybody stopped and just looked dreamy as Anzio couldn't believe it. "What you do to them?" he says, so surprised. "Are you really that slow a learner? It's my voice! If you're hearing's not impaired, that's what happens," I say and really hope he gets it. "So that makes you think you come from siren?" he asks honestly. "Can you think of another reason I can do what I do? Cuz I can't. Gonna help me or not? There will be more money in it for you. And trust me, I can afford it," I say to him as he looks at all the money in his hand and instantly spits out, "Yeah, sure."

So I find myself in his overly small car going towards where the ships are, he told me. He told me a lot of things. He talked incessantly, like I was his new best friend. It was like being stuck in a checkout line with miss frumpy talking about her gall bladder. I was trapped with the bane of my existence in this canned ham-sized tin can with wheels and all I had to do was get out—but no! I had to see my mythical mom that might not even exist. What I saw in the clouds over Sturgis might have been her or it might have been just another game played upon me. Let the universe screw with Reg! Anyway, I'll stick to my haphazard plan while I'm here, until I find her—find something!

So we arrive at the marina, or docking area or where the ships were congregated. It was a bit different here in Italy than where I was from. "There ships. You pick one," Anzio states. "Those aren't ships, they're boats. They're all too small! Now that! That's a ship," I said as I pointed to an old-looking sailing ship farther away out in the water. "Why you want one so big? Why not get speedboat? You can sail around all islands real fast," he informs with the only good idea he's had yet. "That's an idea, but I wanted to do it like they did in the old days, on a ship like the Argo with real sailing men who knew the sea, even with pirates–rrrrrrr matey!" I amused him. "You think pirates are like in old movie, with eye-patch and peg-leg? Pirates dress like metrosexual, like tourist, all friendly. They cut your throat and toss you over side of boat while you not looking," he says. "They'll do what I tell them to do. Only those like you, you know, the deaf or stubborn are free to choose. That's the power I possess. Go on this adventure with me, Anzio, and I'll make you a rich man," I tell him with my eyes drilling right into him. He would know that I am serious in what I had to do. All he had to decide was to go along for the ride.

So Anzio rented a little motorboat for me and we motored out to the ship that I pointed to out in the water. He seemed to think we would have to keep searching if the ship I liked wouldn't go along with my plans. The ship I want is the ship I'll get is all I had to say to him. We motored close enough to their ship to almost worry those on board as they looked us over. "Ahoy!!!" is all I had to say to the crew. Anzio watched their expressions change from concern to pleasure beyond pleasure. They were ready to take orders from their new captain. "You make them seasick. They going to fall off boat," he worries. "Ship! And you're the captain now. I'll tell you what to say and you'll give the orders. And don't worry, they'll follow them. They'll sail over the edge of the earth if I tell them to," I tell him to give him that worried look again.

And we're off to see the sea! I leaned against the starboard side of the ship with Anzio close by. He could barely believe everyone would just drop everything and follow any order I gave them without question or complaint, orders I had already given them in Italian after Anzio gave me pointers on what to say. I looked over the crew. I couldn't tell if they were pirates or former shoe salesmen, though some looked like I wouldn't turn my back on 'em if they had anything more dangerous in their hand than a potato peeler. I kept noticing Anzio's uncomfortable looks at all the wannabe robots on the ship. "Still think I'm not a siren?" I ask. "Man should not have power like that," he concerns. "I didn't ask for it. I just wanna know where it came from," I could only say. "What do we do if we find these sirens?"

he questioned well. "What indeed? I only need to find one," I assumed. "Yes, but if real sirens still exist, they can destroy us, make us crash boat!" he thinks. "Ship! Ship! This ship goes where I tell it to go! No siren, or destiny or anything else will alter its course! I know she's here and I'm gonna find her," I said and went quiet.

So we sailed for hours. We sailed around scenic islands and passed ships of sightseers doing the same. We sailed into the night, finally past Ponza and other islands in the Pontine Islands and not a peepsy from mumsy. The gentle rocking motion of the ship was a free sleeping pill and I fell asleep astern.

I was jolted awake as the ship was being tossed about in a storm. "Where are we?" I asked. "I don't know. I couldn't wake you up!" he said all frantically and it made sense. The men on board's only concern now was to continue onward—to survive! I woke up into a giant churning madness. I had no idea where I was or what to do even if I did. And the water! It kept splashing up onto the ship as it rocked violently in great Neptune's ocean. Was Neptune to blame? Then I heard it. We all did, the siren's song. It was faint at first. Then her song became louder. I knew I had found her and she had found us. "Come home. Come home to us, Reg," the sickeningly sweet voice called to me.

Then from the light of the moon, we saw the rocks. We were close to an island—too close! But what island? Is this how it ends for me, to be battered against some unknown rocky shore and sink into the lonely sea? And what of the men? I yell to them to stop. What do I say? She had more sway over them than I, than Reg, the one that makes time stop for all. They could only sail on, closer to the shore and the jagged rocks. For the first time in my life my voice was useless. I couldn't help them. I couldn't save them. "I'm sorry, Anzio," I said as I just looked at him. Not thinking anything else would work or just not thinking, I threw out my arms as the seawater splashed over me and I yelled, "Don't do this! Take me. Take me! Let my men go! Let them go or I will never follow you. I will destroy you!! If this ship is destroyed, I will survive. I always survive!!! And I will find you!"

I heard laughing, her laughing. She must have thought me only boasting. Reg means what he says. "Come to the island and I will spare them ... but you must come alone," my siren songstress sings. I turn to Anzio and say, "You heard her." Then I took a running start and jumped off the ship—what's that light?

Where am I? I thought for sure gravity would land me down into the depths of the unforgiving sea. Instead I am hurling upward, protected by soft but brilliant light surrounding me, light with colors I have never seen before. I have very little sense of movement, yet it seems I am being propelled upward and forward in every direction the colors take me. I reach out, hesitating to touch the light. Something tells me it's okay. So I reach for the lights, feeling a different feeling with every color I touch. Only good feelings, like good memories. I pull the colors toward me, bending color and light my way like the energy filled taffy they appear to be. I let them go as they spring back into the protective tunnel all about me. Openings now appear in the lights for me to see, to truly see all the things no one has ever seen before. My astral body has taken trips into space before, but nothing like this! I am seeing stars, spirals and new galaxies that I just know no earthly telescope has ever scoped out before. Then there they are ... I see faces, faces made out of stars. No, they are not a few stars strung together to make up a constellation named after a pagan god. These faces were composed of millions of stars and they moved as their owner's starry expressions changed. Seemingly infinite numbers of stars moving together in perfect unison as their owners smile at me or show me their inquisitive looks. How could they be alive? But they are. Are they as curious about me as I am about them, or are they merely letting me pass through their space freely?

I plunge into the water with no time to process what I have just seen. After sinking and rising at the mercy of all that salt water, I simply swam towards the island, hoping that shark, or squid or angry sea wouldn't have its way with me. Land wasn't close, but it wasn't that far either. Hey, if Jack Lalanne could tow seventy boats with seventy people in them at seventy years old, Reg can do it! Hell, I'm just towing myself. The water isn't all warm and fuzzy, though. The sea is an entity in its entirety and it is trying to drag me down. I must resist every stroke, every instant and every thought of giving up. I keep swimming, yet it seems I am getting no closer. Am I being pulled back by some unseen force, or am I just not trying hard enough? I give out a scream—and I swim!!! I swim for my life and for the lives of my crew, because she did say I had to come to the island if she is to spare them. Maybe that is the real test here? She's testing me. Well, here I come!

I see the sandy shore. I am so damn close now! I have arrived!!! I walk in and up onto the sand and collapse onto my knees on the island. Then it crosses my mind—no, dammit! I stand triumphantly and proclaim, "This island is mine! This place belongs to no man, beast or siren! This island belongs to Reg!!!" The clouds ever so quietly dispersed from the sky and the sea became as calm as a lamb. By the fullness of the moon, I see my ship safely at sea. My men are safe. Is this my journey's end? If I don't get off this island it is. I just had to throw my phone away. How much fish will I have to eat before a ship sails by? At least I know how to cook 'em now.

By moonlight only, I think I see someone walking towards me from up in the distance. The walker walks the sand just far enough away to avoid the waves rolling up onshore where his or her feet won't be touched. I don't think this is a mirage, one of my dreams intruding upon my sanity again, but I can never be sure. Then I see the figure more clearly now. The person wears a long robe with a large hood about the head. As the figure approaches more, I can see the robe is of high quality, like one someone well-to-do might wear, or someone with power. The figure now stops about twenty feet away from me. As the hood is pulled back, I can see the features of a man about forty-years-old, yet something about him makes me feel he was far older; that look in his eyes as if he has seen all that can be seen in every dark place in the universe. This was no normal man. I turned to face him as he came closer. "Is this your island?" I asked him. "No, it is yours. I heard you say it," he says and no more. Another one of those types. "You know a way off?" I simply asked cuz I was tired! He simply motioned with his arm to the sea. And as he did, I saw a crystalline rod in his hand over a foot long and much wider than an old nightstick with a crystalline ball capping it. Something told me it was special. Somehow I knew it was the wand Gnome had described, and so I knew who it must be who possessed it. But I asked anyway, "Are you Merlin?" He smiled. He smiled as if he was happy that I had passed some sort of test, or that I was just very perceptive. "That is my title, yes. And you are the one called Reg. All the world knows of Reg," he mystifies. "I think they've known about you a lot longer," I assume. "Merlin's life is one but of legend, one that can only live in the fancies of one's imagination," he says and I just knew he'd say something like that. "Okay, I have to ask, why are you here?" I must know. "Why are you here?" he says to annoy me. Not philosophy at a time like this. I wanna get outta here my brain screamed. "You may leave at any time," he said, obviously probing my brain like Luna or Gawanii. They oughta start a club. "Can't wait, huh? Does all that mind reading save a lot of time? And what do you mean I can leave at any time? I don't think I'm that good a swimmer," I explained. "You are fortunate Merlin came when he did. The one who brought you into this world was about to remove you from it. Merlin could not have that," he said with a smile that meant something. So I asked him, "Are you saying you stopped her?" "The wind, the violence of the sea, those Merlin stopped. As for your mother, her wise decisions stopped her," he implied. "So all the gods, those mythical mayhem makers are all afraid of you? It's because of that wand you're holding, isn't it? Gnome told us about it. A fantastical story, but somehow I believe it now," I said and I did believe. He held the wand out in his hand, approached me and said, "Take it." "Oh, I'm not ready for power like that. I wouldn't know what to do with it," I confessed. He gestured for me to take it, so I reluctantly took the wand into my hands. It swirled with light and colors I had never seen before, and I could see stars and planets come alive inside of it. Were they just images from the past trapped in the crystal or were they real, real planets and stars compressed into this tiny vessel of limitless power? Then I realized that I couldn't let go of the wand. Some kind of energy was flowing out of the wand and into my body. It wasn't really painful, just extremely odd and unnerving. "I can't let go!" I blurted out. He stood there quietly and waited. I noticed my whole body was aglow now. The dark of night made it so very obvious and kinda spooky. Then just as quickly as the glow came on, it disappeared, except it disappeared into me like it was sucked inside of me. Then the wand simply floated out of my hands and back over into the hand of Merlin. "What do you feel?" he said with that smile. "I don't know. Am I supposed to feel something?" I curious. "You are immortal, Reg, as immortal as Merlin. And the power you now possess will protect you always. Use it wisely, as it may be taken away as easily," he explained. "Why me? I'm a screwup. I never asked for such power. I don't crave it!" I needed him to know. "You would not have been given it if you did," he says to make me think. "Then why me? Why bestow such power in my fumbling hands?" I asked without understanding. "It is merely enough power to sustain and protect you. Although even such minuscule power could change destinies and destroy worlds. Be mindful that you possess it or it will surely possess you," he said to worry me. "But why me? Why did you choose me?" I would have him tell me. "You are a rare soul, Reginald. And the power you speak forth is even more rare. It will serve you well on this world and many to come. You have outgrown your world," he says like a punch. And I came to a realization. "You mean I have to leave? Excuse me, but do they speak English on a lot of other planets, like on *Star Trek*? Cuz I ain't goin', at least not without my Luna. I'd rather you took the power back. I'd rather you killed me than make me leave without her," I truly mean with my sad eyes. "Then no longer run from her. Run with her. Run to the ends of the universe with her and back," he said to only make me wonder further. "You mean we can come back one day?" I ask. "If you like. Merlin spends time on many worlds with many delights. Why deny yourself? Merlin admires you," he shocks me. "You admire me?" I say as I think at least I'm not the only one crazy on this island. "There is no lunacy involved. Merlin merely admires the adventures you are about to begin, to see places and worlds Merlin can only dream of seeing again. But Merlin's place needs to be here for now. This is your time," he said to make me wonder again. "It's to keep them away from me, isn't it? The power you gave me. Were the gods from mythology real? I mean I know they're not gods, just probably arrogant space travelers who were never told no by anyone, kind of like the kids in Beverly Hills," I deduce. "Arrogant? Yes. Gods? They thought of themselves so highly. It was merely the power they possessed that fueled their arrogance and foolhardiness. No doubt they have been interfering in your life since you sprang into being ... even in your dreams," he sets me straight. "That explains a lot. All those weird ass dreams were because of them? I don't get it. Did they invade my head to influence me or just to screw with me?" I had to know. "Reg is free now, free to choose. They will bother you no longer," he says with a smile. "Free, huh? The only place I wanna be right now is home. How do I make that happen?" I needed to know because I was away from Luna long enough. My journey of discovery was truly over and I feel a really long journey awaited us all, but would Luna want to go on that journey with me? Luna, here I come! "Mr. Goodtrips! Your trip begins. Follow me," he says to spoil my plans. I guess my new mentor had a few things to show me and possibly teach.

33) HOME

The doors to my palace fling open by themselves. Then I suddenly appear in the palace in a flash of light as everyone currently sitting at my round table turns their heads to witness the event. After all, it was an event—Reg was back! Looking dumbfounded, Luna just looks at me as I casually walk past everyone and say with a big smile, "I met Merlin." Then I continued to walk to the kitchen. While grubbing in the kitchen for a tasty treat, Luna comes in to confront me saying, "You don't stop to say hello? Where have you been? We were making plans—we thought you were dead! No one's seen you. It's like you fell off the edge of the earth." I stop my fridge foraging to say to the less than mellifluous magpie, "Good guess. I wasn't on earth." Then looking tired—cuz I am! I sit down. She notices how tired I look. "Are you alright?" she asks as I ask, "Pass over that cheesecake, would you?" "You don't eat this stuff. Why you starting now?" she complains. "Cuz I haven't eaten in forever and it looks sooooooooo good! Gimme," I beg. So she grabs the cake, slams the fridge shut and sits herself down at the table with such supreme cheesey deliciousness staring me in the face. I just sit there. "May I have a fork?" I had to ask cuz I haven't started to eat like a dog yet. She gets up, gets two forks, sits down and starts eating the cheesecake. I reach for a fork and she grabs it up, along with the whole cheesecake. "Uh uh, start talking," she says with all that creamy, yummy goodness tumbling out of her mouth. "Why don't you just read me? It's quicker,"

I say as she looks around oddly thinking. "I don't know, can't right now. Talk!" she barks. "Well, I went sailing on a big ship ... 'round Italy. Met mumsy siren. She tried to kill me. Met Merlin ... let me hold his wand," I guffaw and continue, "Shoulda phrased that better. The wand that Gnome said he had, I held it, held it in my hands. It gave me some of its power. He said I was immortal," I say as she just stares at me and says, "I can't read you anymore." "I'm not lying to you. Gimme some cake, pleeeease!" I tiredly request as she finally shoves it over with the fork, while she continues to shovel it down. So we both gorge ourselves, talking between bites. "What's he like?" she asks with her mouth full. "Merlin? You'll get to meet him before we leave," I inform. "Where we going?" she asks and nibbles cake. "He said we can see the universe. Just think of it, all the star children will really be able to see the stars," I tantalize. "Really? When is this big event?" she asks like I'm wacko, and barfs down more cake. "Not sure. He said we'll know when it happens," I gobble. "What happens?" she gobbles. "When we decide to go. Look, I know you'll never believe, oh, anything I say till you can read me again, so I'm going to give you something," I say to totally mystify her. Then she crams down more cake. "What?" was her final question.

I stand and motion for her to stand. She starts to stand—but first! She has another bite of cake. We stand before each other. I am totally serious for once, and she keeps chewing. "It's good, isn't it? And to think I almost had some," I remark about the cake she keeps chewing between smiles and giggles. I take her hands as I look into her eyes and say, "I'm always gonna be me, gonna be Reg, whatever that is? Can't escape it. But part of me has changed. Merlin's not the only one who helped me make that change. Joe helped, Otto, Gawanii, Sunny, everyone here at the palace, and most of all ... you. Merlin said never to share your power unless you can trust who you are sharing it with. And the only person that will ever be is you. I trust you and I love you more than anyone anywhere! Will you share all my power, all my strengths and all my weaknesses forever and ever till the never never? Because ..." "Stop talking," she says with her weepy eyes as she grabs me and kisses me. And as we kissed, I could feel my power flow out through me into her body and back into mine. But it was more than that. Love is a force all its own and it was the only ruler in our kingdom now, and I could taste her cheesecake.

She releases me and looks strange saying, "I feel the same, but different. Oh no, I sound nutty like you now. Is that what's supposed to happen?" "You'll get used to it. How long was I gone?" I ask. "Almost a week!" she complains as I smile and tell her, "Actually I was gone for a lot longer than that. Time is different from where I was. And, uh, I only came back for one reason." She finally catches on, being able to read me again. "For me, huh? Hey, your mind's an open book again!" she delights. "Only if I want it that way. I can't be photographed anymore either. No more worries about big brother," I explain. "Then how will you sing, have concerts?" she wanders. "I can turn it on or off. I spent no wasted time with Merlin. He taught me things and showed me things I could never learn anywhere else, and I mean in the universe! In time and space, he taught it all. Hey, he even gave me my own ship. Would you like to see it?" I say to see such anticipation in her widening eyes.

Luna and I run hand in hand towards the front doors as Luna says to everyone at the round table, "Who wants to see Reg's surprise? This way!" We rush out of the house, followed by the rest of the star children and Joe, who moves fast for no one. Standing out near the garden, Luna just has to say, "Okay, where is it?" "Yes, where is this big surprise that does not involve us planning your funeral? How did you manage to disappear in front of the whole world?" Joe nags. "Disappear? Hey, why don't you? Who wants to see my spaceship?" I smile. "Reg, I just noticed I can understand you without my headphones. Did you like, totally lose your voice?" Aphrodite wanders. "I can turn it off or turn it on now. If I'm being nagged by anyone, I'll turn it on and turn them off. Not you, just saying. And now for your viewing pleasure, I give you ... the Trippyship!" I say smacking my hands together as a huge spaceship appears above the palace and psychedelic colored shapes of sixties bands playing are seen dancing all over the ship's surface, while sixties music plays to fill the air with groovy sounds. Everyone looks up, annnnnnnnd—it's a big hit! "Like it, huh? Is that not better than your old van? In that, we will see the stars! And you won't be in need of anything. My ship has it all or can replicate it all. All you need to do is wonder and desire and the magic happens," I thrill. "When?" Aphrodite can't wait. "No time like this instant!" I thrill more. "Reg, you don't just fly off to some unknown adventure all willy-nilly. You must plan a trip, especially one as far as that thing may take us," Joe surmises. "That thing shall take us anywhere we wish to go. You just have to wanna go there. Hey, this is what all of you have always wanted! Come with me and see everything you could ever possibly imagine appear before your eyes. You don't even have to dream to have your dreams come true, because they're waiting for you out there," I finally say as I point to the heavens and watch the smiles and hear all the racing sugarplum candy confection thoughts of such wondrous adventures yet to come dancing through all their swimming heads.

And at that moment when all minds and ultimate desires were in agreement, an ever widening beam of twinkling light so friendly to the eyes beamed down about us and gently floated us all upwards towards our new home for our foreseeable future and maybe then some. On the way up, I could only see smiling, exhilarated faces of what lay ahead, including on my Luna. Our minds were one in what was happening, and this was a happening! It's what my extended family always wanted and I gave it to them. Looking directly at Luna, she simply said, "I do love you, Reg. I never thought it would end like this." "It's only the beginning," my trippy Goodtrips voice amplified for all of us here on earth to hear and enjoy.

With all safely onboard, I thought it best to say a few words to my earthly home before leaving. I figured I owed them at least that much. My voice, my trippy, feel good voice, now pleasantly popped on every TV screen, computer screen, phone and device you can imagine at once, while a sound wave amplified by yours truly spread over all of the home planet I will soon be leaving. So I say,

"Is everybody listening? Of course you are. It's funny how time stops when such a simple thing as a familiar tune starts playing. You just hafta stop to listen to it. Whether you ever liked hearing what I said or just that I said it, I'm grateful, grateful that you cared to listen. I'm grateful that you put up with me when things didn't always come out the way I'd hoped. I'm grateful that you stopped everything and thought only of me. You don't need to do that anymore. I don't mean to tell you what you need, but you need yourselves more than you ever needed me. I only ever wanted to add to your lives, not replace them. So when I'm no longer here, just remember what makes you happy. It's the simple things in life that really make you happy, you know. So Reg says to find your own bliss without him. I know you can do it. And now our Trippyship begins its trippy trip into a universe of pure imagination," I imagine as my Trippyship passes over fantastic LA and up and out into that place out in space that's just waiting for us to arrive. I have no idea what I will find, only that I will find it with all my hopes, and my friends and my Luna. Will I be back? After we all have a few trips on the Trippyship. Until then ... "Far out, man?" Roger would have the last word.

THE END

www.ingramcontent.com/pod-product-compliance
Lightning Source LLC
LaVergne TN
LVHW090548110826
845146LV00001B/66

* 9 7 9 8 9 9 4 2 1 3 5 1 3 *